PENGUIN

GREEK FICTION

CHARITON is widely assumed to be among the earliest of the Greek novelists but his dates are uncertain. *Callirhoe* was most probably written between 100 BC and AD 150, and no later (papyri finds make clear) than AD 160.

LONGUS is usually dated between the mid-second and the mid-third centuries AD; the author remains a mystery.

The ANONYMOUS author of *Letters of Chion* wrote them probably some time during the first or second century AD, but possibly as late as the fourth century AD.

HELEN MORALES was born in 1969 and educated at New Hall and Newnham College, Cambridge. She held academic positions at universities in Reading and Arizona before joining the Faculty of Classics at the University of Cambridge, where she lectured for eight years. She is the author of *Vision and Narrative in Achilles Tatius' 'Leucippe and Clitophon'* (2004) and *Classical Mythology: A Very Short Introduction* (2007), and the co-editor of the classical literary journal *Ramus*. In 2009, she moved to the USA and now teaches at the University of California, Santa Barbara.

ROSANNA OMITOWOJU was born in 1968 in Carlisle, Cumbria, where she attended Trinity School before going on to study Classics at King's College, Cambridge. She completed her BA, PGCE (teacher training) and PhD at Cambridge and is now a Fellow of King's College and Senior Language Teaching Officer in the Faculty of Classics. She is the author of *Rape and the Politics of Consent in Classical Athens* (2002), and is currently working on a book about Menander and a reader on Virgil's *Aeneid* 7.

JOHN PENWILL was born in Yeovil, but migrated to Australia at the age of 11. He read Classics at the universities of Tasmania and Cambridge, and taught at Monash University, the University of Tasmania and for the twenty-two years prior to his retirement in 2009 at the Bendigo campus of La Trobe University where he was

Head of the Arts Program. He has published articles on the Greek epistolary novel and other works of ancient fiction, notably Apuleius' *Golden Ass*. He was President of the Australasian Society for Classical Studies (2006–9) and has for thirty-five years been Associate Editor of the classical literary journal *Ramus*.

PHIROZE VASUNIA was born in Mumbai and educated in India and the USA. He is the author of *The Gift of the Nile: Hellenizing Egypt from Aeschylus to Alexander* (2001); the editor of *Zarathushtra and the Religion of Ancient Iran: The Greek and Latin Sources in Translation* (2007); and the co-editor, with George Boys-Stones and Barbara Graziosi, of *The Oxford Handbook of Hellenic Studies* (2009), with Susan Stephens, of *Classics and National Cultures* (2010), and, with Edith Hall, of *India, Greece, and Rome, 1757 to 2007* (2010). He lives in London.

Greek Fiction

Chariton: *Callirhoe*
Longus: *Daphnis and Chloe*
Anonymous: *Letters of Chion*

Translated by ROSANNA OMITOWOJU,
PHIROZE VASUNIA *and* JOHN PENWILL
Edited with an introduction and notes by
HELEN MORALES

PENGUIN BOOKS

PENGUIN CLASSICS

Published by the Penguin Group
Penguin Books Ltd, 80 Strand, London wc2r orl, England
Penguin Group (USA), Inc., 375 Hudson Street, New York, New York 10014, USA
Penguin Group (Canada), 90 Eglinton Avenue East, Suite 700, Toronto, Ontario, Canada m4p 2y3
(a division of Pearson Penguin Canada Inc.)
Penguin Ireland, 25 St Stephen's Green, Dublin 2, Ireland (a division of Penguin Books Ltd)
Penguin Group (Australia), 250 Camberwell Road, Camberwell, Victoria 3124, Australia
(a division of Pearson Australia Group Pty Ltd)
Penguin Books India Pvt Ltd, 11 Community Centre, Panchsheel Park, New Delhi – 110 017, India
Penguin Group (NZ), 67 Apollo Drive, Rosedale, Auckland 0632, New Zealand
(a division of Pearson New Zealand Ltd)
Penguin Books (South Africa) (Pty) Ltd, 24 Sturdee Avenue, Rosebank, Johannesburg 2196, South Africa

Penguin Books Ltd, Registered Offices: 80 Strand, London wc2r orl, England

www.penguin.com

First published 2011

013

Callirhoe translation copyright © Rosanna Omitowoju, 2011
Daphnis and Chloe translation copyright © Phiroze Vasunia, 2011
Letters of Chion translation copyright © John Penwill, 2011
Introduction and notes copyright © Helen Morales, 2011
All rights reserved

The moral right of the translators and editor has been asserted

Set in 10.25/12.25 pt Postscript Adobe Sabon
Typeset by Palimpsest Book Production Limited, Falkirk, Stirlingshire
Printed and bound in Great Britain by Clays Ltd, Elcograf S.p.A.

isbn: 978-0-140-44925-9

www.greenpenguin.co.uk

Contents

Acknowledgements

I would like to thank Phiroze Vasunia and John Penwill for contributing to the notes, John Penwill substantially so, and to Francesca Griffin for discussions about *Letters of Chion* while supervising her Cambridge MPhil thesis *A Literary Study of Epistolarity in Chion of Heraclea: Reading the Text as a Chio-paideia* (2004). Thanks are also due to Anthony Boyle and, above all, Peter Carson.

Helen Morales

We would like to thank Helen Morales, and Phiroze Vasunia would like to thank Miriam Leonard and Joe Boone.

Rosanna Omitowoju, Phiroze Vasunia and John Penwill

Abbreviations

FGrH   *Die Fragmente der griechischen Historiker*, ed.
              F. Jacoby et al., 1st edn (Berlin, 1923–)
Hunter 1994   R. L. Hunter, 'History and Historicity in the
              Romance of Chariton', *Aufsteig und Niedergang
              der romischen Welt*, 2.34.2 (Berlin and New York,
              1994), pp. 1055–86
Malosse   *Lettres de Chion d' Héraclée*, ed. Pierre-Louis
              Malosse (Salerno, 2004)

Chronology of Greek Fiction

The dates are mostly estimates, and historical and cultural events important for the works in this volume are included. All works were written in Greek unless stated otherwise.

BC

7th–6th century	Homer, *Iliad* and *Odyssey*
	Sappho
5th century	Herodotus, *The Histories*
490–479	Persian Wars
c. 469–399	Socrates
c. 450–380s	Aristophanes
431–404	Peloponnesian War
	Thucydides, *The History of the Peloponnesian War*
c. 428–348	Plato
415–413	The 'Sicilian Expedition' during the Peloponnesian War
405–367	Dionysius I rules Syracuse
404–358	Artaxerxes II Memnon rules Persia
4th century	Xenophon, *Cyropaedia*
367–357, 346–344	Dionysius II rules Syracuse
364–353/2	Clearchus rules Heraclea
c. 335	Aristotle, *Poetics*
mid 4th–early 3rd century	Menander's comedies
3rd century	Theocritus, *Idylls*

AD

1st century?	Anonymous (possibly Chariton), *Chione*
	Anonymous, *Joseph and Asenath*
	Anonymous, *Letters of Chion*
	Anonymous, *Metiochus and Parthenope*
	Anonymous, *Ninus*
	Chariton, *Callirhoe*
	'Dictys of Crete', *The Diary of the Trojan War* (Latin novel)
	Petronius, *Satyricon* (Latin novel)
2nd century?	Achilles Tatius, *Leucippe and Clitophon*
	Antonius Diogenes, *The Wonders Beyond Thule*
	Apuleius, *Metamorphoses* or *Golden Ass* (Latin novel)
	Longus, *Daphnis and Chloe*
	Lucian, *True Stories*
	Pseudo-Lucian, *Ass*
	Xenophon of Ephesus, *Ephesian Tales*
3rd century?	Anonymous, *The Clementine Romance*
	Anonymous, *The Story of Apollonius, King of Tyre* (Latin novel)
	Pseudo-Callisthenes, *The Alexander Romance*
4th century?	Heliodorus, *Ethiopian Tales*

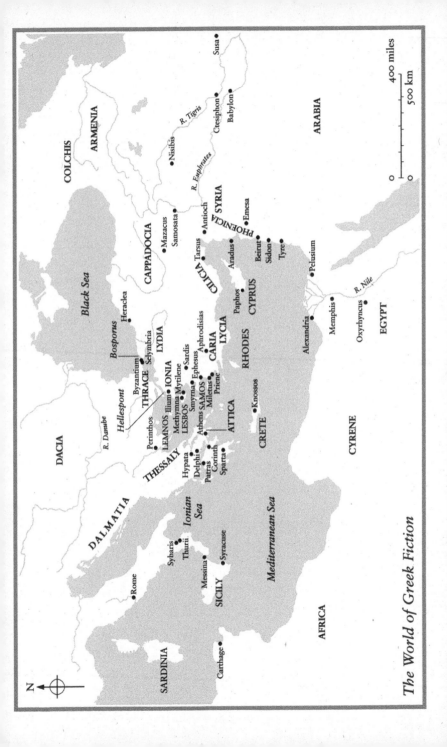

The World of Greek Fiction

Introduction

*New readers are advised that this Introduction
makes details of the plots explicit.*

It may seem surprising to talk of ancient Greek *fiction*, when we
are accustomed to associating ancient Greece's literary achievement with epic and tragedy, with the haunting love poetry of
Sappho and the outrageous comedies of Aristophanes. Everyone
has heard of Homer; who of Chariton? And yet it is not epic
that has survived to be the supreme genre in the modern world,
but the novel. Indeed, the novel seems to be such a modern genre,
by far the most commonly read form of literature today, and the
myth of its originating in the eighteenth century has proved so
tenacious in academic circles, that it's hard to imagine readers
in antiquity settling down to enjoy their versions of *Pride and
Prejudice* or *Harry Potter*.

Hard to imagine or not, Greek fiction was a literary phenomenon that flourished during the Roman Empire, in the first few
centuries AD. Of course, by our criteria, all Greek literature that
is not *factual* could be considered Greek fiction. Epic, tragedy,
comedy and love poetry: all of these would fit the bill. But in
ancient thought the lines of classification were drawn rather
differently. In the first century BC it was not a problem for Cicero
to proclaim Herodotus 'the Father of History' and then go on
to criticize him for inventing innumerable tall tales. Homer,
Herodotus and the playwrights all conjoined myth and history,
which were not then discrete categories, though Thucydides and
Plato would go on to challenge writing that misrepresented the
truth. The body of work that I am referring to as 'Greek Fiction'
is distinctive from earlier writing: it consists of narratives written in prose, not based on myth or historical accounts (though,
as we shall see, some of them feature 'historical' figures and

revise mythic tales), and self-consciously aware of their own fictive status.

Typically 'Greek Fiction' has been used as shorthand for the Greek novel, fantastic tales of love and adventure starring a young man and girl whose union (or reunion) in marriage provides the happily-ever-after ending to the story. 'The good ended happily, and the bad unhappily. That is what Fiction means', as Miss Prism in Oscar Wilde's *The Importance of Being Earnest* puts it. Two of the works in this volume are of this type: *Callirhoe* by Chariton and *Daphnis and Chloe* by Longus. The third piece, however, is rather different and shows just how varied in form and content Greek fiction actually is. This is *Letters of Chion*, a collection of seventeen fictional letters written by an anonymous writer and based on the life of Chion, a young disciple of the philosopher Plato, who lived in Heraclea on the Black Sea during the fourth century BC. The letters build up to the urgent question of whether or not to assassinate the tyrant Clearchus (who was in fact murdered in 353/2 BC). The date of the collection is uncertain, but it was probably written in the first or second century AD and has, therefore, a strong claim to being the very first epistolary novel in the Western literary tradition. That it has taken until the early twenty-first century for Ingemar Düring's 1951 translation of *Letters of Chion* to be superseded (by Patricia Rosenmeyer in her 2006 anthology: *Ancient Greek Literary Letters: Selections in Translation*, and now in this volume by John Penwill) is perhaps unsurprising; those works of Greek fiction that have not fitted the recognizable novel type have been marginalized, at least by Anglophone scholars. One of the aims of this volume is to show the fascinating diversity of Greek fiction. Reading *Callirhoe* and *Daphnis and Chloe* alongside *Letters of Chion* reveals patterns and connections that reading them solely in the context of similar narratives does not, and gives us a richer understanding of ancient Greek fiction and the societies that produced it.

The reason that our generic categorization of these ancient works is haphazard and that using terms like 'fiction' and 'novel' to describe them requires some justification, is that there are no designated Greek or Latin terms for them, beyond weak and general definitions including *plasma* (made-up tale), *fabula* (story) or *dramatikon* (dramatic narrative). 'Novel' was not used in its present sense until the seventeenth century; it comes from the Italian *novella*, 'new story', coined to describe short tales like those in Boccaccio's medieval collection, *Decameron*. Whether the absence of ancient commentary on Greek fiction is due to the lack of any great literary critic working at this time – no one to do for *these* works what Aristotle did for epic and tragedy – or because the textual fluidity and sheer variety of the narratives made them difficult to categorize, or because of some snobbery about the content of certain works, is hard for us to say. In such circumstances, it seems sensible and convenient for us to speak in terms of ancient fiction and of ancient novels.

Callirhoe and *Daphnis and Chloe* are two of five Greek 'love and adventure' novels that survive in full; the others are *Ephesian Tales* by Xenophon of Ephesus (so called to distinguish the author from the historian Xenophon who lived in the fifth to fourth centuries BC), *Leucippe and Clitophon* by Achilles Tatius, and *The Ethiopian Adventures of Charicleia and Theagenes* (often known simply as *Ethiopian Tales* or *Charicleia and Theagenes*) by Heliodorus. There are also three Latin novels: Petronius' fragmentary *Satyricon*, Apuleius' *Metamorphoses* (also known as *The Golden Ass*) and the anonymous *Apollonius, King of Tyre*. Greek fiction that did not take love as its central theme includes the *Alexander Romance*, a flamboyantly fictionalized biography of Alexander the Great and his conquests that proved an astonishingly popular and widely disseminated narrative (surviving in over eighty different versions and in twenty-four languages), Lucian's *True Stories* (tall tales that inspired Jonathan Swift's *Gulliver's Travels*), the anonymous *Ass* (a Greek man-turns-into-donkey tale, falsely attributed to Lucian) and an anonymous *Life of Aesop*, a fictional biography of the slave who wrote the famous fables.

Related to the fictional biographies are collections of letters that dramatize events in the life of a historical character as seen through the eyes of a first-person narrator. *Letters of Chion* is one of these; others purport to be by figures such as the philosopher Socrates, the playwright Euripides and the Athenian statesman Themistocles. The dates of these are uncertain and range widely, but the genre appears to have flourished in the early imperial period. In the Byzantine and modern periods at least (we have no evidence about their original readerships), these letter collections were thought genuine. The 'scandal' of the *Letters of Phalaris* was a turning point in their modern-day fortunes. This collection of 148 letters was attributed to Phalaris, the tyrant of Agrigentum in Sicily in the sixth century BC (*c.* 570–554). Phalaris was notorious for his cruelty: he was said to have roasted men alive inside a hollow bronze bull, enjoying the conceit that their screams made the bull sound like it was bellowing. The *Letters of Phalaris* present a revisionist picture: Phalaris comes across as a kind and cultivated ruler. They were thought to be genuine autobiography until the scholar Richard Bentley published an essay in 1697 proving the impossibility of their having been written in the sixth century BC, and the likelihood instead that they date to the first century AD (there is still no consensus on the date, though most scholars would place it even later than Bentley). For a long time the taint of being 'forgeries' led to the neglect of these letter collections. More recently, they have begun to be appreciated as fiction, and as designed to give the reader an imaginative insight into the inner worlds of well-known and controversial figures from the past.

We also have summaries of two lost novels (*The Wonders Beyond Thule* by Antonius Diogenes and *Babylonian Tales* by Iamblichus) written by the Byzantine bibliophile Photius, and a large number of fragments of novels, including *Phoenician Tales*, *Ninus* romance, *Sesonchosis*, *Metiochus and Parthenope*, *Chione*, *Calligone* and *Herpyllis*. Excavations of papyri are ongoing, leading to new discoveries of fragments of Greek fiction with exciting frequency. The summaries and fragments allow us tantalizing glimpses into some of the more sensationalist aspects of Greek fiction: ghost stories, human sacrifice, necrophilia and cannibalism.

The titles of the novels, while not always guaranteed to be original, nonetheless clearly show the distinctive concerns of Greek fiction. Many comprise the name of a girl (like *Callirhoe*) or of a girl and boy (*Daphnis and Chloe*). These novels follow a similar pattern. Boy and girl (beautiful, and from elite families)

fall in love and swear fidelity to one another. They are separated
and endure threats to their lives and their chastity, but are eventually reunited. The novels end with marriage or, in the case of
Callirhoe where, unusually, the couple are married before they
are separated from one another, a celebration of their reunion
as a married couple. This privileging of virginity and conjugality,
and the attention given to desiring women as well as desiring
men, forms what the philosopher and cultural historian Michel
Foucault called a 'new erotics'. In his *Care of the Self*, the third
volume of his influential *History of Sexuality*, Foucault observes
that the Greek fiction of the imperial period celebrates a 'hetero-
sexual relation' that 'organizes itself around the symmetrical
and reciprocal relationship of a man and a woman, around the
high value attributed to virginity, and around the complete union
in which it finds perfection'.[1] There is certainly nothing quite
like this in earlier literature. The love between a man and woman
and the importance of marriage are, of course, celebrated in
Homer's *Odyssey*, which is a foundational text for the Greek
novels, but the heroines of Greek fiction are allowed to do much
more than sit at the loom and wait for their husbands to return.
They have as many adventures as the heroes (Anthia, in *Ephesian
Tales*, faces attempted assaults on her chastity no less than
sixteen times; her skewering of one would-be rapist through the
stomach is told with memorable relish). They are given as many
speeches as the heroes, and, crucially, are allowed to desire without negative consequences: unusual in earlier Greek literature.
Penelope in the *Odyssey* loves Odysseus, but there are no descriptions of her desiring him like Chloe is shown desiring Daphnis.
Greek tragedy is very much concerned with female desire, but
its emphasis is on the threat that it poses to the household and
to society. Medea and Phaedra are monstrous; Callirhoe and
Chloe are not.

Marriage is represented as a strongly social and civic affair. In
Callirhoe, for example, the marriage is arranged by the assembly
of citizens who lobby Callirhoe's father to let the couple marry:
'The city proposes the marriage today of these two young people,
as they are worthy of each other.' Hermocrates agrees, because,
we are told, he is 'unable to refuse what the city asked', and the

wedding itself is celebrated by the whole of Syracuse. Far from
the sweetly sentimental hearts-and-flowers concept of many a
modern idea of romance, the Greek *eros* (both an emotion or
feeling – love, lust, desire – and a god who has dominion over
these) was a wilful and destructive force that overwhelmed its
victims and threatened social stability. Greek fiction repeatedly
dramatizes the importance of harnessing desire and making it
serve the social institution of marriage. Along the way, of course
(and here the novels have their moral cake and eat it), the readers, as well as some of the characters, have licence to indulge in
some erotic adventures. If love is a social and political affair in
Greek fiction, it is also a philosophical and literary one too.
Daphnis and Chloe is preoccupied with the nature and origins
of *eros*. Are falling in love and making love something natural
or something cultural, the novel asks? Can we ever really be
educated about love, or do we have to experience it for ourselves?
The countryside on Lesbos in which *Daphnis and Chloe* is set
purposefully recalls the pastoral setting of Plato's philosophical
dialogue on *eros*, the *Phaedrus*, as well as the love poetry of
Sappho of Lesbos, and the pastoral love poetry of Theocritus.
The Greek novelists' explorations of love were very much in
dialogue with a long literary and philosophical tradition.

   The other form that titles of works of Greek fiction take is
toponymic: *Ephesian Tales*, *Phoenician Tales*, *Babylonian Tales*,
Ethiopian Tales. Indeed, much Greek fiction is geographically
adventurous, with a taste for the exotic and unknown, and travel
to far-flung places (even, in Lucian's *True Stories*, to the moon!).
Daphnis and Chloe is a notable exception, set as it is in a small
area of the countryside, but the protagonists of *Callirhoe* travel
to Persia, Babylon and Egypt. This expansiveness reflects (and
promotes) a new world and outlook. In classical Athens, Greece's
victory over Persia in the Persian Wars led to the creation of the
'barbarian', an 'us versus them' mentality that, as Edward Said
memorably showed in *Orientalism*, has been remarkably tenacious since that time and throughout Western 'civilization'.
However, the Roman Empire changed the cultural rules; you
could be, for example, at one and the same time Greek, Syrian
and Roman; the 'us and them' model of Hellenism was challenged.

So we can see some old stereotypes at play in *Callirhoe* (the scheming Persian Artaxerxes, for example, and the fact that the Greek girl, Callirhoe, is more beautiful than any of the Persian girls), but we also find non-Greeks portrayed in ways that do not stress their difference, like the sympathetic Persian queen Stateira. An important literary antecedent to this is Herodotus' *Histories*, an account of the Persian Wars written *c.* 440–*c.* 430 BC that, exceptionally, embraced diversity. *Callirhoe* takes the same geographic framework, that of the old Persian Empire, as its literary landscape.

It is striking that Greek fiction, written as it is during the Roman Empire, features no *Roman Tales*. Indeed, many works of Greek fiction, including *Callirhoe*, *Letters of Chion* and *Daphnis and Chloe*, deliberately avoid any mention of the contemporary Roman world. This is in stark contrast to Latin fiction written in the same period, especially Petronius' novel *Satyricon* and Apuleius' *Metamorphoses*, both of which are explicitly concerned with recognizably Roman characters and contemporary concerns. The absence of Rome from Greek works can be interpreted as a form of cultural resistance to Roman rule, by harking back to times before Rome came to power and the 'golden age' of Greek civilization. However, it is also worth considering that, even when Greek fiction omits *overt* reference to Rome, Rome is very much a presence in the novels. One might see, for example, Chariton's representation of the Persian Empire as decadent and corrupt as a veiled comment on the workings of the Roman Empire. *Letters of Chion*, of course, while explicitly set in the fourth century BC, is centrally concerned with the abuse of power by a ruler and how best to respond to it, ongoing preoccupations for Roman citizens whose emperors often behaved like the worst of tyrants.

Despite their extraordinary adventures around the world, and the sheer number and variety of events that take place between their separation and reunion (shipwrecks, pirates, assault, heartbreak, mistaken identity, to name but a few), Chaereas, Callirhoe and the protagonists of the other novels appear remarkably unaltered. There is little sense in the novels that time, and the events that unfold in time, result in significant change. Of course, this reinforces the fantasy of fidelity *no matter what*. But it is also an aspect of the novels that modern readers tend to find unsatisfactory. Much of the pleasure in reading *Pride and Prejudice* or *Portrait of a Lady* comes from observing the characters' psychological journeys: their insights, maturations and changes of heart. There is little of this in the Greek novel, and the characters, as a result, come across as rather one-dimensional. Like characters from melodrama, the protagonists of Greek novels are often best appreciated as the embodiments of social values (the good virgin, the predatory villain, the parasite, etc.) than as psychologically rounded individuals. Once again, *Letters of Chion* proves something of an exception. The letters plot Chion's emotional and intellectual journey towards the conviction that a good philosopher should act on his beliefs. The strengthening of the young man's resolve, and the reader's growing realization that he is moving towards an act that will inevitably lead to his own death, creates much of the tension in this work.

Simplicity of characterization is not matched by simplicity of narrative, however: most Greek fiction, even the relatively uncomplicated *Callirhoe*, is marked by narrative sophistication. *Callirhoe* is at one end of the spectrum: it is largely written in clear, paratactic Greek (simple sentence construction with fewer subordinate clauses), as Rosanna Omitowoju's faithful translation elegantly conveys. On the other end of the spectrum lies Heliodorus' *Ethiopian Tales*, a tour de force of elaborate, convoluted descriptions and intricate, interlocking narratives that flash backwards and project forwards. *Daphnis and Chloe* lies somewhere in between. The artistry of Longus' narrative, beautifully captured in Phiroze Vasunia's translation, is truly impressive with its precise structuring, vividness of description and stylized use of rhetorical devices. The introductions to *Callirhoe* and *Daphnis and Chloe* reveal the contrast between these two works. *Callirhoe* begins by introducing its author:

> I am Chariton of the city of Aphrodisias, a secretary to the lawyer Athenagoras, and I shall relate a love story which took place in Syracuse.

It then launches straight into the story, introducing the principal characters and their drama. *Daphnis and Chloe* is altogether more elaborate. Its four books are prefaced by a prologue (the first paragraph in Book 1) which begins:

> When I was hunting in Lesbos, I saw in the grove of the Nymphs the most beautiful sight I have ever seen, a painting of an image, a love story.

After describing the painting, the narrator continues:

> While I was looking on and admiring these scenes, I was so moved that the desire took me to repaint the painting and respond in words. So I sought out an interpreter of the picture, and then elaborated it in four rolls . . .

So the whole novel is an extended description of a painting, a verbal depiction of a visual image, otherwise known as an *ekphrasis*. Longus, Achilles Tatius and Heliodorus were keen on *ekphrasis* and other showy rhetorical displays that were much prized by orators and sophists (professional debaters and teachers who flourished in the fifth and fourth centuries BC and were characterized by Plato as dangerous manipulators of rhetoric). For this reason they are sometimes known as the 'sophistic novels', in contrast to the less extravagant 'non-sophistic' novels of Chariton and Xenophon of Ephesus. Indeed, the early imperial period is sometimes referred to by scholars as the 'Second Sophistic', and Greek fiction as 'Second Sophistic literature', precisely because it has been viewed as a renaissance of the classical period's love of rhetoric (and the artifice and superficiality that were often thought to accompany it). But even the so-called non-sophistic novels presume an educated readership. Chariton frequently quotes Homer and alludes to the canon of Greek works that any educated person in the Roman Empire would be expected to know: epic, tragedy and Plato.

This brings us to the bigger question of who wrote – and who read – Greek fiction. In a nutshell, we have frustratingly little evidence about either. A large number of Greek fictional works were anonymous or falsely attributed to prominent figures, like the *Letters of Chion*. Longus was too common a Roman name to tell us anything distinctive. The name is attested on Lesbos where the novel is set, but, of course, it does not follow that the author came from Lesbos, and it would not get us very far even if we knew that he did. The first few lines of *Callirhoe* introduce the author, but it is not clear how to interpret these. Aphrodisias was a real city in Caria, Asia Minor (near the modern village of Geyre, in Turkey), and it took its name from Aphrodite, Greek goddess of love. The name Chariton is attested there, so it is perfectly plausible that the persona offered in the introduction reflects the profile of the author. However, the name Chariton means 'Mr Grace', and 'Mr Grace from the City of Love' might well be a pseudonym, appropriate for the author of a love story. A letter from the Emperor Julian in AD 363 forbids the priests of Asia Minor from reading 'fictions from previous generations in the form of history, stories of erotic desire and all such things' (*Letter* 89). This may be a comment on Chariton, Longus and the like (though 'previous generations' may suggest he has even earlier literature in mind). Another possible insight comes from the Roman satirist Persius, who derides his unappreciative audience with the sneering judgement: 'To those people I offer in the morning the programme of public entertainment, and in the afternoon Callirhoe' (*Satires*, 1.134). If the 'Callirhoe' in question refers to Chariton's novel (and not a mime or play by the same name) then this would indicate one reader's disdain for the work, but it remains an enigmatic snippet of 'evidence'.

Studies of papyri fragment finds and literacy rates suggest that Greek fiction was read all over the Roman Empire but far less than Homer, Thucydides and the other authors in the classical canon. This was not, then, 'popular fiction' in our sense of the term. Women, who were not educated as widely as men, cannot have been the majority of the readership, but it would be a mistake to assume that no women read Greek fiction, and the fact that female as well as male characters in the novels are shown reading and writing may be a telling reflection of their real-life readership. The novels would have been read on either a papyrus roll (a sheet of papyrus that, unrolled, would measure approximately 23 centimetres in height and over 10 metres in length), or a codex (sheets of parchment – treated animal skin – that were bound together at one end: an early version of the modern book). The papyrus was the most common form at the time that the earliest fiction, like *Callirhoe*, was written, but the codex was increasingly used and in the fifth century AD superseded the papyrus roll for good. The technological innovation of the codex will have had a bearing on how Greek fiction was read. The papyrus roll was impossible to manoeuvre easily so the reader could flip it backwards. The codex, though cumbersome, made checking backwards and looking forwards more feasible. The novels and letters often invite the reader to look backwards and revise his or her understanding with hindsight; the codex changed how Greek fiction was written and read.

If the picture of the original reception of Greek fiction, and indeed its reception in the late antique and medieval periods, remains murky, some clarity comes in the Byzantine period, when writers modelled their novels upon the ancient Greek novels, especially those of Achilles Tatius and Heliodorus. They were creatively rewritten and re-evaluated from moral and Christian perspectives. From this twelfth-century revival onwards, Greek fiction has been hugely influential upon the development of prose fiction in Europe and North America. A history of this development is well beyond the scope of this introduction, but a key moment was the publication of Pierre-Daniel Huet's *Traitté de l'origin des romans*, originally published as the preface to the novel *Zayde* by Marie-Madeleine de la Fayette, in 1670, and a few years later, extended and published independently. Huet was the first to create the canon of the ancient novel (dividing it up into Greek novels and Latin novels) and was also the first to attempt a systematic history of the novel, identifying three phases: ancient, medieval and modern. Huet inscribed ancient fiction into a history of the novel; other writers translated, adapted, raided and imitated ancient fiction. It is estimated that from the mid sixteenth century to the end of the eighteenth century hundreds and possibly thousands of novels in Western Europe in some way appropriated translations of ancient Greek fiction.

However, Huet's account was also prejudicial. The ancient novel was, according to him, distinctly inferior to its modern relative. The main reason for this was that the genre originated in the literature of the East. This prejudice against 'oriental' literature, together with censorship of erotic literature in the Victorian Age, and a suspicion that the novel was a derivative, feminized and 'popular' form of literature, and therefore inherently inferior, led to the denigration and marginalization of Greek fiction in the nineteenth century and well into the twentieth. It is one of the ironies of literary history that the qualities that once ensured the devaluation of the genre are the very same qualities that are proving attractive to scholars and readers now. An expanded world-view (what we would now call globalization), shifting ideas about cultural diversity, a keen interest in sexuality, the inclusion of slaves' perspectives, an assumption that women are active agents in control of their destinies: all of this has led to the increased legitimization and interest in Greek fiction in the late twentieth and early twenty-first centuries. This volume is in response to, and now part of, the exhilarating surge in popularity of ancient Greek fiction.

Chariton, *Callirhoe*

Callirhoe is one of the earliest, if not *the* earliest, of the surviving Greek novels. It was almost certainly written between 100 BC and AD 150, but more precise dating proves difficult (our dating is largely on stylistic grounds, but papyri that date from around AD 160 rule out it having been written later than that).

The title is also uncertain. One papyrus gives *Narratives about Callirhoe* and a major manuscript has *The Erotic Narratives about Chaereas and Callirhoe*. However, as the novel itself concludes with the words, 'This is all I have to write about Callirhoe', it is now usually referred to simply as *Callirhoe*.

It tells, in eight chapters, the adventures of a young Sicilian woman whose extraordinary beauty leads her first into love and marriage with the handsome Chaereas, but then on to a perilous journey around the Persian Empire. Callirhoe is attacked, buried alive, kidnapped and enslaved, and suffers the amorous attentions of every man of status who sees her, including the King of Persia. She is subject to the whims of both Fate and Aphrodite, the goddess of desire, but, through ingenuity as well as endurance, Callirhoe is eventually reunited with her husband.

Callirhoe is unique among the Greek romances that survive in that it is what we would call 'a historical novel'. It is set in the classical past and includes recognizable figures from history. Hermocrates (Callirhoe's father) was a Syracusan politician who was a major player in organizing Sicily's successful defence against Athenian attack in 415–413 BC (an attack known as the 'Sicilian Expedition') during the Peloponnesian War, the long war between Athens and Sparta. Artaxerxes, the Persian King, is clearly identifiable as Artaxerxes II Memnon, who ruled 404–358 BC. The real king did indeed have a wife called Stateira, as in the novel, and Hermocrates' daughter (whose name was not recorded) did indeed marry a man called Dionysius (Dionysius I who ruled Syracuse after Hermocrates' death, 405–367 BC). However, Chariton's picture of the past is, as we should expect with a fictional account, plausible, rather than historically accurate. The several anachronisms, for example, that according to the historical record Hermocrates died in 408/7 BC and so was not even alive during the reign of Artaxerxes II, or that the Sicilian Expedition was not the end of the Peloponnesian War as the novel suggests, should not detract from the novel's pleasures, for ancient or modern readers. Indeed, *Callirhoe* shows a strong awareness both of its sophisticated relationship with Greek historiography (drawing on Thucydides and Herodotus, Xenophon's *The Education of Cyrus* and Plutarch's *Life of Artaxerxes*, as well as, in all probability, lost works such as Ctesias' history of Persia and Assyria), and its own striking innovation (through repeated emphasis throughout the narrative on 'novelty'). Chariton makes interesting reading alongside *Letters of Chion*: whereas *Letters of Chion* is explicitly concerned with tyranny, *Callirhoe* approaches the subject more obliquely. It offers a fantasy account of the origins of Dionysius I: typically portrayed as an evil tyrant, he is given romantic beginnings by Chariton who thus invites us to entertain the possibility of an alternative, rosier history.

Callirhoe did not enjoy the wide readership and reception from the Renaissance and into the modern period that *Daphnis and Chloe* had. It is possible that its accounts of adultery, bigamy and crucifixion made the novel repellent to Christian sensibilities. In any case, it was not until 1750 that M. Jacques-Phillipe D'Orville published the Greek text alongside a Latin translation. The first English translation came in 1764 and the (anonymous) editor explained that he only came to produce the work after setting it as a translation exercise for his daughters from an Italian edition. He then revised their translation 'with as much attention as many other indispensable duties would permit' before checking it against the Greek: hardly a ringing endorsement of the novel's value. However, in a more general and diffuse way Chariton's influence can be detected in later ancient Greek fiction and in early English novels that celebrate female characters, notably Samuel Richardson's *Pamela* and *Clarissa* and Daniel Defoe's *Moll Flanders*, and what we now call the 'historical novel'.

Longus, *Daphnis and Chloe*

Daphnis and Chloe is a love story set in the countryside in Mytilene on the island of Lesbos. It is a tale of a simple country boy and girl whose love for one another grows in rhythm to the swell and ebb of the seasons. It is a thoughtful novel, concerned not only with the adventures of the lovers but also with the nature of love itself: what it is and what it means to be in love, whether love is different for men and women, and whether it is something that can be taught or something that happens naturally.

Written in sophisticated Greek, the novel can be dated to between the mid second and mid third century AD. We have no information about the author except his name, Longus, a common Roman name. Neither do we have any insight into how the work was received in antiquity, and modern readers have been divided in their opinions. Many have been touched by the innocence of Daphnis and Chloe who are naive about their feelings and how to act upon them. The pastoral setting has also appealed. This is an unusual feature of Greek prose fiction where the action normally takes place in cities and involves international travel, as in *Callirhoe*. Longus drew on a literary tradition of bucolic poetry, most strikingly the work of Theocritus and, probably, that of Philetas of Cos, who is reputed to have taught Theocritus and whose work is largely lost to us; it is surely pointed that Longus named the shepherd who teaches Daphnis and Chloe about love Philetas. Thus Goethe, famously, and with what now seems like rather over-heated enthusiasm, wrote of the novel's astonishing beauty. He advised that it be reread every year, the better to learn from it and appreciate its beauty.

The prologue to the novel announces that the work will 'bring back memories for those who have known love, and to give instruction to those who have not'. It is not clear that the reader totally ignorant about love making (if there be such a reader) will learn anything of use from *Daphnis and Chloe*, but the more knowledgeable reader is likely to find the couple's repeated attempts to make love (copying the behaviour of the goats and sheep to no avail) together with the narrative's arch knowing-ness, either gently humorous or irritatingly faux naïf. Among the critics of Longus was the classical scholar Erwin Rohde, who wrote in his monumental study on the Greek novel *Der Griech-ische Roman und seine Vorläufer* (1876) of 'the revolting, hypocritical sophistication of the work'.

Love had its philosophical and religious aspects too, and both can be seen in *Daphnis and Chloe*. Eros is called a 'sophist' (4.18) and was also linked to Dionysus, a god who was associated with the fecundity and regeneration of nature. Dionysus can be felt throughout the narrative, in the festivals and sacrifice in his honour, and in the figure of Dionysophanes, the aristocratic land owner and master of Daphnis' foster-parents, who is ultimately revealed to be Daphnis' true father and whose name means 'Dionysus Manifest'. Despite the air of mystery that the name Dionysophanes conjures, it is a distortion of the narrative to read it as a cultic text that *systematically* encodes Dionysiac religion, as some scholars have suggested.

Partly because of Goethe's endorsement, *Daphnis and Chloe*

has enjoyed one of the richest modern receptions of any work of Greek prose fiction. Chief among the highlights must be the ballet based on the dazzling score by Maurice Ravel. This premiered in June 1912 in a production by the Ballets Russes, with the great dancer Vaslav Nijinsky playing Daphnis. A critic in 1926 discussed how the librettist, Michel Fokine, dealt with the adaptation. Because the 'charm and monotony of the fields and the seasons' of the original narrative had 'none of the glitter of life which appears so well on the ballet stage', Fokine beefed up the episodes of sexual predation and tension, including having Lycaenion perform a striptease.[2] A production of the ballet in Paris in 1958 had a set designed by the artist Marc Chagall. His lithographs of scenes from the novel are sensuous and vibrantly colourful, and were later reproduced as illustrations to Paul Turner's translation (1988). The novel *The Sound of the Waves* (1954) by controversial Japanese writer and filmmaker Yukio Mishima is a rewriting of *Daphnis and Chloe*. It transposes Longus' idyllic love story to the island of Uta Jima where a poor fisher boy and pearl diver fall in love. There's no 'hypocritical sophistication' here, rather a celebration of simple values and idyllic first love, in harmony with nature.

Anonymous, *Letters of Chion*

Should a man use any means to bring down tyranny?
(Cicero, *Letters to Atticus*, 9.4)

From 364 BC the city of Heraclea on the Black Sea (modern Karadeniz Eregli in the Zonguldat province of Turkey) was ruled by the tyrant Clearchus. He was a leader renowned for his arrogance and brutality: it was even said that he carried a thunderbolt and made up his face so as to appear like Zeus, the king of the gods. Clearchus ruled for twelve years, until he was assassinated by a group of conspirators led by Chion, a citizen of Heraclea. One account imagines how, as Clearchus lay dying from his stab wounds, he was haunted by visions of all the men he had murdered during his tyranny. It was, as Chion must have known, a suicide mission: Clearchus' bodyguards killed the assassins on the spot. The fictional letters conventionally known as *Letters of Chion* (the title most commonly given in the manuscripts, though one expands it to *Letters of Chion, the Platonic Philosopher of the Black Sea*) are written as if by Chion himself, and they take us on the emotional and intellectual journey of a tyrant-slayer.

Tyrant-slayers had long been glamorous, if controversial, figures. In the sixth century BC the poet Alcaeus celebrated the death of Myrsilus, tyrant of Miletus; and Harmodius and Aristogeiton, who were thought to have liberated Athens from tyranny, became icons, with statues and a cult established in their honour. *Letters of Chion* is, in part, a thriller that draws on the popular fascination with political assassination and builds up a suspenseful narrative around the young man's gradual resolve to make an attempt on Clearchus' life.

Now that *Letters of Chion* is no longer thought to be a collection of authentic letters written by the historical Chion, it is generally agreed, largely on stylistic grounds, to have been written some time during the first–second century AD, and so around the time of Chariton's *Callirhoe* (although one editor, Pierre-Louis Malosse, argues for a date as late as the fourth century). It is possible that the work was intended as a veiled political manifesto with a specific target (such as the Emperor Domitian), but the uncertainty about its date, and the absence of reference to contemporary events, makes it hard to interpret a precise agenda.

The assassination of Clearchus is attested in several other works, and the differences between them and that in the *Letters of Chion* are telling. First, Clearchus is generally agreed to have ruled as a tyrant for twelve years before being assassinated (see, e.g., Diodorus Siculus 15.82, 16.36; Memnon, *FGrH*, 434.4), whereas in this work Chion returns home soon after he hears of Clearchus' assumption of power (see Letter 12). The author has telescoped the events into a few months and, taking into account other events in the work, forty-eight years into six (see the table in Malosse, p. 78). The effect of this condensation is to concentrate our attention on the character of Chion himself, the events that shape it, and on the moral issues his actions raise.

Secondly, the author suppresses the fact that Clearchus and Chion were related. According to the historian Memnon (as recorded in the epitome of Photius: cod. 224, *FGrH* 526), Clearchus was killed 'by Chion, the son of Matris, a high-minded man and one who had a common tie of blood with him'. The *Letters of Chion* does not increase the moral complexities of the political murder (and stray into the arena of Greek tragedy) by presenting this as the killing of a relation. Thirdly, whereas other accounts portray Chion as one of a pair or trio of assassins, the *Letters of Chion* all but elevates Chion to the position of sole slayer and thus the one true hero (or villain) of the story.

How to deal with tyrants was not just a political, but also a moral and philosophical issue. The central question of the letters – what action should the good man take against a tyrant – was also asked by Cicero a century before the likely date of composition of *Letters of Chion*, when he was deciding whether or not to side with Pompey against the dictator Caesar (in the end he chose to do so). For guidance, Cicero turned to Plato's influential discussion about tyranny in his work about the ideal city, *Republic*. Indeed, Plato is an important figure in *Letters of Chion*, for at the beginning Chion has left home to study with him at the Academy in Athens. The letters chart his growing realization that an education in philosophy can lead to political action. Contrary to the image that philosophers are all talk and no action, *Letters of Chion* shows how philosophers should be politically engaged and ready to make sacrifices for the safety of their families and communities. The final letter, his suicide note, is addressed to Plato. Clearchus, too, was said to have been a student of Plato's: a sharp irony, then, that it is through Platonic philosophy, and at the hands of another of Plato's students, that Clearchus met his downfall.

Plato's most well-known relationship with a tyrant was with Dionysius II, who ruled Syracuse (376–357, 346–344 BC). Dionysius' uncle, the philosopher Dion, invited Plato to visit Syracuse and help improve the city's governance. This appears to have been Plato's sole attempt to implement his philosophical ideas about how best to run a city in the real world. It was an experiment that failed disastrously: Plato's ideas were rejected and he was unable to leave Syracuse for a time, while Dion was exiled. This episode is the subject of the seventeenth letter in another spurious letter collection (considered genuine until the fifth century AD) attributed to Plato. It is clear that the author of *Letters of Chion* knew this work, as well as Plato's philosophical dialogues, and expects his readers to pick up on where the novel engages with ideas in them.

Most readers detect a coherence and design to *Letters of Chion* (as opposed to its being a random anthology), which would make this the first known epistolary novel (or one of the first: *Letters of Themistocles* also has a claim). As such, it has a privileged position in Western literary history. It might also contribute to the modern debates on tyranny and sovereignty, such as the dialogue between Leo Strauss and Alexandre Kojève (which are themselves rooted in the ancient discussions of Plato and Xenophon).[3] Certainly, our pressing dilemmas about contemporary tyrannies and political resistance and, more pointedly, about the morality of suicide bombing, invite a fresh and engaged reading of this remarkable work.

NOTES

1. Michel Foucault, *The Care of the Self* (1986), tr. Robert Hurley (London, 1986), p. 232. Originally published as *Le Souci Le Soi*.
2. Scott Godard, *Music and Letters*, 7:3 (July 1926), pp. 209–20.
3. Leo Strauss, *On Tyranny*, ed. Victor Gourevitch and Michael S. Roth (Chicago, 1961; reprinted 2000), includes the Strauss–Kojève correspondence.

Further Reading

Greek Fiction

This list is restricted to recent and major works in English, but details of further reading on Greek fiction in all languages can be found on the website of the electronic journal *Ancient Narrative*: www.ancientnarrative.com.

Margaret Ann Doody, *The True Story of the Novel* (New Brunswick, 1996) is a rewriting of literary history, arguing that the modern novel has its origins in ancient fiction.

Simon Goldhill, *Foucault's Virginity: Ancient Erotic Fiction and the History of Sexuality* (Cambridge, 1995) focuses on gender and sexuality in Greek fiction and their role in the history of sexuality.

Judith Perkins, *The Suffering Self: Pain and Narrative Representation in the Early Christian Era* (London, 1995) discusses ancient fiction side-by-side with Christian writings and Stoic ideas of the same periods.

Patricia A. Rosenmeyer, *Ancient Greek Literary Letters: Selections in Translation* (London and New York, 2006) is an anthology of Greek epistolary fiction.

S. A. Stephens and J. J. Winkler (eds.), *Ancient Greek Novels: The Fragments* (Princeton, 1995) contains the texts, translations and commentaries of the fragmentary novels.

Tim Whitmarsh (ed.), *The Cambridge Companion to the Greek and Roman Novel* (Cambridge, 2008) is the best introduction to ancient Greek fiction.

Callirhoe

Tomas Hägg, 'Callirhoe and Parthenope: The Beginnings of the Historical Novel', *Classical Antiquity*, 6 (1987), pp. 184–204.

Richard Hunter, 'History and historicity in the Romance of Chariton', *Aufstieg und Niedergang der römischen Welt*, 234.2 (Berlin and New York, 1994), pp. 1055–86, discusses *Callirhoe* as a 'historical novel'.

Bryan Reardon, 'Theme, structure and narrative in Chariton', in *Oxford Readings in the Greek Novel*, ed. Simon Swain (Oxford, 1999), pp. 162–88, is a literary study. Reprinted from *Yale Classical Studies*, 27 (1982).

Steven D. Smith, *Greek Identity and the Athenian Past in Chariton: The Romance of Empire* (Groningen, 2007) is an in-depth analysis of the politics of *Callirhoe* (*Ancient Narrative*, supplement 9).

Froma I. Zeitlin, 'Living bodies and sculpted portraits in Chariton's Theater of Romance', in *The Ancient Novel and Beyond*, ed. S. Panayotakis et. al. (Leiden, 2003), pp. 71–84, focuses on the extraordinary play with figuration in *Callirhoe*.

Daphnis and Chloe

G. Barber, *Daphnis and Chloe: The Markets and Metamorphoses of an Unknown Bestseller* (London, 1989) focuses on the reception of Longus.

R. L. Hunter, *A Study of Daphnis and Chloe* (Cambridge, 1983) is a foundational work (though the Greek is untranslated).

Bruce MacQueen, *Myth, Rhetoric and Fiction: A Reading of Longus's Daphnis and Chloe* (Lincoln, NE and London, 1990) explores Longus in its literary contexts.

J. J. Winkler, *The Constraints of Desire: The Anthropology of Sex and Gender in Ancient Greece* (New York and London, 1990) has a chapter that interprets *Daphnis and Chloe* as critical of gendered education.

Froma I. Zeitlin, 'The Poetics of Eros: Nature, Art and Imitation in Longus' Daphnis and Chloe', in *Before Sexuality: The Construction of Erotic Experience in the Ancient Greek World*, ed. D. Halperin et al. (Princeton, 1990), pp. 1–49, analyses the poetry and politics of the novel.

Letters of Chion

Ingemar Düring, *Chion of Heraclea: A Novel in Letters* (Göteborg, 1951) is still a valuable commentary.

David Konstan and Phillip Mitsis, 'Chion of Heraclea: A Philosophical Novel in Letters', *Apeiron*, 23 (1990), pp. 257–79, is a good introduction.

John L. Penwill, 'Evolution of an Assassin: The Letters of Chion of Heraclea', *Ramus*, 38 (2009), pp. 24–52, is the best analysis of *Letters of Chion* and its moral questions.

Patricia A. Rosenmeyer, *Ancient Epistolary Fictions: The Letter in Greek Literature* (Cambridge, 2001) opened up the field of Greek fictional letters.

Michael Trapp, 'Biography in Letters; Biography and Letters', in *The Limits of Ancient Biography*, ed. Brian McGing and Judith Mossman (Swansea, 2006), pp. 335–50, reads *Letters of Chion* as 'epistolary biography'.

A Note on the Texts

For Greek and Roman names the translators and editor have chosen the forms most familiar to readers. Thus we have used the Latinized forms of some names but not others; e.g., Plato (not Platon) and Chion (not Chio).

Callirhoe: I have used the Loeb edition of the text edited by G. P. Goold (Harvard, 1995) and have attempted to produce a readable translation that is nonetheless close to Chariton's Greek. *R.O.*

Daphnis and Chloe: I have used the Greek text edited by Michael Reeve for the Teubner series (3rd edn, 1994) as the basis for the translation. I have taken poetic licence on several occasions, where my translation varies slightly from the Greek. This should make little difference to the general reader, and scholars of Longus will have no difficulty in working out where I have done so. *P.V.*

Letters of Chion: The text used is the most authoritative currently available, that of Ingemar Düring (Göteborg, 1951), with minor variations indicated in the Notes. I have attempted to make the translation readable (something that cannot always be said for Chion's Greek), while at the same time preserving some of the pomposity which is an integral part of the author's characterization of his protagonist. *J.P.*

A Note on the Text

CHARITON

CALLIRHOE

BOOK 1

[1] I am Chariton of the city of Aphrodisias, a secretary to the lawyer Athenagoras, and I shall relate a love story which took place in Syracuse.

Hermocrates, the Syracusan general who had defeated the Athenians, had a daughter called Callirhoe. This girl was an amazing example of femininity and an icon for all of Sicily, for her beauty was not merely mortal, but of a sort which is practically divine – again, not like the beauty of a Nereid or a mountain spirit, but like that of Aphrodite herself when she was in her prime. Rumours of this stunning vision spread everywhere and suitors poured into Syracuse. These suitors were heads of state and the sons of potentates and came not only from Sicily, but also from Italy, the Greek mainland and the surrounding continental peoples. However, Eros wanted to have his say in the tying of any matrimonial knots. For there was a certain handsome young man called Chaereas whose beauty surpassed all others, just like Achilles, Nireus, Hippolytus and Alcibiades look in statues and drawings. His father was Ariston who was the second most important man in Syracuse, after Hermocrates. In fact, there was a political rivalry between the two of them which was so extreme that they would prefer to make marital alliances with any family rather than each other's. However, Eros likes a good fight and takes great pleasure in winning against the odds: this was exactly the kind of challenge he was looking for.

There was at that time a communal festival of Aphrodite and almost all the women went to her temple. It was the first time Callirhoe had attended a public festival, but her mother took her, since the god Eros had ordered them to pay homage to the goddess. At exactly that time, Chaereas was walking home from the gymnasium, gleaming like a star: the rosy glow from exercise was added to the natural bloom of his radiant face, just like gold inlaid on silver. As chance would have it, they both approached a certain rather narrow bend in the road – and walked straight into each other! Of course this was the god Eros' way of ensuring that each caught sight of the other. It was love at first sight for both of them, a true union of beauty and nobility.

Chaereas, then, smitten with such a wound of love, could scarcely manage to make his way home. He was like some noble warrior wounded in a vital spot in war, ashamed to fall but unable to stand. The young girl, on the other hand, threw herself down at the feet of the goddess Aphrodite and kissing her, said, 'Mistress, give me as my husband this man you have shown me.' The night came on – dreadful for both of them since the fire of love was burning them. The girl, however, suffered more terribly as a result of the silence she had to maintain, ashamed to have her secret revealed. But Chaereas, who was after all a fine and confident young man, when he began – literally – to waste away, dared to approach his parents and said that he was in love with Callirhoe and could not live without her as his wife. His father groaned when he heard this and said, 'Son, I think it's a lost cause. For it is clear that Hermocrates would never give his daughter to you in marriage, since he has so many rich and regal suitors for her hand. So you must not even try, in case we are openly humiliated.' He then set himself to comforting his son, but the young man's torment increased to such an extent that he was unable to follow his usual pursuits. The gymnasium, for instance, was abandoned by him and was practically deserted by the rest of the local young men since Chaereas was so popular with them. Concerned and curious, therefore, they soon discovered the cause of his malady. When they realized that the handsome youth was in serious danger because of the torment of love in his noble soul, they all felt pity for him.

The time came round for the usual assembly meeting. When the populace had seated themselves, they immediately shouted this one thing: 'Noble Hermocrates, great general, save Chaereas: this will be your most important victory. The city proposes the marriage

today of these two young people, worthy as they are of each other.'
Who could describe such an assembly – of which Eros was the
agitator! Hermocrates was unable to refuse what the city asked.
When he had nodded his head in assent, the whole people leapt
up and left the theatre, and while the young men went off to find
Chaereas, the council and the state officials followed Hermocrates.
The Syracusan women as well were there to attend the bride. The
wedding hymn was sung throughout the city, and the streets were
full of garlands and torches while the doorways were sprinkled
with wine and perfumed oil. The Syracusans considered this day
sweeter than the day of their great military victory.

But the maiden Callirhoe, knowing nothing of all of this, had
thrown herself down upon her bed with her head covered, weeping and refusing to speak. Her nurse came up to the bed, 'Child,
get up! The day we have most longed for is here! The city is
attending your wedding!' To quote the bard, 'At this her knees
and her dear heart were loosed', for she did not know to whom
she was to be married. She was immediately speechless, darkness
poured down over her eyes and she nearly expired: to those who
were watching this seemed the expression of her modesty. When
her maids had quickly arrayed her, the crowd stood back from
the doors and his parents led the bridegroom forward to the
girl. Chaereas ran up and kissed her, and Callirhoe, recognizing
the man she loved, became stronger and more radiant, just like
the light of a lamp that is dying down but, when more oil is
poured in, glows again. When she came forward into the public
view, amazement seized the whole populace, just as when Artemis
appears to huntsmen in a lonely spot. Many of those present
even fell down and worshipped Callirhoe. They were awed by
her and kept telling Chaereas how blessed he was. Poets sing of
such a wedding: the wedding of Thetis on Mount Pelion. They
say the goddess Strife was present then, just as a jealous daemon
was found here in this situation.

[2] For the other suitors, failing in their object of marriage, mixed
bitter disappointment with their anger. Previously fighting among
themselves, at this point they found themselves on common
ground. As a result of this, and because they considered themselves

to have been insulted, they met to take counsel together and Envy became their strategic adviser in the war against Chaereas. First, a certain young Italian, the son of the tyrant of Rhegium, stood up and said the following: 'If one of us had married her, I would not have been angry: just like in athletic competitions, one of the contestants has to win. But since someone who has made no effort on behalf of this match has been valued above us, I am unable to bear the insult. We have stretched ourselves to the limit, spending sleepless nights outside her door, making up to nurses and maidservants, and sending gifts to the people who look after her. For how long have we been slaves? And, worst of all, we have hated each other as rivals in love. But that shiftless, common nobody, who is superior to none of the royal princes taking part in the contest, has himself carried off the prize without any effort. But may the prize do him no good and let us ensure that the marriage spells death for the groom.'

Everyone praised him and only the ruler of Acragas spoke in opposition: 'I oppose the plan, but not because of any goodwill towards Chaereas, rather for the sake of a safer course of action. Remember that Hermocrates is by no means a negligible man and therefore an open battle between us and him would be impossible. It would be far better to proceed with guile: for we get our power more by trickery than by open force. Vote for me as your general in the war against Chaereas: I promise to dissolve the marriage, for I will arm the goddess Jealousy against him and she, taking Love as her ally, will do much evil. Although Callirhoe is sweet tempered and incapable of mean-minded suspicion, Chaereas, bred in the gymnasium, is not without experience of the follies of youth and is quite capable of becoming suspicious and being struck by a young man's fierce jealousy. It is easier to approach him and spread rumours.'

Even as he was still speaking, everyone voted in favour of the plan, and they put the job in his hands as a man with the capability to carry anything out. He then began planning such a scheme.

[3] It was evening time and someone announced that Ariston, Chaereas' father, had fallen from a ladder on his farm and had

only a small chance of survival. When Chaereas heard this, although he loved his father, he was even more greatly grieved that he would have to go alone since it was not possible for him to take his bride. During that night, no one dared to serenade her openly, but coming secretly and surreptitiously they planted the evidence of a revel. They garlanded the outer doors and anointed them with myrrh, they spilt the lees of wine and they dropped half-burned torches.

Day broke and each person who passed the house stopped, struck by a common sense of curiosity. Chaereas hurried straight back to his wife as soon as his father's state of health improved. At first he was surprised to see the crowd around his door, then when he learned the reason he rushed into the house in a passion. Finding the bedroom door still locked, he pounded on it violently and when the maidservant opened it, he fell upon Callirhoe, his anger turning to grief, tearing his clothes and weeping. When she tried to find out what was wrong, he was unable to say, since he was able neither to distrust what he had seen, nor to lend credence to things that he did not want to believe. While he was in confusion like this and trembling, his wife, suspecting nothing of what had happened, kept begging him to tell her the cause of his anger. He, with bloodshot eyes and a strangled voice, said, 'I am weeping at my misfortune, because you have forgotten me so swiftly', and he threw an accusation about the revel at her. She, as the daughter of a general and full of spirit, felt anger at the unfair criticism and said, 'No one came revelling to my father's house, but it is your doors which seem to be accustomed to these revels and perhaps your getting married has upset your lovers.' With these words she turned away, covered her head and gave vent to a stream of tears. Reconciliations are easy for lovers and they joyfully receive any apology from each other. Chaereas, therefore, began to modify his behaviour and restrain himself, and his wife quickly welcomed his change of heart. This made their love burn even more brightly and both sets of parents counted themselves blessed, seeing the harmony between their children.

[4] The man from Acragas, failing in his first plan, fixed for his next one on something more dramatic and prepared the following

scheme. He had a certain hanger-on, a smooth-talker, pleasing and full of every charm. He ordered this man to act the part of one in love and, cultivating an acquaintance with the most lovely and trusted of Callirhoe's maidservants, to make her fall in love with him. He only succeeded with great difficulty but he led the young woman astray with very expensive gifts and by claiming that he would hang himself if he did not succeed in her love: a woman is easily captured when she believes she is loved. Having prepared the ground like this, then, the director of the drama found another actor: this time not so charming, but ready for anything and a persuasive talker. Priming him in advance with what it was necessary for him to do and say, he sent this stranger to Chaereas. Approaching Chaereas as he hung around at the wrestling ground, he said, 'I used to have a son, Chaereas, about your age who greatly admired and loved you while he lived. Now that his life is over, I think of you as my son and your welfare is to the common good of all of Sicily. Therefore, give me your attention and you will hear some very important matters affecting the whole of your life.'

With such comments that shameful man stirred up the young man's soul and made it full of hope, fear and curiosity. But when Chaereas asked him to speak, he shrank from it and gave an excuse that the present moment was not an appropriate one, that a delay was needed and more time. So Chaereas argued for it even more, since he now was anticipating something really serious. The other man, stretching out his right hand to him, led him to a deserted spot; then, knitting his brows into a frown and acting like someone who is distressed, he even managed to cry a little bit and said, 'O Chaereas, it is without any pleasure that I mention this shocking matter to you and for a long time I have shrunk from telling you. But since you are being openly insulted and the dreadful matter is being talked about every-where, I can no longer remain silent. For my nature is to hate what is base and I am especially well-intentioned towards you. Know then that your wife has been seduced into infidelity, and so that you believe this I am ready to show you the adulterer in the act.'

Thus he spake: and a black cloud of grief enveloped him and
taking the sooty dust in both his hands he poured it down onto
his head to defile his lovely face.

For a long time Chaereas lay there senseless, unable to use either
his mouth or his eyes. When he spoke it was with a low voice
unlike his usual one: 'I ask a painful favour from you,' he said,
'and the favour is to be able to see the crimes against me with my
own eyes. But do show me, so that I can destroy myself with good
reason. For I will spare Callirhoe even if she is wronging me.'
'Pretend that you are going to the farm in the country,' the other
man replied, 'but keep a watch on the house in the depths of the
evening; you will see the adulterer entering the house.'
The two of them agreed to this plan, and Chaereas sent a
message (for he himself could not face going in) which said, 'I
am going away to the farm in the country.' Thus that evil and
slanderous man set the stage for the drama. When evening came,
Chaereas went to his lookout point, and the other man, who
had seduced Callirhoe's maidservant, rushed into the narrow
lane, acting like one who was plotting to carry out secret deeds
and was taking every care to escape anyone's notice. His hair
was oiled and his curled locks breathed out perfume; he wore
eyeliner, a fine cloak and beautifully-made sandals; heavy rings
glowed on his fingers. Then, constantly looking around, he
approached the door, knocked lightly and gave the accustomed
signal. At that, the maidservant, herself extremely fearful, quietly
opened the door, took him by the hand and led him in. Seeing
these things, Chaereas was no longer able to hold back but ran
in to catch the adulterer red-handed and kill him.
But the man he was after hid behind the courtyard door and
immediately slipped out. Meanwhile, Callirhoe was sitting on
the couch longing for Chaereas and had not even lighted a lamp
because she was feeling so miserable. When the sound of footsteps reached her, she at once realized that it was her husband
by the sound of his breathing, and joyfully ran to greet him. He
had no voice left to reproach her, but overcome as he was by
anger, he kicked her as she approached. His well-aimed foot
caught her just beneath her diaphragm and robbed the girl of

her breath. Her maidservants picked her up from where she had
fallen and laid her on the couch.

[5] Callirhoe then lay without speaking or breathing, giving the
appearance of someone who was dead to anyone who saw her.
Rumour, the messenger of suffering, ran through all the city,
arousing wailing throughout the streets right down to the sea.
And on all sides, lamentation was heard and it was as though
the city had been captured. Chaereas, still seething in his heart,
shut himself away for the whole of the night and interrogated
the maidservants with torture, first and last the one who was
most special to Callirhoe. As they were being burnt and cut, he
learnt the truth. Then pity overcame him for the dead woman
and he wanted to kill himself, but he was stopped by Polycharmus, his best friend, just as Homer made Patroclus a best friend
for Achilles. When day came, the archons selected a jury for the
murder: they were particularly expeditious in setting up the case
because of Hermocrates' high position in the city. But the whole
populace came to the marketplace vociferously giving vent to
diverse opinions. The unsuccessful suitors were currying favour
with the crowd – above all the ruler of Acragas who was showing off and swaggering about as if he had successfully completed
some deed no one would have expected. But a new event
occurred, something which has never previously happened in a
law court. Once the charge had been read, the killer, even though
the water clock was measuring out his allotted time to speak,
instead of a defence speech, accused himself even more bitterly
and cast the first vote for conviction without saying any of the
justifiable things he could have said in his own defence, nothing
about the slanderous misinformation, nor about his own jealousy, nor his lack of premeditation. But he begged them all:
'Stone me to death in public; I have taken away the city's crowning glory. It would be an act of charity to give me over to the
public executioner. I ought to suffer this even if I had killed
Hermocrates' maidservant. Seek out the most unspeakable form
of punishment. I have committed an act worse than temple
robbery or patricide. Don't allow me burial, don't so defile the
land, but cast my impious body into the sea!'

As he said this a mourning wail broke out and everyone, putting aside the thought of the woman who was dead, began to feel grief for the man who was still alive. Hermocrates first spoke in support of Chaereas: 'I know,' he said, 'that the deed was unintentional. I realize that there have been men plotting against us. They will not be allowed to have two corpses nor will I cause grief to my dead daughter. I have heard her saying many times that she wants Chaereas to live more than herself. Therefore, let us stop this unnecessary trial and go on to the necessary burial. Let us not surrender the corpse to the passing of time nor let the body lose its beauty in decay. Let us bury Callirhoe while she is still beautiful.'

[6] The judges cast their votes for acquittal, but Chaereas would not acquit himself; he wanted to die and devised all sorts of means to fulfil his wish. Polycharmus, seeing that it was impossible to save him in any other way, said, 'Traitor to the dead woman, will you not wait to bury Callirhoe? Will you entrust her to the hands of others? For it is the right time now for you to ensure that she has a luxurious shroud and a funeral procession fit for a queen.' This argument was successful for it summoned up his feelings of both pride and concern.

Who would be able to describe that funeral procession as it deserved? Callirhoe lay on a golden couch wearing her bridal clothes, looking so magnificent and amazing that everyone likened her to the sleeping Ariadne. First, all the Syracusan knights bedecked in all their finery and on their horses preceded her bier, then, after them, the infantry carrying the symbols of Hermocrates' victories; then came the council, and in the middle of the people all the archons as a ceremonial guard for Hermocrates.

Ariston was also carried on a bier, still ill and calling Callirhoe his daughter and a noble lady. After all of these came the wives of the citizens, clad in black and following them, the gifts for the dead, worthy of royalty: first, the dowry of gold and silver; then, the beautiful finery of rich clothes (Hermocrates had sent many from the spoils he had won); next, the gifts of relatives and friends. Right at the end came Chaereas' wealth. For he wanted, if it was possible, for all his possessions to be burnt along with his wife. Syracusan youths carried the couch and the throng of people followed. All were lamenting, but the grief of Chaereas was heard the loudest. The fine and noble tomb of Hermocrates' family was near the shore and was visible to those sailing far away. The abundance of the funeral gifts filled this tomb as if it was some treasury. But what appeared to be for the honour of the dead woman put in motion a series of greater events.

[7] There was a man called Theron, one capable of any wickedness, who sailed the high seas pursuing a life of crime: along with him there was a group of dubious characters who put into harbours under the pretence of running a passenger ferry, but who were really organized into a pirate band. This man by chance witnessed the funeral procession and thus clapped eyes on the gold. Lying in bed that night, but unable to sleep, he kept saying to himself, 'Am I to risk my life fighting on the sea and killing the living for the sake of paltry booty, when it is possible to get rich from one corpse? Let the die be cast! I will not throw away this opportunity for gain. But who shall I take with me on the job? Think, Theron, who is the most appropriate out of those you know? Zenophanes from Thurii? He is clever, but a coward. Menon the Messanian? He is bold, but untrustworthy.'

He went through each one, weighing them up just like someone testing coins and although he rejected many, nevertheless he decided that some would be useful. So he ran down to the harbour at dawn and sought out each one of them. He found some in the brothels, others in taverns – a perfectly appropriate army for such a general. Then, after he said that he had something important to discuss with them, he led them to the back of the harbour and began with these words: 'I have found some treasure and have chosen you out of everyone to be my partners. For the booty is too much for one man, and yet does not require much effort: on the contrary, one night will be enough to make you all rich. We are not inexperienced in such enterprises. Even though they attract criticism from small-minded men, they provide benefits for those who have the wit to capitalize on them.'

They knew immediately that he was putting forward piracy or tomb-robbing or temple-robbing and they said, 'Stop trying to persuade us right now and explain what the deed is so that we don't lose the opportunity.' Answering in turn, then, Theron said, 'You have seen the gold and the silver belonging to the dead girl. It would be fairer for us, who are alive, to have this. So it seems to me a good plan to open the tomb during the night, then for us to embark on a light, speedy yacht and sail wherever the wind carries us and sell the booty abroad.' When the others agreed, he added, 'So now return to your usual pursuits; but let each of you come down to the yacht in the depths of the night bringing a piece of builder's equipment.'

[8] They got on as instructed. Meanwhile, Callirhoe was experiencing a second birth. The condition which had interrupted her breathing passed off because her whole system was cleansed and purged by the enforced fast of the past few days. Slowly and little by little, her breathing returned, then she began to move each limb and then her body, and as she opened her eyes, she felt as if she was waking from sleep and called out to Chaereas expecting him to be asleep beside her. When neither her husband nor her maidservants responded to her and she realized that all around her was an empty darkness, fear and trembling seized the girl and she was unable to grasp the truth in her mind. Slowly as she sat up, she touched the garlands and ribbons tied around her and knocked against the gold and silver which made a noise. There was a strong smell of aromatic spices and herbs. Then she remembered the kick and the fall which resulted from it and managed to work out that she must be in her tomb because she had been unconscious. She shouted out in as loud a voice as she could manage: 'I am alive! Come and help me!' But when nothing happened although she had shouted many times, she abandoned hope of being saved and put her head on her knees and wept, saying, 'Alas for these troubles! I am buried alive, although I have done no wrong and I am going to die a terrible death. They mourn me now, although I am perfectly healthy! Who will get word out? Unjust Chaereas, I blame you not because you have killed me, but because you rushed to throw

me out of your house. You shouldn't have buried Callirhoe so
quickly when she was not truly dead. Perhaps you are already
planning some other marriage!'

[9] Thus she was absorbed in all manner of lamentations when
Theron, after waiting until the very middle of the night,
approached the tomb in silence, lightly touching the surface of
the sea with his oars. Disembarking first, he organized his crew
in the following manner: he set four to keep watch in case anyone
should approach the place, with orders to kill them if they could
but otherwise to alert him to their arrival with a prearranged
signal; another four, with himself as a fifth, were to approach
the tomb; the remaining seven (for there were sixteen in all) he
ordered to remain in the yacht and keep their oars at the ready
so that if something unforeseen should occur, they could swiftly
snatch up the men from the shore and sail away.

When the crowbars were applied and a violent effort was made
to open the tomb, all sorts of feelings seized Callirhoe at once
– fear, joy, grief, amazement, hope, doubt. 'Where does this noise
come from? Is some supernatural spirit approaching me in my
wretchedness as is normal for the dead? Or is it not a noise as
such, but the voice of those beneath the earth calling me to them?
It seems more likely to be tomb-robbers: and this misfortune is
to be added to all the others. Wealth is useless for a corpse!' As
she was still reasoning like this to herself, one of the robbers
pushed his head inside the tomb and came in a little way.

Callirhoe threw herself towards him, wanting to beg his help,
but he leapt back in terror. Trembling, he addressed his companions, 'Let's flee from here. A supernatural spirit is guarding what's
inside and won't allow us to get in.' Theron laughed at him,
saying that he was a coward and deader than the dead woman.
Then he ordered another of the band to enter, but when no one
could face it he went in himself with his sword raised in front
of him. When she caught sight of the sword, Callirhoe was afraid
that she would be killed so she lay down in a corner and from
there supplicated him in her melodious voice: 'Whoever you are,
have pity on one who has not been pitied by either husband or
parents. Don't kill the one whom you have saved.'

Theron – a man who was never slow on the uptake – took courage at this and realized what the situation was. He stood for a moment deep in thought and at first decided to kill the woman on the grounds that she would get in the way of the whole enterprise; but he almost immediately changed his mind thinking of the additional profit, and said to himself, 'She can be part of the grave-goods. There is lots of silver here, lots of gold but the beauty of this woman is more valuable than all of that!' So he took her hand and led her out, then called to his companion and said, 'Look – here is the supernatural spirit you feared! A fine robber you are, afraid of a woman! But for the moment, guard her, for I want to give her back to her parents. We will carry off all the stuff which is inside, now there is no longer even a corpse watching over it.'

[10] When they had filled the yacht with the booty, Theron ordered the guard to stand a little aside with the woman. Then he consulted the men about what they should do with her. There were different opinions, all conflicting with each other. First, someone said, 'We came for something different, comrades, but by luck an even better reward has turned up: let's make the best use of it since we are able to do so without any danger to ourselves. My suggestion is that we leave the grave-goods here on the land and give Callirhoe back to her husband and father, saying that we moored here to do some fishing as we usually do but heard a voice and accordingly opened the tomb out of compassion so that we might save the one who was locked inside. We can make the woman swear to all of this as a witness for us. She will gladly do us this favour believing that she owes it to the benefactors who saved her. Can you think how much joy we will fill the whole of Sicily with? How many gifts we will receive? And at the same time we will be doing what is just towards men and pious towards the gods.'

Before he had finished speaking, another one interrupted, 'What a stupid thing to say, you idiot! Are you telling us now to be philosophers? Has tomb-robbing given us hearts of gold? Are we to have pity on a girl whose own husband had no pity and killed her? Because she has done us no harm? But she will do us harm and of the greatest kind! For a start, if we give her back to those she belongs to, it is not clear what opinion they will have about what has happened, and it is impossible that they wouldn't suspect the real reason that we entered the tomb. And even if the woman's relations don't press charges against us, the city archons and the people themselves won't let tomb-robbers go free, taking their booty with them. Someone will be quick to say that it is much more profitable to sell the girl: she will fetch a price in proportion to her beauty. But such a plan carries with it this danger: because gold doesn't have a voice nor will silver reveal where we took it from, it is possible to make up some story about them. But who would be able to hide merchandise which has eyes and ears and a tongue? Nor is her beauty of a normal human sort which we could disguise. Will we say that she is a slave? Who would believe this once they have seen her? Let us kill her here and not take our own accuser along with us.'

Although many of the men agreed with these suggestions, Theron supported neither of the two views which had been put forward. 'For you,' he said to the first, 'court danger, but you,' (to the second speaker) 'lose us our profit. I will sell the girl rather than destroy her. For if she is sold, she will keep silent out of fear; once that's done she can accuse us as much as she wants, because we won't be there. This life of ours is not one which comes risk free! So let's embark and get going for it is already nearly day.'

[11] Once launched the boat made excellent progress. For they were not forcing themselves against the waves and the wind by setting their own course, but rather whatever direction the wind favoured seemed good to them and they let it direct their prow. Theron tried to reassure Callirhoe attempting to deceive her with carefully-crafted ideas. But she realized how things stood for her and that she had been saved in vain. She pretended, however, not to understand this, but to believe Theron, afraid that she would be killed if she appeared angry. So she said that she could not bear the sea and covered her head and wept. 'Oh Father,' she said, 'you defeated three hundred Athenian ships in this sea, but now a small yacht has snatched your daughter from

you and you can't do anything to help me. I am being taken to an alien land where I must become a slave – me, a nobly born girl! In a trice, some Athenian master will buy the daughter of Hermocrates at market! How much better it was for me to lie as a corpse in the tomb! Eventually Chaereas would have been united with me there; now we are parted whether we are alive or dead!'

She was lost in lamentations of this sort, but the robbers sailed on past small islands and cities, for their cargo was not for poor men: they were seeking rich customers. They anchored right opposite Attica in the lee of a certain hooked promontory. There was a stream there with abundant clear water and a beautiful meadow. They led Callirhoe there and told her to wash and rest a little after the voyage because they wanted her to look after her beauty. Once alone, they planned what harbour they should put into. One of them said, 'We are near Athens, a great and prosperous city. There we can find a great number of merchants, and a great number of rich men. For just as a normal market throngs with men, so in Athens the marketplace throngs also with the people of a thousand other cities.' Everyone thought that it was a good idea to put in to Athens, but the city's reputation for meddlesomeness made it less attractive to Theron. 'Have you alone not heard what busybodies the Athenians are? The people are gossips and lawsuit lovers: in the harbour ten thousand would-be lawyers will find out who we are and where we have brought this cargo from. Base suspicions will take hold of those dubious characters. Their high court is just right there and their magistrates are harder than tyrants. We should fear the Athenians more than the Syracusans. The country that is right for us is Ionia – there royal wealth pours in from the great land of Asia and men live in luxury without asking endless questions. I hope to find some wealthy customers there.' So they took on water and got a store of provisions from a merchant ship moored alongside them, then sailed immediately for Miletus and on the third day put into a fine natural harbour which was eighty stades from the city.

[12] There Theron ordered them to put up their oars and to construct some sort of temporary quarters for Callirhoe and to

provide her with everything she needed. He did not act out of a
sense of humanity but from his greediness for profit, more like
a merchant than a robber. He himself rushed to the town with
two of his crew. At that point he was not planning to seek a
buyer openly nor to advertise what he was up to, but secretly
to rush through a sale by direct payment. But this was hard to
manage because Callirhoe was not to become the possession of
an ordinary person nor one whom he chanced to meet, but of
some wealthy king – and he was afraid to approach such people.
After a considerable period of time passed like this, he was no
longer able to endure the delay. Night came on but he was unable
to sleep and he said to himself, 'Oh Theron, you are an idiot.
For you have already abandoned your gold and silver in a
deserted place for so many days as if you were the only robber
in the world. Don't you realize that other pirates also sail the
seas? I even fear my own comrades in case they desert and put
out to sea. For, to be sure, you didn't gather together a band of
the most honest and upright men, so that you might rely on their
loyalty, but of the most criminal men you knew. Now therefore,'
he continued, 'you need sleep because tomorrow when day comes
you must run to the boat and throw that useless nuisance of a
woman into the sea and never again take on such an awkward
cargo.' But when he fell asleep, he dreamed of locked doors and
therefore decided to keep going for that day. So he wandered
about and eventually sat down in a certain workshop, exhausted
and confused.

   In the meantime, a crowd of men, both slave and free, was
passing by, in the middle of which stood a man in the prime of
life but dressed in black and with a grief-stricken expression.
Theron jumped up (for human nature is curious) and asked one
of the men in the crowd, 'Who is that?' He got this reply: 'You
must be a foreigner or have come from a long way off if you
don't know Dionysius who surpasses all other Ionians by his
wealth, birth and education and is a friend of the Great King
himself.' 'Why is he dressed in black?' 'His wife, whom he loved,
has just died.' Theron got yet more from the conversation, finding out that he was rich and a man with an eye for the ladies.
So he did not let his informant go yet but asked him, 'What is

your relationship to him?' The other man replied, 'I am the administrator of the whole estate and I look after him and his daughter, a young child, orphaned before her time by her poor mother.' Theron said, 'What are you called?' 'Leonas.' 'Oh Leonas,' said Theron, 'it is lucky for you that I ran into you. For I am a merchant and I have just sailed from Italy and therefore I know nothing about what goes on in Ionia. But a woman of Sybaris, the most prosperous lady in that city, had a very beautiful maidservant whom she sold out of jealousy – and I bought her. This can be to your advantage whether you want to obtain a nurse for the child (for she has been suitably trained) or whether it suits you to make the most of a chance to do your master a favour. It is more to your advantage for him to have the slave girl so that he won't subsequently provide a stepmother for the young girl.' Leonas listened to all of this with great enthusiasm and said, 'Some god has sent you down to do a good turn for me! For you are offering me in real life what I have dreamt of: come now to the house and on the strength of this be my guest and friend. The woman's appearance will decide the question about her whether she is to be a possession of my master or is more for the likes of us.'

[13] When they came to the house, Theron was amazed at its size and luxuriousness (for it had been got ready to receive the Persian King), and Leonas asked him to wait while he first saw to his master's comfort. Then he took him to his own dwelling, itself very civilized, and asked him to join him for a meal. Theron, a rogue through and through and very skilled at adapting himself to any situation, started on the meal and cemented his friendship with Leonas by many toasts, some of which were to give him the appearance of sincerity, but other, genuine ones were for the successful undertaking of their shared enterprise. Meanwhile, there was much conversation about the woman and Theron praised her character more than her beauty realizing that what cannot be seen requires advertisement but that her appearance would recommend itself. 'Let us go,' said Leonas, 'and you can show her to me.' But Theron replied, 'She is not here. We stayed on the outskirts of the city because of the customs officers and

our boat is moored eighty stades away', and he explained about
the place. 'You have dropped anchor on our estate,' exclaimed
Leonas. 'This is even better: Fortune is already leading you to
Dionysius. Let us go to the country estate so that you can refresh
yourselves from the sea journey. For our country house is nearby
and lavishly prepared.' Theron was even happier to hear this,
thinking that the sale would be more easily transacted not in the
marketplace but in private, and he said, 'Let's go off at dawn,
you to your country house, me to my ship and I will bring the
woman to you there.' This was agreed and they shook hands on
it and parted. For both of them the night seemed long, the one
eager to make a purchase, the other eager to make a sale.

During the course of the following day Leonas sailed along
to the country house taking a sum of cash with him so that he
was ready for the merchant. Theron meanwhile was on the beach
with his comrades – who by this stage were getting rather nervous – and was explaining to them what was going on. He also
began to try and pacify Callirhoe. 'Daughter,' he said, 'I did
indeed first of all want to return you to your relatives, but an
opposing wind sprang up and I was prevented from doing so by
the sea. You know how much forethought I have shown for you:
most of all we have kept you chaste and Chaereas will get you
back entirely unmolested, as if we had rescued you from your
very own bedchamber. Now, therefore, it is necessary for us to
head on for Lycia, but it is not equally necessary for you to be
made wretched in vain by your dreadful seasickness. I will leave
you with some trustworthy friends, and when I return I will
collect you and take you then back to Syracuse with the greatest
care. So come and get any of your things you want. We will look
after the rest for you.'

At this, Callirhoe laughed to herself although she was very
worried. She thought he was completely stupid for she knew she
was being sold, but she reckoned that this would be an improve-
ment on her current situation, since she was very keen to escape
from the robbers. 'Thank you, Father,' she accordingly said, 'for
the kindness you have shown me. May the god give all of you
your just deserts. But I consider it to be unlucky to use the grave-
goods. Guard them well for me. This small ring, which I had

when I was a corpse, will be enough for me.' Then modestly covering her head she added, 'Theron, take me wherever you want. Anywhere is better than a ship or the sea.'

[14] When he got near to the country estate, Theron thought out the following strategy. Taking the veil off her head and loosening her hair, he opened the door and told her to enter first. Leonas, and all those who were inside, were struck dumb at the sight of her suddenly standing there. They thought they were seeing a goddess, for there was a rumour in those parts that Aphrodite could appear. While they remained dumbstruck at the sight, Theron followed Callirhoe in and went up to Leonas, 'Come and get ready to receive the girl, for this is she whom you want to buy.' Joy and amazement followed his words and Callirhoe was led off to the finest of the bedchambers and allowed to lie down, for she very much needed a rest from the grief and mental and physical stress and fear she had been under. Meanwhile, Theron was shaking Leonas by the hand and saying, 'What I promised has been faithfully carried out, and right now you have the woman. So, on the strength of our friendship, go now to the city and get the registration certificate and then pay me the price you want.' But Leonas, wanting to respond with equal friendliness said, 'Not at all! I will trust you with the cash before getting the registration certificate.' At the same time too he wanted to seize the initiative in the business, afraid that Theron might change his mind. For there were many in the city who would want to buy Callirhoe. Accordingly, he brought out a talent in cash and insisted on him taking it, and Theron took it, although feigning indifference. But when Leonas was trying to get him to stay for dinner (for the hour was far advanced), he said, 'I want to sail to the city this evening but we will meet tomorrow at the harbour.'

After this, he left. When he came to the ship, Theron ordered his crew to raise the anchor and set sail as quickly as possible before they were discovered. So they secretly escaped where the wind took them, but Callirhoe, left alone, finally had the chance to bewail her own fate. 'Look,' she said, 'another tomb in which Theron has locked me, and this one more remote and lonely than the last one! For there my father and mother would have come to visit me and Chaereas would have poured out his libation of tears. I would have felt that, even though I was dead. Who shall I call upon here? Envious Fortune, pursuing me over land and sea, you have not yet completed the sum of my troubles! First, you made my lover my murderer: Chaereas who had never even struck a slave, kicked me who loves him, with such fatal results. Then, you let me fall into the hands of tomb-robbers and led me out of the tomb into the sea, where I was among pirates more fearsome than the waves. I suppose I have been given my famous beauty for this: so that Theron the robber can get a good price for me! I have been sold in this deserted spot and not taken to the city as some other slave might have been because you, Fortune, were afraid that someone might see me and realize that I am nobly born. Because of this I have been handed over like a piece of property, to whom, I don't know – Greeks, foreigners or robbers again.' As she beat her breast she caught sight of the ring on her hand with Chaereas' image on it. She kissed it. 'Truly I am lost to you now, Chaereas, separated from you by so much sea!' she exclaimed. 'And you are grieving and repenting as you lie by my empty tomb, bearing witness to my chastity now after my death, while I, the daughter of Hermocrates, your wife, have today been sold to a master.' Consumed by these laments, sleep was barely able to overcome her.

BOOK 2

[1] Leonas told Phocas the steward to look after the young woman with the greatest of care, and he himself went off to Miletus before dawn, hurrying to take the good news concerning the young girl to his master and believing that he was bringing him a great source of consolation in his grief. He found Dionysius still in bed: for, labouring under his affliction, he hardly went out at all, even though his country needed him. On the contrary, he spent his time in his private apartments as though his wife were still with him.

When he caught sight of Leonas he said to him, 'I slept well last night for the first time since my poor wife's death. For I saw her clearly, made bigger and more beautiful but as if she was really present with me. I thought it was the first day of our marriage and I was leading her as a bride from my beachside estate and you were singing the wedding hymn for me.' Before he had even finished his last sentence, Leonas cried out, 'Master – you are in luck, both in your dream and in waking reality! You are about to hear such things as I have seen –' and he began to explain to him. 'Well, a certain merchant approached me, offering a very beautiful woman for sale – because of the customs officers he had anchored outside the city and near your country estate. By arrangement I went out to the estate and there, discussing it together, we did indeed complete the deal. I gave him a talent and he handed over the woman. But we must do the legal registration here.' Dionysius was very pleased to hear about the woman's beauty (for he truly was a connoisseur of women), but he was by no means so taken with the idea of her being a slave. For he was a man of high lineage, outstanding throughout the

whole of Ionia for his integrity and his culture – to such a one
the idea of a relationship with a slave was not attractive. 'Leonas,'
he said, 'it is just not possible for someone who is not freeborn
to be physically beautiful. Do you not remember how the poets
say that the beautiful are children of the gods, and far more
likely to be the offspring of nobly-born mortals? She impressed
you because there was no one else around and you were compar-
ing her to the local peasant women. But, since you have bought
her, go to the marketplace: Adrastus, the most experienced of
the lawyers, will sort out the registration.'

Leonas was perfectly happy that so little credit was given to his
description, because then his master would be even more amazed
when it unexpectedly proved true. But although he went round
all the harbours in Miletus and all the bankers' stalls, he could
not find Theron anywhere. He asked the traders and the ferrymen
but no one knew him. So in desperation he took a row boat out
and went round to the beach and even then to the estate: but he
was not likely to find a man who had already set sail. Reluctantly
and slowly therefore, he made his way back to his master. When
Dionysius saw the expression on his face, he asked what had
happened. Leonas replied, 'I have lost you a talent, master.' 'This
experience will make you more cautious in the future. However,
what actually happened? Did the girl run away?' 'No, not her,' he
replied, 'but the man selling her did.' 'So he must have been a
kidnapper and sold you someone else's slave – that's why it was
in such a deserted spot. Where did he say the woman came from?'
'From Sybaris in Italy, sold by her mistress because she was jealous of her.' 'Go and find out if there is anyone from Sybaris in
town at the moment. In the meantime, leave the woman where
she is.' So Leonas went off, upset that his plans had not worked
out for the best. Instead he decided to wait for a good moment
to persuade his master to go out to his country estate, since his
one remaining chance was if his master actually saw the girl.

[2] Meanwhile, the peasant women of the area went to visit
Callirhoe and straightaway began addressing her and appealing
to her as if she were their mistress. Plangon, the steward's wife,
who was a very practical person, said to her, 'My dear, I know

you miss your own people deeply, but don't let that stop you from settling in with those whom you find around you now. Dionysius, our master, is, you know, a good and well-intentioned man. Luckily, the gods have led you to a good home – just as if you remained in your fatherland. Wash off the dirt from your long sea voyage: there are maidservants here to look after you.' Although Callirhoe was reluctant, she managed to lead her to the bath. So Callirhoe went in and the maids anointed her with oil and carefully massaged it off, and they were even more amazed by Callirhoe when they saw her undressed. When dressed they had been astonished by her face, claiming that it was divine, but now seeing what was normally covered, they forgot about her face. For her skin was radiant in its white brilliance, shining out like a sparkling star. Her flesh was so delightfully soft that you would fear that even the touch of a finger would bruise it cruelly. Quietly the women murmured to one another, 'Our mistress's beauty was much celebrated: but she would seem like a maidservant in comparison with this girl.' Their praise upset Callirhoe and she had no notion of what it would lead on to. When she was washed and her hair was being arranged, they brought her fresh clothes, but she declared that they were not suitable for a newly-bought slave. 'Give me a slave's tunic, for you are superior to me.' So she put on something more appropriate – but this too suited her and, glorified by her beauty, gave the impression of expensive luxury.

After the women had had a meal, Plangon said, 'Come to the temple of Aphrodite and pray to her to help you. For the goddess makes herself manifest here, and not only the local people but also people from the city come to sacrifice to her. She is especially ready to listen to Dionysius and he never bypasses her temple.' Then she explained about the epiphanies of the goddess and one of the countrywomen said, 'Lady, when you see Aphrodite, you will seem to be looking at an image of yourself.' When she heard this Callirhoe was filled with tears and said to her, 'Alas for my misfortunes! And here is the goddess Aphrodite, the cause of all my troubles. But I will go, because I want to level many accusations at her!'

The temple was near the farm buildings beside the main road

itself. Callirhoe threw herself down prostrate and, taking hold of Aphrodite's feet, said, 'First, you showed Chaereas to me, then, you joined us in a glorious union – but now you have abandoned us, even though we honoured you! Since that is how you want it, I beg one favour from you: make me not pleasing to anyone after him.' With a toss of her head, Aphrodite rejected this request, for she is the mother of Love and was already plotting another marriage though she had no intention of letting that one last either. Callirhoe, then, released from the pirates and her tribulations on the sea, regained her customary loveliness and the local country people were amazed to see her grow more beautiful with each passing day.

[3] Leonas then, spotting a good opportunity, approached Dionysius with these words, 'Master, you haven't been to visit your beachside estate for a long time and the people there are longing for your visit. You need to go and see your flocks and crops and that the fruit harvest is proceeding apace. It is also important that you make use of the magnificent villa, which we built on your orders. You will be able to bear your grief more easily there, distracted by the pleasures and the concerns of a country estate. And if you are pleased with some herdsman or shepherd, you can reward him with the newly-bought slave girl.' This plan found favour with Dionysius and he announced his intention of setting out on a particular day. As word of this pronouncement went round, the drivers prepared their vehicles, the grooms got the horses ready and the crew of his yacht got ready for the voyage. Friends were invited to accompany him and a large retinue of ex-slaves was also assembled. Dionysius had a natural inclination to the magnificent. When everything was ready, he gave orders that the baggage and the majority of his companions be conveyed by sea, while the carriages should follow on when he set out – but well behind since it was not suitable for a man in mourning to arrive in great state. So, just at dawn, without anybody knowing, he mounted his horse as the fifth in a small group. Leonas was also one of them.

While Dionysius was riding out to the fields, Callirhoe, having seen a vision of Aphrodite during the night, was planning to go and worship her again. As she stood there praying, Dionysius jumped down from his horse and entered the temple ahead of everyone else. Hearing the noise of his footsteps, Callirhoe turned; Dionysius caught sight of her and cried out, 'Oh Aphrodite, be propitious and may your appearance mean good luck for me!' As he threw himself to the ground, Leonas raised him and said, 'This, Master, is the girl I just bought. Be calm, sir! And you, woman, approach your master.' At the word 'master', Callirhoe, with downcast eyes, shed forth a stream of tears finally having to accept that she had lost her freedom. Dionysius, striking Leonas, said, 'You impious blasphemer! Do you speak to gods as you would to men? Are you telling me that you bought this girl with silver? No wonder you couldn't find the seller! Have you not heard what Homer teaches us?

> 'Like strangers from a foreign land, the gods
> bear both the insolence and the virtuousness of men.'

At this point, Callirhoe broke in and said, 'Stop mocking me and calling me a goddess when I am not even a particularly lucky mortal.' But when she spoke her voice sounded divine to Dionysius, for her tone was musical and had a resonance just like a harp. Thus Dionysius was in a state of confusion and was too embarrassed to stay in her presence, so he went off to his house already burning with love.

Not long afterwards his entourage arrived from the city and swiftly the rumour of what had happened spread. As a consequence, everybody rushed to see the woman, although they claimed that they were going to worship Aphrodite. Callirhoe was highly embarrassed by the crowd and had no idea what to do, for all the customs were foreign to her, and she could not even see Plangon, whom she was used to, as she was very preoccupied with arrangements for their master. The hour advanced. No one returned from the temple because everyone was held captivated there in a state of amazement. At last Leonas realized what had happened and went to the sacred precinct to bring Callirhoe away. It was then possible to see that royal status comes in their very nature, just as it works for a king-bee in a hive – for they all automatically followed her as if she had been unanimously voted their mistress because of her beauty.

[4] Callirhoe went off to her usual room; Dionysius was utterly smitten but tried to hide the wound, because he was an educated man who always strove to behave in a morally upright way. Nor did he want to appear as a figure of fun to his household staff or seem to his friends to be acting like a teenager, so he kept a tight rein on himself throughout the evening, believing that he was concealing his feelings but in reality being more conspicuous because of his silence. Serving out a portion of food from the meal, he said, 'Have someone take this to our guest. Don't let them say, "From your master," but "From Dionysius".'

He let the drinking continue for a long time because he knew he would not be able to sleep. If he was going to be wakeful, he wanted at least to be with his friends. Late into the night he broke the party up, but still sleep did not come: he could remember everything as if he was still there in the temple of Aphrodite – her face, her hair, how she turned towards him, how she looked into his eyes, her voice, her gestures, her words. Even his tears burned him with desire.

Then came a contest between reason and emotion. Although engulfed by passion, he tried to fight nobly against it. As if trying to struggle up out of a billowing wave, he said to himself, 'You should be ashamed of yourself, Dionysius, that you, a man who ranks first in Ionia for rectitude and reputation, who is admired by satraps, kings and cities, is suffering like some callow youth! You fell in love at first sight and have started moping about this before you are even out of mourning! Was it for this that you came to the country? To make preparations for a wedding when you are still in funeral garb: a wedding with a slave who is perhaps the property of someone else! You don't even have the proper documentation for her!' But Eros loves to get the better of anyone who tries to be sensible and treats self-control as a personal insult, so he burned the poor man all the more savagely because he was trying to be rational about his love.

No longer able to keep it bottled up inside him, he sent for Leonas, who knew perfectly well why he had been summoned but pretended to be ignorant and at a loss about it. 'Why are you awake, Master? It's not still grief for your dead wife, is it?' 'It's about a woman,' said Dionysius, 'but not my dead wife. I know I can say anything to you because of your regard for me and your loyalty. But you have destroyed me, Leonas; you are responsible for all my troubles. You have brought a burning brand into my house and even into my soul! The uncertainty about her is tormenting me. You told me some story about a merchant, without knowing who he was, where he came from or where he was going. And you say that he sold an object of such great beauty for a talent, here in the middle of nowhere, when she is worth a king's ransom? Some god has addled your wits! Think, then, and remember what happened! Who did you see? Who did you speak to? Tell me the truth! You didn't see the ship, did you?' 'No, Master, but I heard it.' 'This is more like it. One of the Nymphs or Nereids has come up out of the sea. At special times you can come across divinities taking their due share of contact with men. Poets and writers tell us the story of these things.' Dionysius enthusiastically talked himself into believing that she was some goddess and used to more august association than mere mortals. Leonas, wanting to oblige his master, said, 'Let's not bother ourselves about who she is, Master. I will bring her to you if you want, and don't let your grief get in the way of your passion.' 'I couldn't do anything,' said Dionysius, 'until I know who the woman is and where she comes from. First thing in the morning let's find out the truth from her. I won't send for her here in case it raises a suspicion of compulsion, so let the meeting take place in the temple of Aphrodite, where I first set eyes on her.'

[5] This seemed a good plan and on the following day, Dionysius took with him some friends, freedmen and the most trustworthy of his slaves, so that he would have them with him as witnesses, and went to the shrine. He had dressed for the occasion with care and even with some real attention to detail on the grounds that he was going to meet the woman he loved. He was already naturally handsome and tall and, most importantly of all, he seemed noble. So Leonas, taking with him Plangon and Callirhoe's usual maids, approached her and said, 'Dionysius is a most just

and most law-abiding man. Come now to the temple, lady, and tell him the truth about your identity: you won't fail to meet with appropriate assistance. Just explain it to him straightforwardly and tell him the whole truth. For this will persuade him to be even more sympathetic towards you.'

When she heard this, Callirhoe set off, cheered by the fact that the meeting was to take place in the temple. As soon as she arrived, everyone was even more amazed by her appearance. Dionysius himself was struck dumb, but after a long silence he just about managed to say, 'Everything about me, lady, is well-known to you. I am Dionysius, the first citizen of Miletus and almost of the whole of Ionia, renowned for my piety and generosity. You really must tell me the truth about yourself. For those men who sold you said that you were a Sybarite, sold by your mistress because of her jealousy.'

Callirhoe blushed and, lowering her head a little, said, 'I have just now been sold for the first time. I have never seen Sybaris.' 'I told you,' said Dionysius, glancing at Leonas, 'that this is no slave girl. And I'd swear to it that she is well-born. Tell me everything, lady – but first of all, tell me your name!' 'Callirhoe,' she said – which Dionysius instantly thought charming – but she remained silent about the rest. But when he kept on importuning her, she said, 'Master, I beg you to allow me to remain silent about my misfortune. My origins and the story of my life are a dream: I am now what I have become, a slave and a foreigner.' As she said this, although she tried to hide it, the tears poured down her cheeks. This made Dionysius cry and all those who were standing around as well. One would think that even the statue of Aphrodite herself looked rather downcast. Dionysius, however, continued even more strongly in his quest to find out about her, and said, 'I beg this favour from you first. Tell me your story, Callirhoe! You will not be speaking to a stranger for there is some sort of affinity between us. Don't be afraid, even if you have done something dreadful.'

Callirhoe was piqued at this and said, 'Don't insult me, for I know of nothing to my discredit. However, since my origins are more noble than my present situation would suggest, I don't want to seem like an impostor or to be offering explanations that would seem unbelievable to anyone who didn't know. For the beginning of my life is no true indicator of my current situation.' Dionysius was full of admiration at her confidence. 'I already understand you,' he said. 'Even if you don't tell me – but do tell me! For you will say nothing about yourself which is as amazing as what we can see. Any explanation pales in comparison with you!'

With difficulty she began to tell her story: 'I am the daughter of Hermocrates, the Syracusan general. When I became unconscious as a result of a sudden fall, my parents buried me with no expense spared. Tomb-robbers opened my grave and found me inside still breathing. They brought me here and Theron handed me over to this man Leonas in a deserted spot.' She told him everything and was silent about Chaereas alone. 'But I ask you, Dionysius (for you are a Greek, come from a city with a reputation for benevolence and are well-educated), neither to be like those tomb-robbers nor to deprive me of my homeland and kinsfolk. It is a small matter for a rich man like you to set me free: you will not lose honour if you give me back to my father. Hermocrates is not an ungrateful man. We all honour and love Alcinous because he sent a suppliant back to his fatherland. Thus I supplicate you: save a captured orphan. If I am not able to live as a noble woman, I will choose to die freely.' When he heard this, Dionysius wept – in theory for Callirhoe, but in reality for himself. For he realized that what he wanted was slipping through his fingers. 'Take courage, Callirhoe,' he said, 'and be of good heart, for you will not fail to meet with the things you ask for. I call Aphrodite here as witness. In the meantime you will have the treatment of a fine lady rather than of a slave.'

[6] So she went off, convinced that she was going to suffer nothing against her will; Dionysius, on the other hand, returned home in a state of distress. He called just for Leonas to come to him and said, 'I am unlucky in everything and hated by Eros! I have buried my wife and now this newly-bought woman flees from me. I was hoping she was going to be a gift from Aphrodite to me, and I was trying to make my life seem blessed – unlike that

Menelaus who was married to the Spartan woman. Nor, I suspect, was Helen as beautiful as this woman is: and she also has the ability to speak persuasively. My life is over! In the course of this very day, Callirhoe will be set free from here – and I'll be set free from life.' At this Leonas exclaimed, 'Master, don't curse yourself! For you have power over her and she is your property, so that willingly or unwillingly she will do what you think is right. I paid a talent for her, remember.' 'You scoundrel, you bought a nobly-born woman! Don't you know that Hermocrates is solemnly declared to be the general of the whole of Sicily, whom even the King of the Persians admires and loves and sends gifts to each year because he defeated the Athenians, the Persians' enemies, at sea? Am I going to tyrannize over a free person, and I, Dionysius, famous for my moderation, am I going to ravish an unwilling woman whom even the bandit Theron did not insult?'

So he said all this to Leonas, but in reality he did not give up his intention of persuading her, since Eros is by nature prone to inspire hope, and he took heart in the thought that his desire would be achieved by care and attention. So he called for Plangon and said, 'You have already given me sufficient proof of your concern. I hand over to you the greatest and most honourable of my possessions – the foreign woman. I want her to lack nothing but even to approach a state of luxury. Take her as your mistress, care for her, adorn her and make her love me. Praise me to her many times and tell her what you know of me. Make sure that you don't call me her master.' Plangon agreed to the request for she was naturally easy-going, and taking a pretty shrewd view of the matter she began to move things forward. Consequently, going to Callirhoe she did not reveal that she had been ordered to attend her, but instead showed a genuine benevolence to her. She wanted to gain her trust as a confidante.

[7] But it happened like this: Dionysius was lingering on in the country on some pretext or other, but in reality because he could neither leave Callirhoe nor was he willing to take her with him, because once she was seen she would become famous and her beauty would enslave the whole of Ionia and give her a reputation which would reach even the Great King. During his stay,

while he was looking more closely into the business of the estate, he found reason to criticize his steward, Phocas, in some matter. The bit of criticism did not in fact go beyond a telling-off, but Plangon seized on it as her chance and ran to Callirhoe in a state of terror, tearing her hair. Grabbing her by the knees, Plangon said, 'I beg you, Mistress, save us! Dionysius is angry at my husband and he is by nature as stern as he is kind. No one can save us except you! For Dionysius will happily give to you the very first thing you ask for.' Callirhoe really dreaded approaching him, but with Plangon begging and pleading she couldn't refuse, since she felt that she was already under an obligation to her because of her kindnesses. So that she did not seem ungrateful then, Callirhoe replied, 'I am a slave and have no right to speak, but if you believe that I have the power to make a difference, I'm ready to join you in supplication. And good luck to us!'

When they went, Plangon instructed the slave at the door to announce to his master that Callirhoe was there. Dionysius happened to have thrown himself to the ground in a grief which was physically wasting him away. So when he heard that Callirhoe was there, he was speechless and darkness poured down over his eyes in response to such an unhoped-for event. Barely able to pull himself together, he said, 'Let her come in.' When Callirhoe approached with her head bowed low, she was overcome with blushes but nevertheless just managed to get her words out, 'I have a sense of obligation to Plangon here because she loves me as a daughter. I beg you, Master, not to be angry with her husband but to grant him his life.' She wanted to say more, but was unable to.

Dionysius then recognized Plangon's strategy and said, 'I am indeed angry and no one would be able to protect Phocas and Plangon from death after what they have done. However, I freely pardon them for your sake: and you two, know that you are being saved because of Callirhoe.' Plangon fell at his knees but Dionysius cried, 'Throw yourself at Callirhoe's feet since it is she who has saved you!' Plangon saw that Callirhoe was delighted and really pleased at the granting of the favour, so she nudged Callirhoe forward and said, 'You therefore, must join

with us in thanking Dionysius on our behalf.' Somehow Callirhoe
tripped and grabbed at Dionysius' right hand as she fell: he, as
if it was barely polite only to give her his hand, drew her to him
and kissed her, then immediately released her so that he did not
seem to have engineered the situation.

[8] The women went away at that point, but the kiss embedded
itself, like poison, in Dionysius' heart. He was able neither to
see nor to hear but was besieged from every side and could think
of no remedy for his passion: gifts would do no good because
he recognized the woman's sense of pride; nor did he think he
would get his way through threats or violence, since he was
persuaded that she would choose death rather than be forced.
So he seized on Plangon as his only means of assistance. Sending
for her he insisted: 'You planned that first bit and I am grateful
to you for the kiss – a kiss which has either saved me or destroyed
me! Now work out how to get round her, using your inside
knowledge as a woman, and I'll be your ally. Let me tell you
that freedom awaits you as your reward – not to mention something which I know is far more important to you than your
freedom, your master Dionysius' life!' With these orders, Plangon
directed the full force of her experience and skill on to the problem, but Callirhoe remained completely unconquerable and
stayed faithful only to Chaereas. She was, however, outmanoeu-
vred by Fortune against whom alone human stratagems have
no power. For she is a goddess who relishes a trial of strength
and about whom nothing should surprise us. At this point then,
she brought about an event that was contrary to expectation,
or was even unbelievable.

It is worth hearing the way in which Fortune plotted against
the woman's chastity. For when Chaereas and Callirhoe were just
about to take the first erotic step on their marital path, they had
a reciprocal desire to enjoy each other, and the equality of their
passion ensured that their union was not unfruitful. Thus she
quickly became pregnant, sometime before her fall, but because
of the danger she had been through and the distress which
followed it, she did not readily realize her condition. But as the
third month began, her stomach began to swell which Plangon,

with her experience of women's matters, observed as she bathed her. She recognized the situation but kept quiet since there were so many slave women around, but in the evening time when they were at leisure, she sat down beside her on the bed and said, 'My child, you know that you are pregnant, don't you?' Callirhoe started to cry, bewailing her fate and tearing her hair. 'Oh Fortune, you add this to my troubles as well – so that I will give birth to a slave!' Hitting herself on the stomach she exclaimed, 'Wretched child, before your birth you were in a tomb and then entrusted to the hands of pirates! What sort of life will you have? With what sort of hopes am I going to bear you, orphan, alien and slave? Face death rather than birth!' But Plangon caught hold of her hands, telling her that on the following day she would provide a less distressing way of aborting the child.

[9] When they were both by themselves, they became absorbed in their own deliberations. Plangon, for her part, was saying to herself that this was a god-sent opportunity for her to advance the cause of her master's love, while she had the contents of Callirhoe's womb to help her argue her case: she would find it a useful tool of persuasion and a mother's tender love would conquer a wife's chastity. Accordingly she put together a persuasive plan. Callirhoe, on the other hand, intended to get rid of the baby, saying to herself, 'Am I to produce a child who is a descendant of Hermocrates but also a slave to be offered to a master? A child whose father no one has heard of? In a flash someone malicious will say, "Callirhoe got pregnant when she was with the pirates." It is enough that I suffer misfortune on my own: there is no advantage for you, child, in leading a wretched life from which you ought to escape if you are born. Depart still free, innocent of suffering! May you know nothing of your mother's experiences!' However, she changed her mind again and pity for the child in her womb came over her. 'Are you planning infanticide? Most wicked of women, you are mad taking on the reasoning of a Medea. You even seem more savage than the Scythian, for she treated her husband like an enemy, but you want to kill Chaereas' child and leave no memorial of that celebrated marriage. What if it was a boy? What if it was like its father? What if it is fated to

enjoy much better fortune than I? Should its own mother kill the
child that was saved from the tomb and from pirates? How many
children of the gods and of kings do we hear about who, born in
slavery, later regain their fathers' high estate, for instance Zethos
and Amphion and Cyrus? You, too, my child, will sail to Sicily,
you will find your father and your grandfather and you will
explain to them what has happened to your mother. A rescue
mission will be sent for me. You, my child, will give back your
parents to each other!' As she reasoned thus through the whole
night, sleep came over her, but only shallowly. Then, the image of
Chaereas came to her, like him in every particular:

> like unto him in size and noble visage,
>   and voice and the raiment which was around his limbs.

And as he stood there he said, 'Wife, I entrust our son to you.'
Although he still had more he wanted to say, Callirhoe leapt up,
eager to embrace him. Believing her husband was her adviser,
she decided to keep the child.

[10] On the following day when Plangon arrived, she told her
of her decision. Plangon did not hold back from commenting
on the inappropriateness of Callirhoe's plan. 'It is impossible for
you, my dear girl,' she said, 'to have a child here with us. For
our master has a passion for you and while he won't force you
since you are unwilling, because of his own sense of self-respect
and moderation, he would not allow a child to be reared because
of his jealousy. He would think it was an insult if you so eagerly
take the part of a man who is absent, but overlook himself
although he is here. It seems to me that it would be better to
destroy the child before its birth – or when it is born. You will
only gain fruitless labour-pains as well as a pointless pregnancy.
Because I care for you, I give you this honest advice.'

Callirhoe heard this with a heavy heart and, throwing herself
at Plangon's knees, begged her to help her find some scheme by
which she might be able to keep the child. Plangon refused her
over and over again and she stuck to this refusal for two or three
days, so that she drove Callirhoe to even more heated supplications

and made herself seem even more trustworthy. First, she made Callirhoe swear not to tell anyone about the plan, then knitting her brows and rubbing her hands, said, 'The most difficult things are brought about by great inventiveness. I am going to betray my master because of the high regard I have for you. Rest assured, therefore, that one of two things will be necessary: either the child must be completely destroyed or it must be born the richest of the Ionians, heir to the most noble estate – and make you, his mother, blessed. Choose then, whichever you want.' 'Who would be so crazy that they would choose infanticide over prosperity? You seem to me, however, to offer something impossible and unbelievable, so explain it more clearly.' In response, Plangon asked, 'How long do you think has it been since you conceived?' 'Two months,' the other replied. 'Time is on our side then. You can make it look like you have produced a seven-month child by Dionysius.' Callirhoe cried out at this, 'Rather let it die!' Plangon pretended to go along with her, 'You are absolutely right, my dear, in preferring an abortion. Let's do that, for it is less dangerous than tricking our master. Cast aside once and for all the memory of your noble birth, and retain no hope of getting back to your fatherland. Accustom yourself to your present position and really become a slave.'

Callirhoe had no suspicion of Plangon as she gave this advice, being a well-born young girl and ignorant of slavish deceitfulness. But the harder she was pushed towards the idea of abortion, the more she pitied the child that was in her womb and she said, 'Give me some time to think, for it is a choice about really important things: either chastity or a child.' Again Plangon praised this sentiment, because she was not choosing one option precipitously: 'There are persuasive arguments on both sides: on the one hand a woman's good faith, on the other a mother's love. However, now is not the right time for long delays, you must choose one or the other tomorrow before your condition becomes obvious.' They agreed to this and then separated.

[11] Callirhoe went up to her room and closed the door. She held her picture of Chaereas against her stomach and said, 'Look, we have become three: husband, wife and child. Let us plan

together what's for the best. I will express my opinion first: I want to go to my grave the wife of Chaereas alone. This is sweeter to me than parents, fatherland and child – to have experience of no other man. But you, child, what do you choose for yourself? To be finished off with poison before seeing the light of day, cast out with your mother, perhaps not even granted a proper burial place – or to live and have two fathers: one the leading man in Sicily, the other the leading man in Ionia? When you grow to be a man you will be easily recognized by your relatives, because I am convinced that I will bear you to look like your father. And you will sail home gloriously with a fleet of Milesian triremes, and Hermocrates will joyfully welcome a grandson who is already able to be a general. You cast your vote in the opposite way, child, and you don't put your trust in death for us both. After you, let's find out about your father. But actually he has already spoken because he himself stood beside me in a dream and said, "I entrust our son to you." I call you to witness, Chaereas: you are giving me in marriage to Dionysius!'

For the rest of the day and the following night she was wrapped up in these thoughts, and she was persuaded to live, not for her own sake, but for that of the child. On the following day, Plangon came to her and at first sat down beside her with a sad expression and presenting a sympathetic appearance. There was silence between the two of them. After a long time, Plangon asked, 'What have you decided? What are we going to do? Because now is not the time for hanging about.' Callirhoe was not able to reply easily because she was crying and constrained, but she just managed it: 'The child betrays me against my will: do what seems for the best. I am afraid that even if I submit to this violation, Dionysius will despise my status and, thinking of me as a concubine and not as a wife, he won't raise the child of another man and I will have lost my chastity in vain.' While she was still speaking, Plangon started her reply: 'I have thought about this before you did, because I already love you more than I do our master. I trust Dionysius in this respect, for he is honourable. Nevertheless, I will get him to swear an oath, even though he is my master. We must do everything carefully and you, child, can trust him once he has sworn the oath. But off I go to carry out my mission.'

BOOK 3

[1] Dionysius, failing to secure Callirhoe's love and no longer able to bear it, decided to starve himself to death and wrote a final will and testament setting down how he was to be buried. In this document he addressed Callirhoe in the hope that she would visit him, even if he was a corpse. Plangon was very keen to go in to her master but was prevented by a servant who had orders that no one was to be allowed in. Dionysius heard them arguing at the door and asked who was creating the disturbance. When the servant replied that it was Plangon, Dionysius said, 'She has come at a very bad time,' (for he no longer wanted to see any reminder of his passion) 'but call her in anyway.' When she opened the door, she cried, 'Why are you wearing yourself out with grief, master, thinking that you have failed. For Callirhoe is proposing marriage to you! Dress in your finest clothes, start sacrificing and receive the bride whom you love!' Dionysius was almost dumbstruck at such unhoped-for news, a darkness poured down over his eyes, all his senses failed him and he presented the appearance of one who was dead. Plangon's shriek brought a crowd running to the spot and the whole house went into mourning on the grounds that its master was dead. Nor did Callirhoe hear this news without tears: so great was everyone's grief that she wept for Dionysius like a husband.

When finally he had just about recovered his senses, he said in a weak voice, 'Which of the gods is deceiving me and throwing me off my course? Is it a true vision or just a dream which announces these things to me? Does Callirhoe want to marry me or does she not even want to be seen by me?' Standing right by him Plangon replied, 'Stop torturing yourself unnecessarily and start believing in the good things which are coming your way! I would not deceive my own master: Callirhoe really has sent me as a special envoy of marriage.' 'Do your job, then,' said Dionysius, 'and tell me her exact words. Leave nothing out and add nothing, but recount it all faithfully.' 'She said, "I come from the first family in Sicily. I have suffered misfortune, but I still have my pride. I have lost my homeland and my parents: the only thing I have not lost is my nobility. If Dionysius wants to take me as his concubine and satisfy his own personal passion, I would hang myself rather than hand my body over to such slavish outrage. But if he wants to take me as his legally wedded wife, I myself am willing to become a mother, so that the race of Hermocrates may have an heir. Let Dionysius consider this, not by himself or in a rush, but with friends and relatives so that no one may later say to him, 'Will you raise children born from a slave and bring shame to your house?' If he does not want to be a father, let him not be a husband."' These words inflamed Dionysius even more and he had a faint hope that he was loved in return. Stretching up his hands to the heavens, he said, 'O Zeus and Helios, if only I might see a child born to Callirhoe, then I would seem more blessed than the Great King! Let us go to her. Lead the way, my dear Plangon, kindest servant a master ever had.'

[2] After running upstairs, Dionysius was at first eager to fall at Callirhoe's feet, but nevertheless he held himself back and calmly sat down. 'Lady, I have come to you,' he said, 'to acknowledge the gratitude I owe you for saving my life: for I had no intention of compelling you against your will, and if I failed, I had resolved to die. I have survived because of you. But although I feel immense gratitude towards you, I still blame you in some ways: because you did not trust that I would have you as a lawful wife "for the begetting of children" according to Greek law. If I had not loved you, I would not have begged for such a marriage. But you seem to have judged me guilty of madness, thinking that I was going to have a nobly-born woman as a slave and that a descendant of Hermocrates was unworthy of me. "Think about it," you say. I have thought about it. Do you, who are most dear

to me of all, fear my friends? Who would dare to say that a child
of mine was unworthy when it has a grandfather more noble
than its father?' Saying this with tears in his eyes at the same
time, he approached her. Blushing, she kissed him gently and
said, 'I do trust you Dionysius, but I don't trust my own luck
because I have already fallen from the midst of great good
fortune, and I am afraid that my bad luck has not yet run its
course. Although you are noble and just, I would like you to call
the gods to witness – not on your own behalf, but on behalf of
your citizens and relatives so that no one may be able to plan
something bad against me because they know that you have
sworn such an oath. A woman who is alone and a foreigner is
all too easily despised.' He replied, 'What sort of oaths do you
want? If it were possible I would be ready to go up to heaven
and swear an oath at the feet of Zeus himself!' 'Swear,' she said,
'by the sea which brought me to you, by Aphrodite who showed
me to you and by the Eros who leads a bride to her wedding.'
This found favour and was swiftly done.

The erotic passion felt by Dionysius increased and brooked
no delay to the marriage: desire is too powerful to be rationally
controlled. Dionysius, although a well-educated man, was
entirely overcome by the storm of his passion and his soul was
overwhelmed by its tide. Nevertheless, he struggled to get his
head above the triple-crested wave of desire. At that point he
went through the following thought process: 'Am I about to
marry her in a deserted spot as if she really is a slave? No, I am
not so mean spirited that I would fail to celebrate my marriage
to Callirhoe in style. In this first act it is essential that I show
honour to my wife. It also provides a degree of insurance against
future eventualities: of all things Rumour is the most dangerous,
as it flits away through the air with nothing to restrain it. Because
of it, nothing unusual is ever able to remain private, and already
it is racing about taking this fresh piece of news to Sicily:
"Callirhoe lives; tomb-robbers excavated the tomb and stole her
and she was bought in Miletus." Already a Syracusan trireme is
putting to sea and the general Hermocrates is demanding his
daughter back. What am I going to say? "Theron sold her to
me"? But where is Theron? And, even if I am believed, am I still

a receiver of stolen goods? Get your defence speech ready, Dionysius! Before you know it you will be making it in front of the
Great King. Best then to say, "I found out somehow that she was
a freeborn woman, away from her native land. With her consent,
I married her officially in the city according to the laws." If I do
it like this, I will have a better chance of persuading my father-
in-law as well that I am not unworthy of the marriage. Be
resolute, my soul, and cut short the intervening days so that you
may – in safety – enjoy a longer period of pleasure. I will be in
a stronger position to meet the crisis if I have the rights of a
husband and not just of a master.'

This was the decision Dionysius came to and so he called
Leonas and said, 'Go to the city. Get everything ready for the
wedding in magnificent style. Get the flocks driven up; have food
and wine imported over land and sea; I would like the whole
city to feast at public expense.' He organized everything carefully,
then on the following day he himself made the journey in his
chariot. However, he gave orders that Callirhoe was to be taken
round by boat in the evening (for he did not yet want her to be
widely seen) and brought to his town house which lay right by
the harbour called Docimus. For this he entrusted her to Plangon's care.

Just as she was about to leave the estate, Callirhoe first wanted
to pray to Aphrodite so she went to the temple, got everyone
else to leave and then addressed the goddess with the following
words: 'Lady Aphrodite, would I be right to feel anger towards
you – or gratitude? When I was a young girl you married me to
Chaereas and yet now you are leading me as a bride to another
man after him. I would not have been persuaded to swear alle-
giance to you or your son if I had not been put in a difficult
position by this child' – she gestured towards her stomach – 'But
I beg you,' she said, 'not on my own behalf, but on that of the
child. Allow me to keep my strategy secret. Since he doesn't have
a father, let him seem to be Dionysius' child; once he is grown
up he will find his real father.' When the sailors saw her walking
out of the sanctuary towards the shore, they were struck with
fear, thinking that it was Aphrodite herself coming to embark.
As one man they rushed to prostrate themselves before her. With

greater eagerness the rowers bent to their oars and the ship reached the harbour, in less time than it takes to relate.

At the break of dawn, the whole city was garlanded. Each man sacrificed not only in the temples but also in front of his own house. There were all sorts of speculation as to who the bride could be. The mass of common people were persuaded by her beauty (and because she was unknown) that a Nereid had come out of the sea or that she was a goddess from Dionysius' country estate; for this is what the sailors were saying. Everyone shared an intense desire to see Callirhoe and a great crowd gathered together around the temple of Concord, where it was customary for grooms to receive their bride. For the first time since being in the tomb, Callirhoe was dressed in all her finery; when once she had decided to get married, she thought that her beauty should be worthy of her noble family and fatherland.

So when she had put on a gown of Milesian wool and bridal garlands, she went to see the crowd. Everyone shouted, 'It's Aphrodite who is getting married!' They spread purple tapestries for her to walk on, and roses and violets; they sprinkled myrrh on her as she walked; and no one stayed inside their houses, neither young nor old – even in the harbours themselves, where the crowd was so dense some people went up on the roofs! But a jealous spirit again got its pound of flesh on that day: I will tell you how in a moment. But first I want to tell you what was going on in Syracuse during that same period.

[3] There, the tomb-robbers had closed up the tomb very carelessly in their rush to get away in the night. Chaereas sat up waiting for the dawn and when it came went to the tomb with the excuse of taking a wreath and libations, but in reality with the intention of taking his own life there. For he could not bear to be parted from Callirhoe and thought that death alone could provide a cure for his grief. When he arrived he found the door stone moved and the entrance clearly visible. Flabbergasted at the sight he was overcome by a terrible confusion at the thought of what could have happened. Swift Rumour soon took the message of the extraordinary event to the Syracusans, and everyone rushed to the tomb, but no one dared to enter until he was

instructed to do so by Hermocrates. Someone was sent in and
reported back in detail; but it seemed unbelievable that the
corpse should no longer be lying there. At that point Chaereas
demanded to enter the tomb himself, desperate to see Callirhoe
again even if she was a corpse. Searching the tomb, he found
nothing. Many others entered unable to believe the news.
Nobody knew what to do and one of the bystanders said, 'The
grave-gifts have been stolen; it is the work of tomb-robbers. But
where is the corpse?' There were many conflicting answers to
that question among the crowd. Chaereas, however, looked up
to the heavens and raised his hands, crying, 'Which of the gods
hates me so much that he has taken Callirhoe from me and now
keeps her with him against her will, at the mercy of a more
powerful fate? That's the reason why she died so suddenly – so
that she would not become ill. It was like Dionysus took Ariadne
from Theseus and Zeus took Semele from Actaeon: nor did I
realize that I had a goddess as a wife who was more sublime
than we mere mortals. But she didn't need to leave the world of
men in such a way. Thetis was a goddess, but she lived with
Peleus and he had a son with her: I have been robbed of Callirhoe
at the very climax of our love. Why do I have to suffer like this?
Am I jinxed? Should I kill myself? With whom shall I be buried?
For I still have this hope even in the midst of disasters that if I
am not to be allowed to share a bedroom with Callirhoe, I will
at least find a shared tomb. Lady, I defend my continued existence because you compel me to live. For I intend to seek for you
across land and sea – and would do so in the heavens above if
I were able. But I ask this of you – wife – don't flee from me!'
The assembled multitude broke down weeping at the words and
everyone began to mourn Callirhoe as if she had just died.

Triremes were immediately hauled down to the sea and a great
number of men were allotted to the search. Hermocrates himself
searched through Sicily and Chaereas through Libya; some were
sent to Italy and others ordered to go through Ionia. But human
efforts were utterly deficient and only Fortune (without whom
no task is accomplishable) could bring the truth to light, as you
will learn from the events themselves.

For the tomb-robbers, after they had sold their problematic

cargo, left Miletus and set off for Crete. They had heard that it was a great and prosperous island where they thought that they would easily be able to offload the rest of their haul. However, a fierce wind blew them off course to Ionia and there they drifted in open sea for a long time. Thunder and lightning and exceptionally long hours of darkness assailed the criminals, revealing that it had been the presence of Callirhoe that had been responsible for the good sailing conditions they had experienced before. Every time they came close to death, the gods refused to grant them a speedy release from fear, prolonging their nightmare voyage yet further. The wretches were unable to land and forced to remain at sea for such a long time that they experienced dreadful shortages, especially of water. Their ill-gotten gains were no use now, and they were dying of thirst surrounded by gold. In the end they were forced to accept that they were wrong and shouted to each other that it was all 'no use'. All the others were dying of thirst and in that crisis Theron showed that he was the worst of all, for he secretly stole the remaining water and robbed his fellow robbers. He thought that he was doing something clever, but Providence's plan was to keep him alive for the torture of crucifixion.

The trireme carrying Chaereas fell in with the yacht when it was becalmed and at first they avoided it, thinking that it was a pirate ship. When they realized that it was without a helmsman and was being carried randomly with the ebb and flow of the waves, one of the men from the trireme piped up, 'It doesn't have a crew! We don't need to be afraid. Let's move up close and inspect this strange vessel.' The captain was happy to go with this suggestion, for Chaereas was off, hidden in his cabin, weeping. When they drew alongside they first shouted out to anyone on board. Since no one answered, one of the men from the trireme boarded the yacht and found nothing except gold and corpses. He reported back to the other sailors who were delighted, thinking themselves blessed by Fortune to have found a treasury floating in the sea. The outcry brought Chaereas on to the scene, who at once learnt the cause of the noise and wanted to see it for himself.

Recognizing the grave-goods, Chaereas tore at his clothes and let out a great and far-resounding cry: 'Alas, Callirhoe! These are your things. Here is the garland which I myself put around you; your father gave you this and your mother gave you this. Here is your wedding dress! The ship has become a tomb for you. I see your things, but where are you? Your body alone is missing from the tomb's inventory.'

When he heard this, Theron lay like one dead – he was indeed already half dead. Over and over he repeated to himself his determination not to utter a word or a sound because the consequence was entirely predictable for him. However, man is a creature with a natural impulse to cling to life and even in the worst crises still hangs on to the hope that things will change for the better. The god who made man planted this fallacy like a seed in everyone so that they would not try to escape this mortal coil. So, consumed by thirst, the first word which Theron uttered was 'Water!' When it had been brought to him and he had received everything which he needed, Chaereas sat down beside him and asked, 'Who are you? Where are you sailing to? Where are these things from? Why do you have them in your possession?' But Theron had recovered his sense enough to reply deceitfully and said, 'I am a Cretan and I am sailing to Ionia in search of my brother who is serving with the army. But there was a sudden crisis and I was abandoned in Cephallenia by the rest of the crew. From there I boarded this yacht which happened to sail by at the right time. We were driven to this spot in the sea by extreme winds and then becalmed for such a long time that everyone died of thirst; I alone survived as a result of my piety.' When he heard this, Chaereas ordered that the yacht be tied on behind the trireme, and at the break of dawn he sailed into the Syracusan harbour.

[4] Rumour beat them to it; naturally speedy, she is even swifter when she has news which is both fresh and bizarre. Everybody ran down to the shore and there was altogether a patchwork of shouts, amazement, questions and incredulity, as the new situation overwhelmed them. When her mother saw her daughter's grave-goods, she wailed aloud, 'I recognize everything! You alone, child, are missing! Peculiar tomb-robbers, though – they have looked after the rich clothes and gold and only stolen my daughter.' The beaches and the harbours echoed with women

beating their breasts and they filled the land and sea with their wails. Hermocrates, however, a general and a practical man, said, 'We don't need to stand here wondering about it: what we need is to get on with the appropriate legal proceedings. Let's go to the assembly. Does anyone know if we need a jury?'

The whole speech had scarce been spoken

and already the whole theatre was full. Even women took part in that assembly.

All of the citizen body was on the edge of its seat as Chaereas came in first, dressed in black, pale, dishevelled, just as he had been when he took his wife to the tomb. Nor did he want to mount the rostrum, but stood at its foot crying for a long time, and although he wanted to speak, was unable to do so. The crowd shouted, 'Take courage and speak!' Just about managing to look up, Chaereas said, 'The present moment is suited to mourning and not to public speaking, but the same compulsion that makes me cling to life forces me to speak now – to find out about Callirhoe's disappearance. That was the reason I set out on my voyage, the success of which still hangs in the balance. I caught sight of this vessel drifting in fair weather but labouring under some difficulty and taking on water despite the calmness of the conditions. Wondering what was going on, we came alongside and I thought I was looking at my wife's tomb as all her things were there; only she herself was missing. There was a crowd of corpses but all of men unknown to me. We found this man in among them, himself half dead. I have looked after him with the greatest care and brought him to you.'

Meanwhile public officials led Theron into the theatre, bound and under suitable escort. For the circular rack, instruments of torture, fire and whips were being brought along with him, since Providence was paying out to him the rewards of his efforts. When he was in the middle of the assembly, one of the magistrates asked him, 'Who are you?' 'Demetrius,' he said. 'Where do you come from?' 'Crete.' 'What do you know? Tell us.' 'When I was sailing to Ionia to meet my brother, I was left behind by my ship, then I boarded this yacht which was sailing past. I found' what I thought were merchants but now know were tomb-robbers. As we drifted at sea for a long time, the others all died from lack of water, I alone was saved because I have lived a blameless life. Please, Syracusans, people known far and wide for your kindness, don't be more savage to me than raging thirst and the sea!' At such a speech, the crowd were moved to pity for him and he would have persuaded them and earned himself a free passage home had a spirit, avenging Callirhoe, not stirred up resentment against him because of his deceitful persuasion. For it would have been the most outrageous thing ever for the Syracusans to have been persuaded that he alone had been saved because of his piety, when in reality he alone had been saved because of his impiety, so that he could be punished even more.

So sitting among the crowd was a fisherman who recognized him and said quietly to those sitting next to him, 'I have seen this man before – knocking about around our harbour.' The word swiftly passed on to others in the crowd and someone shouted out, 'He's lying!' Everybody craned round and the magistrates ordered the man who had spoken first to come down, and although Theron denied it the fisherman was more convincing. They immediately called for the torturers and had the scoundrel whipped. Burned and cut, he still insisted on denying it and indeed only narrowly failed to outlast the torture. But in every one of us conscience is a powerful thing and the truth comes out in the end: slowly and with difficulty then, Theron admitted his guilt. He began to explain: 'Seeing the treasure buried in the tomb, I gathered together a band of robbers. We opened the tomb – and found the corpse alive! We took everything and stowed it on the yacht, but when we reached Miletus we only sold the woman and took the rest to Crete. We were then blown out into the Ionian Sea and you have seen what we suffered there.' He told everything and only left out the name of the man who had bought her.

At these words, joy and grief took hold of everyone: joy because Callirhoe was alive, but grief because she had been sold as a slave. A sentence of death was passed on Theron but Chaereas begged that he should not die yet, 'So that he can come with me and point out the men who bought her. Consider the constraints I am

under – helping to plead the case of the man who sold my wife!'
But Hermocrates prevented this happening by saying, 'It is better
to make the task of finding her more difficult than to go against
the laws. I beg you, men of Syracuse, bearing in mind my position
as your general and the battles I have won, repay the gratitude
you owe me by helping my daughter. Send out an embassy on
her behalf so that we can reclaim her freedom.' He was still
speaking when the crowd shouted out, 'Let's all sail!' For the
most part the council backed such a wish, but Hermocrates said,
'I thank you all warmly for the honour, but two ambassadors
from the people should be sufficient and two from the council.
Chaereas himself should sail as a fifth.'

These suggestions all seemed good and were decided upon
and consequently he dismissed the assembly. The majority of the
crowd escorted Theron as he was led away. He was impaled in
front of Callirhoe's tomb and from the stake looked out across
the sea over which he had carried Hermocrates' daughter as a
captive: a sea which not even the Athenians had succeeded in
capturing.

[5] Everyone thought that it would be best to wait for the sailing
season and to set out at the beginning of spring: it was still winter
at that point and it seemed impossible to cross the Ionian Sea.
Chaereas, however, was in a fret of impatience, and, because of
his love, ready to get hold of any sort of vessel and launch himself
on to the sea for the winds to carry off. Accordingly, out of
respect for him and even more for Hermocrates, the ambassadors
were unwilling to cause any delay; on the contrary, they were
perfectly ready to set sail. The Syracusans sent out the expedition
at state expense so that this also should lend weight to the
embassy and brought into harbour the warship that still carried
the trophies of the recent victory. When the day appointed for
the launch arrived, a mass of citizens rushed down to the harbour,
not just men but women and children too, and there were, on
all sides, tears, prayers, cries of grief, advice, fear, encouragement,
despair, hope. Ariston, Chaereas' father, a man of extreme old
age and ill, threw his arms around his son's neck and, clinging
there in tears, said, 'Son, why are you abandoning me when I

am an old man close to death? It is clear that I will never see
you again. But wait just a few days, so that I can die in your
arms. Then bury me and go!' His mother threw her arms about
his knees too and said, 'I beg you, son, don't leave me abandoned
here but take me on board your trireme like a light cargo. If I
am heavy and hard to bear, throw me into the sea which carried
you!' As she spoke she tore open her dress and bared her breasts,
saying:

'Child, respect these and have pity for me
If ever the breast I offered you soothed away your cares.'

Chaereas was utterly broken by his parents' supplications and
threw himself off the ship into the sea, hoping to end it all and
to avoid either of the fates: the failure to find Callirhoe or causing such grief to his parents. Swiftly the sailors jumped overboard
and just about managed to drag him in. Then Hermocrates sent
the crowd away and also ordered his captain to get going.
Another example of truly noble friendship occurred, for Polycharmus, one of Chaereas' friends, was likewise nowhere to be
seen but had previously said to his parents, 'I am a friend of
Chaereas' and so is he of mine, but not of such a degree that I
should run the most terrible risks for him. So I will lie low until
he moves off to sea.' But when the vessel set sail, he was there
on board waving goodbye to his parents: he did this so that they
would not be able to stop him.

As Chaereas left the harbour, he looked out to the open sea.
'O sea,' he cried, 'take me on the same route you took Callirhoe!
I beg you, Poseidon, that either I bring her back with me or I
don't return here without her! If I am not able to bring my wife
back, I want to be a slave along with her.'

[6] A favourable breeze carried the trireme along and it followed
the yacht's course as if it could follow its tracks. They came to
Ionia in the same number of days and weighed anchor in the
same bay on Dionysius' estate. The others were exhausted as
they came on shore and they got on with refreshing themselves,
putting up tents and preparing a meal, but Chaereas was pacing

about with Polycharmus. 'Now, how can we find Callirhoe?' he
was saying. 'I am especially afraid that Theron was lying to us
and that the poor woman is dead. But if she really has been sold,
who knows where? Asia is an enormous place.' As they walked
about they came upon the temple of Aphrodite and since it
seemed a good idea to make obeisance to the goddess, Chaereas
ran up to grasp her knees and said, 'Mistress, you showed me
Callirhoe in the first place at your festival. Now give back the
woman whom you gave me as a gift.' He was just lifting up his
head when he saw a gold statue of Callirhoe next to the image
of the goddess, which Dionysius had given as an offering.

> His knees buckled and his dear heart faltered.

Everything went dark and he fell to the ground. Seeing him, a
temple servant brought him some water and, as she helped the
poor man, said, 'Take heart, child. The goddess has overwhelmed
many others too. But this is a very lucky sign. Do you see this
gold statue? She was a slave, but Aphrodite has made her mistress
of all of us.' 'Who is she?' asked Chaereas. 'She is the mistress
of this estate, my child, the wife of Dionysius, the most important
man among the Ionians.' When he heard this, Polycharmus sen-
sibly did not let Chaereas say anything more, but helped him to
rise and hustled him out, not wanting anyone to discover who
they were until they had discussed everything fully together and
come up with a plan.

   While the temple servant was still there, Chaereas said nothing, but was completely silent at first, except that tears sprang
from his eyes as if of their own free will. But going as far out on
the shore as he could, he threw himself down and cried, 'Kindly
sea, why did you insist on saving me? Was it so that after a fair
voyage I might see Callirhoe the wife of another? I hoped never
to see this – not even after my death. What am I to do, ill-starred
as I am? I was hoping to take you from a master and I was
assuming that I could persuade the man who had bought you
with ransom money. Now I have found you rich and probably
a princess. How much happier I would have been if I had found
you dissolved in tears. Going up to Dionysius, I would say, "Give

me back my wife!" But who says this to a man who has just got married? And if I were to meet you I would not be able to go up to you nor to greet you as a fellow citizen in the most ordinary of ways. I would probably be in danger of being killed as the adulterer of my own wife!' Polycharmus tried to calm him as he made these laments.

[7] In the meantime, Phocas, Dionysius' steward, caught sight of the warship and was rather worried. Striking up an apparently casual conversation with one of the sailors, he discovered the truth of who they were, where they had come from and why. He realized, therefore, that the trireme brought great disaster for Dionysius and that the man who had snatched Callirhoe away would not be allowed to live. He was a man who was well-disposed towards his master, and who wanted to prevent something terrible happening and to avert a great war – great for Dionysius' household at any rate if not in general; for this reason, he rode off to the nearby barbarian garrison and announced that a warship was lying hidden, secretly moored, possibly on a spying mission, possibly for piracy, and that it would be very much in the King's interests for it to be captured before it could carry out its nefarious business. This argument persuaded the barbarians and he brought them back with him once they had decided what to do. In the middle of the night they fell upon the trireme and torched it, taking captive all those who escaped alive and leading them back in chains to the garrison. In the allotment of prisoners, Chaereas and Polycharmus begged to be assigned to the same master and the man who took them sold them in Caria. There, dragging heavy chains, they toiled on Mithridates' property.

Now, Chaereas appeared to Callirhoe in a dream, bound and wanting to approach her but not able to. She gave a great and piercing wail in her sleep, 'Chaereas, come here!' That was the first time that Dionysius heard the name and he realized that his wife was in a state of distress: 'Who is it you are calling to?' Her tears betrayed her and she was unable to suppress her grief, but gave full rein to her feelings. 'A wretched man,' she answered, 'my first husband, an unlucky man even in my dreams, for I saw him bound. But you, poor man, have you died searching for me (for it is clear that your bonds represent death) while I live in luxury, lying on a golden couch with another man? But before long I will come to you. Even though we have been separated in life, in death we will have each other!' At these words Dionysius was prey to conflicting emotions. Jealousy got its claws into him because Callirhoe loved the dead Chaereas, but on the other hand, fear gnawed at him in case she should kill herself. However, he took courage from the thought that his wife believed her first husband to be dead and would surely not leave him if Chaereas were no longer alive. Accordingly, he was as sympathetic as possible to her and kept an eye on her for many days to prevent her doing anything terrible to herself. For her, hope drew the sting from her grief: hope that perhaps he lived and her dream had been false, and even more the hope inherent in her pregnant stomach. In the seventh month after her marriage, she gave birth to a son – ostensibly Dionysius', but in reality Chaereas'. The city held a great festival and embassies arrived from everywhere to join the Milesians in celebrating the new addition to the family of Dionysius. He, overcome with joy, put everything into his wife's hands and made her truly the mistress of his house; he filled the temples with offerings and regaled the city en masse with sacrificial feasts.

[8] Callirhoe, on the other hand, was caught in a frantic struggle not to betray her unspeakable secret, and she decided that it would be a good idea to free Plangon, the only other person who knew that she had been pregnant when she came to Dionysius. Thus she would have her loyalty not only as a result of the natural sympathy between the two women, but also in gratitude at the material change in Plangon's circumstances. Dionysius said, 'I am very happy to repay Plangon for her romantic services, but I think that we would be behaving unfairly if we honour the servant but do not give our thanks to Aphrodite in whose presence we first saw each other.' 'That can only be more true for me than for you,' said Callirhoe, 'for I owe her greater gratitude. But for the moment I am still in childbed: if we wait for a few days, we will be able to go off to the country estate safely.'

She soon recovered from the birth and became plumper and

more blooming, no longer a maiden but in the full flower of womanhood. While they were travelling to the country, Phocas prepared magnificent sacrificial feasts because they brought with them a great entourage from the city. Getting started on the huge number of sacrifices, Dionysius said, 'Lady Aphrodite, you are responsible for all the good things in my life. I have Callirhoe because of you; because of you I have my son; because of you I am a husband and a father. Callirhoe is all I need. She is sweeter to me than my homeland and my parents, and I love my child because he has made his mother more securely mine. I thus have a pledge of security guaranteeing her affections. I beg you, Mistress, protect Callirhoe for me and protect our son for Callirhoe.' The mass of people who were standing round cheered him and pelted them – some with roses, others with violets and others again with whole garlands so that the precinct of the temple was filled with flowers. Dionysius then said a prayer in front of everyone but Callirhoe wanted to speak to Aphrodite alone. She first took her son into her arms, a vision of exquisite beauty, such as, before now, no painter has managed to paint, no sculptor to sculpt and no poet to describe; for none of them has shown Artemis or Athena with her baby in her arms. Seeing her, Dionysius wept with joy and in silence made obeisance to Nemesis. Callirhoe then ordered Plangon alone to stay and sent the rest on ahead to the house.

When they had left, she stepped up close to Aphrodite and held up her baby in her hands. 'Mistress,' she said, 'I feel great gratitude to you on behalf of this child, but not on my own. I would have been grateful to you if you had spared Chaereas for me. You have, however, given me a child who is the image of my dear husband and so have not taken Chaereas entirely away from me. Allow my son to be more fortunate than his parents, and let him be equal to his grandfather; let him command a war fleet and let people say when he fights a sea battle, "Hermocrates' grandson outdoes his grandfather!" His grandfather will rejoice to have someone to inherit his talents and his parents will rejoice even though we are dead. I beg you, Mistress, exchange your enmity for friendship towards me from now on because I have suffered enough. I have died, I have come back to life, I have been stolen by bandits, I have gone into exile, I have been sold and I have been a slave – and I consider this second marriage as still a heavier misfortune than these. However, I ask one favour in return for all of these from you and through you from the other gods: protect my fatherless child!' Although she had more to say, her tears prevented her.

[9] A little while later she called the priestess and the old lady heard her and replied, 'Why do you cry, child, when you are in the midst of such good fortune? Already strangers prostrate themselves before you as a goddess. Just now, two fine young men – sailors – came here. One of them, when he saw your statue, almost expired on the spot, so like her representative on earth has Aphrodite made you.' This struck right to Callirhoe's heart and, like one bereft of her senses, with fixed eyes she cried out, 'Who were these strangers? Where had they sailed from? Why did they speak to you?' At first the old woman was afraid and stood there speechless, then with difficulty she managed to get out, 'I only saw them, I didn't hear them.' 'What did they look like? Try to remember their appearance.' The old woman said something, but nothing very precise; nevertheless, Callirhoe guessed at the truth, for we are all ready to believe the thing we want to be true. Looking across at Plangon she said, 'Somehow, my lost Chaereas found his way here. What has happened to him? Let's look for him, but we must keep it a secret.'

When she saw Dionysius, she only told him what the priestess had said, for she knew that Eros is by nature meddlesome and that Dionysius would try on his own account to tease out what had happened: which is just what he did. Realizing immediately what the situation was, he was struck with jealousy and although he was far from guessing that it was Chaereas, he was afraid that there was someone hiding on his estate with a plan of seduction. For his wife's beauty made him suspicious and fearful of everything, and he was not only afraid of the strategies of men but he even thought that it was possible that a god might come down from heaven as a rival lover.

Accordingly he summoned Phocas and grilled him with questions: 'Who were those young men and where did they come from? I imagine they were rich and noble? Why were they worshipping at the temple of Aphrodite on my estate? Who told them about it? Who let them use it?' Phocas, however, did not reveal the truth, not because he feared Dionysius but because he knew that Callirhoe would ruin him and his family if she found out what had happened. So he denied that any foreigners had been there, not realizing that Dionysius would imagine a far worse scenario: that he was part of the plot himself. Enraged by his denial, therefore, Dionysius called for whips and the rack for Phocas and summoned not only him but all the men who worked on his estate, convinced that he was hot on the scent of the planned seduction.

Realizing that he was in terrible danger whether he spoke out or not, Phocas said, 'Master, I will tell you the truth.' Dionysius sent everyone else away. 'Look, we are alone,' he said. 'Don't lie any more: tell me the truth even if it is shameful.' 'It is nothing shameful,' he replied. 'In fact I have some very important and positive news for you. If the first part of it seems really bad, don't get distressed by this or upset until you have heard the whole story, because it turns out really well for you in the end.' Dionysius was waiting impatiently to hear what he had to say and was hanging on his every word. 'Hurry up!' he urged. 'Tell me all now!'

At that, Phocas began to speak, 'A trireme sailed in from Sicily, bringing ambassadors of the Syracusans demanding Callirhoe back from you.' Dionysius fainted when he heard this and darkness poured down over his eyes. He had a vision of Chaereas standing beside him and tearing Callirhoe away from him. Lying on the ground, he bore the appearance and colour of a corpse. Phocas was in a terrible quandary because he did not want to call anyone who would then be a witness to such an unspeakable sight. Gradually and with difficulty he himself managed to bring his master round. 'It's all right,' he said. 'Chaereas is dead. His ship has been destroyed. There is nothing to fear.' These words roused Dionysius and little by little he came to himself and understood everything fully. Phocas explained how one of the sailors had told him where the trireme was from, on whose behalf it had set sail and who was on it; also he recounted his stratagem with the barbarians, the night, the fire, the shipwreck, the deaths, the prisoners taken away in shackles.

It was just as if a cloud or shadow lifted from Dionysius' spirit and he embraced Phocas, saying, 'You are my benefactor; you have truly protected my interests and shown yourself most trustworthy in a terrible crisis. I have Callirhoe and my son because of you! I would not have asked you to kill Chaereas, but I do not blame you for having done so, because the only crime is of loving your master. There is only one thing which you have done less than fully: you have not made it your business to find out if Chaereas was among the dead or one of the ones who were captured. We must search for the body for then he could be properly buried, and my mind could more securely be put at rest. I am not able to be completely reassured because of the prisoners. We do not even know where they were sold.'

[10] He told Phocas to be quite open about all the other events, but to keep silent about two things: his own stratagem and the fact that some of the men from the trireme had survived. He went to Callirhoe with a very sad expression and then he summoned local people whom he had carefully primed so that his wife, realizing what had happened, would accept the loss of Chaereas more fully. Coming before her, they all told her what they knew, that at some point during the night barbarian pirates had attacked and set fire to a Greek trireme which had been moored on the headland the previous day. 'At dawn we saw the water mixed with blood and corpses floating in the waves.'

When she heard this his wife began to tear her clothes and, beating her eyes and cheeks, she ran into the room she had first entered when she had just been sold. Dionysius accepted this as a sign of her grief, fearing to seem coarsely insensitive by his unwanted presence. He consequently ordered everyone else to leave her alone and for Plangon alone to sit with her in case she should do anything terrible to herself.

Callirhoe desperately seized the opportunity for solitude. Sitting on the ground, filthying her head with dust and tearing at her hair, she began the following laments: 'I begged to die before you or with you, Chaereas, even if it was necessary for

you to die well after me. What hope is there left for me in life?
Unlucky already yet still I counted on this – "I will see Chaereas
at some point and I will recount to him all that I have suffered
on his account. These things will make me more worthy in his
eyes. What joy he will be filled with when he sees his son!" How
useless such thoughts were, and keeping his fatherless child is a
self-indulgence which has already cost me dear. Unjust Aphrodite, you alone saw Chaereas and you didn't let me see him when
he came. You handed his beautiful body over to bandits, and
you had no pity for one who had sailed the high seas for you.
Who would appeal to such a goddess who kills her own suppliant?
On that fearful night you did not help a young man – beautiful,
in love – even when you saw him being killed next to your
temple. You have taken away from me my age mate, my fellow
citizen, my lover, my beloved, my bridegroom. Give him back
to me even if he is a corpse. I contend that we have been born
the unluckiest of mortals. What harm did the trireme do so that
the barbarians should burn it? – a boat which never oppressed
anybody except Athenians. Now both our parents are sitting
beside the sea, waiting for the outcome of our voyage, and when
a ship is spotted from afar, they say, "Here comes Chaereas
bringing Callirhoe!" They are getting my bridal bed ready, the
wedding chamber is being decked out – for us who don't even
have our own tomb! Cursed sea, you took Chaereas to Miletus
to be killed and me to be sold into slavery.'

BOOK 4

[1] So Callirhoe passed the night in lamentation, grieving for Chaereas who was actually still alive. She had only just fallen asleep when she had a dream about barbarian brigands bringing torches, the trireme being set on fire and she herself coming to Chaereas' aid. Dionysius was upset at seeing his wife waste away in case some of her beauty should also be destroyed, but he still assumed that her full acceptance of the loss of her former husband would be most profitable for the success of his own passion. Wanting to show his affection and generosity, he said to her, 'My dear, get up and prepare a tomb for the poor wretch. Why do you strive for what's impossible and ignore what's necessary? Imagine he is standing beside you saying:

"Bury me with all speed so I may pass through the gates of Hades."

And if you don't find the poor man's body there is still an ancient Greek custom of honouring even those who have disappeared with a tomb.'

He persuaded her easily because the advice pleased her. After she had decided on this, her grief lessened and, getting up from her couch, she searched for a place in which she could build a tomb. A spot near to the temple of Aphrodite appealed to her on the grounds that there would be a memorial of their love for those in the future. But Dionysius resented the idea of Chaereas being such a close neighbour and insisted on keeping that spot for himself. To delay the project then, he said, 'Let's go to the city, my dear, and there build a high and magnificent tomb,

'So that it might be clearly visible from afar to men on the high seas.

The harbours of Miletus are very fine and Syracusans too have
moored there many times. In this way your desire to honour
him will be known even among your own countrymen.'

The suggestion pleased Callirhoe but for that moment she kept
her enthusiasm in check. When she reached the city, however, she
began to build the tomb on a certain steep headland, a copy of
her own tomb in Syracuse in every way: in overall appearance, in
size, in extravagance and, just like that one, for someone who was
alive. By importing many statues and employing many workmen,
the job was soon completed and at that point she carried out a
burial service which was the twin of her own. The day for the
burial was chosen and published and not only did the great majority of Milesians come to it, but pretty much the whole of Ionia.
Two eastern satraps were also present who happened to be in the
city anyway: Mithridates, the ruler of Caria, and Pharnaces, of
Lydia. Everyone's professed motive for attending was the opportunity to show their respect for Dionysius; their real reason was
the chance to see Callirhoe. Her immense fame had spread to all
of Asia and her name had reached as far as the Great King, a feat
which even the names of Ariadne and Leda had failed to do. On
top of that, Callirhoe's appearance more than lived up to its reputation; she walked at the front of the procession, black-robed and
with her hair loose, but emitting a blinding radiance from her
face. With her bare arms and feet she outshone the 'white-armed'
and 'lovely ankled' goddesses who appear in Homer.

No one there was able to bear the brilliance of her beauty,
and some fell back as if struck by a ray of light while others
prostrated themselves before her. Even children felt it. Mithridates, the ruler of Caria, fell to the ground his mouth wide open
in wonder, just like someone unexpectedly struck by a bolt from
a catapult, and his servants were scarcely able to get him up and
provide support to move him away. An image of Chaereas was
carried in the procession copied exactly from the engraving on
his signet ring, but no one looked at this image even though it
was very beautiful, because Callirhoe was there and she alone
monopolized everyone's gaze.

How could one do justice to the procession's finale? For when they got close to the tomb the bearers put down the bier, and Callirhoe got up on it and embraced and kissed Chaereas' image. 'You first buried me in Syracuse, I am now doing the same to you in Miletus. We are not only very unlucky, but unlucky in an almost unbelievable way. We have buried each other but neither of us has the other's corpse. Malevolent Fortune, when we died you begrudged us burial in the same land, and you have made first exiles and then corpses of us.' The assembled multitude broke down weeping and everyone pitied Chaereas, not because he was dead, but because he had lost such a woman.

[2] Callirhoe, then, was burying Chaereas in Miletus while he was working on a chain gang in Caria, and soon his body was whittled down with hard agricultural labour. Many things wore away at him: beatings, neglect, chains and, more than all these, his love. For even though he longed for death, he was held back by an insidious hope that perhaps he would see Callirhoe at some point in the future. Polycharmus, therefore, his friend and companion, seeing that he could work no more but was constantly beaten and mercilessly mistreated, went up to the foreman and said, 'Measure out a specific piece of land for us so that you don't charge the other prisoners' laziness to our account. We will get each day's allotted job done.' The foreman was persuaded by this argument and did as Polycharmus suggested. Thus Polycharmus – a youth but with a man's strength and spirit and not enslaved to the cruel tyrant, Love – worked the double plot pretty much single-handedly, gladly taking on the lion's share of the work so that he might spare his friend.

As they experienced such hardships, they finally came to understand that their freedom really had gone. The satrap Mithridates returned to Caria, not the same man who had gone off to Miletus, but pale and thin and like a man who has received a wound – but a wound in his soul – short-tempered and bitter and eaten-up by his love for Callirhoe: he would have been completely finished if he had not come across the following shred of comfort. Certain of the workers who were chained with Chaereas (there were sixteen in number, all in the same dark little room) broke out at night, killed their overseer and tried to escape. They did not make it, though, because the dogs' barking alerted the others. They were all caught that night and carefully fastened in the stocks. When day came the supervisor informed Mithridates of what had happened, and he, without seeing them or hearing their defences, immediately ordered that all sixteen roommates be crucified. They were accordingly brought out, with ropes round their necks and feet, and each one carrying a cross. Those carrying out the punishment added this austere public ritual to the necessary punishment in order to instil fear in any who might have the same idea.

Chaereas got on with it in silence, but Polycharmus, carrying his cross, said, 'We are suffering this on your account, Callirhoe! You are responsible for all our troubles.' When the overseer heard these words, he got the impression that a woman was an accomplice to what had gone on. So that she might also be punished and an investigation made into the plot, he swiftly released Polycharmus from his shared chains and took him to Mithridates. Mithridates was in his garden, lying dejected and distraught, imagining for himself Callirhoe as he had seen her at the funeral. He was completely lost in such a reverie and he looked with disfavour on the arrival of his servant. 'Why are you bothering me?' he said. 'It is urgent, Master. I have found the source of this dreadful trouble and this abominable creature here knows the accursed woman who conspired in the murder.' When he heard this, Mithridates drew together his brows and shot out a terrifying look: 'Tell me who was your accomplice and partner in these crimes!' Polycharmus denied all knowledge and that he had at all been a party to what had gone on. So whips were called for, fire and instruments of torture brought in, and one who was skilled in inflicting pain growled, 'Tell us the name of the woman whom you claimed was responsible for all your troubles.' 'Callirhoe!' confessed Polycharmus.

The name was like a blow to Mithridates but he assumed that there must be some unfortunate coincidence of names between the women. He no longer had any enthusiasm for continuing the interrogation, afraid that he would be put in a position where he had to violate the name of his dreams. But when his friends and household called for a proper investigation, he said, 'Let Callirhoe be brought before me.' Beating Polycharmus then, they kept asking who she was and where they could get hold of her. Although the poor man was at the end of his tether, he did not want to make a false accusation against any woman and said, 'Why do you shout at me in vain, trying to get hold of someone who is not here? I called on Callirhoe the Syracusan, daughter of the general Hermocrates.' When he heard this, Mithridates was covered in a deep blush and a sweat over all his body. He was powerless to stop tears starting from his eyes, so that even Polycharmus fell silent and everyone there was thrown into confusion. Eventually, and with difficulty, Mithridates pulled himself together and said, 'What business of yours is Callirhoe and why did you call on her when you were about to die?' Polycharmus replied, 'It is a long story, Master, and pointless for me to tell. I don't want to bother you with such nonsense at the wrong moment, and I am afraid that if I waste time my friend will steal a march on me. I want to die with him.' His audience's anger dissipated and his courage moved them to pity. Mithridates felt the greatest sympathy of all and cried, 'Don't be afraid! You are not troubling me by telling me the story for I am deeply humane. Have the courage to tell me everything and leave nothing out. Who are you and where do you come from? How have you come to Caria and why are you working the land in chains? Especially tell me about Callirhoe and who your friend is.'

[3] Polycharmus began to speak: 'We are of Syracusan stock, we two prisoners. The other one is the foremost young man in Sicily, in honour, wealth and, formerly, nobility of appearance. I, on the other hand, am a nobody, except that I am his comrade and his friend. We left our parents and sailed away from our homeland: I went for his sake, but he went for the sake of his wife, called Callirhoe, whom he had buried in the most costly fashion, believing her to be dead. However, tomb-robbers found her alive and sold her in Ionia, as we were all told by Theron the pirate under torture. The city then sent out a trireme and ambassadors to search for the lady, but barbarians set fire to the ship, slaughtered the majority, led my friend and me off in chains and sold

us here. We have endured this disaster with dignity, but some of
our fellow prisoners, unknown to us, broke their bonds and
committed murder. You then ordered that we all be taken out
for crucifixion. My friend, even on the point of death, did not
utter his wife's name, but as I was being led out I named her as
the source of my troubles, the woman for whom we had put to
sea.' He was still speaking when Mithridates burst in, 'What is
your friend called?' 'Chaereas,' replied Polycharmus. 'But please,
Master, order the executioner not to place our crosses far apart!'
Tears and groans met this speech and Mithridates sent everyone
to Chaereas to prevent him from being killed first. They found
the others already fastened up on their crosses and Chaereas just
about to go up on his. From afar they all shouted out different
things: 'Spare him!' 'Come down!' 'Don't harm him!' 'Let him
go!' The executioner stayed his hand and Chaereas came down
– grieving because he had been happy at the thought of escaping
from a wretched life and a disastrous love.

Mithridates went to meet him as he was led away and
embraced him, saying, 'Brother and friend, you have brought
me within an inch of committing an act of impiety through your
self-disciplined but untimely silence.' Straightaway he ordered
his servants to take the pair to the bath and to see to their
physical needs and once they were bathed to dress them in fine
Greek clothes. He himself invited friends to a party and carried
out a sacrifice on behalf of Chaereas' safety. There was plenty
to drink, great kindness and everything that could possibly be
needed. But as the feasting went on and Mithridates became
heated with wine and love, he said, 'I don't pity you your bonds
and the cross, Chaereas, but I do pity you for losing such a
wife!' Chaereas cried out in astonishment, 'Where did you see
my Callirhoe?' 'She's not yours any more,' said Mithridates.
'She is the legal wife of Dionysius of Miletus. They already have
a child.'

Chaereas could not contain himself when he heard this and
threw himself at Mithridates' knees. 'I beg you, Master, put me
back on the cross! You are torturing me much more by compelling me to live knowing this. Faithless Callirhoe, most unjust
of all women, I have been sold as a slave for you, done hard

labour, carried a cross and been in the very hands of the executioner, but you have lived in luxury and celebrated your wedding
while I was held in chains. It wasn't enough for you to become
another man's wife while Chaereas still lived: you had to
become a mother too!' Everyone began to cry and the party
began to take on the appearance of a wake. Only Mithridates
was happy at this point, nursing his secret erotic hopes that he
would be able to further his designs on Callirhoe while seeming
to help a friend. 'It is just about night-time,' he said. 'Let's go
off now, but tomorrow, when we are sober, let's think it all
through. The problem needs more time.' At this he stood up
and brought the party to a close, and he himself went off to bed
in the usual way after he had shown the young Syracusans to
his finest guest suite.

[4] The night, full of anxieties, stretched out in front of everyone
and no one was able to sleep. Chaereas was angry and Polycharmus was trying to calm him, while Mithridates was
rejoicing in the hope that, sitting on the sidelines of the athletic
contest between Chaereas and Dionysius, he might manage to
carry off the prize of Callirhoe without getting his hands dirty.

When the discussion started on the following day, Chaereas
immediately wanted to go to Miletus and demand his wife from
Dionysius. He was sure that Callirhoe would not remain there
once she had seen him. But Mithridates argued, 'As far as I am
concerned, you are welcome to go, for I don't want you to be
separated from your wife for another day. I wish that you had
never left Sicily and that nothing terrible had befallen the pair
of you. But since fickle Fortune has imposed such a grim situation on you, you must plan carefully and logically. Right now
you are ready to rush into things on impulse rather than planning them carefully, and without thinking through what the
consequences will be. Are you going to go alone to enter a huge,
unknown city? Are you planning to snatch away the wife of a
man who is not only rich but one of the most powerful in Ionia,
and who feels himself tied with the closest of bonds to her?
Against this, what have you got? Your only allies, Hermocrates
and Mithridates, will be far away, more able to wring their hands

over you than to help you. I think that the place itself is unlucky
for you – you have already suffered terribly there. I am afraid,
though, that what happened then might seem lucky by comparison: the Miletus you experienced might then seem like a bed of
roses. You were captured, but survived. You were sold into slavery, but to me. But now, if Dionysius realizes that you are
plotting against his marriage, which god would be able to save
you? You would be handed over to the cruellest of hands, those
of a rival lover, and perhaps no one would believe that you were
Chaereas. Mind you, you would be in greater danger if they
found out your true identity! Are you the only one who doesn't
realize what sort of a god Eros is? That he takes delight in decep-
tions and tricks? I think that you should first approach your
wife by letter to find out if she remembers you and wants to
leave Dionysius, or if she

> Would like to live happily in the house of whichever man might
> marry her.

Write her a letter. Make her sad, make her happy, make her
search for you, make her call out your name. I will organize the
delivery. You, go and write!'

Chaereas was persuaded by this argument and went off on
his own. He was desperate to write but the words just would
not come, as tears flowed down his face and his hand trembled.
After crying over his disastrous situation, he finally managed to
write this letter:

> To Callirhoe from Chaereas.
> I am alive and I owe my life to Mithridates who has thus performed
> a great service to me – and I hope to you. I was sold in Caria by
> barbarians after they had burnt the fine trireme (your father's
> warship) on which I came. Our city had sent me with an embassy
> on your behalf. I do not know what happened to the other citizens,
> but my friend Polycharmus and I were saved from the brink of
> death by our master's pity.
>   But Mithridates outweighed his friendship by the grief he caused
> me when he told me about your marriage. As a mortal, I am

prepared to face death – but not your marriage! I beg you: change your mind. I sprinkle this letter of mine with tears and kisses. I am that Chaereas of yours, whom you saw as you walked to the temple of Aphrodite when you were still a girl, and on whose behalf you spent sleepless nights. Remember our bridal chamber and our wedding night, when you first experienced your husband and I my wife. It's true that I was jealous, but that is what comes with being in love. I have been punished: I have been sold, I have been a slave, I have been in chains. Don't hold a grudge about that thoughtless kick: I have been up on the cross for you, but I didn't reproach you. If you still remember me, then my sufferings are as nothing. If you think otherwise, you will hand me a death sentence.

[5] Mithridates gave the letter to a man called Hyginus in whom he had great faith and to whom he had previously entrusted the running of his whole Carian estate. He had earlier revealed to him his own love. Mithridates also wrote a letter to Callirhoe himself, explaining his goodwill towards her and his care for her interests. He told her that he had saved Chaereas for her sake and he advised her not to underestimate the claims of her first husband, saying that he himself promised to mastermind their reunion if that was what she wanted. Along with Hyginus he also sent three attendants, expensive gifts and a great quantity of gold. He told the other servants that he was sending these things to Dionysius as a way of avoiding suspicion. However, he ordered Hyginus that when they got to Priene, he should leave the others there and journey into Ionia alone (for he could speak Greek), entering Miletus as a spy. When he had worked out how best to deal with the situation, he should bring the others from Priene to Miletus.

Hyginus went off and was in the process of carrying out his orders, but Fortune had decided on a different outcome and turned this into the starting point for greater events. For when Hyginus set out to Miletus, the slaves, who were left on their own without anyone in charge of them, immediately started to squander the plentiful gold which they were looking after. In a city that was small and full of Greek busybodies, such foreign wealth soon attracted everyone's attention. Since these unknown men were spending money like water, it was assumed that they were thieves, or at least fugitives of some sort. So the chief magistrate came to the inn and after a short search found the gold and all the expensive gear. Thinking it was stolen, he asked the slaves who they were and where the stuff came from. They were terrified of being tortured and immediately came out with the truth that Mithridates, the ruler of Caria, was sending all this as a gift to Dionysius, and they showed him the letters. The magistrate did not open the letters, however, because they were sealed on the outside, but instead he handed everything over to his officials to be sent to Dionysius, thinking that he was doing him a great favour.

Dionysius happened to be holding a banquet for his most important citizens. The party was a glittering success and already, I imagine, both flute playing and singing had been heard. In the middle of a song someone brought the following note to Dionysius:

> Bias, the chief magistrate of Priene, salutes his benefactor, Dionysius. Worthless slaves were appropriating the gifts and letters that were on their way to you from Mithridates, the ruler of Caria, but I have apprehended those men and send them on to you.

Dionysius read the note in the middle of the party, and felt rather smug about the princely gifts. Then he ordered the seals to be broken and started to read the letters. He saw the words, 'To Callirhoe from Chaereas. I am alive . . .'

> But his knees went weak and his dear heart faltered,

and a darkness poured down over his eyes. However, although he had almost taken leave of his senses, he managed to hang on to the letter because he was afraid of anyone else getting hold of it. He was roused by the noise of everyone dashing about in panic, and when he realized what had happened, he ordered his servants to take him to another room so that he could be alone. The party thus ended on a melancholy note because everyone

thought that Dionysius had had a fit, and Dionysius himself was
shut away on his own, reading the letters over and over again.
He was a prey to conflicting emotions: hope, despair, fear, uncertainty. He did not believe that Chaereas was alive because he
profoundly did not want it to be true, but he suspected an adulterous plot by Mithridates, trying to offer the hope of Chaereas
as a way of corrupting Callirhoe.

[6] When daylight came he increased the provisions for Callirhoe's
protection, so that no one would be able to approach her or tell
her anything of what was going on in Caria. He adopted the
following strategy for his own protection. By a happy coincidence, Pharnaces, the ruler of Lydia and Ionia, was in town, a
man who seemed to be the most powerful of the officials sent
by the Great King to the coastal provinces. Dionysius went to
him as a friend and asked his advice. In a private tête-à-tête,
Dionysius said, 'I beg you, Master, help me and protect yourself!
Mithridates is a very dangerous man and he is jealous of you.
Even though he had been my guest, he plotted against my
marriage and sent adulterous letters and gold to my wife.' At
that point, he read out the letters and explained Mithridates'
strategy. Pharnaces gladly listened to all this, partly because of
Mithridates (for their proximity had caused any number of
niggling irritations between them) but mostly because of his own
love. For he too burned with desire for Callirhoe and it was for
her sake that he spent so much time in Miletus and had invited
Dionysius and his wife to his banquets. Consequently, he promised to help him as much as he could and wrote the following
top secret letter:

Pharnaces, satrap of Lydia and Ionia, sends greetings to his own
master, Artaxerxes, King of Kings. Dionysius the Milesian is your
slave, as were his fathers before him, eagerly devoted to the interests of your dynasty. This man has made a complaint to me that
Mithridates, the ruler of Caria, and his own guest, is trying to
corrupt his wife. Mithridates is giving a bad name to your rule
and, even more importantly, causing unrest. Any act of lawlessness
by a satrap should be censured, but especially this, for Dionysius

is the most powerful of the Ionians and the beauty of his wife is
legendary so there is no way that such an insult would escape
publicity.

When it arrived, the King read this letter to his friends and
asked them what he ought to do. Various opinions were voiced.
Those who were jealous of Mithridates and who believed they
had a hope of succeeding to his satrapy, thought that a plot
against the marriage of an honourable man ought not to be
overlooked; those who were of an easier-going temperament or
who respected Mithridates (for he had many supporters) were
not happy at the idea of a respectable man being arrested on the
basis of slanderous hearsay. With almost equal support for both
sides, the King made no decision that day but put further consideration of the matter to one side. In the course of the evening he
began to feel resentment because the good name of his rule was
being put in jeopardy, and he was concerned about the future,
as Mithridates might begin to hold his authority in contempt.

He decided then and there to bring Mithridates to trial and
the idea of summoning the beautiful wife also took hold of him.
Wine and the darkness of the evening were his counsellors as he
sat there alone, and the King remembered the part of the letter
about her. In excitement he also remembered a rumour that a
certain woman called Callirhoe was the most beautiful woman
in Ionia. He was only sorry that Pharnaces had failed to include
the wife's name. On the off chance that perhaps there was
another woman even better than the one he had heard of, he
decided to summon the wife. So he wrote to Pharnaces, 'Send
me Dionysius, my Milesian slave, and send his wife with him.'
To Mithridates he wrote, 'Come and defend yourself against the
charge of plotting against Dionysius' marriage.'

[7] Mithridates was astonished at this and at a loss to know the
source of the accusation, but when Hyginus returned he explained
what had happened to the slaves. Betrayed then by the letters,
he planned not to go to the court, afraid of the strength of the
accusations and of the King's anger. Instead, he decided to
capture Miletus, kill Dionysius, the cause of all this, snatch

Callirhoe and revolt against the King. 'Why do your best to betray your freedom and put yourself in the hands of a master?' he thought. 'Perhaps you will be more successful by remaining here because the King is far away and his generals are no good. Even if this just provokes a different mode of attack, things can't get any worse for you. In such a crisis do not betray the two finest things in the world, your love and your power to rule. Leadership is a noble thing to take with you to the grave and death will be sweet with Callirhoe.'

While he was still forming these plans and making preparations for his revolt, a messenger came saying that Dionysius had left Miletus taking Callirhoe. Mithridates heard this news with a heavier heart than when he had received the summons to trial. When he had wept over this new disaster, he said, 'What hope do I still have? Fortune has betrayed me on all sides. Perhaps the King will pity me since I have done nothing wrong, and if I have to die, perhaps I will see Callirhoe again. And I will have Chaereas with me in the court and Polycharmus, not only to help me plead my case, but as witnesses.' Ordering all his personal staff to accompany him, he set out from Caria, with such high hopes that he would be acquitted that everyone sent him on his way not with tears but with sacrifices and celebration.

So, Eros sent this expedition out from Caria and another, of greater celebrity, from Ionia: it had a far more glittering reputation for beauty. Rumour ran ahead of the woman, announcing to everyone that Callirhoe was coming whose reputation spread far and wide, the greatest marvel in nature,

Like unto Artemis or golden Aphrodite.

The news of the trial made her even more famous. Whole cities came out to meet her and the roads were blocked by the crowds who had come to see her, but still, for everyone, the reality of the woman surpassed her reputation. Dionysius was made utterly miserable by the constant congratulations and the enormity of his good fortune made him even more fearful, because he was an educated man who knew that Eros is fickle. It is for this reason that poets and sculptors show him carrying the bow and the

torch – both weapons which move and flicker, not wanting to
stand still. The memory of ancient stories, in which beautiful
women constantly change their loyalties, preoccupied Dionysius.
He feared everything and saw everybody as a rival, not only his
opponent, but the judge himself, with the result that he had
second thoughts about the wisdom of having told Pharnaces,

When it was possible to sleep holding his beloved in his arms.

It was one thing to keep watch over Callirhoe in Miletus but
completely different to guard her throughout the whole of Asia.
Nevertheless he kept his secret until the end and did not tell his
wife what was really going on, but offered the excuse that the
King had summoned him because he wanted to consult him over
matters in Ionia. Callirhoe was unhappy, journeying far away
from the sea which connected her to Greece, for while she looked
on Miletus' harbours, Syracuse seemed to be near. She also had
great comfort there from Chaereas' tomb.

BOOK 5

[1] How Callirhoe was married to Chaereas – the most beautiful woman to the most beautiful man – as the result of Aphrodite's machinations; how it was thought that she was dead after Chaereas struck her in a fit of passionate jealousy; how she was buried so magnificently but then came to life in the tomb and was taken from Sicily by tomb-robbers who sailed to Ionia and sold her to Dionysius; about Dionysius' love; about Callirhoe's loyalty to Chaereas but the necessity of her marriage because of her pregnancy; about Theron's confession and Chaereas' expedition to find his wife; about his own capture and sale in Caria along with his friend Polycharmus; how Mithridates identified Chaereas just as he was about to be killed and how he made attempts to reunite the lovers, but how, discovering this from his letters, Dionysius denounced him to Pharnaces, then Pharnaces to the King and that the King called both of them to trial – all this, I told you in the previous books. Now I am going to tell you the rest.

As far as Syria and Cilicia, Callirhoe coped with the journey easily because she could hear Greek voices and see the sea which led to Syracuse. But when they came to the river Euphrates, beyond which the whole continent stretches out endlessly, and which is itself the starting point of the King's enormous empire, at that moment a longing for her homeland and family crept over her along with a sense of despair about ever going back again. Standing on the riverbank, she ordered everyone to keep back except Plangon, her one confidante. She began, 'Malevolent Fortune, so eager to fight with one poor woman, you have shut me in a tomb when I was still alive, then taken me from there not out of pity, but so that you could hand me over to robbers.

The sea and Theron are jointly responsible for my exile. And I, the daughter of Hermocrates, was sold into slavery! Even more upsetting than my lonely exile, I became the object of a man's attentions and have had to marry someone else while Chaereas is still alive. Yes, you even begrudged me this because you no longer allow me to remain in exile in Ionia. There I had a home in a land which was foreign, but still Greek-speaking, where I had great comfort because I was near to the sea. Now you thrust me from my accustomed sphere and leave me cut off, a world away from my native land. You have taken me away from Miletus just as you did before from Syracuse. I am an island dweller being taken away across the Euphrates and buried deep in foreign lands far from the sea. How can I hope for a ship to sail here from Sicily? I am cruelly separated from your tomb. Noble spirit of Chaereas, who will bring offerings for you? For the rest of my time, Bactra and Susa will be my home and my final resting place. I am only going to cross you once, Euphrates. The length of my stay scares me less than the fear that there too someone may take a fancy to me.' As she said this, she kissed the ground, then got on to the ferry and was taken across.

Dionysius was blessed with enormous wealth which he used to ensure that his wife travelled with every possible comfort. The kindness and hospitality of the local people also made their journey even more majestic: one community escorted them to the next, one satrap entrusted them to the next one's care and, of course, her beauty charmed everyone. Moreover, a further consideration spontaneously moved these foreign people: the expectation that this woman would one day have great power, and for this reason everyone rushed to offer her gifts or to perform favours which would excite her gratitude.

[2] This is how things were going with them. Meanwhile, Mithridates travelled hurriedly through Armenia, particularly afraid that it would come to the King's attention if he seemed to be following in Callirhoe's footsteps and at the same time eager to arrive at the city first and get things organized for the trial. So he arrived in Babylon (where the King was currently residing) and spent the first day quietly in his own personal quarters, which

he, like all the other satraps, had had specially assigned to him. On the following day he went to the foyer of the palace and there greeted the Persians who equalled him in rank and Artaxates, the eunuch who had the greatest power and influence with the King. First he honoured them with gifts, then said, 'Announce to the King, "Mithridates, your slave, is here to defend himself against the slanders of the Greek and to show his obedience to you."' The eunuch returned quickly and gave the reply, 'The King hopes that Mithridates has done nothing wrong. He will judge the cases when Dionysius arrives.' Mithridates paid his respects to the King and then went away. Since he was on his own, he called Chaereas to him and said, 'I am being taken to court and judged because I wanted to restore Callirhoe to you. Dionysius claims that I wrote the letter that you sent to your wife and thinks that it is evidence of adultery. He believes that you are dead – and let him believe it until the trial, so that you can appear unexpectedly. All I ask is that you pay back this act of kindness by hiding yourself and by holding off trying to see Callirhoe or doing anything to make contact with her.'

Unwillingly Chaereas agreed and tried to hide his feelings but could not help the tears coursing down his cheeks. Saying, 'Master, I will do what you ask', he went to the room which he was staying in with his friend Polycharmus and threw himself to the floor, tearing at his tunic, and

> With both hands scooping up the sooty dust
> He poured it down over his head, and fouled his noble face.

Then, in tears, he said, 'O Callirhoe, we are close, but cannot see one another. You have done nothing wrong because you do not know that Chaereas is alive. I, on the other hand, am the wickedest man in the world. Ordered not to see you, I have given in to such tyranny because I am a coward and I want to live. If someone had laid this injunction on you, you would not have remained alive.'

While Polycharmus tried to comfort Chaereas, Dionysius was already approaching Babylon and Rumour raced on ahead into the city, announcing that the woman was arriving, a woman whose beauty was not human, but divine, the like of whom the sun had never seen in all its course. Barbarians are by nature women-mad and so every house and every street was full of the news. The rumour even reached as far as the ears of the King himself and he asked his eunuch Artaxates if the Milesian woman had arrived. For a long time his wife's celebrity had been a source of unhappiness to Dionysius (for it made him feel insecure), and when he was about to enter Babylon he became even more uncomfortable about it. Groaning to himself, he said, 'This is no longer your own city of Miletus, Dionysius! Even there you had to be on your guard against men plotting against you. As if you can't see what could happen, are you now rashly bringing Callirhoe to Babylon where there are many men like Mithridates? Menelaus couldn't protect Helen even when he was in austere Sparta, and a barbarian shepherd imposed upon him even though he was a king. There are many Parises in Persia! Do you not see that the danger is already starting? Cities welcome us with open arms and satraps fawn over us. She is already feeling flattered by all this attention and the King hasn't even seen her yet! My one chance of security is if I can keep her secretly hidden, because she will be safe if I can avoid her being seen.' These were the calculations he was making, as he mounted his horse, handed Callirhoe into the carriage and drew the curtains securely around her. Perhaps it would have turned out as he wanted if the following incident had not taken place.

[3] Some of the wives of the most aristocratic Persians went to visit Stateira, the King's wife, and one of them said, 'Mistress, this Greek creature – this female – is waging war against us! We have always been famed for our beauty, but now the reputation of Persian womanhood is in danger of being trampled underfoot. Join with us in planning how we can avoid being imposed upon by this foreigner.'

The Queen laughed in disbelief at the rumour and, still laughing, said, 'Greeks are vagabonds and beggars and consequently are impressed by anything. Rumour has it that Callirhoe is very beautiful, but it also claims that Dionysius is rich! So let one of us appear beside her when she comes in, and we can extinguish this poor slave's pretensions.' All the women prostrated themselves before the Queen and said how impressed they were by her plan immediately, with one voice crying out, 'If only it were possible for you to appear, Mistress!' After that, opinions were divided and the names of various women, foremost for their beauty, were called out. There was a vote, just like in the theatre, and Rhodogune, daughter of Zopyros and wife of Megabyzos, was chosen, whose beauty was a famous phenomenon. Just as Callirhoe was to Ionia, so was Rhodogune to Asia. Taking her off, the women helped her dress and adorn herself, each one adding her own touches to the ensemble. The Queen gave her bracelets and a necklace.

When they had finished arming her so beautifully for the contest, she made her appearance as if coming to welcome Callirhoe. Indeed, she had a perfectly acceptable excuse since she was the sister of Pharnaces, the man who had written to the King about Dionysius. All of Babylon rushed outside to see the spectacle and the throng of people made the gateways almost impossible to pass. At the most conspicuous spot, Rhodogune waited, attended royally. Exquisite and very sure of her own beauty, she stood there provocatively, and all the women looked round at her and whispered to each other, 'We have won! The Persian woman will outshine the foreigner! Just let them be judged together! Let the Greeks learn that they are boorish beggars!' At this point, Dionysius arrived and, aware that Pharnaces' sister was there, leapt down from his horse and ran up to her eagerly. She blushed and as she approached the carriage, said, 'I would like to greet my sister.' It was consequently impossible for Dionysius to keep Callirhoe hidden, and so, unwilling and groaning to himself, out of respect he let her approach Callirhoe. Immediately, everyone strained to see and almost knocked each other down in their eagerness to get as close as possible and have a better view than their neighbour. Callirhoe's radiant beauty blazed out and dazzled everyone's eyes with a bolt like lightning appearing suddenly in the deep darkness of the night. Utterly amazed, the barbarians prostrated themselves, forgetting even the existence of Rhodogune. She recognized that she was beaten and, unable to leave, but not wanting to be looked at, she slipped in under the curtain with Callirhoe, accepting her defeat. Callirhoe was still in the carriage, and it was beginning to move forward, hidden again by the curtain; but the people, without being able to see her any more, were trying to kiss the car itself.

When the King heard that Dionysius had arrived, he ordered Artaxates, his eunuch, to summon him to receive the following message, 'Since you are accusing a trusted man who holds high office, you ought not to have taken so long to get here: however, I can see that the reason was that you were travelling with your wife. I am currently holding a festival and am just going off to carry out a sacrifice. I will hear the case thirty days from now.' Dionysius paid his respects and left.

[4] On both sides preparations were being made for the trial as if it was for a great war. The people's loyalty was divided: Mithridates had the support of as many as were in favour of the satraps' rule, for he was born in Bactra and only later moved to Caria. Dionysius, on the other hand, had the goodwill of the common people because it was felt that he was being wronged against the laws and – of even greater significance – that he was being plotted against because he had such a wife. The women of the country had their own views as well, though their loyalties were divided. On the one hand, those who prided themselves on their good looks were jealous of Callirhoe and wanted her to be humiliated by the trial; but the majority, jealous of the women who fancied themselves the elite, were hoping that the foreign woman would be vindicated. Each of the two men thought that victory was within his grasp. Dionysius took heart from the letters that Mithridates had written to Callirhoe in Chaereas' name (for he never suspected that Chaereas was still alive), while Mithridates, knowing he could produce Chaereas, was sure that he could not be convicted. However, he pretended to be worried and engaged professional advocates, so that his defence would seem all the more dazzlingly effective because of its unexpectedness. For the whole month, the Persians and their women could talk of nothing else except the trial so that, to be honest, all of Babylon was like a law court. The appointed day seemed to take a terribly long time to arrive, not only to everyone else but to the King himself. What sort of Olympic Games or Eleusinian Nights were ever awaited with quite such eagerness?

When the day itself arrived, the King took his seat. There is a special building in the palace which is set aside as a law court, outstanding in both size and beauty. There, in the middle, lies the King's throne and on either side are seats for his companions, men who, even among the ruling elite, are foremost in reputation and honour. In a circle around the throne stand captains and generals and the most influential of the King's freedmen, so that one could fittingly say of that company,

> Seated, the gods hold court, with Zeus at their centre.

The litigants were brought in, silent and fearful. That morning it was Mithridates who came up first, escorted by a group of friends and kinsmen, not looking particularly bright and cheerful, but rather sorry for himself like a defendant should. Dionysius followed, dressed in Greek style with a cloak of Milesian wool and holding the letters in his hand. When they had been brought in, they prostrated themselves before the King. After that, the King ordered his secretary to read out the letters, including the one from Pharnaces and his own in reply, so that his fellow judges would know the full history. In response, a great flood of praise broke out expressing its admiration of the King's sensitivity and judgement.

When silence had been restored again, it was necessary for Dionysius to begin speaking as the plaintiff and everyone turned towards him. But Mithridates jumped in first, 'I am not trying to make my defence speech too early, Master, but I know how things should be done. It is essential, before the speeches start, that all the relevant parties are present. Where then is the woman over whom this trial is taking place? You thought that she was important to the case because of the letter and accordingly wrote to instruct that she be present and she is here. Don't let Dionysius hide, then, what is at the heart and hub of the whole affair.' To this Dionysius replied, 'This is so typical of an adulterer, to bring another man's wife into the public gaze against the will of the husband and when she herself is neither bringing the charge nor having it brought against her. If she had been seduced it would have been necessary for her to be present as the injured party. But as things are, you hatched your plot without her knowledge, and I am using my wife neither as a witness nor as someone to speak on my behalf. Why then is it necessary for someone to be present when they have no formal part in the case?'

What Dionysius said was legally correct, but it persuaded no one because everyone wanted to see Callirhoe. Although the King was ashamed to give the order, his companions used the letter as an excuse and it was declared to be necessary. 'How strange it would be,' said one, 'when she has come all the way from Ionia for her to let us down at the last minute when she is actually in Babylon.' Thus it was decided that Callirhoe should be present, but Dionysius had still not told her anything, having all the time until now concealed the reason for their journey to Babylon. He was afraid to take her unexpectedly into the courts when she knew nothing about it (for it would only be reasonable for his wife to be annoyed that she had been deceived) and so he got an adjournment of the case to the following day.

[5] So at that point the court adjourned. Dionysius went home and, inasmuch as he was a sensible and educated man, addressed a speech to his wife which was as persuasive as possible in the circumstances, going through every detail carefully and gently. Callirhoe certainly did not hear this account without tears, weeping at the mention of Chaereas' name and very upset at the thought of the trial. 'This is the last straw, having to go into a courtroom! I have died, I have been buried, tomb-robbed, sold, enslaved. Look, Fortune, now I am being put on trial! It obviously was not enough for you to have slandered me unjustly to Chaereas: now you have accused me of adultery to Dionysius! Then you pursued me to the grave with your slanders, now to the law court of the King. I have become the talking point of Asia and Europe. With what sort of a look can I face the judge? What sort of speeches will I have to listen to? O malevolent beauty, given to me for this alone, so that the earth could be filled with slanders about me. Hermocrates' daughter is being judged but without the support and advocacy of her father. Whenever other people are in a courtroom, they pray for good-

will and mercy, but I am afraid that I will be only too pleasing to the judge.'

She passed the whole day in misery, going over these complaints and Dionysius was even more wretched than she. In the course of the night she had a dream that she was still a young girl in Syracuse, going into Aphrodite's precinct and coming back, then that she was seeing Chaereas and the day of their wedding. The whole city was hung with garlands and she herself was being led in a procession with her father and mother to her bridegroom's house. She was just about to kiss Chaereas when she was roused from sleep and calling Plangon (for Dionysius had already got up first to practise for the trial), she told her about the dream. Plangon replied, 'Have courage, Mistress, and cheer up because you have had a propitious dream. All your problems are about to be solved: everything that appeared in the dream is going to happen in reality. Go off to the King's court as if to the temple of Aphrodite, have confidence in yourself and regain the beauty you had as a bride.' While she said this she dressed and adorned Callirhoe whose spirits automatically rose, as if she could foretell the future.

Early that morning there was a jostling crowd outside the palace and the narrow streets around were all full. Everybody had gathered there, ostensibly to hear the trial, but in reality to see Callirhoe. But she seemed even to outshine herself to the same degree as she had previously outshone other women, and she came into the courtroom just as the divine bard describes Helen standing with the elders,

With Priam, Panthoos and Thymoites . . .

The sight of her caused amazement and an uncanny silence, and

Everyone prayed to lie in bed by her side.

If it had been necessary for Mithridates to speak first he would not have been able to find his voice, because he was suffering under this new blow, like a man receiving a more dangerous wound on the site of an old trauma.

[6] Dionysius began his speech like this, 'I am grateful to you, Sire, for the honour you have shown to me, and also to chastity and to the marriage vows of us all, for you have not overlooked a private man being plotted against by a man in power. Instead, you have called me to trial so that you can pass judgement, on my behalf, on this act of licentiousness and outrage, and so that you can enact punishment on behalf of us all. The deed also deserves a greater penalty because of who committed it. To explain: Mithridates who plotted against me was not my enemy, but my guest and friend. Nor were his designs against any other part of my property, but against my wife whom I honour more highly than my own body and soul. He was a man who ought to have come to help me if anyone else had tried to harm me, if not on behalf of his friendship with me, then on behalf of you, his King. For you gave him great power which he has unworthily abused, or rather he has betrayed the one who entrusted him with this power. I am not unaware of the entreaties Mithridates has used in relation to this trial or the influence and resources he has at his disposal; I know that we are not on an equal footing. But, Sire, I put my trust in your sense of justice and the laws which you uphold impartially on behalf of us all. If you are going to acquit him, it would have been far better not to bring him to trial, because previously everyone was afraid that their crime would be punished if it came to court. But you will be openly disrespected if, although he has been judged by you, he is not punished.

'My argument is straightforward and succinct: I am the husband of Callirhoe here and she has made me a father; I did not marry her as a virgin but as a woman who had previously been married: her former husband was called Chaereas, but he died a long time ago and has a memorial near where we live. Mithridates happened to be in Miletus and was introduced to my wife according to the laws of hospitality, but he did these later deeds not as a friend or as a sensible and civilized man, such as you would want to entrust your cities to, but appearing wantonly tyrannical. Knowing my wife's chastity and loyalty, he realized that it would be impossible to seduce her with persuasion or bribes and thus devised what seemed to him a most cunning plan. For he pretended that her former husband, Chaereas, was alive and fraudulently wrote letters to her in his name, sending them via slaves. But your fortune, Sire, appointed you as a worthy judge and the foresight of the other gods brought the letters into the open. For Bias, the general of Priene, sent slaves to me with the letters, and I, after discovering what was going on, reported it to Pharnaces, the satrap of Lydia and Ionia, and then he referred it to you.

'This is my account of the matter which you are judging. The proof is unmistakable. It must be one of two things: either Chaereas is alive or Mithridates is proved an adulterer. And it is not possible for him to claim that he did not know that Chaereas was dead, because he was in Miletus when we built the tomb and he joined with us in our mourning. But when Mithridates wanted to commit adultery, he brought the dead to life. I will finish by reading the letter that this man sent to Miletus from Caria by means of his own slaves. Take it up and read it: "From Chaereas. I am alive." Let Mithridates prove this and be acquitted. Just think, Sire, how shameless is an adulterer who fraudulently takes the identity of the dead!'

Dionysius stirred his audience to anger with this speech and was immediately assured of their vote. Annoyed, the King directed a bitter and disappointed glance at Mithridates.

[7] Mithridates, however, was unmoved. 'I beg you, Sire,' he said, 'because you are just and humane, don't convict me before you have heard both sides of the argument, and don't let this Greek creature, by fabricating wicked slanders against me, be more persuasive to you than the truth. I know that the woman's beauty weighs heavily against me, for it seems so believable that someone would want to seduce Callirhoe. But I have lived a virtuous life and this is the first breath of scandal which has attached to my name. Even if I were an incorrigible and licentious man, I would have been made a better one by your entrusting me with the government of such great cities. Who would be so crazy that he would choose to undermine such advantages for the sake of one moment of pleasure and shame? If I had known I was guilty, I could have brought a counter suit against Dionysius, because

he is bringing me to trial over a woman who is not legally married to him. Rather, he bought her when she was up for sale. The law of adultery is not a law that governs the treatment of slaves. Let him first read out her registration of freedom and then talk of marriage! Do you dare to name a woman whom Theron the pirate gave to you for a talent after he had stolen her from the tomb? "But," he says, "I bought her, but she was really free." Then you are a slave dealer and not a husband. Even still I will now address my speech to you as if you were a husband. Let's call the sale a wedding and the price you paid a dowry; let the Syracusan seem to be a woman from Miletus for today. But learn further, Master, that I have wronged Dionysius neither as a husband nor as a master. First, he is bringing an indictment not for adultery that occurred but for adultery that was going to happen, and since there is no deed, the letters he read out are worthless. The laws punish acts. Second, you produce a letter, but I did not have the chance to respond, "I did not write it. It is not in my hand. It is Chaereas who is searching for Callirhoe. Judge him guilty of adultery." "Yes," he says, "but Chaereas is dead and you are trying to seduce my wife by impersonating a dead man." Dionysius, don't offer me such a dangerous challenge! I bear witness: I am your friend and your guest. Stop the trial – it's in your interests! Ask the King to dismiss the case. Offer a retraction, "Mithridates did nothing wrong. I brought him to court for no reason." But if you persist, you will regret it and you will be casting a vote against yourself. I warn you, you will lose Callirhoe. The King will find that you are the adulterer and not me.'

At this point he fell silent. Everyone looked at Dionysius to see, when the choice was put in front of him, whether he would abandon the case or remain firm. While they did not understand what Mithridates was alluding to so cryptically, they had a strong suspicion that Dionysius did. He, however, was in the dark, because he did not think for one second that Chaereas was alive and so he said, 'Make whatever announcement you want. You won't deceive me with your clever rhetoric and your carefully crafted threats, nor will Dionysius ever be found to be a sycophant.'

Taking over then, Mithridates raised up his voice and, just as if he was at some ceremony of divination, said, 'Royal gods of the heavens and of the earth below, come to the aid of a good man who has many times prayed justly to you and offered you magnificent sacrifices. Give back to me the reward of my piety, now while I am beset by this false accusation. Grant me Chaereas, if only for the trial. Noble soul, appear before us! Your Callirhoe is calling for you. Stand between us both, Dionysius and myself, and tell the King which of us is the adulterer!'

[8] While he was still saying this (for he had not yet reached his conclusion), Chaereas himself appeared. When she saw him Callirhoe cried out, 'Chaereas, you are alive', and ran towards him. Dionysius, however, standing in the middle of the room, caught her and prevented them from embracing each other. Who could do justice to the scene in the courtroom? What poet could put such an amazing story on the stage? You would have thought you were in a theatre full of a thousand conflicting emotions. Everything was there at the same time: tears, joy, amazement, pity, suspicion, prayers. People were congratulating Chaereas, rejoicing with Mithridates, commiserating with Dionysius and uncertain what to do about Callirhoe, for she stood speechless, utterly confused by all the noise around her, able only to look at Chaereas with glowing eyes. I think that at that point even the King would have happily changed places with Chaereas!

Open conflict is a normal and immediate response for rival lovers, and for them the sight of the prize kindled their fighting spirit even further, so that if it had not been for their sense of respect towards the King, they would have come to blows with each other then and there. However, they went as far as they could in words, Chaereas saying, 'I was her first husband', and Dionysius replying, 'I was the more reliable one.' 'Don't take my wife away from me!' 'But you buried her.' 'Show me the divorce papers!' 'Do me a favour! You only need to look at her tomb.' 'Her father gave her to me!' 'She came to me of her own free will!' 'You are not good enough for Hermocrates' daughter.' 'And I suppose you are, though you are still in bondage to Mithridates?' 'I demand Callirhoe back.' 'I'm not letting her go.' 'You are coercing someone else's wife.' 'You killed yours!' 'Adulterer!' 'Murderer!' This is how they warred with words against each other and all the rest listened, not without enjoyment.

Callirhoe, meanwhile, stood looking down at the ground and crying, in love with Chaereas but feeling great respect for Dionysius. The King dismissed everyone and, now that Mithridates was no longer the issue after his brilliant defence, took counsel with his companions as to whether there would have to be a legal ruling about the woman. Some thought that it was not a decision for the King: 'You have correctly heard the complaint against Mithridates, because he was your satrap, but all the rest of the people involved are private individuals.' However, the majority gave the opposite advice because the woman's father was someone who had been supportive of the King's interests. They also said that this judgement was not a separate issue, but was practically a part of the case he had already been judging. The bottom line was that they did not want to agree with the others because Callirhoe's beauty had such power over all who saw her.

Those who had been sent out were called back in again and the King said, 'I acquit Mithridates and let him go away tomorrow back to his own province, taking with him gifts from me. Let Chaereas and Dionysius each lay out their legal claim to this woman, for it is only right for me to protect the interests of the daughter of Hermocrates, a man who joined with me in defeating the Athenians, the greatest enemies of the Persians and myself.' When the case had been dismissed like this, Mithridates prostrated himself before the King, but the others did not know what to do. When the King saw that they were at a loss, he said, 'I am not hurrying you. You can come once you have prepared for the case. I grant an adjournment of five days. In the meantime my wife, Stateira, will look after Callirhoe since it would not be right for someone who is about to be legally awarded to a husband to be accompanied by one of the men into court.'

Everyone else left the courtroom with heavy hearts: Mithridates alone was pleased with the situation. He collected his gifts, stayed one night and then set off bright and early to Caria, more confident than before.

[9] Eunuchs escorted Callirhoe to the Queen without any warning, for whenever the King wants to send something to her he does so without prior notice. As soon as she saw her, Stateira jumped up from her couch, thinking that Aphrodite stood before her, a goddess whom she honoured above all others. Stateira prostrated herself before her, but a eunuch, seeing her amazement said, 'This is Callirhoe. The King has sent her to you so that she can be looked after until the trial.' Stateira heard this with great pleasure and, putting aside her female competitiveness, liked Callirhoe even more because of the honour she had mistakenly paid her. In fact she took great pride in the task entrusted to her and, taking her by the hand, said, 'Cheer up, my dear, and stop crying. The King is sensible. You will have the husband you want. You will be married more honourably because of the legal judgement. Go and rest now, for you are exhausted, as I can see, and still have very confused emotions.' Callirhoe was very glad to hear this because she longed to be on her own. As soon as she was lying down to rest, she put her hand to her eyes and said, 'Did you really see Chaereas? Was that my own Chaereas or are my wits wandering? Perhaps Mithridates sent his ghost for the trial. For they say there are magicians among the Persians. But yet he spoke and said everything as if fully conscious. How could he bear to stand by and not embrace me? We have been parted without even exchanging a kiss.' As she was pondering this, she heard the noise of feet and the cries of women. They had all rushed to the Queen, thinking this was a great opportunity to see Callirhoe. But Stateira said, 'Let's leave her be. She is not in a very good state and we have five days to see, listen and talk.' They went away rather downhearted, but they came back on the following morning, and the same thing happened increasingly every day in ever larger numbers, so that the Queen's apartments became thronged with many people. The King came to visit the women rather more often than usual, as if he was just coming to see Stateira. Expensive gifts were sent to Callirhoe, but she refused to receive them from anyone, still locked in the role of a woman in the midst of misfortune, wearing black clothes without any adornment. These things, though, just made her seem all the more admirable. But when the Queen asked which husband Callirhoe preferred, she made no reply and just cried.

This is how things were for Callirhoe, but Dionysius was bearing the situation as nobly as he could, as a result of the natural stability of his character and the discipline of his upbringing. The strangeness of his misfortune, though, was enough to overpower even the bravest man, for he burnt with an even greater passion than when he was in Miletus. For when he first fell in love he was attracted only by her beauty, but then many other things added to his love: their life together, the bond of a shared child, her coolness towards him, his own jealousy and, especially, the unexpectedness of it all.

[10] So he suddenly shouted out, 'What sort of Protesilaus is this who has come back to life to attack me? Which of the gods of the Underworld have I wronged, so that I find as a rival lover a corpse whose tomb I built with my own hands? Lady Aphrodite, although I founded a temple to you on my own estate, and sacrificed to you many times, you have ambushed me. Why did you show me Callirhoe if you weren't going to let me keep her? Why did you make me a father although I couldn't even be a husband?'

Meanwhile, embracing his son he said, through his tears, 'Poor child, you used to seem to me to be lucky, but now you seem to me to have come along at the wrong time, because I have you as the last thing left to me of your mother and as a memorial of my unlucky passion. You are a little child, but you are not totally unaware of your father's misfortunes. This journey of ours has been a bad idea: we could have stayed in Miletus. Babylon has brought us to this. I have been defeated in the first trial which Mithridates brought, and I am very worried about the second one. This one represents a greater danger and the way it has started has left me without hope. My wife has been taken away from me without a trial, and now I have to go to law with someone else over my own wife, and, what's even more difficult, I don't know whom Callirhoe wants. But you, child, can find this out from your mother. Now go to her and supplicate her on your father's behalf. Weep, kiss her, say, "Mother, my father loves you", but don't reproach her. What do you say, tutor? No one will allow me to enter the royal quarters? What monstrous tyranny! They will lock out a son going to his mother as his father's ambassador?'

Dionysius then spent the time until the trial being the umpire in a battle between love and logic, while Chaereas spent it locked in inconsolable grief. Pretending to be ill therefore, he ordered Polycharmus to take a message to Mithridates, their joint benefactor. When he was alone, he fastened up a noose and was just about to get up to it when he said, 'I would have had a fortunate death if I had gone up on the cross, when I was falsely accused during the time I was a slave in Caria. For then I would have departed this life in the false belief that I was loved by Callirhoe, but as things are, I have lost not only my life, but any comfort I might have had in death. When she saw me, Callirhoe neither came over to me nor kissed me. Although I was right there in front of her, it was another's wishes she respected. I don't want her to be embarrassed so I will forestall the outcome of the trial. I am not going to wait around for an ignominious conclusion. I know that I am an insignificant adversary for Dionysius, a foreigner, a beggar and a guest in a strange land. My dear wife, good luck to you! I am going away and I won't be a nuisance at your wedding. Be rich and enjoy the luxuries of bounteous Ionia. Have everything you want. But now that Chaereas really is dying, Callirhoe, I beg you for one last favour: when I die, approach my corpse and, if you can, weep over it. For this will mean more to me than immortality. As you bend over the tombstone, even if your husband and child are looking on, say, "Chaereas, you are truly gone, now. Now you really have died. But I was going to choose you in the King's courtroom." When you say this, I will hear you, wife. Perhaps I will even believe you. You will make me more honoured than the gods below. Even if they forget the dead in Hades I will remember you, my dear one, there.' With these laments, he kissed the noose, saying, 'You are my comfort and my advocate. I will win because of you. You have been kinder to me than Callirhoe.'

Just as he was getting up and fastening the noose around his neck, his friend, Polycharmus, suddenly appeared and restrained him, though Chaereas was like a madman, when trying to talk him out of it had failed. Already the day appointed for the trial was at hand.

BOOK 6

[1] When it got to the day before the King had to decide whether Callirhoe ought to be Chaereas' wife or Dionysius', the whole of Babylon was waiting in suspense, and everyone, either in their own homes or bumping into each other in the street, was saying, 'Today is Callirhoe's wedding! Who's going to be the lucky man?' The city was divided. Some were enthusiastic supporters of Chaereas: 'He was the first husband. He married her when she was a virgin and they love each other. It was to him that her father gave her in marriage and it was her country that buried her. He has not gone back on his marriage vows nor has he been abandoned by her. Dionysius, on the other hand, bought her – he didn't marry her. Pirates sold her even though it is illegal to buy a free woman.' But Dionysius' supporters said the opposite: 'He rescued her from the pirates' nest when she was about to be killed. He gave a huge sum of money to ensure her safety. First he saved her, then he married her: Chaereas married her, then killed her. Callirhoe ought to remember her tomb! And Dionysius has the strongest card: they have a child together.' This was what the men said. The women, on the other hand, were in a position not just to make speeches, but to offer advice, since Callirhoe was there with them. 'Don't turn away from the man who married you when you were a girl. Take the man who first loved you and who comes from the same city: then you will be able to see your father. Otherwise, you will live in a strange land like an exile.' But the others said, 'Take the man who looked after you, the one who saved you, not the one who killed you. What if Chaereas gets angry again? Another tomb? Don't betray your son: honour the father of your child.' So many comments

like these were flying around that you would say that all of Babylon was a courthouse.

The last night before the trial arrived. The royal couple lay next to one another, but the views they held were very far apart. The Queen was praying for the day to come quickly, so that she could fulfil a duty which had turned into a burden: she was beginning to feel weighed down by the constant comparison with Callirhoe's beauty. Not only this, she was suspicious of the King's frequent visits and the way he kept suddenly wanting to be sociable at all sorts of strange hours. He had previously only visited the women's quarters on rare occasions, but since Callirhoe's arrival had practically haunted the place. Watching him closely when he was with them, she saw him looking secretly at Callirhoe, his eyes stealing towards the sight of her as if uncontrollably attracted there. Consequently, Stateira was looking forward to the next day with great pleasure, but this was not true of the King who lay awake the whole night.

> Sometimes lying on his side. Then sometimes again
> On his back, sometimes face down,

he was turning everything over in his mind and saying, 'The trial is at hand. How precipitate I was to set such a short period of preparation! What am I going to do in the morning? Callirhoe will go away for ever either to Miletus or to Syracuse. Poor eyes, you have only one hour left to drink your fill of such an exquisitely beautiful sight! Then a man, so far below me in status that he is practically my slave, will be luckier than I! O my soul, consider what can be done! Be true to yourself! I have no other counsellor except Eros himself, a suitable adviser for a man in love. First of all ask yourself this: Who are you? Callirhoe's lover or her judge? Don't deceive yourself. You don't yet know it, but you are in love and it will be proved the moment you stop seeing her. Why do you want to give yourself this grief? The Sun, your ancestor, chose her for you, the most beautiful of all the living creatures he looks upon. Are you throwing away a gift from a god? I suppose I am taking all this trouble for Chaereas and Dionysius, unworthy slaves of mine, so that I can be an umpire in this nuptial contest, and so that I, the Great King, can do the work of a matchmaking old crone! But I have acted too hastily in taking on this decision and everyone knows it. I also have great respect for Stateira. So I must not let my passion be publicly known – but just don't let the trial reach any conclusion! It will be enough if I can at least keep seeing Callirhoe. Delay the case: this is possible even for an ordinary judge.'

[2] At dawn, attendants were preparing the royal courthouse. The populace were rushing to the palace and the whole of Babylon was in a state of agitation. Just as it is possible to see the athletes in the Olympic Games arriving in the stadium with a crowd of supporters, so it was for these men. The majority of the Persian aristocrats accompanied Dionysius, and the common people came with Chaereas. The air rang with the thousands of cries of good luck and support from their well-wishers, 'You are the better man! You will win!' Here, though, the prize was not the olive bough, apples or pine cones, but beauty, over which even the gods rightly compete. The King called his chief eunuch, Artaxates, and said, 'In a dream, royal gods were standing over me demanding sacrifices and I must first fulfil that sacred duty. So announce that the whole of Asia must carry out a month of sacred observance, holding festivals and suspending all trials and public business.' The eunuch made this announcement and immediately the whole country was garlanded and making sacrifices. The flute echoed and the pipes blared out and the sound of singing could be heard. The foyers belched out incense and every house and street was in constant party mode,

> The savour of sacrifice rose to the heavens, twirling up around the smoke.

The King offered up magnificent sacrifices at the altars. He first sacrificed to Eros and called on Aphrodite over and over again, in the hope that she would intercede for him with her son.

In the middle of all this happiness, three people alone were suffering: Callirhoe, Dionysius and, above all, Chaereas. Callirhoe was not able to grieve openly in the palace, but in secret she complained and cursed the festivals. Dionysius cursed his own stupidity for ever leaving Miletus. 'You fool,' he said, 'you must endure the disaster which you brought on yourself. You are your own worst enemy. It would have been possible for you to have Callirhoe even if Chaereas was alive. You were in control in Miletus and the letter would not have been given to Callirhoe if you didn't want it to be. Who saw her? Who approached her? It is you who have thrown yourself into this lions' den. If only it was just you! As things are, it is also the thing which is dearer to you than your own soul. Because of this, a war is threatening you from all sides. Do you think it is a good idea, you idiot, to have Chaereas as your opponent? You have got yourself a rival lover who will get the better of you. Now the King has all these dreams and they insist that he carry out the sacrifices which he is doing today. O, the shamelessness of it! He drags out the trial while he keeps someone else's wife in his house, and at the same time, claims to be a judge!'

While Dionysius was listing his grievances like this, Chaereas was refusing to eat and had completely lost the will to live. When Polycharmus tried to prevent him from starving himself to death, he said, 'You really are a wolf in sheep's clothing! You hold me in torment and gladly watch me suffer. If you were my friend, you would not begrudge me my freedom from slavery to a cruel god. I have been robbed of so many chances to be happy! If I had been buried in the tomb in Syracuse with Callirhoe, I would have been very fortunate, but you prevented me from dying then, even though I wanted to, and you prevented us being together. Perhaps she would not have gone out of the tomb if she had to leave my dead body. At least if I was lying there, I would be avoiding the troubles which came next, being sold, the pirate attack, being in bondage, the cross and, even worse than the cross, the King. O lovely death, after you I would be able to have a second marriage with Callirhoe! You destroyed another perfect opportunity for death after the trial. I had seen Callirhoe, but had not got near her or kissed her. O, what a new and incredible source of misery: it is to be judged by law whether Chaereas is Callirhoe's husband! But the envious deity does not even allow this trial, such as it is, to reach a conclusion. In dreams and in

real life, the gods hate me.' As he said this he attacked himself
with a sword, but Polycharmus grabbed his hand and, all but
tying him up, kept a very close eye on him.

[3] The King called to him his most trustworthy eunuch, but at
first felt too much shame to speak even to him. Seeing him blushing with embarrassment and wanting to say something, Artaxates
said, 'What are you hiding from me, Master? I am your loyal
slave and I know how to keep my mouth shut. What terrible
thing has happened? How distraught I am that some plot . . .'
'Yes, a plot,' replied the king, 'and a serious one: not by men but
by a god. In the past I heard stories and poems about what Eros
is like, that he has power over all the gods and even Zeus himself.
Nevertheless, I did not believe that anyone could be stronger
than I. But this is a god! A powerful and violent Eros has taken
up residence in my soul. It is hard to admit it, but I am truly at
its mercy.'

As he said these things, his eyes filled with tears and he was
no longer able to get his words out. As he fell silent, Artaxates
immediately realized how he had got his wound, for he had
previously not been entirely without suspicion, and he recognized
that there is rarely any smoke without fire. In addition it was
hardly either likely or reasonable that, with Callirhoe present,
the King would have fallen in love with someone else. However,
he pretended to have no idea what the King was talking about
and said, 'What beauty has got this power over you, Master? It
is you who have control of everything worth valuing in this
world, gold, silver, rich clothes, horses, cities, peoples. You have
thousands of beautiful women, but Stateira is the most beautiful
of all and you have sole enjoyment of her. However, unlimited
access to someone can be a passion killer, unless one of the gods
should come down from heaven or another Thetis come up from
the sea. For I believe that even the gods love your company.'

The King replied, 'What you say may indeed be true because
this woman is one of the gods. There is nothing human about
her beauty, even though she denies it: she pretends to be a Greek
woman from Syracuse. But this is just a sign of pretence, because
she doesn't want to be found out by naming one of the cities

which belongs to me; instead, she sets her story out beyond the Ionian Sea and over the greater sea beyond that. On the pretext of the trial she has come to me and she has armed herself with this whole melodramatic story. But I am amazed that you could dare to say that Stateira is the most beautiful woman of all, when you have seen Callirhoe. You must try to think of a way to relieve this anguish of mine. You must search high and low to find a cure.' 'The cure you seek has been found,' he replied, 'by both Greeks and non-Greeks alike. For there is no other remedy for love except the love object itself. This was surely the logic of the refrain "the one who deals the blow, heals it"?' But the King was rather shocked by this advice and exclaimed, 'Don't say such things, by trying to encourage me to seduce someone else's wife! I remember the laws that I laid down myself, and my own sense of justice which I have exercised in all things. You can find me guilty of no lack of self-control. I haven't gone that far yet!' Artaxates, afraid that he had been overhasty in his advice, changed tack to flattery. 'You are so right, Sire. Don't apply the same romantic rules to yourself as to others; use instead ones that are more noble and kingly, and really wrestle with your conscience. You alone, Master, are able to have power even over a god. So treat yourself to any pleasure which might distract you. You particularly love hunting and I know you sometimes go without food or drink when overcome by your obsession for that hobby. It would be a better idea to spend time out hunting than in the palace near the source of the fire.'

[4] This suggestion pleased him and a magnificent hunt was announced. Both the Persian nobles and selected men from the non-Persian battalions rode out in full dress. Although all were worth seeing, it was the King himself who most caught the eye. He was seated on a towering Nisean horse of great beauty, fitted with a gold bridle, golden bosses, cheekpieces and breastplate. He was dressed in Tyrian purple (though the cloth was Babylonian) and wore a tiara dyed the colour of hyacinths. With a golden dagger fastened at his waist, he wielded two javelins and had slung about him a bow and quiver of very costly Chinese workmanship. He sat there in all his finery, for love, of its own

accord, promotes a bit of glamour, and he wanted to seem impressive to Callirhoe: all the way through the city he kept looking around in case she was watching the procession as it left. In no time at all, the mountains were filled with the sounds of men running and shouting, dogs barking, horses neighing and wild animals being chased. All the excitement and noise would have been enough to drive even Eros mad, for delight was mixed with agony, joy with fear and danger with pleasure.

But the King saw not a single horse out of all the many prancing along beside his own, nor a single beast out of all the many they were hunting, nor did he hear the barks of a single dog or the shouts of any man. He had eyes only for Callirhoe, even though she was not there, and he could hear only her voice, even though she was not speaking. This was because Eros was right there with him on the hunt. Given that Eros is a god who always rises to the challenge, when he saw that the King thought he had hit on a successful strategy against him, he turned that strategy back on itself and burnt his soul by means of the very precautions he was trying to take. Getting right inside his soul, he whispered, 'What it would be to see Callirhoe here, wearing little greaves, with bare arms, her face covered in blushes and her breasts quivering! Truly,

> She will come just like Artemis, the arrow-shooter, down from
>   heaven,
> Or over lofty Taygetus or Erymanthus,
> Rejoicing in the boars and the swift deer.

By conjuring up this picture, the King ignited his passion even more violently.
[There is a lacuna in the text, so we are missing the beginning of the conversation between the King and Artaxates.]

. . . Barely had he finished saying this, when Artaxates replied, 'Master, you have forgotten the real situation. Callirhoe has no husband for the judgement as to whom she should marry is still waiting to be made. So it is fair to say that the woman you love is separated: nor need you fear the laws which exist in relation to marriage, nor be concerned about adultery, because first there would have to be a wronged husband before there could be an adulterer who was wronging him.' The logic of this pleased the King since it was an argument in favour of the thing he desired, and taking the eunuch by the hand, he kissed him and said, 'I am so right to have more respect for you than for anyone else. You are my greatest supporter and an excellent guardian of my interests. Go then, and bring Callirhoe. But I charge you with two things: bring her neither unwillingly nor openly. I want you to use your powers of persuasion but in secret.'

Immediately the hunt was cancelled and everyone began to turn back. The King was obsessed with these new hopes and rushed everyone back to the palace, rejoicing as if he had hunted down the finest quarry. Artaxates was happy too, since he thought that he had secretly done the King a great favour and would be in the driving seat in the future over royal policy, with not only the King bound to him by gratitude but Callirhoe even more so. As a eunuch, a slave and a barbarian, he thought the task ahead of him a very easy one, for he had no notion of the Greek nobility of mind or, for that matter, of Callirhoe's chastity and loyalty.

[5] Watching out for a good opportunity, he approached her and, getting her on her own, said, 'I bring you something of the greatest value, but you must remember that it was I who did you this service. I am sure you will be suitably grateful.' At the beginning of this speech, Callirhoe was over the moon, because it is human nature to believe what one wants to be true. She immediately thought that she was going to be given back to Chaereas and in her eagerness to hear this, promised the eunuch that she would return the favour of the good news he was bringing her. Starting up again after this interruption, he began the opening of his speech: 'You, Lady, have been blessed with divine beauty, but from it you have reaped no great or noble reward. Up until today the high repute and celebrity of your name, known across the whole world, has not brought you either a husband or a lover who is worthy of you. Instead, you are stuck between these two, the one a poverty-stricken islander, the other

a slave to the King. In what way has either of them raised you to the great and glorious position you deserve? Where is the prosperous country you should have? What sort of costly adornments do you own? What cities do you rule? How many slaves prostrate themselves before you? Babylonian women have maidservants who are better off than you! But you are not completely forgotten: the gods are taking an interest in your affairs. That is the reason they brought you here, using the trial as an excuse, so that the Great King could see you. This is the really good news for you: he likes what he sees! And I keep you constantly in his mind and sing your praises to him.' He added this last bit because every slave is accustomed to bring attention to himself when he is talking about his master, in the hope of getting some personal benefit from the conversation.

Callirhoe was immediately cut to the quick, as if the words themselves were daggers in her heart. However, she pretended not to understand and said, 'May the gods always be favourable to your gracious King, and he to you, because you have had pity on an unfortunate woman. I beg that he may release me swiftly from this anxiety by resuming the trial so that I will no longer be trespassing on the Queen's hospitality.' But the eunuch, thinking that he must have explained what he wanted unclearly and that she was still in the dark, said, 'It is this very point in which your good fortune lies, that you won't have to have slaves and paupers as your lovers, but instead the Great King! He is the one who is easily able to give you Miletus itself and the whole of Ionia and Sicily and other, greater tribes. Sacrifice to the gods, congratulate yourself and start working out how you can please him more: and when you are rich, don't forget me!'

Callirhoe was at first about to tear out, if she could, the eyes of the man who was trying to corrupt her, but then, educated and intelligent woman that she was and swiftly remembering the place she was in, who she was and who was addressing her, she covered up her anger and gave a carefully coded answer to the Persian: 'I am not so mad that I have persuaded myself that I am worthy of the Great King! I am like one of the maidservants of the Persian women. I beg you, don't keep reminding your master about me. Even if he isn't angry to start with, after this he certainly will be cross because you have thrown the master of the world at the feet of Dionysius' slave. I am amazed that someone as intelligent as you doesn't understand the King's benevolence. He does not love me, poor unfortunate woman that I am, but he pities me. Anyway, let's not talk about it in case someone slanders us to the Queen.' With this she rushed off leaving the eunuch standing there with his mouth open. Brought up under the most extreme form of autocratic rule, he had never imagined that anything could be impossible, not just for the King, but even for himself.

[6] On his own and completely taken aback by the answer he had received from Callirhoe, he was left prey to a thousand emotions, anger at Callirhoe, disappointment for himself and fear of the King because perhaps he would not believe that he had spoken to her but been unsuccessful: it might appear that he had treacherously abandoned the task in order to curry favour with the Queen. He was afraid that Callirhoe would repeat his words to the Queen, and that Stateira, in a great rage, would plot some terrible revenge against one who had not only helped but actually brought about the love affair.

At the same time as the eunuch was considering how he might safely tell the King what had happened, Callirhoe, back on her own, was saying: 'Oh, I saw all this coming! Euphrates, I have you as my witness. I predicted that I would not cross you again! Fare-well, father, and you, mother, and my Syracusan homeland. I will see you no more! Now truly Callirhoe is dead. Then I came back from the grave, but in the future not even the robber Theron will lead me out again! O treacherous beauty, you are responsible for all my troubles. Because of you I was killed, because of you I was sold, because of you I was married again after Chaereas, because of you I was brought to Babylon and because of you I have been present at a trial. How many problems have you presented me with? Bandits, the sea, the tomb, slavery, the trial. But the King's love is more unbearable to me than all the rest! I have not yet mentioned the King's anger and I think that the Queen's jealousy is to be feared even more. Chaereas, a Greek man, was unable to control his jealousy, so what will a haughty barbarian woman do? But pull yourself together, Callirhoe, and work out what is the noble thing to do, worthy of Hermocrates: kill yourself! But not yet. So far this is the first time that the eunuch has made contact. If I find out more accurately what is going on, that will be the time to show my loyalty to Chaereas, with him right there.'

The eunuch, meanwhile, went to the King but concealed the truth of what had happened, instead claiming that lack of time and the Queen's close vigilance had ensured that he had no opportunity to approach Callirhoe. 'You told me, Master, to make sure that it all remains secret. You were right to make this stipulation. You have taken on the most holy role of judge and you want to be respected among the Persians. For this reason everybody sings your praises. But Greeks are the type who find fault over the smallest things and they are also gossips. They would ensure that what happened became widely known, Callirhoe out of boasting that the King loved her, Dionysius and Chaereas out of jealousy. Nor would it be right to upset the Queen over a foreign woman whose glamour was really exaggerated by the trial.' This was the counter argument he tried to spin, so that he might perhaps be able to turn the tide of the King's love and release himself from a burdensome task.

[7] At the time these arguments proved very persuasive, but when the night came, the King burned more fiercely again and Eros recalled to his mind what Callirhoe's eyes were like, and how beautiful her face was. He praised her hair, her walk, her voice, what she looked like as she entered the courtroom, and as she stood there, how she spoke, how she was silent, how she looked down modestly in shame and how she cried. Awake for most of the night and falling asleep for only as long as it took to see Callirhoe in his dreams, when morning came, he called for the eunuch and said, 'Go and spend the whole day watching out for an opportunity. For you will certainly get a chance for a private conversation even if it is only a very short one. If I wanted to fulfil my passion openly and with force, I would have used armed guards.' The eunuch prostrated himself and promised to do as he was asked, for it is impossible for anyone to refuse when a king gives a direct order. But he knew that Callirhoe would give

him no opportunity, and rather would elude him by deliberately staying close to the Queen. To deal with this problem and attributing the cause not to the one who was supposedly being watched but to the one doing the watching, he said, 'Master, if you think it is a good idea, could you summon Stateira, as if you want to discuss something privately with her? For her absence would give me an opportunity to get to Callirhoe.' 'Do it,' said the King.

So, going up to the Queen and prostrating himself before her, Artaxates said, 'Mistress, your husband is asking for you.' When she heard this Stateira acknowledged him and hurried off to the King. The eunuch, seeing that Callirhoe was left alone, took her right hand and, as if he was a benevolent man and a philhellene, led her away from the crowd of maidservants. She understood at once and immediately went pale and lost the power of speech, but nevertheless she followed him. When they were standing alone he addressed her, 'You have seen the Queen and how, once she heard the King's name, she acknowledged it and rushed off. Yet you, a slave, do not understand your good fortune, nor are you satisfied when someone invites you who is perfectly capable of ordering you. But because I respect you I have not told the King about your madness; in fact on the contrary, I have offered him a promise on your behalf. So it is possible for you to choose which of the two paths you want to follow. Let me recap both paths for you: if you let yourself be persuaded by the King, you will receive the finest gifts and the husband you want (for of course the King does not intend to marry you, but you will be there to offer him pleasure when the time is right); if you do not obey, let me tell you what the King's enemies have to suffer. They are the only people who long to die, but are not allowed to.'

Callirhoe laughed at the threat and said, 'It won't be the first time I have had to suffer: I am no stranger to misfortune. What can the King do to me which is worse than the things I have already experienced? I was buried alive; a tomb is more cramped than any prison! I fell into the hands of bandits, but just now I suffered the greatest of all my troubles when I didn't see Chaereas even though he was there.' This speech betrayed her, for the eunuch, who was naturally quick on the uptake, realized that she was in love. 'You must be crazy,' he said. 'You prefer the slave of Mithridates to the

King, don't you?' Callirhoe was angered at this slight on Chaereas and said, 'Hold your tongue, you! Chaereas is nobly born, a leading light in a city which even the Athenians could not defeat – but at Marathon and at Salamis they defeated this precious Great King of yours!' As she said this, tears coursed down her face, but the eunuch pressed her even harder, 'You are the one causing the delay! Would it not be better to have a judge who is on your side so that he would give you back your husband? And perhaps Chaereas may not find out what had happened, or even if he did know, he may not be jealous of someone who is so much more powerful than he. He will regard you as more worthy of respect because you have attracted the attentions of the King.' He added this last comment not on Callirhoe's account, but because that was what he really believed. All barbarians stand in great awe of the King and think him a god on earth. But Callirhoe would not have welcomed marriage even with Zeus himself, nor would she have chosen immortality over even just one day with Chaereas. When he could see he was getting nowhere, the eunuch said, 'Lady, I am going to give you a chance to think this over. Don't just consider yourself but think of Chaereas too who is in danger of meeting a most pitiable end: for the King will not take lightly being beaten in love.' With that he left, but this parting shot touched Callirhoe.

[8] However, the goddess Fortune swiftly turned all thoughts away from romantic considerations and directed them towards completely new affairs. Messengers arrived for the King announcing that Egypt was in the grip of a huge revolt; that the royal satrap had been killed by the Egyptians and they had elected a native king; that this king had launched an expedition out of Memphis and had crossed the Nile at Pelusium; that already this expedition had overrun Syria and Phoenicia, completely overwhelming their cities like a flood or a sudden fire rushing down upon them. The King was thrown into great confusion by this news and the Persians were thunderstruck: a cloud of depression descended on the whole of Babylon. Then prophets and other unofficial sorcerers said that the King's dream had predicted the future: that the gods, in demanding sacrifices, were predicting danger, but victory as well. Then, all the usual things that occur at the outbreak of an unexpected war

were said and done, for all of Asia was deeply affected by what
was happening. The King called together a meeting of all the noblest
of the Persians and as many of the leaders of other tribes as were
available and with whom he usually discussed important affairs,
and he took counsel with them in regard to the present situation.
Many different suggestions were made, but everybody agreed that
speed was essential and that matters should not be put off even
for a single day, if at all possible, for two reasons: so that they
should stop the enemy forces from increasing in number and so
that they should encourage those who remained loyal by showing
them that help was at hand; furthermore, they agreed that delay
would ensure the opposite, because their enemies would hold them
in contempt, thinking that they were afraid and their allies would
give themselves up, thinking that they had been abandoned. It was
a great piece of good fortune for the King that he had received the
news neither in Bactra, nor in Ecbatana, but in Babylon which was
near to Syria so that after crossing the Euphrates he would have
the rebels in his power. It seemed a good idea, therefore, to set out
with the forces he already had around him and to send a message
ordering the army to muster at the Euphrates from all sides. The
Persian forces were very easily gathered because it had all been
drawn up by Cyrus, the first Persian king. He had laid down which
of the tribes were to provide cavalry for war and how many, which
were to provide infantry and how many, and which to provide
archers; also how many open chariots and how many scythed ones
each person was to provide, and where the elephants were to come
from and how many, and then financial contributions, in what
form they were to be made and how much each had to provide.
In this way everything was prepared in the same amount of time
it would take one man to get himself ready.

[9] On the fifth day after the message had arrived, the King marched
out of Babylon, issuing a blanket order that all of military age were
to follow him. Among them went Dionysius because he was an
Ionian and none of the King's subject peoples was allowed to stay
behind. Decked out in the finest armour and gathering a body of
men which easily bore comparison even with those that surrounded
the King, he placed himself in a very conspicuous position in the

front ranks and was clearly a man who was going to perform some noble deed such as is done by men who are by nature ambitious for honour and who consider their manly excellence not as some sort of accidental addition, but as the finest of their possessions. He was also motivated by a thread of hope that if he appeared to advantage in the war, the King might give him Callirhoe as the prize for his deeds of bravery, quite separately from the trial.

The Queen did not want Callirhoe to be taken along and for this reason did not mention her to the King or ask what his orders were concerning the foreign woman. Artaxates also kept silent as if not wanting to distract his master with such romantic foolishness when the state was in danger, but in reality because he was as glad to escape from the situation as he would have been from a wild beast. I think, in fact, he was grateful to the war for ridding the King of a passion which had been nurtured by idleness.

But, of course, the King had not forgotten Callirhoe. Even in the midst of an almost indescribable flurry of decision making and organization, the memory of her beauty kept coming to him. He was ashamed to say anything about her in case everyone thought he was like some infatuated adolescent, obsessed by an attractive woman during a war of such magnitude. Although still under the compulsion of passion, he said nothing to Stateira or to his eunuch, even though he knew about his feelings, but he came up with the following plan. The King and the Persian nobles have a custom that whenever they go to war they take everything with them: their wives and children, gold and silver, clothes, eunuchs, concubines, dogs, furniture and all their costly possessions and luxuries. So the King summoned the steward in charge of these things and after a long discussion went through a list of other things and what should happen to each item, then finally he mentioned Callirhoe with as bland an expression as possible as if it was of no concern to him, 'As for that foreign creature, whose trial I have promised to hold, I guess we must take her along with the other women.'

So this is how Callirhoe left Babylon. Nor was she unhappy to go because she had hopes of catching sight of Chaereas. War brings many things, none of them certain, and for those who are in misfortune, change is a good thing: perhaps peace would come speedily and the trial too would take place there and come to an end.

BOOK 7

[1] When everybody set out to the war against the Egyptians
with the King, no one gave any instructions to Chaereas. He was
not subject to the King and in fact at that time was the only free
person in Babylon. He was delighted, assuming that Callirhoe
was also staying, and so on the following day he went to the
palace looking for his wife. When he saw that the gates were
shut and heavily guarded, he went round the whole city searching for her and, as if he were going out of his mind, constantly
asking Polycharmus, 'Where is Callirhoe? What has happened?
Surely she hasn't gone off to war!'

When he could not find Callirhoe, he decided to look for
Dionysius, his rival, and went to his house. There was someone
standing outside the house, like a doorkeeper, and he passed on
to Chaereas what he had been told to say. For Dionysius wanted
to dash Chaereas' hopes of reunion with Callirhoe without waiting for the trial and had accordingly come up with the following
strategy. When he set out for the battle he left this man behind
to tell Chaereas that the King of the Persians, needing allies, had
sent Dionysius to raise an army against the Egyptian king and,
to ensure that he fulfilled this task faithfully and enthusiastically,
had given him Callirhoe.

When he heard this, Chaereas instantly believed it, for an
unhappy man is easily deceived. Rending his clothes and tearing
at his hair, he beat his breast at the same time and said, 'Treacherous Babylon, you have offered an evil hospitality and been like a
desert to me. What a fine judge! You have been a pimp handing
over another man's wife. A wedding party in the middle of a war!
And while I have been in training for the trial, putting all my faith

in speaking the truth, I have had a judgement against me in my absence and Dionysius has won without saying a word. But his victory will do him no good because Callirhoe will refuse to live on when Chaereas is near but separated from her. In the first place he deceived her with the belief that I was dead. Why then do I delay and why do I not kill myself in front of the palace, my blood an offering at the threshold of the courtroom? Let the Medes and Persians know what sort of judgements their King made here!'

When Polycharmus saw that he was unable either to console or to save Chaereas, he said, 'For a long time, my dearest friend, I have comforted you and many times I have prevented you from dying. But now I think you have the right idea and so far am I from trying to prevent you that I am ready and willing to die with you. So let's consider what would be the best way to die. The method that you are planning will stir up a certain resentment against the King and bring him shame in the future, but is no just requital for what we have suffered. It seems to me that deciding the way we die is our one chance of really getting revenge on the tyrant. Wouldn't it be great if we could hurt him enough to make him regret how he had behaved and leave a noble legacy for those who come after us: that two wronged Greeks were able to get their own back on the Great King and die like men.'

'But,' replied Chaereas, 'how can we – who are only two men, poor and in a strange land – do such damage to a man who is lord over so many and has all the power which we ourselves have witnessed? He has bodyguards and guards who guard the bodyguards, and even if we were to kill one of his men or to burn some of his possessions, he would be completely oblivious of the loss.' 'You would be right,' said Polycharmus, 'if it wasn't for the war. As things presently stand, we know that Egypt has gone into revolt, Phoenicia has been captured and Syria overrun. The war will come to meet the King before he has crossed the Euphrates. So we are not just two men: we have as many allies as the Egyptian king leads, as many weapons, as much money and as many triremes! Let's use someone else's power to get our own revenge.'

Nor was the speech completed

before Chaereas was eagerly calling out, 'Hurry, let's go! In the war I will be able to exact legal punishment on the judge!'

[2] Getting ready swiftly, they set off after the King, pretending that they wanted to enlist with him and hoping that this pretext would ensure their safe crossing of the Euphrates. They caught up with the army at the river and mixed themselves in with the rearguard, but once they arrived in Syria, they deserted to the Egyptian king. When his guards captured them, they were interrogated very fully to find out who they were since, not having the insignia of ambassadors, they were particularly suspicious that they might be spies. Even then they would have been in very grave danger if a Greek who happened to be there had not recognized their speech. They demanded to be taken to the king since they were bringing something which would be greatly to his advantage. When they were brought before him, Chaereas said, 'We are Greeks, Syracusans of good family. This man who is my friend went to Babylon on my account, but I went for the sake of my wife, the daughter of Hermocrates – if perhaps you have heard of the general Hermocrates who defeated the Athenians in the sea battle.' The Egyptian king nodded in agreement for there are no people on earth who remain in ignorance of the disastrous defeat which the Athenians suffered in the war in Sicily. 'Artaxerxes has treated us like a tyrant,' continued Chaereas and told them the whole story, concluding, 'So we hand ourselves over to you as loyal friends who have the two most powerful motivations for courage that there are: desire for death and revenge. I am as one already dead in view of my misfortunes and for the time which remains to me, I live only to cause grief to my enemy.

May I not perish without a struggle and without fame,
But achieving some great deed to be remembered by men to come.

When he heard this, the Egyptian king was very pleased and took Chaereas by the hand saying, 'Young man, you have come at a good time for yourself and for me.' He immediately ordered them to be given weapons and a tent and shortly afterwards made Chaereas his messmate and then an adviser because he showed intelligence and courage, followed closely by loyalty, such qualities as emerge from a noble nature and a well-planned education. In addition, his animosity towards the Great King and his desire to gain respect spurred him on and made him an even more glamorous figure.

He immediately showed his worth by means of the following great achievement. Everything was going well for the Egyptian king and he was suddenly gaining control over western Syria, and Phoenicia was in his power except for Tyre. But the Tyrians are a race who are bellicose by nature and who want to keep their reputation for bravery lest they should lose face with Heracles the god, who is most important to them and to whom alone they have pretty much dedicated their city. They have great faith in the security of their fortifications, because the city is founded virtually on the sea with only a narrow causeway giving access to it and joining it to the land and thus preventing it from being an island. The city is like a ship at anchor with its gang-plank leading towards the land, and is thus largely impregnable on all sides. Against a land force they are almost totally protected by the sea, since all they have is the one gate; against a hostile fleet they are protected by the walls, since the city is heavily fortified and the harbours can be locked up like the doors of a house.

[3] When all around them had been captured, the Tyrians alone were scornfully indifferent of the Egyptians and kept faith with Persia. Irked by this, the Egyptian king summoned his council, the first to which Chaereas had been invited, and addressed it in the following way:

'Allies – for I would never call my friends "slaves" – you can see the difficulty because just like a ship that has for the most part enjoyed favourable weather we are now caught by an opposing wind and Tyre remains a nut we cannot crack however hard we try. We have also realized that the King is pressing us hard. So what shall we do? It is neither possible to capture Tyre nor to bypass it since, like a wall lying in the middle, it closes off all of Asia to us. I think that we should leave here as quickly as we can before the Persian might is added to that of the Tyrians. It would be very dangerous for us to be caught in enemy territory, but Pelusium is strong and there we need fear the attacks of neither the Tyrians nor the Medes nor of any other men. This is because the sand is virtually impassable, the access routes are narrow and both our sea and the Nile would lend friendly protection to us Egyptians.' With this excessively cautious advice, silence and depression descended on everyone. Chaereas alone dared to speak.

'My king – for you are truly our king, not that Persian monster – you grieve me by turning our thoughts to flight when we should be preparing for victory. We will be victorious, if the gods wish it, and not only take Tyre but Babylon as well. There are always many setbacks in war but we must not shrink from them. Rather we should struggle against them, armed with a noble optimism. These Tyrians who now mock us, I will set before you naked and in chains! If you don't believe me, you are welcome to abandon me here, because while there is breath in my body I will never share your flight. Or if you would like, leave with me the few who are willing to stay:

> We two, Polycharmus and I, we will fight on,
> . . . for we have come by the will of god.

Everyone was ashamed not to agree with Chaereas' view. The king was amazed by his strength of mind and agreed that he could take as big a portion of the army as he wanted. He did not do this immediately but, mingling secretly with the rank and file and ordering Polycharmus to do the same, he first discovered what Greeks there were in the army. Consequently, he found a good number serving as mercenaries and he chose Spartans, Corinthians and other Peloponnesians; he even found twenty Sicilians. From these he selected a squad of three hundred and he addressed them in the following way:

'Greek men, since the king has given me the opportunity to select the best men out of the army, I have chosen you. I myself am Greek, a Syracusan, ethnically Dorian. It is necessary for us to surpass the others not only in nobility but also in courage.

No one should be alarmed at the deed which I am asking you to do, because we will find it possible and even easy; its difficulties lie in its reputation, not in its reality. Such a small number of Greeks withstood Xerxes in Thermopylae. There are not five million Tyrians; instead, they are few and they are motivated by arrogance and boastfulness, not by resolution and good sense. Let them find out how much better Greeks are than Phoenicians! But I am not hankering after the role of general; rather I am ready and willing to follow whomever you want to be your leader. He will find me ready to obey him because I am striving after collective, not personal, glory.' At this everyone shouted out, 'You be our general!'

'Since that is what you want and you have given me this mandate, I will be your leader,' he said. 'And I will try and do everything I can so that you do not choose to withdraw the goodwill or trust that you have towards me. But, if the gods are willing, in this life you will be renowned and admired from all sides as well as become the richest of the allies, and in the time to come you will bequeath an undying reputation for courage. You will all be sung about and, just like the three hundred with Othryades or those with Leonidas, the men who follow Chaereas will be hymned to the heavens.' Before he had finished speaking, everyone shouted out, 'Lead us on!' and rushed to get their weapons.

[4] Then Chaereas equipped them with the finest armour and led them to the Egyptian king's tent. When he saw them, the king was amazed and assumed that he was seeing other men and not his usual troops and he promised them great rewards. 'We know you are as good as your word,' said Chaereas. 'Have the rest of the army at the ready but don't march on Tyre until we have taken control of it. We will go up on to the battlements and signal to you.' 'May the gods be willing,' replied the king, then Chaereas led them off against Tyre, marshalling them into a close-packed formation, so that they would appear to be much fewer than they really were. Thus truly,

Shield pressed on shield, helmet on helmet and man on man.

At first they were not spotted by the enemy, but as they got nearer men on the walls saw them and signalled to those inside the city, who were expecting anything rather than the approach of the enemy. For who would have expected that so few would come against the most powerful city against which even the full might of the Egyptians had never dared to mobilize itself? When they came right up to the walls, the Tyrians asked who they were and what they wanted. Chaereas replied, 'We are Greek mercenaries. We have been denied pay by the Egyptian king and have also discovered a plot against us. Thus we have come wanting to join with you in attacking our common enemy.' Someone relayed this to those inside and one of the generals opened the gate and came outside with a small number of men. Chaereas killed this man and attacked the others:

He struck all around him and an unspeakable groan rose from them.

Other men fell on the rest and slaughtered them like lions attacking an unguarded herd of cattle. Groans and laments rose from the whole city and although few could see what was going on, everyone joined in the clamour. A confused mob went out through the gate wanting to see what was happening. This is particularly what destroyed the Tyrians because those who were inside the city were forced to come out and those outside, struck and goaded with swords and spears, tried to flee back in again. Meeting each other in the narrowest place, they gave a golden opportunity to those who were trying to kill them. Nor was it possible to shut the gates because of the corpses heaped within them.

In the midst of this indescribable confusion, Chaereas alone kept his head. Forcing a path against those in his way and getting inside the gates, he and nine others leapt up on to the wall and shouted the signal to the Egyptians. In less time than it takes to tell, they arrived and Tyre was captured. While all the others were celebrating, Chaereas alone neither sacrificed nor garlanded himself. 'What good are victory celebrations to me, if you, Callirhoe, can't see them? After that wedding night of yours I will never again wear a garland, for if you are dead, I am committing a terrible impiety and if you are alive, how could I feast lying on a couch without you?'

This was the situation for them, but meanwhile the King of the Persians had crossed the Euphrates and was hurrying as quickly as possible to get to grips with the enemy. Now that he knew that Tyre had fallen, he was afraid for Sidon and for the whole of Syria, seeing that his enemy was now a match for him. For this reason he thought that he should no longer travel with all the comfort of his great retinue, but tighten his belt so that nothing would reduce his speed. So, taking with him a select few from his army, he left those who were not really of the most appropriate military age with the Queen, as well as all the money he had brought with him, his costly garments and royal wealth. Since everywhere was full of confusion and danger and the cities as far as the Euphrates overrun with war, he thought that it would be safer to put those he was leaving behind on the island of Arados.

[5] This is an island which is thirty stades away from the mainland and there is an ancient temple of Aphrodite on it. The women could pass their time there in security as if they were in their own home. When Callirhoe saw the statue of Aphrodite, at first she stood right opposite it in silence and weeping, only reproaching the goddess with her tears. With difficulty she managed to speak, 'Look at Arados here, a tiny island in comparison with huge Sicily and with not a soul here who is known to me. That is enough now, Lady. But I suppose you will be declaring war on me next? If I have offended you in some way, you have taken your punishment. If this wretched beauty has excited your resentment, it has destroyed me. Now I have experienced war, the only thing left out of all my misfortunes I had still to suffer. In comparison to my present situation, Babylon was a doddle! There Chaereas was near me. Now he is dead for certain; he would not live on now that I have left Babylon. And I do not have the chance to ask anyone what happened to him. All foreigners, all barbarians, all are jealous of me or hate me, and those who like me are worse than the ones who hate me! But you, Lady, show me whether Chaereas still lives.' She left as she

said these final words. Rhodogune, daughter of Zopyros, wife of Megabyzos, both from the Persian aristocracy, came over and comforted her. She herself was the first Persian woman Callirhoe had met when she arrived in Babylon.

The Egyptian king, when he heard that the Great King was near and was readying his troops on land and sea, called for Chaereas and said, 'I have not had a chance to repay you for your first successes when you gave me Tyre, but still I am calling on your help with the next stage so that we do not lose what we have already won. I will make you my partner in these gains because Egypt is quite enough for me: you can have Syria. Come then, let's think what must be done, because the war is at its height on both land and sea. I am offering you the choice of whether you want to command the army or the fleet. I think it would be more appropriate for you to fight at sea because you Syracusans had that great naval victory over the Athenians. Today's conflict is against the very Persians whom the Athenians defeated. You have Egyptian triremes, greater in size and number than the Sicilian ones: emulate your father-in-law's success at sea!' Chaereas replied, 'Any danger is sweet to me. For your sake I will prosecute this war against the King who is the most hateful person on earth to me. Give me my three hundred men along with the triremes.' 'Take them,' said the Egyptian king, 'these and as many others as you want.'

No sooner was it said than done because the crisis was imminent. The Egyptian king led out the infantry to meet the enemy while Chaereas took up his naval command. At first the infantry were thrown into gloom by this, because Chaereas was not marching with them. Already they loved him and always had high hopes whenever he was leading them: without him they felt like a strong body with its eyes missing. The fleet on the other hand were elated and full of resolution because they had the bravest and most glamorous leader. Their minds were focused on nothing trivial though; rather, all the captains, pilots, sailors and men-at-arms equalled each other in their eagerness to show the greatest devotion to Chaereas.

In the course of that same day, the battle began on both land and sea. For a long time the Egyptian infantry withstood the

Medes and Persians but then it began to give ground, overcome by the superior numbers. The Egyptian forces were eager to flee to Pelusium but the Persians were determined to capture them. Perhaps they might have managed to escape if Dionysius had not performed an amazing feat. He had acquitted himself nobly in the field, always fighting near the Great King so that he would attract his attention and always being the first to rout the enemy before him. When the Egyptians' retreat had gone on steadily for several days and nights, he could see that the King was very upset by this, and said, 'Don't be upset, Master. I will stop the Egyptian king escaping if you give me a force of hand-picked cavalry.' The King agreed. So, taking five thousand men, he completed two days' journey in one day and attacking the Egyptians unexpectedly at night, he took many alive and killed even more. The Egyptian king was taken alive, but killed himself and Dionysius took his head to the King. When he saw it, he said, 'I am officially recording your name in the list of men who have done great service to my house, and right here and now I am giving you the sweetest gift of all, which I know you desire above all others, Callirhoe as your wife. The war has decided the case. You have the finest prize for your deeds of bravery.' Dionysius prostrated himself before him and considered himself as equal to the gods, persuading himself that he really was the lawful husband of Callirhoe.

[6] This is what was happening on land. At sea, however, Chaereas was victorious and the enemy fleet proved no match for him. They could withstand neither the ramming of the Egyptian triremes nor their frontal attack, and while some immediately turned and fled, others were forced ashore and captured, men and all. The sea was full of Median shipwrecks. The Great King, however, did not know of the defeat which his men had suffered at sea, nor did Chaereas know about the Egyptian defeat on land: each thought that their own side was equally successful on both fronts. On the same day on which Chaereas fought the sea battle, he sailed to Arados and ordered his ships to encircle the island and guard it.

[There is a lacuna which presumably described Chaereas' capture of the island.]

. . . so that they might take a message to their master. They gathered together all the eunuchs, maidservants and other, less valuable slaves into the marketplace since it had plenty of space. The crowd was so huge that they had to spend the night not only in the walkways but also out in the open. They took the higher class of people into the market's covered area where usually the magistrates hold their business meetings. The women sat down on the floor around the Queen and refused either to approach the fires or have a bite of food, for they believed that the King had been captured, the Persian Empire destroyed and the Egyptians were victorious on all sides.

Night fell on Arados, at once most sweet and terrible. For the Egyptians were celebrating that they were released from war and from slavery to the Persians, but the captive Persians were expecting chains, whips, rape, slaughter and – the least of their troubles – slavery. Stateira was crying with her head on Callirhoe's knee because she, as a well-educated Greek woman and one who was no stranger to difficult times, was a great source of comfort to the Queen.

But then the following incident took place. The Egyptian soldier who had been entrusted with the job of guarding those under cover realized that the Queen was among them. As a result of the innate sense of awe which barbarians feel in the royal presence, he did not dare to approach her, but, standing by the door, called out, 'Do not be downhearted, Lady. For the commander is not aware now that you are shut in here with the prisoners of war, but once he knows, he will make sure you are treated kindly. He is not only a brave man, but . . .'

[There is a lacuna, and presumably one of the Egyptians sees Callirhoe and tells Chaereas of her beauty (both unaware of her identity). Chaereas sends for her and the Egyptian suggests to the woman that she is to be married.]

'. . . He will make you his wife because he is naturally chivalrous where women are concerned.' When she heard this,

Callirhoe gave a great wail and tore at her hair, saying, 'Now I truly am a prisoner of war! Kill me rather than order me to do this! I will not endure a marriage. I pray for death. Let them torture me and burn me. I will not move a step from here. This spot is good enough for a tomb for me. But if, as you say, your general is a humane man, let him grant me this favour: let him kill me here!'

He pleaded with her again, but she would not move; instead she fell to the floor and lay there with her head covered. This left the Egyptian with the problem of what he should do, because he did not dare use force and persuasion had again been unsuccessful. Accordingly he turned round and went back to Chaereas looking downcast. When he saw him, Chaereas said, 'What is it now? Has someone stolen the best bits of the spoils? They'll be sorry if they did!' The Egyptian answered as follows, 'Nothing bad has happened, Master. But the woman whom I found in such distress refuses to come here; instead she has thrown herself on the ground, asking for a sword and saying she wants to die.'

With a laugh, Chaereas said, 'Oh, you are the most naive man I've ever met! Don't you know how a woman can be manipulated with entreaties, flatteries, promises, especially if she thinks she is loved? You were probably rough and violent with her.' 'I wasn't, Master,' he replied. 'I did all the things you said to do – twice! I even pretended that you would marry her! She was especially upset at that bit.' Then Chaereas said, 'I must be a really charming and attractive prospect if she rejects me with every sign of loathing before she's even seen me! But this woman seems to have a resolution which is not without a sort of nobility. No one be violent towards her; allow her to get on with things as she chooses. It is only right for me to respect such chastity. Perhaps she too is grieving for her husband.'

BOOK 8

[1] The preceding book revealed how Chaereas, thinking that Callirhoe had been handed over to Dionysius and desiring revenge on the Great King, transferred his loyalty to the Egyptian king, was appointed naval commander and won a sea victory. Also how, after that victory, he took control of Arados where the King had placed his wife and his entire household, including Callirhoe.

The goddess Fortune was about to bring about an event which was as unbelievable as it was sad, so that although Chaereas had Callirhoe in his possession, he was ignorant of the fact and sailed off with other men's wives in his triremes, leaving his own wife there alone, not asleep like Ariadne, nor with Dionysus as a bridegroom, but as spoil for his enemies. But this seemed too awful to Aphrodite. She was already beginning to be reconciled to Chaereas, even though he had previously angered her very much by his inappropriate jealousy, for when she had given him the finest gift, such as not even the Alexander who is known as Paris had, he had acted with violence instead of gratitude. But since Chaereas had shown his contrition to Eros by his countless sufferings as he wandered from west to east, Aphrodite took pity on him. Now, after she had run them hard across land and sea, she wanted to retie the marital knot with which she had fastened this beautiful pair in the beginning.

I think also that this final book will be the most pleasurable one for my readers because it contains the resolution of all the problems in the first ones. It is no longer full of robbery and slavery, trials and battles, self-starvation, war and capture; it contains instead a well-deserved love and lawful marriage. How

the goddess brought the truth to light and revealed the unsus-
pecting pair to each other, I will tell you.

It was evening and much of the booty still remained. Exhausted,
Chaereas got up so that he could organize things for the voyage.
As he was going across the marketplace, the Egyptian soldier
said, 'There is that woman, Master, who refused to come to you
and is instead starving herself to death. Perhaps you can persuade
her to get up. I still think it is a shame if you have to leave the
most beautiful bit of the booty!' Polycharmus joined in, wanting,
if possible, to open him up to a fresh love which might comfort
him for the loss of Callirhoe. 'Let's go and have a look, Chaereas,'
he said.

Chaereas stepped over the threshold then, and caught sight
of a woman cast on the floor and with her head covered. Immediately, his soul was whirled into confusion and suspense at the
sound of her breathing and her shape. He would have recognized
her fully if he had not been so completely convinced that Dionysius had got Callirhoe back. He approached her quietly, saying,
'Whoever you are, my dear, don't worry, we will do you no harm.
You will have the husband you are longing for.' Before he finished
speaking Callirhoe had recognized his voice. She threw off her
covering and they cried simultaneously, 'Chaereas!' 'Callirhoe!'
Locked in each other's embrace and swooning, they fell to the
floor. At first Polycharmus was speechless and stood in amazement at the unbelievable sight, but then as time passed he said,
'Get up, you have got each other back. The gods have answered
your prayers and filled your cups to the brim. Remember that
you are not in your own homeland, but in hostile territory and
you must first plan everything carefully to ensure that no one
will separate you again.' Although he was shouting this, they
were like people who are submerged in deep water, scarcely able
to hear the voices from above. They would slowly rise up, then
seeing each other and kissing again, slide back down. They did
this a second and a third time, sighing with one voice, 'I have
you, if you really are Callirhoe.' 'If you really are Chaereas . . .'

The rumour ran around that the commander had found his
wife. Not a single soldier remained in his tent nor a sailor in
his trireme nor a sentry at his door. From all sides they ran up

saying excitedly, 'You lucky woman, you have got the most gorgeous husband!' But when Callirhoe appeared no one continued praising Chaereas, and everyone stared at her as if only she was there. She walked forward with great style, accompanied by Chaereas and Polycharmus on either side, like bodyguards. The men threw flowers and garlands on them, wine and myrrh were poured at their feet and it was a moment which encapsulated all that is sweetest in war and in peace: victory celebrations and a wedding.

Chaereas' usual practice was to sleep in his trireme during the night and then be up with the dawn to get on with business. But that was then. On this occasion he entrusted everything to Polycharmus' care, and without even waiting for the night to fall, set off for the royal apartments. Every city in the Persian empire has a carefully chosen suite set aside for the use of the Great King. In it lay a bed of gold made up with coverlets of Tyrian purple and Babylonian tapestries.

Who could describe that night, filled as it was with so much talk, so many tears and, of course, the acts of love? First, Callirhoe began with her history, how she had come to life in the tomb, been taken away by Theron, how she had sailed far away and been sold. Up to this point Chaereas listened with tears in his eyes, but when she came to the part of the story when she was in Miletus, Callirhoe could not bring herself to go on. When Chaereas, however, began to express his deep-seated jealousy, the explanation about the child appeased him. 'Tell me,' he said, 'how you came to Arados and where you left Dionysius and what dealings you had with the Great King.' She immediately swore that she had not seen Dionysius since the trial and that although the King had fallen for her, there had been nothing between them, not even a kiss. 'I have been unjust then,' said Chaereas, 'and too bitter in my anger, behaving in such a dreadful way to a King who had not actually done you any wrong. You see, when I had to leave you, I thought that the only course open to me was to betray the King and go over to the other side. But I have brought no shame on you: in fact I have filled the land and the sea with my victories.' He went on to tell her the full story, actually rather touchingly vain about his triumphs.

When there had been quite enough talk and tears, they wound
themselves around each other and

Rejoicing, they performed the ancient rites of the marriage bed.

[2] While it was still night-time a certain Egyptian nobleman
arrived by boat and, disembarking hurriedly from his yacht,
asked where Chaereas was. When he was taken to Polycharmus
he said that he could not deliver his secret message to anyone
other than Chaereas and it was very urgent. For a long time,
Polycharmus prevented him from going in to Chaereas, not
wanting to disturb him at an awkward moment, but since the
man was so desperate, he opened the door just a crack and told
him about the emergency. Like a good general, Chaereas said,
'Fair enough: war brooks no delay, I know!' The Egyptian was
brought in and stood by the bed in the still shadowy room. 'You
need to know that the King of the Persians has killed the Egyptian king and sent part of his army to Egypt to establish control
there. He is leading the rest here and is almost upon you. When
he found out that Arados was captured he was very upset, partly
about all the wealth that he had left here, but especially in
anguish about his wife Stateira.'

When he heard this, Chaereas jumped up. But Callirhoe,
putting her arms around him said, 'Where are you rushing off
to before thinking through what's happening? If you make this
public, you will bring a great war crashing down about your
ears, and everyone will know what's happened and despise you
for it. And if we fall back into other people's hands again, we
will suffer more seriously than the first time.' He was swiftly
persuaded by this advice and only came out of the bedroom
when he had decided on a plan. Shaking the Egyptian by the
hand, he summoned his whole force and addressed them: 'Men,
we are victorious over the Great King's army on land as well!
This man has just brought me the good news along with letters
from the Egyptian king. We must sail as quickly as possible to
the place he has appointed. Everyone, get your kit together and
embark.'

After he said this, the trumpeter sounded the recall to the

triremes. The men had loaded up the booty and prisoners on the previous day, and now nothing was left on the island except things that were too heavy or useless. Then they released the mooring cables and raised the anchors and the harbour was filled with shouts and confusion as everyone carried out their various tasks. Going round each of the triremes, Chaereas secretly gave coded instructions to the captains to make Cyprus their goal, since it was necessary to capture it while it was still unguarded. The next day, a following wind brought them to Paphos where there is a temple of Aphrodite. When they had landed but before anyone could disembark, Chaereas first sent heralds to the local people to announce that they came in peace and under truce. After these terms had been accepted, he disembarked his whole force and sent an offering to honour Aphrodite. Then he brought together a huge number of sacrificial animals and feasted the army. As he considered what he should do next, the priests, who were also seers, announced that the omens were good. Encouraged by this, he called together the captains and his three hundred Greeks and as many of the Egyptians as he knew were well-intentioned towards him and addressed them in the following way:

'Fellow soldiers and friends, partners in my great triumphs, peace is sweetest for me and war safest when I have you with me. Putting it to the test, we have found that this partnership of ours has made us masters of the sea. But a critical decision faces us about what security the future holds for us. Let me tell you now that the Egyptian king has been killed in battle and that the king has got control over all his lands, and we are surrounded by the threat of enemies on all sides. The question is whether anyone would advise us to go to the King and put ourselves in his hands.' They immediately shouted that anything must be done rather than this.

'Where shall we go to now? Everywhere is hostile to us and we can no longer put our trust in the sea, while the land is under the control of our enemies. To be sure, we cannot just take wing and fly away!'

Into the silence which followed this, a Spartan man, a relative of Brasidas and someone who had had to leave Sparta with great urgency, was the first to dare to say, 'Why are we asking where we should go to flee from the King? We have the sea and triremes: both lead us to Sicily and to Syracuse where we need have no fear not only of Persians but even of Athenians!' Everyone approved his suggestion. Only Chaereas pretended not to agree, using the length of the voyage as a pretext, but in reality testing if that was what they really wanted. When they insisted that they were ready to sail at a moment's notice, he said, 'You Greek men give good advice and I thank you for your good intentions and loyalty to me. I will not allow you to change your minds while the gods remain in support of what you do. But there are many Egyptians present who should not be forced against their will. Most of them have wives and children from whom they would not be happy to be parted. You must quickly go among the common troops then and find out about each man so that we only take those who want to come.'

[3] These things happened as ordered. Callirhoe, however, took Chaereas by the hand and led him apart from the others. 'What have you decided, Chaereas? Are you going to take Stateira to Syracuse as well and beautiful Rhodogune?' Chaereas blushed and said, 'I don't take them for my sake, but as ladies-in-waiting for you.' Callirhoe exclaimed, 'May the gods keep me from being so mad that I have the Queen of Asia as my slave, not to mention taking her to a foreign land! If you want to please me, send her back to the King, because she took care of me like a sister-in-law.' 'There is nothing I would not do for you,' said Chaereas. 'You are mistress of Stateira and all the things we took with her, and even more than this, you are mistress of my soul.' Callirhoe kissed him delightedly and immediately ordered her servants to take her to Stateira.

Stateira was with the other Persian noblewomen in the hollow body of a ship, completely unaware of what had happened and that Callirhoe had got Chaereas back, for she was very carefully guarded and it was impossible for anyone to approach her, see her or tell her any of the things that were going on. When Callirhoe came aboard the ship with the captain walking at her side, there was great consternation and confusion with people running this way and that. Then a murmur quietly ran round, 'The commander's wife is here.' Stateira gave a tremendously deep groan and, in tears, said, 'O Fortune, you have brought me to this day, so that I, a queen, should see my mistress! Perhaps she is here to see what sort of a slave she has got herself.' At this she could not hold back a lament and at that moment realized what captivity means for those of noble birth.

However, the god had a swift reversal up his sleeve, for Callirhoe ran in and embraced Stateira, saying, 'Greetings, Queen! For you are a queen and always will be. You have not fallen into enemy hands, but into those of someone very dear to you and whom you have treated with great kindness. It is my Chaereas who is the commander here. His anger towards the King, caused by the delay in getting me back, made him become a naval commander with the Egyptians. But he has stopped now and is reconciled and is no longer your enemy. Get up, my dear, you are welcome to go: go back to your husband. He still lives and Chaereas will send you back to him. You too, Rhodogune, my first friend among the Persians, get up and go to your own husband, and as many others as the Queen wants. But always remember Callirhoe!' Stateira was dumbfounded by all this, unable to believe it or yet not to. But it would not have been Callirhoe's nature to seem to mock them in their misfortune, and the crisis demanded that they respond to the situation immediately. There was, accordingly, a certain Demetrius among the Egyptians, a philosopher, known to the Great King, suitable in age and unlike the other Egyptians in education and character. Chaereas summoned this man and said, 'I want you to come with me, but instead I am going to ask you to perform for me a very important service. I am going to send the Queen back to the Great King through you: this will mean that your standing with the King is increased, but it will also enable you to reconcile him with the others.' Then he appointed Demetrius as the commander of the ships that were being taken back.

Everyone wanted to accompany Chaereas and cared more for him than for their homelands and children. But he chose only twenty triremes, the biggest and the best because they had to cross the Ionian Sea. On to these he embarked all the Greeks there were and as many Egyptians and Phoenicians as he knew were unmarried. There were also many Cypriots who wanted to come with him. He sent all the others home, after allotting to them their share of the booty so that they could return to their own families happily and with increased status. No one failed to receive what they had requested from Chaereas.

Callirhoe took all the royal regalia and jewellery back to Stateira, but she did not want to take it, saying, 'You have it. These royal outfits suit such a physique as you have. You must have it so that you can use it as gifts for your mother and your ancestral gods. I have lots more of this stuff in Babylon. May the gods grant you a good voyage, safety and that you never again be separated from Chaereas. You have always behaved fairly to me and demonstrated a nature which is noble and worthy of your beauty. The King entrusted me with a very fine task!'

[4] Who could describe that day and the many deeds it contained, how different for each individual – the prayers, the hurried preparations, the joy, the grief, the exhortations to each other, the letters home? In the midst of this, Chaereas wrote a letter to the King which went as follows:

> You were intending to give a judgement, but I had already won at the hand of the most just judge there is. For war is the best judge of who is better and who is worse. This has given back not only my wife, Callirhoe, to me, but also yours to you. I have not copied your slowness but return Stateira to you swiftly and before you have even asked for her. Throughout her captivity she has been treated with the utmost respect and as a queen. But you should know that it is not me but Callirhoe who sends you this gift. We ask in return that you should reconcile with the Egyptians because it is fitting for a king to be the most forgiving of all. You will get good soldiers who love you because they have chosen to remain with you rather than follow me as friends.

Chaereas wrote this letter and it only seemed fair and charitable to Callirhoe that she should write to Dionysius. This was the only thing she did on her own away from Chaereas because she was keen to hide it from him, aware as she was of his deep-seated jealousy. Taking up a wax tablet, she inscribed it thus:

> Callirhoe sends greetings to Dionysius, her benefactor. I call you this because you are the man who released me from bandits and slavery. Please don't be angry. I am with you in spirit because of the son we share, whom I entrust to you to bring up and educate in a way which is worthy of us. Don't make him experience a stepmother. You have not only a son, but a daughter too. Two children are enough. When he is a man, join them in marriage and send him to Syracuse so that he can see his grandfather. I send greetings to you too, Plangon. I am writing this to you with my own hand. Farewell, good Dionysius, and remember your Callirhoe.

She sealed the letter and hid it in the folds of her dress and when it was necessary for everyone to go to the ships and embark, she led Stateira on to the ship with her own hand. Demetrius was erecting a royal canopy on the ship, draped with purple and gold Babylonian hangings. Handing her on to the couch with charming deference, Callirhoe said, 'Look after yourself for me, Stateira. Don't forget me, but write often to me in Syracuse. Everything will be all right for the King. I will tell my parents and the Greek gods how grateful I am to you. I put my child in your care because I know you love to see him too. Think that you have him entrusted to you in my place.'

As she said these things her eyes filled with tears and she set her woman off weeping too. On the point of leaving the ship, Callirhoe gently leaned over Stateira and, blushing, slipped the letter to her. 'Give this to poor old Dionysius, whom I entrust to you and the King. Console him. I am afraid that now he has lost me he might harm himself.' The women would still have kept chatting, weeping and kissing each other if the helmsman had not given the signal for departure. Just about to embark on her own trireme, Callirhoe prostrated herself before Aphrodite. 'I thank you, Lady, for my present circumstances. Now you have become reconciled with me: but please allow me to see Syracuse!

There is much sea in between and the frightening depths wait for me unless you sail with me.' Meanwhile, not a single Egyptian would embark on to Demetrius' ships until they had bidden Chaereas farewell and kissed his head and hands. He inspired such great love in everyone. He also allowed the other part of the fleet to set out first, and until they were far out at sea they could still hear their shouts of praise mixed with prayers.

[5] While they set out on their voyage, the Great King secured his grip over his enemies and sent to Egypt someone who could take firm control of everything there. Meanwhile, he hurried to Arados after his wife. When he was near the coast around Tyre and sacrificing the first fruits of victory to Heracles, someone came to him announcing that 'Arados has been sacked and lies empty, the Egyptian ships have carried off everything in it.' Terrible grief seized the King, thinking he had lost the Queen. The Persian nobles grieved too,

With Stateira as the pretext, but each for his own losses,

this one for a wife, another for a sister or a daughter: they all grieved for someone as each had lost someone close to them. While their enemies sailed away, they had no idea which part of the sea held them.

On the second day they saw the Egyptian ships sailing towards them. The reality of the situation was unknown to them, of course, so they were amazed when they saw this: the royal standard flying from Demetrius' ship (which was usually only raised when the Great King was at sea) increased their bewilderment still more. It caused confusion seeing it here on an enemy ship. As soon as they spotted it, they sent word to Artaxerxes, 'Perhaps it will turn out to be some new King of Egypt!' Artaxerxes jumped up from his throne, hurried down to the shore and issued the signal for war, even though he had no triremes. However, his whole force stood at the harbour, ready for battle. Already someone was stretching back his bow and already someone was about to hurl his spear, and they would have done it, if Demetrius had not realized what was happening and told the Queen. Stateira came out of the tent and showed herself, and at that instant everyone dropped their weapons and prostrated themselves. But the King could not hold himself back and before the ship had properly docked, he was the first to leap aboard to her. Wrapping his arms around her and bursting with tears of joy, he said, 'Which of the gods has given you back to me, my darling? For both possibilities seemed beyond belief: that I should lose my queen, or that once lost, she should be found! How have I got you back from the sea after I left you on land?' Stateira replied, 'You have me as a gift from Callirhoe.' When he heard her name, the King felt a fresh blow to the old wound and, looking at his eunuch, Artaxates, said, 'Take me to Callirhoe so that I can thank her.' But it was Stateira who answered, 'I will tell you everything', and straightaway proceeded from the harbour up to the palace. Then, after she had ordered everyone else to go away so that only the King and his eunuch remained, she related what had happened on Arados and in Cyprus and finally gave him the letter from Chaereas. As he read it, the King was filled with a thousand different emotions: he felt anger at the capture of his nearest and dearest; but then repentance at having forced on Chaereas the necessity of deserting to the other side; and finally gratitude to him because he had sent him back his wife. He also felt grief that he would no longer be able to set eyes on Callirhoe. Yet above all it was a wistful envy which touched him, and he said, 'Chaereas is blessed; he is luckier than I.'

When the explanations were complete, Stateira said, 'Sire, comfort Dionysius. This is the injunction that Callirhoe lays on you.' So Artaxerxes turned to his eunuch, 'Let Dionysius come before us.' He came quickly, keyed up with hope because he knew nothing about Chaereas, but thought that Callirhoe was with the other women and that the King had summoned him so that he could give him back his wife as the prize for his dazzling success in the field. However, when he arrived, the King explained to him everything that had happened. In that crisis, Dionysius really showed his mental strength and excellent upbringing, for he was like someone who, when the thunderbolt lands at their feet, manages to keep their head. Just like this, when he heard

those words, more painful than any thunderbolt, that Chaereas
was taking Callirhoe back to Syracuse, he schooled himself to
remain calm and decided that it would be impolitic to show grief
when the good news of the Queen's safety was still fresh. Artaxerxes said, 'If I had been able, I would have given Callirhoe
back to you, Dionysius, in return for all the goodwill and loyalty
you have shown me. But since this is impossible, I give you all
of Ionia to rule and you will be recorded as the foremost benefactor to the King's household.' Dionysius prostrated himself
and expressed his gratitude before rushing away so that he could
give vent to his tears. As he left, Stateira silently handed him the
letter.

In his own room, he turned around and locked himself in. As
soon as he recognized Callirhoe's handwriting, he at once kissed
the letter, then bared his breast and clasped the letter to it as if
it were Callirhoe herself. For a long time he remained like this,
unable to read the letter because of his tears; but as his tears
abated, he began with difficulty to focus on it. At first he kissed
Callirhoe's name, but when he came to the part where she called
him her benefactor, he cried, 'Alas, no longer "husband". But it
is you who were my benefactor: what of any value have I done
for you?' Yet he was pleased at the apology and explanation the
letter contained and read its contents many times, because he
secretly felt that it showed that she had not left him willingly.
This is how subtle Eros is, easily persuading a lover that he is
loved in return. Then he looked at his little child and as the bard
says, 'dandled him in his arms'. 'In time, child, you too will leave
me and go to your mother, since that's what she has ordered. I
will live alone, knowing that I have brought this all on myself.
Empty jealousy has destroyed me, along with you, Babylon!'
After saying this, he prepared to leave for Ionia as quickly as
possible, thinking that the greatest comfort he could find would
be in the long journey, his dominion over many cities and the
images of Callirhoe in Miletus.

[6] This is how the situation stood in Asia when Chaereas
successfully completed his voyage to Sicily. Fearing that the
attack of some cruel deity might drive him back, Chaereas stood

at the prow throughout the entire journey and brought his big
ships across the great sea. When Syracuse came into view, he
gave the order to his captains to deck out the triremes and sail
in formation because they were in calm water now.

When the people in the city saw them, one of them said,
'Where are these triremes coming from? Surely they are not
Athenian? Come on, let's go and tell Hermocrates.' They told
him speedily, 'General, think what you should do! Shall we close
the harbours or shall we launch an attack? We don't know if a
greater fleet follows and this is only the advance guard which
we can see.' Racing down from the town square to the shore,
Hermocrates sent a vessel to row out to meet them. When it got
close enough to ask them who they were, Chaereas ordered one
of the Egyptians to reply, 'We are Egyptian sea merchants bringing a cargo which will delight the Syracusans.' 'Don't approach
en masse until we know if you are telling the truth,' came the
reply. 'I don't see any cargo ships, but big triremes ready for war:
so let most of them remain floating outside the harbour and just
one sail in.' 'Right you are.'

Chaereas' trireme sailed in first. On the top deck it had a tent
covered with Babylonian hangings. As it came in to anchor, the
whole harbour was filled with people, for a crowd is naturally
nosy and this time they had even more reason to gather. Looking
at the tent, they imagined that it contained costly goods and not
people, and made predictions to each other, guessing at anything
but the truth. Since they believed that Chaereas was dead, it was
inconceivable to them that he could appear alive, sailing into
harbour and bringing such riches with him. Chaereas' parents
did not come out of their house, but Hermocrates, who had
remained in public life despite his grief, was standing there but
hidden at the back.

Everyone was utterly bewildered and their eyes were standing
out on stalks, when suddenly the hangings were thrown back
and Callirhoe appeared, lying on a golden couch, clothed in
Tyrian purple, with Chaereas sitting at her side wearing a general's insignia. Thunder has never deafened its audience so much,
nor lightning blinded those who are looking at it, nor has someone striking a rich seam of gold ever set up such a shout of

exultation as the crowd did then, suddenly seeing a sight beyond description. Hermocrates sprang forward to the tent and embraced his daughter, saying, 'You are alive, child, or my wits have gone begging!' 'I am truly returned to life now, Father, because I am here with you.' Everyone shed tears of joy.

Meanwhile, Polycharmus sailed in with the other triremes. He had been entrusted with the rest of the fleet from Cyprus, because Chaereas no longer had time for anything apart from Callirhoe. The harbour swiftly filled up and looked almost as it had after the Attic sea battle: these triremes too sailed in garlanded from battle, under the command of a Syracusan general. There was a great babble of voices, of those from the sea greeting those on land and vice versa, with good wishes, compliments and prayers flying repeatedly from one side to the other. And then Chaereas' father was there, almost swooning from unexpected joy, while Chaereas was surrounded and greeted by an eager crowd of friends and men who had trained with him; there was a crowd of women around Callirhoe too. To them, Callirhoe seemed yet more beautiful still, so that you would have said that you were seeing Aphrodite herself rising up out of the sea.

Going forward, Chaereas said to Hermocrates and his father, 'Please accept the Great King's wealth.' He immediately ordered everything to be taken out; the silver and the countless gold, then the ivory, amber and clothes, and he showed the Syracusans all the costly wooden furniture, including the Great King's couch and table so that the whole city was filled, not as it had been before with Attica's poor spoils from the war, but, strangely, with this Median booty from peace.

[7] Everyone wanted to see them and hear what they had to say and, as one, the crowd shouted out, 'Let's go to the assembly.' In less time than it takes to describe it, the theatre was full of men and women, and when Chaereas entered alone, they all shouted out, 'Call Callirhoe!' Hermocrates led in his daughter and then got up in front of the crowd. At first they all cast their eyes up to heaven, praising the gods and thanking them more fervently for this day than for the day of their victory. Then at

some point they split into two and the men shouted in praise of Chaereas and the women of Callirhoe: then they joined in praising them both again, which the pair of them preferred.

As soon as she had greeted her native land, the crowd led Callirhoe out of the theatre on the grounds that she was exhausted from the voyage and her trials; but they kept Chaereas there, wanting to hear a blow-by-blow account of all his time away. He started at the end, not wanting to upset the people with the sad events which had started it. But the crowd urged him on, 'Start at the beginning, we beg you. Tell us everything, and don't leave anything out.' Chaereas shrank from it, for the most part ashamed of all the senseless things which had happened, but Hermocrates said, 'Don't be ashamed, child, even if you have to say something that is rather upsetting or bitter for us, because the glorious conclusion outweighs all the previous things, and not telling us creates a worse suspicion by your silence. You are speaking to your native people and your parents whose affection for you both is equally balanced. Remember that everyone already knows the first part of the story for they tied the marital knot between you themselves. How, a prey to the rival suitors' plot, you were overcome by unnecessary jealousy and inopportunely struck your wife, they also know: and that when she seemed to be dead she was buried magnificently, while you were tried for murder and voted against yourself in the hope of joining your wife in death. But the people acquitted you, knowing that it had not happened intentionally. They know the next part too: that Theron the tomb-robber dug into the grave by night and when he found Callirhoe alive, put her and all her grave-goods on his pirate ship and sold her in Ionia; that you set out on a search for your wife but did not find her, instead falling in with a pirate vessel on the sea and that although the other pirates were dead from thirst, you brought Theron, who was the only one alive, back to the assembly and that he was tortured and put to the stake; and finally, they know that the city sent out a trireme and ambassadors on Callirhoe's behalf and that Polycharmus willingly went with you as your friend. But tell us what happened after you sailed out of here.'

Chaereas took up the story from here: 'After a safe voyage to

Ionia we landed at the estate of a Milesian man by the name of
Dionysius, foremost in Ionia in wealth, birth and reputation.
This man had bought Callirhoe from Theron for a talent. Don't
be afraid, she was not a slave, because although he had bought
her, he immediately made her into the mistress of the estate and
already in love with her, did not dare to force himself on a well-
born woman, but he could not bear to send the woman he loved
back to Syracuse. When Callirhoe realized that she was pregnant
by me, if she wanted to save this new fellow citizen of yours,
she had to marry Dionysius and spin some fancy lines about the
child's birth, so that it would seem to be Dionysius' and be
brought up properly. Men of Syracuse, there is a fellow citizen
of yours growing up in Miletus, rich and looked after by a very
worthy man. His family is a noble Greek one, so let us not
begrudge him his great inheritance.

[8] 'I learned all this later. At that point, after landing on the
estate and seeing just one statue of Callirhoe in the temple, I had
great hopes. However, during the night Phrygian pirates from
the sea burned our trireme and killed almost everyone, put myself
and Polycharmus in chains and sold us into Caria.' At this, the
crowd broke into lament, but Chaereas said, 'Let me pass over
what happened next in silence for it is even more distressing
than the first part.' But the crowd shouted out, 'Tell us everything.' So he said, 'The man who bought us worked for
Mithridates, the ruler of Caria, and he set us to digging although
we were still in chains. When some men killed the prison guard,
Mithridates ordered that we should all be crucified. I was led
up with the rest of them. When we were just about to be tortured,
Polycharmus shouted out my name and Mithridates recognized
it. For he had been a guest of Dionysius' in Miletus when this
"Chaereas" was being buried. Callirhoe had been told about
what had happened to the trireme and, thinking that I was dead,
she built me a magnificent tomb. Mithridates swiftly ordered
me to be brought down from the cross which I was almost on
and made me one of his closest friends. He was very keen to
restore Callirhoe to me and got me to write to her.

'However, through the carelessness of one of his servants,

Dionysius himself got hold of the letter. He did not believe that I was alive and thought that Mithridates was plotting to get hold of his wife and immediately submitted an accusation of adultery to the Great King. He agreed to hold the trial and ordered everyone to come to him. This is how we came to be in Babylon. Dionysius took Callirhoe and made her famous and a celebrity throughout the whole of Asia, and Mithridates took me. When we got there we argued our cases in a great trial before the King. He immediately acquitted Mithridates and promised an adjudication between myself and Dionysius concerning our wife, entrusting Callirhoe in the meantime to Stateira the Queen. Men of Syracuse, how many times do you think I planned to kill myself since I was separated from my wife, and would have if Polycharmus, my only friend in all this, had not saved me? For the King put the trial on one side, burning with love for Callirhoe himself, though he neither seduced her nor forced himself on her.

'Just at that key moment, Egypt revolted and started a serious war, something which turned out to be the source of great success for me. For while the Queen took Callirhoe along with her, I was falsely informed that she had been handed over to Dionysius and, wanting to get revenge on the Great King, I deserted to the Egyptian king and accomplished great deeds for him. So I subdued the almost impregnable Tyre and after being appointed naval commander, I fought a sea battle against the Great King and became master of Arados where the King had left the queen and the wealth which you see now. And I would have been able to make the Egyptian king of all Asia, if he had not been defeated in a battle without me and killed. But for the rest, I have brought the Great King into friendship with you by giving him his wife back as a gift and sending back the mothers, sisters, wives and daughters of the most noble Persians. I have myself led back here the best of my Greek troops and those of the Egyptians who wanted to come. Another fleet of yours will also come from Ionia, led by Hermocrates' grandson!'

Prayers of gratitude followed this on all sides. Chaereas, however, checked the applause and said, 'Callirhoe and I give thanks on your behalf to my friend, Polycharmus, for he showed kindness and the truest loyalty to us. If it meets with your approval, I would like to give him my sister as a wife, with a share of the booty as dowry.' The people shouted their assent, saying, 'The people are grateful to Polycharmus, a good man and a trustworthy friend. You have benefited your homeland in a way worthy of Hermocrates and Chaereas.' After this, Chaereas spoke again, 'I also ask you to make these three hundred Greek men, my brave army, into citizens.' Again the people shouted their approval, 'They are worthy of being citizens with us! Let it be passed in a show of hands.' The vote was recorded and they were immediately allowed to join in the business of the assembly. Chaereas also gave them a talent apiece while Hermocrates allotted land to the Egyptians for them to farm.

While the crowd was in the theatre, Callirhoe went to the temple of Aphrodite before returning home. Clasping the goddess's feet and laying her head on them, with loosened hair, she kissed them, saying, 'Thank you, Aphrodite! You have presented Chaereas to me again in Syracuse where I saw him first when I was still a virgin, by your will. I do not blame you, Lady, for what I have suffered. These things were allotted to me by fate. But I beg you, don't separate me again from Chaereas but allow us a happy life and to die together.'

This is all I have to write about Callirhoe.

LONGUS

DAPHNIS AND CHLOE

BOOK 1

When I was hunting in Lesbos, I saw in the grove of the Nymphs the most beautiful sight I have ever seen, a painting of an image, a love story. The grove was beautiful, full of trees and flowers and flowing water, and a single spring nourished everything, the flowers no less than the trees. The painting was even more delightful because it showed exceptional skill in presenting the love affair. Many people, even foreigners, were drawn there by its fame and they came to pray to the Nymphs or to see the picture. The painting showed women giving birth, other women dressing babies in clothes, children abandoned, animals nursing them, shepherds raising them, young people making a pledge, pirates rushing down, enemies invading, and all the many wonderful things that make up a romance. While I was looking on and admiring these scenes, I was so moved that the desire took me to repaint the painting and respond in words. So I sought out an interpreter of the picture, and then elaborated it in four rolls, as an offering to Love and to the Nymphs and to Pan, and as a possession from which all men may derive pleasure: it is intended to heal the sick and to console the afflicted, to bring back memories for those who have known love, and to give instruction to those who have not. Because absolutely no one has escaped Love, and no one will escape him as long as there is beauty and as long as there are eyes to see with. And may the god Love permit me to write about the passions of others and keep me moderate with regard to my own.

[1] Mytilene is a city on Lesbos, a large and beautiful one. It is divided by canals that pour in from the sea and decorated by

bridges made of polished white stone, and it looks almost like
an island rather than a city. About two hundred stades from this
city of Mytilene, there was a rich man's estate, a beautiful property that had hills filled with wild animals for game, plains of
golden wheat, sloping vineyards and pastures full of flocks. The
sea here gently lapped the soft sand of the long, languishing shore.

[2] One day, when grazing his flock on this estate, a goatherd
named Lamon found a baby boy being suckled by one of his she-
goats. There was a copse of oak trees thick with brambles and
wandering ivy and soft grass on which the baby boy was lying.
The goat used to run to this place and then often disappear from
sight: she would leave her kid behind and stay with the baby.
Lamon watched the goat running back and forth, and felt pity for
her neglected kid. Then, at noon, following in the goat's tracks, he
saw her stepping about carefully next to the baby, so as not to
harm the infant with her hooves, and saw the baby drawing a
stream of milk from this nanny goat as if she were his mother.
Lamon was amazed, naturally, and coming nearer, he found a baby
boy who was healthy and beautiful and in better clothes than you
would expect to find on an abandoned child. He was wearing a
purple cloak and a golden brooch and a dagger with an ivory hilt.

[3] His first thought was to carry off only the tokens and to
ignore the baby. But then he was ashamed that the goat was
showing greater compassion for a human being than he was, so
he stayed there and watched over the child until nightfall, and
then brought everything to his wife Myrtale, the tokens, the child
and the goat itself. She was astonished to see that the goats were
now giving birth to children, but he told her the whole story, how
he found the baby abandoned, how he saw it nursing and how he
was ashamed to leave it behind to die. And she agreed that
he had made the right choice. They decided to hide the tokens
that had been left out with the baby and pretend that he was
their own son, and they decided as well to entrust the nursing
to the goat. And so that he would have a pastoral name, they
decided to call him Daphnis.

[4] Two years went by. Then a shepherd named Dryas, who tended his flock in the neighbouring fields, had a similar experience: he made the same sort of discovery and saw the same kind of spectacle. There was a cave of the Nymphs, a great rock, hollow on the inside, rounded on the outside. The statues of these Nymphs were made of stone, each with feet uncovered, arms bare to her shoulders, hair loose down to the neck, girdles around the waist and a smile about the eyes. The whole scene was like a chorus of dancers. In the very middle of the cave in the great rock, water gushing out of a spring formed a flowing stream, which spilled over into the smooth, green meadow stretched out in front of the cave and nourished the thick, soft grass with its liquid. Hanging inside the cave were milk pails and flute pipes and pan pipes and reed pipes, offerings left behind by shepherds of old.

[5] A sheep that had recently given birth used to wander often into this shrine of the Nymphs and give the impression of being lost. Wanting to discipline her and to restore her to her earlier habits, Dryas made a leash out of a green shoot, as a snare, and went to the rock to catch her there. This is what he planned to do: what he saw there was nothing that he expected. He saw the ewe giving suck, just like a human mother, to an infant tugging for milk, and the baby greedily, but without crying, holding both teats to its face. The baby's face was clean and bright because each time the baby would drink its fill of milk, the ewe would lick its face clean with her tongue. Unlike the other foundling, this child was a girl, but like the other, this one also had fine tokens among the swaddling clothes: a belt embroidered with gold, gilded slippers and golden anklets.

[6] Thinking he had found a gift from the gods, Dryas followed the sheep's example and decided to take pity on the child and give it his affection. He picked up the child in his arms, put away the tokens in his bag, and then prayed to the Nymphs for their blessings in caring for their little suppliant. And when it was time to drive his flock back home, he went to his cottage, and told his wife what he saw, showing her what he found. He told

her to think of the baby as their daughter and to bring up the forgotten child as they would their own, without telling anyone. Nape (this was her name) straightaway became a mother and loved the child, as if she were afraid of being outdone by the sheep, and to inspire trust in her story, she also gave the girl a pastoral name, Chloe.

[7] As the years passed, the two children grew up very quickly, and they looked much more beautiful than the children of country folk usually do. One night, when Daphnis was fifteen and Chloe two years younger, Dryas and Lamon each had the same dream. They dreamed that the Nymphs from the cave which had the spring in it, where Dryas discovered his baby, were handing over Daphnis and Chloe to a very haughty but beautiful boy who had wings coming out of his shoulders and was carrying tiny arrows that fit his little bow. He shot a single arrow at both of them, and ordered them, from that moment on, to go out into the fields, Daphnis as a goatherd and Chloe as a shepherd.

[8] When they saw this dream, the two fathers were annoyed that their children would become shepherds and goatherds, since the swaddling clothes had seemed to augur a much brighter future for the two foundlings. For this reason, they had raised them with greater care and refinement than usual, and had taught them reading and writing and all the things that seem so fine to the rustic mind. But they decided to listen to the gods since, after all, the children had been saved by divine providence. They told each other their dreams, and sacrificed to the winged boy, whose name these simple people did not know, in the cave of the Nymphs. Afterward, they sent out Daphnis and Chloe to become keepers of their flocks, though first they taught them all the skills that a good herdsman needs to have: how to pasture the flocks before midday, how to graze them when the heat has died down, when to lead them to drink, when to drive them to their beds, which animals responded best to sticks and which to their voices only. These two were thrilled to take up positions of such importance, with the result that they loved their goats and sheep more than is usual among herdsmen: Chloe because she credited her

survival to the sheep, and Daphnis because he remembered that a goat had nourished him when he was abandoned.

[9] It was now the beginning of spring, and the flowers were in bloom everywhere, on the trees, in the meadows and in the hills. The countryside was filled with the buzzing of the bees, the twittering of song-birds and the frolicking of newborn lambs: the lambs were frolicking in the hills, the bees buzzing in the meadows and the birds singing in the groves. So overwhelming was the beauty of the season and so innocent and impressionable were Daphnis and Chloe that they imitated everything they happened to hear and see. When they heard the birds singing, they sang along; they saw the lambs scampering, and they hopped about nimbly too. In imitation of the bees, they gathered together the most fragrant blossoms, throwing some of the flowers into their laps, and weaving others into garlands that they offered to the Nymphs.

[10] They were inseparable and did everything together, tending their flocks side by side. If Daphnis rounded up Chloe's stray sheep for her, just as often Chloe drove down the more intrepid of Daphnis' goats from the high cliffs for him, and if one was distracted by some game or toy, the other would watch over the flocks for both of them. Their toys were simple, designed to amuse children or childlike shepherds. She would spend hours picking stalks of asphodel and weaving a trap for grasshoppers, and concentrate so hard on this that she would forget her flock. He would cut slender reeds, make holes in the joints of these plants, join them to each other with soft wax and play the pipes until nightfall. They shared their milk and wine, and whatever food they brought to the fields from home, that also they shared with each other. A passer-by would have been more likely to see the sheep and the goats parted from each other than Chloe and Daphnis.

[11] While they were playing with these toys, Love devised a way to make things more earnest. A she-wolf was feeding her cubs by stealing sheep from the other flocks in the nearby

countryside because she needed large amounts of food to feed her young. So the villagers came together by night and dug some pits, each of which was six feet wide and four times as many feet deep. The earth that they carried out they spread all over, placed wooden sticks over the opening, and the remaining soil over them, so that the earth looked just like it was before it was dug up. Even a hare running across would have broken the wooden sticks, which were weaker than dry stalks, and then have discovered that this was not land but an imitation of it. They dug many such pits, in the mountains and plains, but they were not able to catch the wolf, since she had seen them and knew that the soil was treacherous. But they did destroy many goats and sheep – and they nearly did the same to Daphnis. This is what happened.

[12] Two he-goats got into an excited state and fell into a fight. One of the two violently shattered the other one's horn; snorting and leaping in pain, he turned and started to escape. The victorious goat followed in his steps, and made sure the other's flight was prolonged. Daphnis was upset at the harm done to the horn of the one goat and the audacity of the other, so he took up a wooden stick and a crook, and he pursued the pursuer. Quite naturally, neither the fugitive goat nor his angry pursuer were very careful about where they were stepping, and they both fell into the pit, the goat first and Daphnis second. In fact, this was what saved Daphnis, for he used the goat to cushion himself against the fall. He waited tearfully for some passer-by to come and pull him out. But Chloe saw the accident, and came running to the hole, and when she discovered that he was alive, she called one of the cowherds from the neighbouring fields for help. He came there, and began to look for a rope that Daphnis might hold on to and be pulled out by. But there was no rope, so Chloe undid her breastband and gave it to the cowherd to let down. And in this way, standing at the edges of the pit, they pulled him out, and he climbed out with his hands as they pulled up the breastband. They also pulled up the poor goat, which had broken both his horns: this was his reward for triumphing over the other goat. They gave this goat as a thank-offering to the cowherd,

and planned to lie and say to the people at home that there was
an attack of wolves if there were any questions about the missing goat. They went back to check the sheep and goats, and when
they were sure that the goats and the sheep were pasturing in
peace, they sat down at the foot of an oak tree to see if any part
of Daphnis' body was bleeding from the fall. Nothing was
broken and nothing bleeding, but his hair and the rest of his
body were plastered with soil and mud, and so they decided to
wash him before Lamon and Myrtale might see what had
happened.

[13] Daphnis went with Chloe to the Nymphs' shrine, and gave
her his tunic and his bag to look after, and he went and stood
in the spring, and washed his hair and the rest of his body. His
hair was black and full, and his body was tanned by the sun; it
looked as though his body had taken its colour from the dark
hues of his hair. Chloe was looking at Daphnis, and he seemed
beautiful to her. And because that moment was the first time he
looked beautiful to her, she thought that the bath was the cause
of his beauty. As she washed his back, his soft flesh yielded to
her hands, so she secretly touched herself many times to see if
her own body was more delicate when she pressed it. Then, they
drove the flocks home since the sun was already at the point of
setting, and Chloe desired in her heart only to see Daphnis bathing again. When the sun rose the next morning, they went out
to the pasture. Daphnis sat under his usual oak tree and played
his pipes, and at the same time was keeping an eye on the goats,
which were lying down and appeared to be listening to his music.
Chloe sat nearby, and cast an eye on her flock of sheep, but was
looking mostly at Daphnis. He again seemed to her to look
beautiful playing the pipes, and this time she supposed the music
was the cause of his beauty. So, after he played, she too took up
the pipes to see if she might not also become beautiful. She
persuaded him to take another bath, and saw him bathing, and
as she watched, she touched him. As she walked off, she was
moved to praise him inwardly and think how beautiful he was –
and this thought was the beginning of love. What she was
feeling she didn't know, since she was a girl and was raised in

the country, and, because no one had told her, she had not even
heard about love. But her heart was vexed, she was not able to
keep her eyes open and she chattered at length about Daphnis.
She cared not for her food, lay awake at night and disregarded
her flock; she laughed, then she cried; she sat down, then she
leaped up; her face was pale, and then again it was fired red. An
ox stung by an insect was never so tormented! When she was
all alone one day, she said these words to herself:

[14] 'I'm sick now, but what my sickness is I don't understand;
I'm in pain, but haven't been injured; I feel sad, but none of my
sheep is lost; I'm burning hot, yet here I am sitting in the dark
shade. The bramble's scratched me so many times, still I never
cried; so many bees have pricked me, and I never shouted out.
But this prick in my heart is more pointed and bitter than all of
those. Daphnis is beautiful, but the flowers are too; the sound
his pipes make is beautiful, but so is the song of the nightingales;
yet none of these other things matters to me. I wish I were his
pipes and he'd blow me; I wish I were his goat and he'd graze
me. You wretched water, how is it you made Daphnis alone
beautiful, and when I bathed in you, you did nothing to me! I'll
soon be dead and gone, dear Nymphs: you're not doing anything
to save this young woman whom you brought up. Who will
garland you after I go? Who will take care of my poor lambs?
Who will look after the chattering grasshopper? I worked hard
to hunt it down, so that it might lull me to sleep in front of the
cave. Now it's sleep that I'm hunting down, because of Daphnis,
and the grasshopper is prattling on in vain.'

[15] These were things she felt and said in her uncertainty – but
the word she was searching for was *love*. The cowherd who had
pulled out Daphnis and the goat from the pit was called Dorcon,
and he was a young man whose beard had just started to grow
and who knew about love in word and action; he had been
struck by a desire for Chloe as soon as he saw her that day, and
with each passing moment burned more and more in his soul
for the girl. He dismissed Daphnis as a young boy, and decided
to accomplish his task through gifts or by force as necessary. To

start with, he brought them gifts, for him a set of pipes, the nine reeds bound together with brass instead of wax, and for her a bacchant's fawnskin, the colour of which was like the colours in a picture. As he came to be considered a friend by them, he gradually stopped giving attention to Daphnis, but to Chloe every day used to bring a soft cheese or a garland of flowers or a ripe apple. One day he brought her a newborn calf and the chicks of some mountain birds and a wooden cup inlaid with gold and with ivy wreaths carved on it. She was inexperienced in lovers' techniques, and was happy to take the gifts, and happier still because she was herself able to make Daphnis happy. Since Daphnis also now had to get to know love in action, one day a beauty contest took place between Dorcon and him. Chloe was the judge, and the prize for the winner was to kiss Chloe. Dorcon spoke first:

[16] 'I, dear girl, am taller than Daphnis, and I am a cowherd, while he's a goatherd; so I am superior to him just as cows are superior to goats. I am as white as milk, and my hair is a fire that sparkles like the red summer corn, and my mother brought me up, not a wild beast. That man is small, he doesn't have a beard, just like a woman, and is as black as a wolf; he looks after goats and smells terrible because of them. He is so impoverished that he can't afford to keep a dog. And if, as they say, he was nursed directly on goat's milk, there's no difference between him and the kids.' These words, and others like them, Dorcon spoke. Then Daphnis replied: 'I was raised by a goat, and so was Zeus. I look after goats that are bigger than his cows. I don't stink because Pan doesn't either, and you know he is more goat than not. I have enough cheese and bread rolls and white wine, and as many possessions as rich country folk need. I don't have a beard, and Dionysus doesn't either, and if I'm dark, so is the hyacinth; but Dionysus is better than the Satyrs and the hyacinth better than the lilies. Dorcon is red-haired like a fox and bearded like a goat and white like some woman from the city. If you have to kiss me, you'll kiss my mouth, but with him, you'll get the bristles of his beard. And remember, dear girl, that a sheep suckled you, but you are quite beautiful.'

[17] Chloe did not wait any longer. She was so delighted with the encomium and had desired to kiss Daphnis for so long that she leaped up and gave him a kiss: it was quite simple and clumsy, but entirely capable of setting his heart on fire. Dorcon was upset, and he ran off, seeking another way to make love. But Daphnis, like someone who has been bitten rather than kissed, instantly became gloomy. He shivered now and again, and could not restrain the pounding in his heart; he wanted to look at Chloe, but whenever he looked at her, he turned all red. Then, as never before, he was filled with admiration for her hair, because it was blonde, and her eyes, because they were large like a cow's, and her complexion, because it was whiter, truly, even than goats' milk. It was as if he had only now, for the first time, come to possess eyes, as if earlier he had been blind. He did not take any food, except just a taste, and as for drink, if he felt compelled to have any, he took just enough to moisten his mouth. He was quiet and lethargic when earlier he had been more chatty than a grasshopper and livelier than the goats. Even his sheep he neglected; even his pipes he threw away. His face grew paler than summer grass. He talked freely to no one but Chloe. When he was alone and away from her, he talked to himself in this way:

[18] 'Whatever did Chloe's kiss do to me? Her lips are softer than roses, her mouth is sweeter than honey, but her kiss is sharper than a bee sting. I've kissed kids many times, I've kissed newborn puppies many times – not to mention the calf that Dorcon gave her. But this kiss is something new. I'm short of breath, my heart is pounding, my soul is melting away: yet I want to kiss her again. An evil victory! A strange illness – I don't even have a name for it! What if Chloe drank some potion before she kissed me? Then why is she not dead? The nightingales are singing, but my pipes are silent; the kids are skipping, but I'm sitting still; the flowers blossom, but I'm not weaving garlands; the violets and the hyacinths are in bloom, but Daphnis withers away. Is even Dorcon going to be better-looking than me?'

[19] This was what our brave Daphnis felt and said: for the first
time, he had tasted love, in word and action. But Dorcon, the
cowherd and would-be lover of Chloe, was on the lookout for
Dryas to plant the vines nearby, and went towards him with
some fine cheeses, and gave them to him as gifts. (He had been
a friend of his from the time he used to take the animals to
pasture.) Then later, after this gesture had taken effect, he threw
in a word about marrying Chloe, and since he was a cowherd,
he declared that if he could take her to be his wife, he would
give many large gifts: a pair of oxen for ploughing, four hives
of bees, fifty apple trees, the hide of a bull to cut into sandals,
and every year a weaned calf. Dryas was so easily charmed by
the gifts that he almost agreed to the marriage. But then he
considered how the girl was worthy of a better husband, and he
grew nervous that if his role in the marriage were discovered,
the consequences would be dire for him. So he rejected the
marriage, asked for Dorcon's forgiveness and declined the gifts
that he had promised.

[20] This was the second time Dorcon was frustrated of his
desires. Now that he had lost his good cheeses in vain, he decided
to lay his hands on Chloe when she was alone. Observing that
they used to drive their herds to drink on alternate days – one
day it was Daphnis, the next day the girl – he devised the sort
of trick that is typical of a shepherd. He took the skin of a large
wolf, which a bull fighting to protect the cows had killed with
its horns, and put it over his body, carrying it on his back down
to his feet, so that the front feet folded over his hands, the back
feet went over his ankles and the gaping mouth covered his head
like the helmet of a hoplite soldier. Making himself look as wild
as possible, he waited beside the spring where the goats and the
sheep went to drink after their pasture. The spring was in a
hollow, and the place all around it was overrun with bear's foot
and brambles and low junipers and thistles: a real wolf could
easily have hidden in ambush there. Dorcon hid himself, and
waited for drinking time. He had great hopes of getting his hands
on Chloe once he had frightened her by his appearance.

[21] After a little while, Chloe drove her flocks down towards the stream. She left behind Daphnis, who was cutting green leaves to feed the kids after pasture, but the dogs were still following her to protect the flocks and the goats. Dogs are experienced at tracking by scent, and these barked furiously at Dorcon as he moved to take the girl. Attacking him as if he were a wolf, they pounced on him before he could, in his surprise, pull himself up fully, and bit him from the head down to his toes. For a time, Dorcon was embarrassed at being found out and, feeling protected by the skin covering him, he lay quietly in the thicket. But when Chloe, who was upset as soon as she saw him, called Daphnis for help, and when the dogs were ripping apart the skin hanging on his body, Dorcon yelled out loudly and pleaded with the girl for help, even as Daphnis arrived on the scene. They quickly calmed the dogs with their familiar voices and commands, and helped Dorcon, who had been bitten on the thighs and shoulders, to the spring, where they washed the bites. After chewing on the green bark of the elm, they applied it to his wounds. Because of their innocence in amour and its audacities, they thought of the disguise as a country prank. They were not angry, but instead they tried to revive Dorcon's spirits, and led him by the hand for some distance before they sent him on his way.

[22] After escaping from such a serious danger, and after being saved not from the jaws of the wolf, as they say, but from the jaws of the dog, Dorcon treated his wounded body. For their part, Daphnis and Chloe worked hard at rounding up the goats and ewes before nightfall. Some of the ewes were disturbed by the wolfskin and upset by the barking dogs, and had climbed up on to the rocks, and some had even run down to the seashore. Indeed, the flocks had been trained to follow their voices, to respond to the pipes and to gather together at the sound of hands clapping; but this time fear had made them forget everything, and it was only with difficulty and by following in their tracks like hares that Daphnis and Chloe recovered them and then led them back to their folds. That one night only, they fell into a deep sleep and found in their weary labours a cure for their love

sickness. But when the daylight returned, they experienced the
same feelings once again: they were happy to see each other, they
were sad to leave: they desired something, they did not know
what they desired. This only they knew, that the kiss had
destroyed him and the bath had destroyed her.

[23] The season also fired up their passions, since spring was
already over, and summer was beginning. Everything was in
bloom: trees were teeming with fruit, fields were filled with corn;
the cries of the cicadas were mellifluous, the smell of the ripe
fruit was sweet, the bleating of flocks was pleasant. It was easy
to imagine that the rivers were singing as they flowed gently,
that the breezes were piping as they blew in the pine trees, that
the apples dropped to the ground because they were under the
effects of love, and that the sun was disrobing all the people in
the country because it was in love with beauty. Daphnis felt hot
because of all these influences, and used to dip into the rivers.
He washed himself, and hunted down the fish that circled around
in the waters, and he often also drank the water to put out the
heat burning inside of him. As for Chloe, after milking the ewes
and many of the goats, she worked for a long time curdling the
milk: the flies were terrible at harassing and stinging her when
they were not chased away. Then she washed off her face,
crowned herself with pine twigs, girdled herself with fawnskin,
and filling a pail with milk and wine, made a drink for Daphnis
and herself to share together.

[24] When it was midday, their eyes caught sight of each other,
and they were captivated. Chloe, seeing him naked, fell completely
for his beauty, and felt herself melting away, unable to find fault
with any part of him; and Daphnis, seeing her in fawnskin and
pine crown, as she held out the pail, thought that he was looking at a Nymph from the cave. He took the pine off her head
and crowned himself, after first kissing the crown; and when he
was naked and washing himself, she kissed his clothes and put
them on herself. They tossed apples at each other sometimes
and combed each other's hair, their tresses streaming down: she
compared his hair to myrtle because it was black, and he

compared her face to an apple because it was white and red. He would teach her to play the pipes, and as she would begin to blow, he used to snatch away the pipes, and run over the reeds with his own lips. He appeared to be instructing her whenever she would make a mistake, but really he was using the pipes as a ruse to kiss Chloe.

[25] As he played the pipes in the midday sun and as the flocks were lying in the shade, Chloe quietly slipped into a sleep, and Daphnis noticed this. Putting down his pipes, he looked at her, all of her, without satiety, without any shame. As he looked at her, he said softly: 'How beautiful her eyes are when she sleeps, how sweet her mouth is when she breathes! Neither apples nor pears compare to them. But I'm afraid to kiss her: kissing her stings my heart, and, like new honey, drives me mad. And I'm afraid that if I kiss her, I'll wake her up. Oh, these chattering cicadas: their loud cries will not let her sleep! The goats also are fighting and striking each other with their horns. Oh, those wolves: they are bigger cowards than foxes if they won't snatch them away!'

[26] While he was lost in these thoughts, a cicada, running away from a swallow that wanted to catch it, fell down the front of Chloe's clothes. The swallow followed closely, and was unable to capture it, but coming near Chloe in its pursuit, the swallow grazed her cheeks with its wings. She let out a huge yell, not knowing what had happened, and woke up with a start. When she saw the swallow still fluttering nearby, and Daphnis laughing at her fright, she put aside her fear, and rubbed her sleepy eyes. Then the cicada chirped out of her cleavage like a suppliant giving thanks for protection, and Chloe let out another loud shriek. Daphnis laughed and, seizing the opportunity, set his hands down between her breasts, and took out the dear cicada; and it still did not go silent even though it was in his hand. She was pleased, seeing this; she took up the cicada, gave it a kiss, and then again put it back chirping into her cleavage.

[27] One day, a wood pigeon singing a country song in the forest was entertaining them. When Chloe wanted to know what it

was saying, Daphnis taught her by reciting this well-known tale: 'There was a young woman, young woman, who was as beautiful as you, and who pastured many cattle in the wood, as you do. She was also fond of singing, and the cattle delighted in her music, and she tended them without sticks and goads: sitting under pine and crowning herself in pine, she sang about Pan and the Nymph Pine, and the cows lingered to hear her voice. A boy grazing his cattle nearby, a good-looking fellow and no less fond of singing than the young woman, entered into a musical competition with her. He responded to her song with a stronger voice, like a man's, but a sweet sound, like a boy's; charming eight of her best cattle into his own herd, he lured them away. The young girl was grieved by the damage to her herd and by the defeat of her song, and she prayed to the gods that she might become a bird before she arrived home. The gods were persuaded, and made her into this very bird, a mountain dweller like the young girl, and as musical as she was. Even now, in her song, she divulges her misfortune and her search for the lost cattle.'

[28] These were the kinds of pleasures that the summer gave them. When the autumn was at its height, however, and when the grapes were ripening, pirates from Pyrrha (who were using a Carian ship so that they would look like barbarians) arrived in the fields. Disembarking with their swords and breastplates, they seized everything that they put their hands upon: fragrant wines, wheat in abundance and honey in the combs. They also drove away some cattle from Dorcon's herd. They captured Daphnis, too, when he was wandering by the sea. (Chloe, being a girl, grazed Dryas' sheep later in the day because she was afraid of the arrogant shepherds.) Seeing a young man who was tall and handsome and a better value than their rustic loot, they no longer wasted time and effort on goats and other fields, but led him down to the ship crying and not knowing what to do and calling out loudly for Chloe. After cutting loose the cable and putting in their oars, they sailed into the sea, just as Chloe drove down her flock, bringing new pipes with her as a gift for Daphnis. Seeing the goats in a state of confusion and hearing Daphnis calling for her in a louder and louder voice, she forgot

the sheep, threw aside the pipes and ran off to Dorcon to ask
for help.

[29] But he lay there, knocked down by strong beatings from
the pirates; he could scarcely breathe, and was losing a lot of
blood. Seeing Chloe revived a little of the flame of his earlier
love. 'I shall die soon, Chloe,' he said. 'Those unholy pirates cut
me down like one of the cows when I was fighting for the cattle.
But you, I say, must keep Daphnis safe, avenge me and kill them.
I taught the cows to follow the sound of my pipes and to respond
to my song whenever they would stray far away. Go, take these
pipes, and blow on them that song I once taught Daphnis and
which Daphnis taught you. Leave the rest to the pipes and the
cows over there. I'm giving you the very pipes with which I
entered into many contests and defeated cowherds and goatherds. But you, in return for this, while I'm still alive, kiss me,
Chloe, and mourn for me when I die. And if you should see
another grazing the cows, then remember me.'

[30] These were Dorcon's last words. He kissed his last kiss, and
with this kiss and with these words, his life slipped out from
him. Chloe took up the pipes, placed them on her lips and played
them as loudly as she could. The cows heard her and recognized
the song, and, in one motion, they bellowed and leaped into the
sea. Since the violent leaping was on one side of the ship, and
since the cows' fall caused the sea to hollow out on that side,
the ship overturned and was destroyed by the enveloping waves.
They all fell out, but they didn't all have the same chance of
survival: the pirates had their swords hanging beside them, and
had put on breastplates covered with scales, and had worn
greaves above their ankles; Daphnis was barefoot, because he
had been grazing his flock in the plain, and half-naked, because
it was still the season of scorching heat. So, the pirates swam
for a short time, and were pulled down into the watery depths
by their weapons. Daphnis easily took off his clothes, but worked
hard at swimming, since he had gone swimming only in rivers
before; but in a while, he learned from necessity what had to be
done, and forced his way into the middle of the cows. Taking in

his two hands two horns of two cows, he was carried along in
the middle, without pain or effort, as if driving a wagon. In fact,
cows can swim like no man, and they are slower only than
waterbirds and, of course, fish. A cow, when swimming, will not
drown, unless its hooves fall away from being drenched through.
The proof of this observation is that to this day many places by
the sea are called Ox-ford.

[31] Daphnis was saved in this way, escaping beyond all hope
from two dangers, piracy and shipwreck. Coming out and
discovering Chloe on land, laughing and crying at the same time,
he fell into her arms and asked what she intended by playing
the pipes. She told him everything: her running to Dorcon, the
training given to the cows, how she was asked to play the pipes,
and that Dorcon was dead. Only their kiss she didn't mention,
out of embarrassment. They decided to honour their benefactor,
and going with his family and friends, they buried the unfortunate Dorcon. They piled on heaps of earth, planted many
pleasant plants and hung up the first fruits of their labour for
him. They also poured libations of milk, and pressed down the
grapes, and broke many pipes over his grave. A piteous bellowing was heard from the cows, and some were seen running
confusedly while they bellowed: these things were believed by
the shepherds and goatherds to be the cows lamenting for the
deceased cowherd.

[32] After Dorcon's funeral, Chloe washed Daphnis; for the bath,
she took him to the Nymphs, and led him into the cave. She
herself then, for the first time as he looked on, washed her own
body, which was white and pure in its beauty and hardly needed
a bath to make it more beautiful. Gathering together the flowers
that were in season, they placed garlands on the statues and
hung up Dorcon's pipes from the rock as a dedication. After this,
they went and looked for the goats and the sheep. They were all
lying down there, neither grazing nor bleating, but, I think, longing for the presence of the absent Daphnis and Chloe. When
they saw the animals and cried out their old cries and played
their pipes, the sheep stood up and started grazing, and the goats

snorted and pranced about, as if they were happy at the safe
return of their familiar goatherd. Yet Daphnis could not bring
himself to be happy now that he had seen Chloe naked and her
once-hidden beauty finally revealed. His heart was in such pain
that he felt it was being consumed by poisons. He was breathing
heavily, as if someone were pursuing him, and sometimes his
breath would fail him, as if it were all spent in the earlier attack.
The bath seemed to him to be more frightening than the sea. He
felt that his soul had remained among the pirates – he was young
and from the country and still ignorant of Love's piracies.

BOOK 2

[1] The autumn was now at its midpoint, the harvest was fast approaching and everyone was in the fields at work, readying the presses, cleaning out jars and weaving wicker baskets. Others were preparing their short hooks to cut the clusters, readying the stones to crush the ripest grapes and pounding dried twigs, so that the new wine might be drawn off at night before first light. Daphnis and Chloe forgot their goats and sheep and gave the others a helping hand. He carried the grapes in his baskets, threw them into the press and trod on them, and drew off the wine into jars, while she prepared the food for the pickers, brought the older wine for them to drink and picked the grapes off the lower vines. In Lesbos all the vine is low-lying, not the kind that shoots up high, and it is not a tree vine, but the branches extend downward close to the ground and trail like ivy; even a child whose hands are just out of its swaddling clothes can reach the clusters.

[2] As was the custom at the festival of Dionysus and the birth of wine, the women were summoned from the nearby fields to provide help. They cast their eyes on Daphnis and praised his beauty as equal to Dionysus', and one of the bolder ones even kissed him and goaded him on – Chloe was dismayed. Then the men around the presses hurled colourful remarks at Chloe, chanted maniacally like Satyrs around a bacchant and prayed to be her sheep and be tended by her, and she in turn was pleased – and Daphnis was dismayed. They both prayed that the harvest would quickly be over and that they could take up their customary haunts again, and that instead of this unmusical shouting

they could hear their pipes or their bleating flocks. And in a few days the vines had been picked, the jars did hold their new wine and there was no need any more for extra hands, so they drove their flocks into the plain and, with much rejoicing, they paid their respects to the Nymphs and offered them grape clusters still on branches as first fruits of the harvest. They never had shown indifference when they passed by the Nymphs before: when they led their flocks to pasture, they would always salute the Nymphs, and when they went out from the pasture, they would pay their respects and bring some offering, a flower or a fruit or green leaves or a libation of milk. Sometime later, they received their just reward from the gods in return for these things, but at that moment, they were, as the saying goes, dogs off the leash – leaping, piping, singing, they wrestled with their goats and sheep.

[3] While they were giving each other pleasure in this way, an old man approached, dressed in a goat's hair cloak and wearing leather shoes, and carrying a bag (such an old bag). He sat down beside them, and said, 'I am Philetas, my children, an old man who sang a good deal to these Nymphs here, and played the pipes many times to that Pan there, and I have led many herds of cows by my music alone. I have come to reveal to you what I have seen, to tell what I have heard. I have a garden, the work of my own hands, which I have cared for from the time I stopped herding because of old age. All the things that the seasons produce, my garden has each of them in due time. In the spring, it has roses and lilies and hyacinths and both kinds of violets; in the summer, poppies and pears and all kinds of fruit; and now, it has vines and figs and pomegranates and green myrtle. In the morning, flocks of birds come together in this garden, some come for food and some to sing; it's thickly covered and shaded and watered by three springs. If the fence were removed, the garden would look like a grove.

[4] 'When I went in at about noon today, I saw under the pomegranates and the myrtles a boy holding these same fruits. He was as white as milk and his hair was as golden as fire, and he

was glistening as if he'd just bathed. He was naked, alone, and was enjoying himself there picking fruit as if he was doing this in his own garden. So, I rushed forward to catch him, fearing that through his arrogance he'd break my myrtles and pomegranates, but he escaped very easily by running under the rose bushes or hiding under the poppies like a partridge chick. Now, I am used to chasing animals: I've had my hands full many times before in chasing suckling kids, and I've tired myself out many times in running after newborn calves. But this was some shifting thing, impossible to hunt down. Well, I grew tired, being an old man, and so, while I leaned on my stick and watched him in case he should escape, I asked him which of the neighbours was his father and what he thought he was doing by picking fruit in someone else's garden. But he didn't answer, and drawing near, he laughed very softly and threw the myrtle berries at me – and in some way or the other charmed me out of my anger. So I told him not to be afraid any more and begged him to come into my arms. And I swore by the myrtle berries that I'd let him go and give him apples and pomegranates as well and allow him always to pick whatever fruit and pluck whatever flowers he wanted, if I could get from him just one kiss!

[5] 'He laughed very loudly in response and let out a sound sweeter than any swallow's or any nightingale's or any swan's, even when the swan's as old as me: "It's no trouble for me to kiss you; I want to be kissed more than you want to become young again. But see if the gift is suitable for a man of your years. Old age will not save you from not pursuing me further after you've had your one kiss. I'm difficult to hunt, and swifter than hawks or doves or any bird faster than them. I am not a boy even though I seem to be one, but am older than Cronus and all time itself. I knew you in the prime of your youth when you tended the scattered herd on this mountain, and I sat beside you when you played the pipes beneath those beeches and were in love with Amaryllis, but you didn't see me though I was standing very close to the girl. So, I gave her to you, and now you have sons, good cowherds and farmers. But for the present I'm looking after Daphnis and Chloe, and after I bring them together in the

morning, I come to your garden and enjoy its flowers and fruit
and bathe in these springs. It is for this reason that your flowers
and fruit are beautiful; they are irrigated by the waters of my
bath. See for yourself whether any of your trees have been broken
down or if any fruit have been picked or if any flowers have
been trampled on or if any spring has been disturbed. And
consider yourself lucky that you alone among old men have seen
this boy."

[6] 'He finished speaking, and hopped up like a young nightingale
into the myrtle, and gliding from one bough to the next through
the leaves he ascended to the top. I saw the wings on his shoulders, the bow and arrows between his wings, and then I saw
none of these things or even him any more. If I have not grown
these grey hairs in vain, if in my old age I do not think useless
thoughts, then I say it is to Love, my children, that you are
consecrated, and Love cares for you.'

[7] They were very delighted and thought they had heard a story
rather than a true account, and they asked him what Love was,
whether boy or bird, and what power he had. So, Philetas spoke
again: 'Love, my children, is a god, young and beautiful and
winged; he rejoices in youth and pursues beauty and gives wings
to souls. He has more power than Zeus himself: he rules the
elements, he rules the stars, he rules over gods like himself. You
have less power over your sheep and goats. All flowers are the
work of Love, all the plants here are his creation, through him
rivers flow and winds blow. I myself have seen a bull in love and
he bellowed as if he were stung by a gadfly, and I have seen a
he-goat loving a she-goat and following it everywhere. I myself
was young once and loved Amaryllis, and I forgot about food
and didn't take any drink and sought no sleep: my soul fell sick,
my heart throbbed, my body shivered in the chill; I cried out as
if I were being beaten, I grew silent as if I'd become a corpse, I
threw myself into rivers as if I was on fire. I called on Pan for
help since he had himself loved the Nymph Pine; I praised Echo
for calling out "Amaryllis" after me; I broke my pipes because
they could charm the cows but couldn't lead Amaryllis to me.

There is no remedy, no cure, for Love, no drink, no food, no spells to chant, nothing – only kisses and embraces and lying down naked together.'

[8] Philetas instructed them in these matters and went away, taking from them some cheeses and a kid with little horns. Now that they were left alone to themselves and had heard for the first time the name of Love, they were distressed in their hearts, and as they wandered back at nightfall to their dwellings, they compared their own feelings to what they had heard: 'Lovers know sadness, and so do we. They do not care for food, and we don't care either. They are unable to sleep; that is what we also are suffering now. They seem to be on fire; there is a fire within us too. They desire to see each other; that is why we pray for day to come quickly. Perhaps, this is love, and we love one another but do not know it. Or is this love, and I alone am in love? Then why are we sad about the same things? And why are we looking for one another? It was true, all that Philetas said. The boy from the garden is the same one who appeared to our fathers in that dream and ordered that we tend their flocks. How might anyone catch him? He's small and will evade us. And how can anyone escape him? He has wings and will overtake us. We must flee to the Nymphs for help. But Pan did not help Philetas when he was in love with Amaryllis. All the cures he mentioned, that's what we need to look for – kisses and embraces and lying down naked on the ground. It will be very cold, but we are strong, like Philetas.'

[9] This was the lesson they learned at night. On the next day, they led their flocks to pasture, and when they saw each other, they kissed, which they had never done before, and throwing their arms around each other, they embraced, but they shrank back from the third remedy, removing their clothes and lying down; that was too bold not only for virgins, but also for young goatherds. So once again night led to sleeplessness and to reflection on what had happened and self-blame for what they had passed over: 'We kissed, and that was no help. We embraced, and that was nothing more. Perhaps, lying down together is the

only cure for love. We must try this as well. That will have more power than a kiss.'

[10] With such thoughts on their minds, it was natural that their dreams should also turn to love's pleasures and to kisses and embraces. And they did in their dreams what they did not do by day: they lay down with each other naked. So they were more possessed by Love's power when they woke up on the following morning, and they rushed to drive down their flocks to get to their kisses, and when they saw each other, they ran forward smiling. Then there were kisses, followed by arms and embraces, but the third remedy was slow to come, since Daphnis did not dare to say it and Chloe did not want to make the first move – until, by accident, they came to do this too.

[11] They were sitting near each other by the trunk of an oak, and having tasted the delight of kissing, insatiably they took their fill of the pleasure; they threw their arms about in order to embrace, and their lips met as they pressed their bodies together. Daphnis hugged Chloe very tightly and she fell over on her side, and he, following her kiss, lay down with her; and recognizing the picture from their dreams, they lay down for a long time as if bound together. They knew nothing of the future, and thought that this was the limit of love's pleasure; they wasted most of the day like this, and then separated, and drove back their flocks, hating nightfall. Perhaps, they would have made their way even to some of love's truths if the disturbance that followed had not seized the whole countryside. This is what happened.

[12] Wealthy young men from Methymna, wishing to mark the harvest by a pleasure trip away from home, launched a small ship and used their servants as rowers and sailed toward the fields of the Mytileneans that lie near the sea. The coast held out many safe harbours and was beautified with expensive houses, and everywhere there were baths and gardens and groves, some natural and others artificial, but all were fine places to spend one's youthful energy in. They sailed by or moored their ship along the coastline, but they did no harm, and indulged in diverse

pleasures: some with hooks attached to reeds fished, from a crag by the sea, with a thin line for fish beneath the rocks; others with dogs and nets hunted the hares that were escaping from the commotion in the vineyards; and some others thought about wild birds and set nets for wild geese and ducks and bustards, so that their pleasure pursuits also contributed to their table. If they needed anything more, they obtained it from the people in the fields, paying more obols than the goods were worth. They needed only bread and wine and shelter; they did not think it safe to spend the night at sea in that autumnal season, and so they hauled their ship to land because of their fear of storms at night.

[13] One of the rustics needed a rope to suspend the stone that crushed the trampled grapes, since his was now broken, and he quietly went down to the sea, reached the unguarded ship, untied the cable and took it home to use for his own needs. In the morning, the young Methymneans made a search for the rope, but since no one confessed to the theft, they complained about their bad hosts and sailed away. They sailed for about thirty stades and landed in the fields in which Daphnis and Chloe lived, since they thought that it was a good plain for hunting hares. Since they did not now have a rope to moor the vessel with, they twisted a long green willow shoot into a rope and with it they tied the stern of the ship to the land. Then, they released their dogs to hunt by scent and set their nets in the most promising trails. And the dogs ran up and down barking and frightened the goats, which abandoned the mountains and rushed down towards the sea. The boldest of the goats, finding nothing to eat in the sand, went straight for the ship and ate up the green shoot with which it was moored.

[14] And there was a slight swell in the sea, which was set in motion by the wind coming down from the mountains. Very soon the backwash of the wave lifted the untied boat and carried it out to the open sea. The Methymneans saw what was happening, and some of them rushed to the sea while others collected the dogs. All of them were shouting, so that all of those who

were in the fields nearby could hear them and come together to help. But it was no use; for the wind reached full force, and the ship was carried away with the current at uncontrollable speed. The Methymneans, having lost a great deal of property, looked for the man who herded the goats and found Daphnis and beat him and stripped him. One of them took a dog leash and twisted his arms behind his back in order to tie him up. And he cried out as he was being beaten and shouted out to the rustics and called out first of all to Lamon and Dryas for help. These hardened old men, made strong by farm labour, came and lent their support to Daphnis, and demanded that an inquiry be held into the events.

[15] And when the others also made the same demand, they appointed the cowherd Philetas as the judge; he was the oldest man present and had a reputation for exceptional honesty among the villagers. First, the Methymneans stated the case for the prosecution, with clarity and concision, because they knew they had a cowherd for judge: 'We came to these fields because we wanted to hunt. We tied our ship with the green vine and left it on the shore, and we ourselves set out for the hunt with the dogs. In the meantime, this man's goats came down to the sea and ate the vine and set loose the ship. Did you see it carried out to the sea? Do you know how many of our possessions were on it? So many clothes lost and equipment for the dogs and silver coins. With that much silver, a man could buy all these fields. For this, we demand the right to seize this worthless goatherd who puts his goats to pasture by the sea as if he were a sailor.'

[16] These were the charges made by the Methymneans. Daphnis was in a bad way because of the beating, but when he saw that Chloe was present, he dismissed all his bruises, and said: 'I know quite well how to pasture my goats. Not a single villager has ever blamed me because a goat of mine has grazed in his garden or crushed the tender vine. But these hunters are vile and their dogs are poorly trained, they run about too much and they bark bitterly and like wolves they drive my goats down from the hills and plains to the sea. "But the goats ate up the willow

shoot." And that's because they didn't have grass or wild strawberry or thyme in the sand. "But the ship was destroyed by the wind and the sea." Yes, and that is the work of the storm, not of the goats. "But the ship had clothes and money." And what sane person would believe that a ship carrying such a load would be held just by a willow shoot?'

[17] With these words, Daphnis burst into tears, and so completely moved the rustics to pity that Philetas the judge swore by Pan and the Nymphs that neither Daphnis nor his goats were in the wrong, but rather the sea and the wind, and over these, he said, there were other judges. Philetas' words did not convince the Methymneans, who in their anger dragged Daphnis away again and wanted to tie him up. The villagers were now annoyed, and set upon them like starlings or jackdaws, and quickly they freed Daphnis, who was fighting in his own right, and quickly they beat them with clubs and put them to flight. They did not cease until they had driven them across their borders and into the fields of others.

[18] While they were pursuing the Methymneans, Chloe led Daphnis gently to the cave of the Nymphs and bathed his face, which was stained with blood from a blow that broke his nose, and from her bag she took out a slice of bread and a piece of cheese and gave these to him to eat, and what was most refreshing of all, she kissed him a honey-sweet kiss with her soft lips.

[19] So close to disaster did Daphnis come on that occasion. And the matter did not end there. When the Methymneans came back to their homes, which they did with difficulty, this time by road rather than by sea, and with bruises rather than with revelry, they summoned an assembly of citizens and taking the role of suppliants, claimed that they had a right to vengeance. They said nothing that was true, lest they become a laughing stock for having been treated in such a humiliating way by mere shepherds, and they accused the Mytileneans of destroying their ship and plundering their money as if they had been at war. Their people believed them because of their wounds and thought it

right to avenge young men who came from prominent homes, and they voted for war against the Mytileneans, without an official declaration, and they ordered the general to launch ten ships for the purpose of making raids on their enemy's shore; since winter was near, it was not safe for them to entrust a larger fleet to the sea.

[20] Straightaway, on the next day, the general put out to sea with soldiers at the oars and raided the coastal farmlands of Mytilene, looting their sheep, their bread, their wine (the harvest had just come to an end), while seizing many of the men who were working there. He also attacked the fields of Chloe and Daphnis, and making a swift raid, drove off as booty whatever animals he encountered. Daphnis was not grazing his goats but had gone up to the wood to cut green leaves so that he might have food for the kids during the winter, with the result that he was up there when he saw the raid, and he hid himself in the hollow trunk of a dry beech tree. But Chloe was among her flocks; she was pursued, and fled to the Nymphs for protection, and she asked them in the name of the goddess to spare her and her flocks. But it was no use. The Methymneans violently ridiculed the statues and drove away the flocks and led off Chloe herself, beating her with willow shoots as if she were a goat or sheep.

[21] Now that their ships were filled with all kinds of plunder, they decided not to sail further but to make the voyage home, fearing both the weather and the enemy. So they sailed away and had to work hard at the oars because there was no wind. As for Daphnis, when it was quiet again, he went down to the plain where they used to graze the flocks, but did not see the goats and the sheep and could not find Chloe. Everything was deserted, and the pipes that Chloe liked were lying thrown on the ground. Crying out loudly and wailing pitifully, he ran to the beech tree where they used to sit, then to the sea in order to see her, and then to the Nymphs, where she had fled when she was being pursued. There he threw himself down on the ground and blamed the Nymphs and called them traitors:

[22] 'Chloe was snatched away from you, and you could bear to see this? She wove garlands for you, she poured libations of new milk for you, she dedicated these very pipes here to you. No wolf has ever seized a goat of mine, but enemies have snatched away the flock and the girl who used to look after it with me, and they will skin the goats and slaughter the sheep, and Chloe will live in the city from now on. How can I walk back to my father and my mother without the goats, without Chloe, without any work? I have nothing to look after. I'll lie down here and wait for death or another war. And you, Chloe, do you feel the same way? Do you remember this plain and these Nymphs – and me? Or are you at least comforted by the sheep and the goats that were captured with you?'

[23] As Daphnis said these words, a deep sleep took him away from his tears and his pain, and the three Nymphs seemed to stand before him, tall women and beautiful, semi-naked and barefoot, their hair loose, just like the statues. At first, they seemed to take pity on Daphnis; then the eldest spoke and encouraged him: 'Don't blame us, Daphnis. We care for Chloe more than you do. We cared for her even when she was a child, and we saw to her nurture when she was lying in this cave. Even now, we are seeing to her well-being: she will not be carried off to Methymna to become a slave and she will not become a part of the enemy's loot. And that Pan there who stands beneath the pine tree, whom you never honoured with so much as a flower, we asked him to be Chloe's protector. He is accustomed more to the military than we are and he has left his country home to fight in many wars, and when they attack him, the Methymneans will see that he is no soft enemy. Don't wear yourself down with your anxieties, but get up and show yourself to Lamon and Myrtale, who are lying on the ground thinking that you also are part of the plunder. Chloe will come back to you tomorrow with the goats and the sheep, and you will pasture your herds together and play the pipes together. Love will take care of the rest for you.'

[24] Daphnis saw and heard these things, and leaped up from his sleep, and weeping tears of pleasure and grief, he kneeled

down before the statues and promised that if Chloe were saved, he would sacrifice the best of the she-goats. He ran to the pine tree where the statue of Pan stood, goat-limbed, horned, holding pipes in one hand and a frisky he-goat in the other, and he knelt down before him too and prayed for Chloe and promised to sacrifice a he-goat, and it was only at sunset that, with difficulty, he put a stop to his tears and prayers. He picked up the leaves he had cut and went back to the farm to Lamon's family, relieved them of their sorrow and filled them with joy, and ate some food and fell asleep, crying softly, and he prayed to see the Nymphs again in a dream, prayed for the day to come quickly, the day on which they had promised him Chloe. Of all nights, that one seemed to him the longest. But what happened in the night was this.

[25] After the general of the Methymneans sailed for ten stades, he wished to give his soldiers a rest because they were weary from their raiding. So he decided on a promontory that stretched out over the sea in the form of an extended crescent inside of which the sea afforded a calmer anchorage than any harbour. He anchored the ships here in deeper water so that none of the peasants might do any harm from the land, and he let the Methymneans go out to indulge their pleasures in peace. Since they had an abundance of all things because of their plunder, they drank, they played and they held a victory festival as it were. The day had just come to a close, and the night was putting an end to their pleasures, when suddenly the whole earth seemed to be blazing with fire, and they heard the dashing and crashing of oars as if a large fleet was about to attack. Someone shouted the call to arms, someone else yelled out for the general, some thought they were wounded and others lay down as though they had died. It was as if they were seeing a night-time battle, but with no enemy there.

[26] The night that passed was like this, but the day that followed was more frightful than the night. Daphnis' he-goats and she-goats had flowering ivy on their horns, and Chloe's rams and ewes howled like wolves. And she herself could be seen, crowned

with pine. Many incredible things happened in the sea itself. The
anchors remained stuck in the deep when men tried to raise
them; the oars shattered when they were lowered for rowing;
and dolphins, leaping out of the brine, struck the ships with their
tails and loosened the bolts and timbers. Above the steep cliff
that was under the headland, the sound of pipes was heard, not
the pleasant sound that comes from pipes, but the terrifying din
of war trumpets. They were thrown into confusion and ran to
their arms and called upon their enemies, though they could not
see any. They prayed that night would return, so that they might
obtain a truce. Those who had any intelligence saw clearly that
all the things that had happened, the apparitions and the sounds,
were the work of Pan, who was angry with the sailors for some
reason, though they couldn't understand why, since they hadn't
pillaged any sanctuary of Pan – then at midday, when the general
fell asleep, thanks to divine intervention, Pan himself appeared
to him and spoke as follows:

[27] 'You are the most impious and irreverent of men – why did
you dare to commit such insane, reckless actions? You have filled
these lands and fields of mine with war, you have driven away
the herds of cows and sheep and goats that were in my care, you
have torn from the altars a virgin whom Love wishes to place
at the heart of a story, you showed no shame before the Nymphs
as they looked on, nor before me. You will not see Methymna
again if you sail away with your loot, nor will you escape these
pipes that panicked you. I will drown you and turn you into
food for fish unless you, very quickly, restore Chloe to the
Nymphs and the flocks to Chloe, goats and sheep both. Get up
and take the girl ashore with the animals I mentioned, and I
myself will guide you by sea and guide her by land.'

[28] Bryaxis, the general, was very greatly disturbed. He leaped
up and summoned the captains of the ships and ordered them
to search immediately for Chloe among the captives. They found
her shortly and brought her into his presence; she had been
sitting down, with the crown of pine on her head. He considered
this sign a confirmation of what he had seen in his dream, and

brought her to land in his own flagship. As soon as she disembarked, the sound of the pipes was heard again from the rock;
it was not, as before, the sound of war and horror, but was rather
the pastoral tune that leads flocks to pasture. The sheep ran
down the gangway slipping on their horned hooves and the goats
ran as well, but more boldly, since they were used to steep rocks.

[29] All these animals stood around Chloe in a circle, like a
chorus, skipping and bleating and showing signs of their pleasure; but the goats of the other shepherds and the sheep and the
cattle remained in their place in the hold of the ship, as though
the melody had not entranced them. Everyone was struck with
amazement and cried out for Pan – but then something even
more amazing than these things was seen in both the elements.
Before the Methymneans had raised their anchors, the ships set
sail, and a dolphin leaped out of the sea and led the flagship,
while the sweet sound of pipes guided the goats and sheep,
though no one saw the piper, and sheep and goats went forward
together and grazed, evidently pleased by the melody.

[30] It was roughly the time for the second grazing when Daphnis, looking out from a high rock, saw the flocks and Chloe. He
cried out loudly 'Nymphs and Pan!', ran down to the plain,
embraced Chloe and collapsed in a faint. Chloe's kisses and
warm embraces slowly restored his life to him, and then he went
to their old oak tree and sat by the trunk and asked how she
had escaped from so many enemies. She told him everything:
the ivy on the goats, the howls of the sheep, the pine flowering
on her head, the fire on land, the noise at sea, the two kinds of
piping (one warlike, the other peaceful), the frightful night, and
how the music guided her back on the road though she did not
know the way. Daphnis recognized his dream of the Nymphs
and the work of Pan in this, and he himself told her all that he
had seen, all that he had heard, and how he was saved by the
Nymphs when he was on the verge of death. And then he sent
Chloe to fetch Dryas and Lamon and their families and the
materials for a sacrifice. In the meantime, he took the best of
the she-goats and crowned it with ivy, just as it had appeared to

the enemy, and pouring an offering of milk on its horns, he sacrificed it to the Nymphs, and then he hung up the carcass, skinned it and made a dedication of the hide.

[31] After Chloe and the others arrived, he lit a fire, boiled a part of the meat, roasted the remainder, and then he presented the first portions to the Nymphs and poured a bowl of sweet new wine as an offering. He spread out a bed of leaves, and then gave himself over to food and drink and play, and at the same time he kept an eye on the flocks so that no wolf might attack them and imitate the enemy's work. They also sang some songs to the Nymphs, the compositions of shepherds from long ago. When night came, they slept in the field, and on the following day they directed their minds to Pan. They crowned the leader of the goats with pine and led him to the pine tree, and they poured offerings of wine, celebrated the god, and then sacrificed the goat, hung it up, and skinned it. And they boiled and roasted the flesh and set it on leaves in a nearby meadow, and they fixed the skin with its horns on the pine tree by the statue, a dedication made by rustics to a rustic god. They made an offering of the first portions of the flesh, and poured offerings from a larger bowl. Chloe sang, Daphnis played the pipes.

[32] They reclined afterward and began to eat. The cowherd Philetas approached, bringing, by chance, some small garlands to Pan and clusters of grapes on vines with the leaves still on them, and he was followed by his youngest son, Tityrus, a boy with red hair, bluish green eyes and pale skin, and also high-spirited, who walked along bouncing lightly like a kid. So they leaped up and together they garlanded Pan and they hung the vines on the foliage of the pine. Then they made the others recline nearby and drink together, and like old men when they are quite drunk, they told each other many stories, how they went grazing when young, how they escaped all those pirate raids; someone boasted that he had killed a wolf, and someone else (actually, this was Philetas' boast) that in playing the pipes he was second only to Pan.

[33] So Daphnis and Chloe pleaded with him in every way to share his skill with them and to play his pipes, since they were celebrating a god who enjoyed pipes. Philetas answered that he was short of breath because of old age, but he still promised to play and took up Daphnis' pipes. But these were too small for his great skill, and were suitable rather to be blown on by a boy, with a boy's mouth. So he sent Tityrus to fetch his own pipes from his farm, which was ten stades away. The boy threw off his coat and set off at a run, just like a fawn, while Lamon meanwhile promised them that he would relate the story of the pipes which a Sicilian goatherd had sung to him for the cost of a goat and pipes:

[34] 'These pipes were, in the old days, not an instrument but rather a beautiful girl who had a lovely, melodious voice. She used to graze her goats, play with the Nymphs or sing, as she does now. When she was grazing, playing and singing, Pan approached her and tried to persuade her to do what he desired by promising that all her she-goats would give birth to twins. But she laughed at his love and said that she would not accept a lover who was neither fully goat nor fully human. Pan gave chase and attempted to take her by force. Syrinx fled Pan and his violence; she fled and grew tired of fleeing, and so hid among reeds, and then disappeared into a marsh. Pan angrily cut down the reeds, but did not find the girl. Then he understood her suffering and invented the instrument: he bound together reeds of unequal length, because their love was also unequal, and blew into the reeds. So what was once a beautiful girl has now become a set of melodious pipes.'

[35] Lamon had just stopped narrating his tale and Philetas was thanking him for telling a story that was sweeter than song, when Tityrus arrived, bringing his father's pipes, a large instrument of large reeds, and decorated with bronze where the reeds were joined with wax. It felt like the very thing that Pan first put together. So Philetas rose and sat upright in a chair, and tried to see, first, if he could blow through the reeds; then, when he saw that his breath raced through unhindered, he blew on them

with full force and vigour. You might have imagined that you had heard many flutes playing together, so great a sound did his pipes make. Little by little, he reduced his force and changed to a sweeter melody and showed every skill in pastoral music; he piped a tune suitable for a herd of cows, another proper to goats, and a third that pleased the sheep. The music for the sheep was sweet, for the cows loud, and for the goats sharp. In a word, his one set of pipes imitated all pipes.

[36] The others lay there, hushed, delighted. But Dryas stood up and asked him to play a Dionysian tune and danced a dance of the harvest for them. First, he danced like a man picking the grapes, then like someone carrying the baskets, then someone treading the vines, then filling the jars, then drinking the sweet new wine. All these Dryas danced so gracefully and so vividly that they thought they were looking at the vines and the press and the jars and Dryas actually drinking.

[37] So then he was the third old man to win acclaim, this time for his dancing, and he kissed Chloe and Daphnis, who got up quickly and danced Lamon's story. Daphnis imitated Pan, and Chloe Syrinx. He begged and urged, and she smiled and feigned indifference; running on tiptoe to give the impression of having hooves, he pursued her, and she gave the appearance of being tired by running away. Then Chloe hid in the wood as if this was the marsh, and Daphnis took Philetas' large pipes and played a mournful song, like a lover, then a seductive song, like a seducer, then an exhortation, like a searcher. Philetas was amazed and leaped up, kissed him, and kissing him again, gave him the pipes as a gift, praying that Daphnis too would leave them with an equally worthy successor.

[38] Daphnis dedicated his own pipes, a small set, to Pan, and kissed Chloe, as though he had found her after a chase that was real, and he drove away his flock, piping beneath the darkening sky. Chloe also drove away her flock, guiding them by the tune of the pipes. The goats walked close to the sheep, and Daphnis walked near Chloe, so that they took their fill of each other until

nightfall. And they agreed to drive down their flocks earlier the next day: and so they did, coming at daybreak to the pasture and offering salutations to the Nymphs and to Pan. Then they sat under the oak tree, and they piped, kissing and embracing each other and lying down together. But they did nothing more, and got up again. Then they turned their minds to food and drank wine mixed with milk.

[39] As the result of all this, they grew hotter and bolder, and they competed with each other in a contest of love, and in little time they progressed to swearing oaths of fidelity. Daphnis went to the pine tree and swore by Pan that he would not live alone without Chloe, not even for a single day, and Chloe went into the cave and swore by the Nymphs that all she desired was to be with Daphnis in life and death. But such was Chloe's simplicity (she was a girl) that when she left the cave, she asked him for a second oath, saying, 'Daphnis, Pan is a god of love and is unreliable: he was in love with the Nymph Pine, he was in love with Syrinx, but he never stops troubling the Dryads and annoying the Nymphs who guard the flocks. If you are careless about keeping your oaths, he will be careless about punishing you, even if you should go to more women than there are reeds in the pipes. Swear to me by this herd of goats and by that she-goat that nurtured you that you will not leave Chloe behind as long as she remains faithful to you. But if she wrongs you and the Nymphs, then shun her, loathe her, kill her like a wolf.' Daphnis was pleased at her lack of trust. He stood in the middle of the herd and, holding a he-goat in one hand and a she-goat in the other, swore that he would love Chloe as she loved him, and that if she preferred another man to Daphnis, he would kill himself instead of her. She was thrilled and trusted him: she was a girl and a shepherd and she believed that, for shepherds and goatherds, goats and sheep were proper gods.

BOOK 3

[1] When the Mytileneans learned of the attack made by the ten ships, and when some people from the fields informed them about the plundering, they thought that the outrages of the Methymneans were intolerable, and decided to take arms against them as quickly as possible. They enrolled three thousand soldiers and five hundred cavalry and sent them under the command of the general Hippasus, by land, since they were hesitant to hazard the sea in winter.

[2] He set out but did not raid the fields of the Methymneans, nor did he seize the flocks or plunder the farmers and shepherds of their other possessions, because he thought such actions suited a pirate more than a general. He made directly for the city itself, hoping to smash through the gates while they were unguarded. He was about a hundred stades short when he was met by a herald offering the terms of a truce. The Methymneans had learned from their captives that the Mytileneans did not know about the things that had happened, and that farmers and shepherds had taken action against young men who had treated them outrageously. They began to regret their action against a neighbouring city as hasty rather than sensible, and they were ready to give back all their spoils and to resume safe relations by land and sea. Hippasus sent the herald on to Mytilene, although he had been appointed a general with full powers, and himself pitched camp about ten stades from Methymna and waited for orders from his city. After two days, a messenger arrived with orders for him to take back the plundered goods and come home without doing any harm.

Given a choice between war and peace, they found peace more profitable.

[3] So ended the war between the Methymneans and Mytileneans, the beginning and the end of which were entirely unexpected. For Daphnis and Chloe, however, the winter that arrived was more bitter than war. All of a sudden, the snow fell thick and fast and blocked the roads and locked the farmers in their homes. Roaring rivers rushed down, the ice froze hard and the trees seemed bowed low and at the point of breaking: all the land disappeared from sight except around a few fountains and streams. No one took his flock to pasture or himself went out of doors, but instead they lit a big fire at cock's crow and used to spin flax or weave goats' hair or devise snares for birds. At that time, they took care to supply the cows in the mangers with chaff to eat, the sheep and the goats in the folds with leaves, and the sties of the pigs with acorns.

[4] Since everyone needed to stay at home, the other farmers and herdsmen took pleasure in the brief respite from work, and they enjoyed taking their meals in the morning and at night and sleeping long hours: to them the winter was sweeter than summer, autumn, and even spring. But Chloe and Daphnis remembered the pleasures they had had to leave behind, their kisses, their caresses and their meals together. They passed sleepless nights and grievous days waiting for the spring to restore them to life after death. They felt the pain anew each time they touched a sack from which they had eaten, or if they saw a pail from which they had drunk together, or saw the pipes (once a lover's gift) flung aside without care. They prayed to the Nymphs and to Pan to release them from these evils and to show the sun again to them and their flocks, and at the same time they prayed that they might find some way to see each other once more. Chloe was completely at a loss and resourceless, since her foster mother was always with her, teaching her to card wool and turn the spindles, and was prattling on about marriage. Daphnis, on the other hand, had greater leisure, and he was cleverer than a girl, so he came up with the following plan to see Chloe.

[5] In front of Dryas' farm, next to the farmhouse itself, there grew two myrtles and some sprays of ivy. The myrtle trees stood near each other, while the ivy grew between them so that it extended its tendrils on either side like a vine and, by entwining its leaves with theirs, formed a sort of cave, while a cluster of berries hung down, as numerous and as swollen as grapes on vine branches. Flocks of birds hovered around the ivy in winter because of the lack of food outside, lots of blackbirds and thrushes, wood pigeons, starlings, and the other birds that feed on ivy berries. Saying that he intended to hunt these birds, Daphnis filled his bag with honeyed cakes and set out, and to lull suspicion took along birdlime and snares. Although the distance between the two places was no more than ten stades, the snow was still frozen and made the going hard. But love knows no bar, not fire nor water nor Scythian snow.

[6] So, at a run, he came to the farm, and shaking off the snow from his legs, he set his snares, smeared long twigs with birdlime, and then sat down to wait for birds and for Chloe. The birds came in large numbers, and many were caught, enough to occupy him while he picked them up and killed and plucked them. Still, no one came out of the farm, not a man, woman or barnyard fowl. All of them were lingering by the fire, shut up indoors, and Daphnis was completely at a loss and thought that he had come at an ill-omened moment. He summoned up the courage to invent an excuse to push through the doors, and thought hard about the most convincing thing that he could say.

'I've come to get a light to kindle our fire.'

'But you have neighbours less than a stade away.'

'I came to ask for bread.'

'But your bag is stuffed with food.'

'I want some wine.'

'But just the other day you had the grape harvest.'

'A wolf has chased me.'

'But where are the wolf's tracks?'

'I came to hunt for birds.'

'So why don't you go home now that you've finished hunting?'

'I want to see Chloe.'

'But who would confess this to a girl's father and mother?'

Coming up against obstacles everywhere he turned, he thought to himself, 'Everything I say sounds suspicious. Silence would be better. I'll see Chloe in the spring, since I'm not fated, it seems, to see her in the winter.' He thought about his plight in this manner, and silently picking up his catch, he started to go away – when, as if Love took pity on him, something happened.

[7] Dryas and his family were at the table. The meat was carved, the loaves of bread were set out, the wine was mixed. One of the sheepdogs, watching for the right moment, snatched a piece of meat and fled through the doors. Dryas was annoyed, especially since it was his portion, and took up a club and gave chase, following in its tracks, like a dog. He had chased it up to the ivy when he saw Daphnis throwing his catch over his shoulders, preparing to hurry away. He immediately forgot about his meat and dog, shouted out a loud hello to the boy, embraced and kissed him, took him by the hand, and led him back into the house. When the lovers saw each other, they almost collapsed to the ground, but finding the strength to stand upright, they greeted and kissed each other, which is what supported them and kept them from falling down.

[8] Surpassing all his own expectations, then, Daphnis won both a kiss and Chloe too, and sitting down near the fire, he unloaded from his shoulders on to the table the wood pigeons and the thrushes, and he described how, vexed at being forced to stay indoors, he had gone hunting, and how, with snares and birdlime, he had caught the birds that were pecking at the myrtle berries and the ivy. They praised his energy and told him to eat what the dog had left behind. They told Chloe to pour him a drink, and she gladly served them, the others first and then Daphnis, and she pretended to be angry that although he had come so far he was ready to run away without seeing her. Nevertheless, she took a small sip before she handed the drink to him, and he, despite his thirst, took his time with it, drawing out the pleasure as much as possible.

[9] Then the table was quickly cleared of bread and meat, and while they remained sitting there, they asked after Myrtale and Lamon and praised their good fortune in having such a son to care for them in their old age. Daphnis was pleased that Chloe should hear these praises, and when they pressed him to stay for the sacrifice of Dionysus the next day, he was so full of joy that he almost kneeled down to worship them instead of Dionysus. He immediately drew out many honeyed cakes from his bag, and the birds he had caught, and they prepared them for their evening meal, and another bowl of wine was set out, and a second fire was kindled, and since night was fast approaching, they put out a second meal, after which they told stories and sang songs, until they went to sleep, Chloe with her mother, Dryas with Daphnis. Chloe found little profit in this arrangement except that she would get to see Daphnis the following day, but Daphnis, on the other hand, enjoyed an empty pleasure: he thought it was delightful to sleep even with Chloe's father, so he threw his arms around him and kissed him repeatedly, dreaming that he was doing all this to Chloe.

[10] At daybreak, the cold was exceedingly sharp, and the north wind was freezing, the land dry, but they got up and sacrificed a yearling ram to Dionysus, and they lit a large fire and made the meal ready. While Nape baked the bread and Dryas boiled the ram, Daphnis and Chloe took advantage of the leisure time and went out of the farm to where the ivy grew, and they set the snares again, and smeared birdlime, and hunted a large number of birds. And they enjoyed their continual kissing, their sweet talk:

'I came to see *you*, Chloe.'

'I know, Daphnis.'

'It's for you that I'm killing these poor blackbirds.'

'What can I do to show you that I –?'

'Remember me.'

'I do, I remember you by the Nymphs whom I swore by in the cave. We'll go there again as soon as the snow melts.'

'But there is so much of it, Chloe, I'm afraid that I'll melt before the snow does.'

'Courage, Daphnis, the sun is hot.'
'I wish that it were as hot, Chloe, as the fire that burns my heart.'
'You're joking, now; you mock me.'
'No, I'm not, by the goats you told me to swear by.'

[11] In this way, Chloe answered Daphnis' questions, like an echo. When Nape called them, they ran inside, bringing a bigger catch than they had the day before, and after offering the first of the wine to Dionysus, they crowned their heads with ivy and ate their meal. And when it was time, the family cried out 'Iacchus!' and 'Evoe!', and sent Daphnis on his way, filling his bag with bread and meat. They also gave him the wood pigeons and thrushes to take to Lamon and Myrtale, and said that they would catch more all through the winter as long as the ivy berries lasted. And then he left, kissing the others first and Chloe last, so that her kiss would remain pure and unsullied on his lips. He made many other visits, on various pretexts, so that for them the winter was not entirely loveless.

[12] And when at last spring began to come in, the snow started to melt, the earth was laid bare, the grass was starting to grow and the shepherds led their flocks to pasture, but ahead of all the others were Daphnis and Chloe, the slaves of a greater shepherd. And at once they ran to the Nymphs and the cave, then to Pan and the pine, and then to the oak, under which they sat and grazed their flocks and kissed each other. Then they looked for flowers, since they desired to put garlands on the gods, but these were only just being encouraged to grow by the nourishing breath of the west wind and the warmth of the sun; still, they found violets and narcissus and pimpernel and the other first fruits of spring. They also obtained new milk from the she-goats and ewes, and placing garlands of flowers on the statues, they poured the milk as an offering to them. Then they made an offering of the music of their pipes, as though they were challenging the nightingales to sing, and they in turn warbled softly in the bushes, and little by little perfected their 'Itys', as if they were remembering the song after a long silence.

[13] Here and there, the flocks of sheep were bleating, and the lambs were frisking, and they knelt under their mothers and sucked the teats. The rams chased the ewes that had not yet lambed: getting the females in position underneath, the males mounted them. The he-goats were, if anything, more passionate in chasing the she-goats and leaping on to them, and they also fought over the she-goats, each he-goat keeping his own females and guarding them against any secret adultery. Such a spectacle would have stirred vehement desires even in old men; as it is, Daphnis and Chloe were young and bursting with vigour and had been searching for love for a long time already, and they were set on fire by what they heard and close to collapse through what they saw, and they too, and especially Daphnis, were yearning for something more than kisses and embraces. He felt that he had been wasting his youth in the winter, languishing indolently at home, and at that moment he was passionate with his kisses, full of lust in his embraces, continually craving more, and bolder than ever.

[14] He asked Chloe to give him everything he desired and that they both lie down naked together for a longer period than they used to before: this was the one thing left from Philetas' instructions, to bring forth the only antidote for love. She asked what more there could be than kisses and embraces and lying down together, and what he had decided to do when they were lying down naked together. 'What the rams do to the ewes,' he said, 'and the he-goats to the she-goats. Don't you see how, after they've done the thing they do, the females don't run away from the males any more and the males don't have the labour of chasing the females? But they graze together in future as if they had together enjoyed the same pleasure. That thing they do must be something sweet, something that wipes out the bitterness of love.' 'But, Daphnis, do you not see the she-goats and the he-goats or the rams and the ewes, don't you see that the males do it standing up and the females also take it standing up? The males leap on the females, the females carry them on their backs. But you're asking that I should lie down and do all this with you, and while naked too? Those animals are much shaggier than I

am when I'm fully clothed.' Daphnis was persuaded by her; he
lay down next to her for a long time, but he didn't know how
to do what he hotly desired, so he made her stand up and clung
to her from behind in imitation of the he-goats. But now he was
even more perplexed, and he sat down and cried because he
was more foolish than rams in making love.

[15] He had a neighbour, one Chromis by name, who farmed
his own land, and was now past his prime. This Chromis had a
wife, imported from the city, who was young and pretty and a
little too chic for the country: her name was Lycaenion. Every
day, she saw Daphnis driving his goats, in the morning to pasture
and at night back home again, and she desired to entice him
with gifts and take him as a lover. On one occasion, she ambushed
him when he was alone and gave him as a gift a set of pipes and
honey in the comb and a deerskin bag, but she hesitated to say
anything because she saw that he was very attached to the girl
and surmised that he was in love with Chloe. She had guessed
that this was so earlier, because of the nodding and the laughter.
But then she went out one morning pretending to Chromis that
she was going to help a neighbour who was about to give birth.
She followed Daphnis and Chloe closely from behind, and from
behind some bushes where she would not be seen, she heard
everything they said and saw whatever they did, and she took
good notice of Daphnis' tears. She felt sorry for them in their
agony and thought that here was a double opportunity, to deliver
them from their troubles and to satisfy her own desire. This was
the plan she devised.

[16] On the following day, again pretending that she was going
to the woman who was about to give birth, she went openly to
the oak tree where Daphnis and Chloe were sitting, and gave a
choice imitation of a woman in distress. 'Save me, Daphnis,' she
said. 'I'm in trouble. I had twenty geese, and an eagle snatched
the best one, then it couldn't lift it up to his high rock over there
because it was so heavy, and now the eagle has fallen down with
it into this wood over here. In the name of the Nymphs and Pan
over there, please come into the wood with me – I'm afraid to

go alone – and save my goose. Don't let the geese be without
one of their number. Perhaps you'll kill the eagle also, and he'll
no longer snatch so many of your lambs and kids. Chloe will
look after your flock in the meantime; the goats must know her
well; after all, she's always with you when you take them to
pasture.'

[17] Not in the least suspicious about what was to come, Daphnis got up right away, picked up his staff and followed behind
Lycaenion. She led him as far as possible from Chloe, and when
they were in the thickest part of the wood, she told him to sit
down near a stream, and said, 'Daphnis, you're in love with
Chloe. I learned this from the Nymphs in a dream last night.
They told me how you cried yesterday and they told me to save
you by teaching you how to make love. Love is not kisses and
embraces and what rams and he-goats do. There is leaping, but
it is far sweeter than theirs, because it takes longer and gives a
longer pleasure. If you would like to be freed from your troubles
and experience the pleasures you are looking for, then come,
give yourself to me as my student, I will teach you your lessons
and oblige those Nymphs.'

[18] Daphnis could no longer hold out, in his pleasure: since he
was a rustic and a goatherd, a lover and a youth, he flung himself
at her feet, and begged Lycaenion to teach him as quickly as
possible the skill through which he could do what he wanted to
Chloe. As if he were going to be taught something truly great
and heaven-sent, he promised to give her a suckling kid and soft
cheeses made from a goat's first milk and the goat as well. Lycaenion found him to be a goatherd through and through, more than
she had expected, and she began to teach Daphnis in the following way: she told him to sit down beside her, as he was, and to
kiss her as often and as warmly as he usually did, and at the same
time as he was kissing her, to embrace her and to lie down with
her on the ground. When he had sat down and kissed her and
lain down, she discovered that he was aroused and bursting with
desire, and so she raised him up from where he was reclining on
his side, placed herself underneath and skilfully guided him on

the road that he had long sought. She did nothing exotic then, and for the rest, nature itself taught him what needed to be done.

[19] When the lesson in love was complete, Daphnis, ever the shepherd, was eager to run to Chloe and immediately practise what he had learned, as if afraid that he would forget it if he delayed, but Lycaenion held him back, and said, 'You still need to learn something, Daphnis. I happen to be a woman, and I haven't suffered any hurt now, because, a long time ago, another man taught me this lesson and took my virginity as his payment. But when Chloe wrestles with you in this kind of wrestling match, she will cry out and weep and will lie there bleeding heavily. Don't be afraid of the blood. When you have persuaded her to give herself to you, lead her to this place, where even if she shouts out, no one will hear her, and if she cries, no one will see her, and if she bleeds, she can wash in the spring. But remember that I made you a man before Chloe.'

[20] After Lycaenion had tendered this advice, she went off to another part of the wood, as if she were still looking for her goose, but Daphnis reflected on what she had said and lost his earlier feelings of urgency, and he declined to trouble Chloe for more kisses and embraces, not wanting her to cry out against him as she would at an enemy, or weep as if she had been hurt, or bleed as if she were wounded. He had just learned about the blood and was frightened by it, since he thought that blood came only from wounds. Deciding to take just his usual pleasures with her, he went out of the wood and came to the place where she was sitting, weaving a little garland of violets. He told her a lie about snatching the goose from the eagle's talons, and then holding her close, he kissed her just as he had kissed Lycaenion in their moments of pleasure. He allowed himself that much, because it was not dangerous. She fitted the garland on his head, kissed his hair, which she said was better than violets, and from her bag she took out a piece of cake and some bread and gave this to him to eat, and while he was eating, she snatched pieces from his mouth and ate them herself like a fledgling.

[21] While they were eating, and it has to be said that they were kissing more than eating, they saw a fishing boat sail by. There was no wind, and the sea was calm, and the sailors must have decided to row – and they were rowing with all their strength since they were hurrying in order to bring their newly caught fish as fresh as possible to the city for one of the rich men there. And as sailors often do to take their minds off work, they lifted their oars while the cox called out sailors' songs to them, and the rest of them like a chorus shouted out in unison in intervals following the beat of his voice. When they sang like this in the open sea, their shouts were inaudible, since the sound dispersed over a large expanse of air. But when they ran in under a headland and rowed into a crescent-shaped curving bay, the shouting rang out louder and the cox's songs travelled clearly up to the land. A deep glen lay above the plain and received the sound into itself, like a musical instrument, only to send out again a precise imitation of every word and noise, the splash of the oars and the voices of the sailors. What a pleasure it was to hear! The sound came first from the sea and then from the land, and the later the sound began on land, the more slowly it faded away.

[22] Daphnis, understanding what was happening, paid attention only to the sea, and took pleasure in watching the ship as it ran past the plain faster than a bird, and he tried to hold on to some of the songs to fit the melodies to his pipes. But Chloe, experiencing for the first time what we might call an echo, gazed first at the sea and the sailors who were calling out, and then she turned to the wood to see who was answering their songs. When they had sailed by and there was silence even in the glen, she asked Daphnis whether there was another sea behind the headland and another ship sailing by and other sailors who sang the same songs and fell silent all at the same time. Daphnis laughed at her sweetly and kissed her a kiss that was sweeter still; then he placed the garland of ivy on her and began to tell her the story of the echo, asking for ten more kisses as the price of his teaching:

[23] 'There is, my girl, a large family of Nymphs: there are Nymphs of Ash and Nymphs of Oak and Nymphs of the Meadow, all

are beautiful and all are musical. Echo was the daughter of one
of them, and she was a mortal born from a mortal father, but
she was also beautiful because of her beautiful mother. The
Nymphs raised her, the Muses taught her to play the pipes, the
flute, the lyre, the cithara, and all manner of song. When the girl
reached her bloom, she danced with the Nymphs and sang with
the Muses, but she fled at the sight of all males, human and
divine, because she loved her virginity. But Pan was angry with
the girl; he was jealous of her music and unable to touch her
beauty, and so he visited such madness on the shepherds and
goatherds that like dogs and wolves they tore her apart and
scattered her limbs, still singing, all over the earth. Earth hid all
her limbs and preserved her music as a favour to the Nymphs,
and by the will of the Muses, she sends forth her voice and, just
as she did when she was a girl, imitates all things, gods, humans,
instruments, beasts. She even imitates Pan on the pipes, and when
he hears the music, he springs up and chases her across mountains, not desiring to take her but rather to learn who his unseen
student might be.' When Daphnis completed his story, Chloe
gave him not ten kisses, but many more, for the echo had
repeated almost the same words he uttered as if to bear witness
that he had not lied.

[24] The sun grew warmer each day, as the spring slowly gave
way to summer, and they enjoyed new pleasures, now of summer.
Daphnis swam in the rivers, Chloe bathed in the springs; he
played his pipes in rivalry with the pines, and Chloe sang in
competition with the nightingales. They hunted chattering grasshoppers, they captured chirping cicadas, they gathered flowers,
or shook trees and ate the fruit. They lay down together naked,
and a single goatskin covered them. Chloe would easily have
become a woman had the prospect of blood not terrified Daphnis. Afraid that he might one day become reckless and lose
control, he would often not allow Chloe to expose her nakedness;
Chloe wondered at this, but she was ashamed to ask the reason.

[25] In this summer season, a large number of suitors arrived to
ask about Chloe; they came from all over to ask Dryas for

marriage, bringing gifts or making large promises to win her
hand. At this Nape's hopes were raised, and she advised that
Chloe be given away in marriage on the grounds that if a girl of
such an age were kept much longer at home, she would very
likely soon lose her virginity while pasturing the sheep and make
a man of some shepherd in return for apples or flowers. Nape
felt that they should make her the head of a household and take
the many presents for themselves and keep them for their own
legitimate son – she had given birth to a male child not long
before. Dryas was at times swayed by her words, especially since
the gifts mentioned by each suitor were well beyond the expectations of a shepherd girl, but then he reflected that the girl was
better than her peasant suitors and that if he ever found her true
parents she would increase his fortune substantially, and so he
postponed his decision, kept putting off an answer from day to
day, and in the meantime did quite well by the suitors' presents.
When Chloe learned of this, she was deeply pained, and avoided
Daphnis for a long time because she did not want to hurt him.
But when he insisted and persisted in asking her, and was plainly
suffering more by not knowing than he would have been if he
did know the truth, she told him everything, how she had many
wealthy suitors, how Nape was asking for a speedy marriage
and how Dryas did not decline them but had postponed his
decision until the grape harvest.

[26] Daphnis was so upset at her words that he sat down and
cried, and said that if Chloe were no longer a shepherd, he would
die, and not only he but all the sheep would die too without a
shepherd like her. Then pulling himself together, he regained his
confidence, and decided to persuade Chloe's father and enrol
himself as one of her suitors, and he hoped that he would prevail
over the others. He was disturbed by one thing: Lamon was not
wealthy. But this was the only thing that made Daphnis' hope
a slim one, and he nevertheless resolved to be a suitor, and Chloe
agreed with him. He did not dare to speak to Lamon directly,
but found the courage to speak to Myrtale and revealed his love
to her and put forward arguments in support of the marriage.
At night, Myrtale disclosed his desires to Lamon, but he reacted

harshly to Daphnis' petition, and abused her for wanting to
marry a shepherd's daughter to a boy whose infant tokens had
promised a great fortune and who, if he were to find his own
kin, would set them free and make them the masters of a large
estate. Myrtale was afraid that Daphnis, on account of his love,
might try to kill himself if his hopes of marriage were dashed,
and so she gave him other reasons for Lamon's refusal: 'We are
poor, my child, and we want a bride who is richer than we are,
while they are wealthy and want wealthy bridegrooms. But come,
go and talk to Chloe and persuade her and her father not to ask
for too much and to give her in marriage to you. She loves you
dearly and would rather sleep with a poor but handsome lover
than some rich ape.'

[27] Myrtale never thought that Dryas with packs of rich suitors
around him would agree to this, but she hoped her reasons for
putting off Daphnis' suit seemed plausible, and Daphnis could
not find fault with her advice. He was far short of what he
desired, however, and so he did what all poor lovers do: he cried
and again called on the Nymphs for help. And in the night they
appeared to him in his dreams, and they stood beside him just
as they had before, and once again the eldest spoke: 'Another
god is looking out for Chloe's marriage, but we shall give you
gifts with which you might sway Dryas. The ship of those young
Methymneans (your goats nibbled at its willow shoot) was that
very same day swept by the winds far from the coast, but in the
night a sea breeze ruffled the waves and then the ship was driven
ashore against the cliffs of the steep headland. The ship and its
cargo were more or less destroyed, but a purse of three thousand
drachmas was thrown out by the waves and is lying hidden
under seaweed near a dead dolphin. No passer-by has approached
the area because of the foul odour. You should go, and when
you get there, pick it up, and after you pick it up, give it to Dryas.
For the moment, it is enough for you not to seem to be a poor
man: later, you will even be rich.'

[28] They spoke and vanished into the night. At daybreak, Daphnis leaped up joyfully, and whistled as he drove his goats to

pasture. He kissed Chloe, kneeled down before the Nymphs and went down to the sea as though to bathe in the water, and he walked on the sand near the line where the waves broke, searching for the three thousand. It wasn't going to be hard: the dolphin lay there in his path, giving off a foul stench, cast up on the shore, clammy from decay. Using the horrible smell as his guide, he went to it at once, removed the seaweed and found his purse of silver. He took it up and placed it into his bag, but before he left the spot, he shouted out in celebration of the Nymphs and the sea. Although he was a goatherd, he loved the sea more sweetly than the land because it was helping him marry Chloe.

[29] Now that he had three thousand, he lingered no more, but thought himself the richest of all men in the world (not just of the farmers there), and he went straightaway to Chloe, told her about the dream and showed her the purse, and then he asked her to watch over the flocks until he should return, and raced off to see Dryas. He found him threshing the grain with Nape, and boldly launched into the subject of marriage: 'Give me Chloe as my wife. I know how to reap well and to prune vines and to plant slips; I know how to plough the land and winnow the grain in the wind. Chloe can bear witness to how well I pasture the flocks. Fifty goats I received, and I made their number double. I've also myself reared fine, large he-goats when previously we used to send our she-goats out to other stud farms. I'm young too, and an honest neighbour, and a she-goat nursed me, as a ewe did Chloe. And my gifts shall be superior to the other suitors' in the same way that my claims are stronger than theirs. They will bring goats and sheep, a yoke of scurvy oxen and corn that's barely acceptable as food for hens, but from me you will get these three thousand. Only, don't let anyone know of this, not even my own father, Lamon.' With that, he handed over the money, threw his arms around him and kissed him.

[30] As soon as Dryas and Nape saw that much silver, beyond what they had ever hoped to see, they immediately swore to give him Chloe and promised to persuade Lamon. Nape remained there at the floor with Daphnis as she drove the cows around

and threshed the corn in the machine, while Dryas stored the
purse in the same place where he had hidden the tokens of
Chloe's birth and then set off hastily to Lamon and Myrtale
intending to ask them – how strange! – for a marriage. He found
them measuring the newly winnowed barley and feeling dejected
because the crop was almost less than the seed that they had
sown. He tried to comfort them and said the problem had
afflicted everyone. Then he asked that their Daphnis be for his
Chloe saying that though other suitors were offering many gifts,
he would take nothing from them, but rather would give the
two of them a present from his own household. Daphnis and
Chloe had been raised together from their childhood, he said,
and by grazing with each other, they were joined by a love that
could not easily be broken, and what's more, they were now old
enough to sleep with each other. He said all this and much more;
in truth, he did stand to win three thousand if he could convince
them about the marriage. Lamon was no longer able to plead
poverty as an excuse (Dryas and Nape were not looking down
on them) or Daphnis' youth (he was already a young man), but
he held back from speaking the truth and from saying that Daphnis was too high for such a marriage, and so after a little pause
he answered in these words:

[31] 'You are right to honour your neighbours before strangers
and you are right not to regard wealth as higher than honest
poverty, and may Pan and the Nymphs love you for it. I too am
eager for this marriage. I would be mad if I, especially now as I
get older and need help with the work, didn't seize on this union
of our families. It would be something worthy. And Chloe is
much sought after too; a radiant girl in the prime of her youth,
she's good in every way imaginable. But since I am a slave and
am not the lord of my own affairs, we must inform my master
and obtain his consent. So come, let us put off the marriage until
the autumn. We have visitors from the town and they say that
he will come then, and at that time they shall be man and wife;
but for now let them love each other like brother and sister. And
may I say this one thing, Dryas, the young man you're taking
all this trouble over is better than we are.' When Lamon finished,

he kissed Dryas and offered him a drink, since the sun was now
at its midday height; and he continued to treat him with all
friendliness and walked with him a part of the way home.

[32] Lamon's parting words were not lost on Dryas and as he
walked he reflected on who this Daphnis might be: 'He was
nursed by a she-goat as if the gods were watching over him, and
he's good-looking and nothing like that snub-nosed old man
and his balding wife. He can come up with three thousand drachmas when no goatherd is likely to have three thousand pears.
Was he abandoned just like Chloe was, and did Lamon find him
just as I found her? Were tokens left with him like those that I
found? If this is really what happened – and by Pan and the
Nymphs, I hope that it is so – then perhaps Daphnis will, in
finding his own parents, also find out something about Chloe's
mysterious birth.' These were his thoughts and dreams as he
reached the threshing floor. When he got there, he found Daphnis waiting in suspense for the news, and so he calmed him by
greeting him as his son-in-law and promised to celebrate the
marriage in the autumn, giving him his hand and pledging that
Chloe would belong to no one but Daphnis.

[33] Faster than the speed of thought, without stopping to eat
or drink, Daphnis ran to Chloe and found her milking and
making cheese; he gave her the good news about the marriage
and kissed her openly as his future wife and then shared in the
work. He drew the milk into pails and set the cheeses on the
baskets and guided the lambs and kids to feeding position
beneath their mothers. When this was done, and all was in order,
they washed and ate and drank, and they wandered about in
search of ripe fruit. And fruits there were in abundance because
it was the season when everything was ripe, lots of pears of all
kinds wild and cultivated, and lots of apples, some fallen to the
ground fragrant and scented like wine, others still hanging on
the branches and gleaming fresh like gold. One apple tree had
been stripped and had neither fruit nor leaves, and all its branches
were bare, except for an apple that hung at the absolute top of
the highest branches, big and beautiful, more fragrant by far

than all the rest. The fruit picker must have been afraid to climb so high and had neglected to take it down: perhaps the beautiful apple had been saved for a shepherd in love.

[34] When Daphnis saw this apple, he was eager to climb up and take it down, and disregarded Chloe's attempts to stop him. But she was annoyed at being disregarded and went away to her flocks. Daphnis climbed up quickly, picked the fruit off the branch and gave it to Chloe as a gift. Then he delivered the following speech to his sulking lover: 'Girl, the finest seasons created this apple, a fine tree nurtured it, the sun made it ripen, and Fortune watched over it. I saw the apple: once I saw it, I couldn't leave it to fall to the ground and be trampled on by some grazing herd, or some slithering snake might poison it, or time could destroy it as it lay there seen and praised by other people. This apple, this prize that Aphrodite took for her beauty, this I give you as a prize for your victory. Her judge and yours are almost alike: he was a shepherd and I am a goatherd.' He spoke, and put the apple in her lap; she kissed him as he drew near, and Daphnis did not regret his daring climb up the high tree, since the kiss he got was better than any apple, even an apple of gold.

BOOK 4

[1] A fellow slave of Lamon's arrived from Mytilene with the news that their master would be coming there a little before the harvest, to see whether the Methymneans' raiding had done any damage to his fields. Since summer was already drawing to an end and the autumn was approaching, Lamon worked to make his master's country home altogether enchanting. He cleaned out the springs so that they could have clean water, carried the dung out of the yard to remove any obnoxious odours and tended to the garden so that it would look beautiful.

[2] In fact, the garden was entirely beautiful, and looked like the gardens of kings. It was a stade in length, lay on elevated ground and was four plethra in width; it was like a large plain. It contained trees of all kinds, apple, myrtle, pear, pomegranate, fig and olive. On one side, there was a lofty vine that spread its ripening grapes over the apple and pear trees, as though the clusters were competing with the other fruit. But in addition to these cultivated trees, there were also cypresses, laurels, planes and pines, all wreathed in ivy; and clusters of ivy berries, which were big and turning dark, seemed to mimic the grapes. The fruit-bearing trees were on the inside as if for protection, and the other trees stood outside them as if to wall them in, and these again were enclosed by a narrow fence. All the parts of the garden were divided and separate; each tree trunk stood at some distance from the next, but higher up the branches joined and intermingled their foliage. This had happened naturally, but it also looked like a work of art. There were beds of flowers too, both wild and cultivated: the roses, hyacinths and lilies were

cultivated by hand, and violets, narcissus and pimpernels were produced by the earth. There was shade in summer, and flowers in spring, and grapes for picking in autumn, and fruit in every season.

[3] From there the view of the plain was very fine, and one could see the shepherds grazing their flocks; the view of the sea was fine too, and the ships sailing by could be seen, and all this added to the luxurious charm of the garden. At the centre of the length and breadth of the garden was a temple and altar of Dionysus, the altar wreathed in ivy, the temple in shoots of vine. Inside the temple were paintings of Dionysus and of stories involving him: Semele giving birth, Ariadne sleeping, Lycurgus in chains, Pentheus being torn apart. There were Indians in defeat and Tyrrhenians being turned into dolphins and Satyrs treading everywhere and bacchants dancing. Nor was Pan forgotten, but he, too, sat there on a rock, playing his pipes, as if he were providing the music for the treading and the dancing.

[4] This was the garden that Lamon tended to, cutting away the dry wood and tying up the vines. He put a garland on Dionysus and watered the flowers from a spring that Daphnis had found for the flowers; the spring was used just for the flowers, but still it was called Daphnis' spring. Lamon encouraged Daphnis to fatten his goats as much as possible, saying that the master would certainly want to see them after such a long absence. Daphnis was confident that he would be praised for them; he had doubled the number he had received, and not a single one had been snatched by a wolf, and they were fatter than sheep. But since he wanted to make his master more ready to consent to his wedding, he devoted all his care and attention to them. He took the goats out very early in the morning and drove them back very late in the evening; twice a day, he led them to drink, and looked out for the richest pastures. He also secured new bowls and many milk pails and larger cheese baskets. He was so careful that he oiled the goats' horns and combed their hair; they looked like a flock that was sacred to Pan. Chloe shared in all the work on them and neglected her own flock to give more of

her time to the goats, so that Daphnis thought that it was because
of her that his flocks seemed more beautiful.

[5] While they were occupied with these matters, a second
messenger came from the city and told them to strip the vines
as soon as possible, and he said that he himself would stay until
they had made the grapes into new wine, and then he would
return to the city to bring his master for the completion of the
autumn harvest. They welcomed this Eudromus (for that was
his name) very warmly, and at once they began stripping the
vines, bringing the clusters of grapes to the presses and pouring
the new wine into the jars; they set aside the most luscious grapes
and left them on their shoots, so that even the people from the
city might have some idea of the harvest and its pleasures.

[6] When Eudromus was about to run off to the city, Daphnis
gave him many presents, especially such as a goatherd might give,
firm cheeses, a late-born kid and a woolly white goatskin so that
Eudromus would have something to put on when running
messages in the winter. He was thrilled and kissed Daphnis and
promised to put in a word on his behalf with the master. And so
Eudromus left with a friendly goodbye, but Daphnis was in
suspenseful agony while he grazed his flock with Chloe. She also
was full of fear: the young man, who was used to seeing goats
and a hill and farmers and Chloe, was now, for the first time,
about to see his master, when previously he had only heard his
name. So she was anxious for her Daphnis and the meeting with
his master, and she was troubled in her heart about their marriage
and feared that their dreams would be in vain. They kissed continually and they embraced each other like two shoots of ivy that
had grown into one, but their kisses were timid and their embraces
had a melancholy aspect, as though their master were already
there and they were frightened by that or were avoiding his gaze.
And then this new development also added to their worries.

[7] There was an arrogant cowherd called Lampis who had also
said to Dryas that he wished to marry Chloe and had already
given him many presents in his desire for the marriage. When he

learned that Daphnis would marry her if his master should consent, he thought of a scheme to make the master turn bitter against Daphnis and Lamon. He knew that the master took special pleasure in the garden, and decided to damage it and spoil its beauty as much as he could. He realized that if he cut down the trees, he would almost certainly be caught because the noise would betray him, and so he decided to destroy the flowers instead. He waited for night, jumped over the fence, and then dug up some of the flowers, smashed others and trampled on the rest like a pig; then he escaped into the night without being caught. On the following day, Lamon came to the garden to draw water for the flowers from the spring; he saw the whole place devastated, the work of an enemy, clearly, and not a thief. He tore his tunic into pieces and shouted so loudly to the gods that Myrtale dropped what she was doing and ran out and Daphnis left his goats and ran up. They saw the ruined garden, they saw it and shouted and wept; theirs was a new kind of lament, a mourning for flowers.

[8] They wept for fear of their master, but even a stranger would have wept had he been there. The place was in a state of complete disarray, and the ground was wholly a muddy ruin, except that the flowers that escaped the violent attack still retained their bloom and shone and were still beautiful though they lay on the ground. Bees settled over them too, buzzing and humming, continually, ceaselessly, as though in sorrow. Lamon was struck by the disaster, and said, 'O, the poor roses, how they're broken! O, the poor violets, how they've been trampled down! And the hyacinths and the narcissus, dug up by some vile man. Spring will come, but they will not bloom; summer will come, but they will not flower; and another autumn, but they will not be a part of anyone's garland. And you, Lord Dionysus, did you not feel pity for these wretched flowers? You used to live with them, to look at them. So often I made garlands for you from them. How shall I show the garden to my master now? What will he do when he has seen it? He'll string up this old man on one of the pines and have him flayed like Marsyas, and perhaps he'll do the same to Daphnis as well thinking that his goats were responsible.'

[9] At the thought of this, the tears they were shedding grew hotter still, and they were in mourning no longer for the flowers but for their own selves. Chloe also went into mourning at the thought that Daphnis would be strung up, and prayed that their master might never come; she lived through days of distress as if she was already watching Daphnis being whipped. At nightfall, Eudromus brought the message that the older master would arrive in three days' time, but that the son would come ahead of him the next day. So they considered and discussed what had happened, and made Eudromus a part of their deliberations. He liked Daphnis and advised him to admit to everything to the young master first and promised he would help him and the others; the young master respected him, he said, because the two were foster-brothers nursed on the same milk. And on the next day, they followed his suggestion.

[10] Astylus arrived riding on his horse, and with him, and also on horseback, was his hanger-on, the kind they call a 'parasite'. Astylus was a young man whose beard was just showing, but Gnathon (that was the parasite's name) had been shaving and trimming his beard for a long time. Lamon fell at Astylus' feet, together with Myrtale and Daphnis, and pleaded with him to take pity on an unfortunate old man and to turn away his father's anger from a man who had done no wrong; and at the same time, he told him everything. Astylus felt pity for his shepherd, and when he went to the garden and saw the destroyed flowers, he said that he would himself intercede with his father on their behalf and blame the horses saying that they had turned violent after being tethered there, and had broken loose and smashed up, trampled on and uprooted the flowers. At these words, Lamon and Myrtale prayed for his happiness in all things, and Daphnis gave him several presents, kids, cheeses, birds with their chicks, clusters of grapes on vines and apples on boughs. Among the gifts there was also a wine with an exquisite bouquet, a Lesbian wine, the loveliest of all drinks.

[11] Astylus thanked and praised them for these gifts, and then turned his attention to hunting hares; he was, after all, a wealthy

young man who never tired of the finer divertissements, and he had come to the country to savour new pleasures. Gnathon was, on the other hand, a man who knew how to eat and drink himself drunk and then have sex while drunk. He was nothing other than the sum of his mouth, his stomach and his loins, and he had observed Daphnis with care when he brought the gifts. He was a pederast by nature, and finding beauty such as he had never seen in the city, he decided to make a pass at Daphnis, and thought he would easily seduce a mere goatherd. With this idea in mind, he stayed out of Astylus' hunt, and went down to where Daphnis was grazing, on the pretext of looking at goats, but in truth to gaze at Daphnis. To soften him, he praised his goats and asked him to play a shepherd's melody on his pipes and said that he would quickly make him a free man since his influence was great.

[12] When he saw that Daphnis was tame and receptive, he lay in wait for him at night as he was driving his goats from the pasture. Running up to Daphnis, Gnathon first kissed him, and then asked him to do for him what the she-goats do for the he-goats. Daphnis slowly realized what Gnathon was saying, and said that it was fine for he-goats to mount she-goats, but that no one had ever seen a he-goat mounting a he-goat, or a ram mounting a ram instead of a ewe, or cocks mounting cocks instead of hens. Gnathon was ready to use force and was laying his hands on him, but since the man was drunk and could barely stand up, Daphnis pushed him back and threw him sprawling to the ground. Then he scampered off like a puppy and left Gnathon lying down, needing a man's hand (not a boy's) to help him to his feet and guide him home. After that, Daphnis did not let him come close at all, but grazed his flocks in different places at different times, keeping far from Gnathon and watching over Chloe. For his part, Gnathon did not persist further, having learned that Daphnis was both strong and beautiful, but instead he looked out for the opportunity to discuss him with Astylus and hoped he would get Daphnis as a gift from the young man, who was often willing to grant great favours.

[13] That moment was not at hand, however: Dionysophanes was arriving with Cleariste, and there was much noise and commotion from pack animals and servants and men and women. Later, Gnathon did begin to compose a lengthy and passionate speech on the subject. Dionysophanes, by now a grey-haired man, was tall and handsome and able to compete with youths half his age; few men were as wealthy as he, and none as worthy. On the day of his arrival, he sacrificed to the gods who watch over the countryside, Demeter and Dionysus and Pan and the Nymphs, and set a large bowl of wine for everyone there to share in. On the next few days, he inspected Lamon's work and saw the well-ploughed fields, the trimmed vine shoots and the beautiful garden (Astylus had taken the blame for the flowers). He was very pleased with what he saw, praised Lamon and promised to set him free. Afterward, he went down to the pasture as well, to see the goats and their goatherd.

[14] Chloe ran away to the wood, because the crowd frightened her and made her feel shy, but Daphnis stood there, wrapped in a shaggy goatskin, a newly sewn bag hanging from his shoulders, his hands full, one holding cheeses freshly made, the other unweaned kids. If Apollo ever worked for Laomedon as a cowherd, he must have looked just like Daphnis did at that moment. He said nothing, but blushing and looking down, held out the gifts. Lamon said, 'This fellow, Master, is the herdsman of your goats. You gave me fifty she-goats to graze and two he-goats, but he has turned them into a hundred she-goats and ten he-goats. Do you see how sleek they are, how thick their hair, how full their horns? He has even given them an ear for music and makes them follow all his instructions through his pipes!'

[15] Cleariste heard him and wanted to test what he said, so she told Daphnis to play the pipes as he did usually, and she promised to give him a tunic and cloak and sandals if he should play. He made them sit down as if they were in the theatre, while he himself stood under the beech tree and brought out the pipes from his bag. He began: first he breathed into them very gently,

and the goats stood still and raised their heads; then he blew the melody for grazing, and the goats lowered their heads and grazed; then he struck up a shrill tune, and the goats lay down together; then he piped a sweet song, and they ran away to the wood as if a wolf was approaching; after a few moments, he sounded the retreat, and they came out of the wood and ran together around his feet. No one had ever seen human slaves so obedient to the orders of their master! All of them were amazed, but Cleariste most of all, and she swore that she would give him her presents since he was an excellent goatherd and an excellent musician. Then they went up to the farmhouse and had lunch, and they sent Daphnis some of the food intended for their own table. He ate his meal with Chloe; he took pleasure in tasting city food and had great expectations of obtaining his master's consent to the proposed marriage.

[16] But the fire in Gnathon's heart was kindled still more by what had happened in the pasture, and he came to think life was not worth living if he could not possess Daphnis. He watched for Astylus to walk into the garden and then brought him into the temple of Dionysus and kissed his hands and feet. Astylus asked him why he was doing this and told him to speak his mind and vowed that he would help him. To this he replied, 'Master, your Gnathon is ruined! Once, I used to love only the food in your house, I used to swear that nothing was lovelier than old wine of a good vintage, I used to say that your cooks were better than all the boys of Mytilene: but now the only thing I consider beautiful is Daphnis. I've lost my taste for rich food; so much of it is prepared every day, meat, fish, honey cakes, but no more for me! I'd much rather be a she-goat and eat grass and leaves, if only I could hear Daphnis' piping, if only I could be pastured by him. Save me, save your Gnathon, and conquer Love the unconquerable. If not, I swear by you, by my own god, I will take a dagger, fill my stomach with food and kill myself in front of Daphnis' door, and then you'll no longer cry out for your little Gnathon as you often like to do when you're playing around.'

[17] Since he was a young man with a large heart and, moreover, since he was familiar with the sickness that love could bring, Astylus could not resist him as he wept and kissed his feet again, but he promised to ask his father for Daphnis and to take him to the city, as a slave for himself and as a lover for Gnathon. But Astylus also wanted to bring the man himself to some level of reflection and he asked, smiling, if Gnathon wasn't ashamed of his love for Lamon's son or of his eagerness to lie down with a young man who grazed goats, and as Astylus said this he sniffed in disgust at the stench of goats. But the other was well schooled in love talk of all kinds, thanks to drinking parties in the city, and he did not miss his mark as he spoke on behalf of himself and Daphnis: 'No lover is bothered by such things, my master. He is captivated by beauty in whatever body he finds it. That's why people have fallen in love with plants and rivers and beasts – and who would not take pity on a lover who would have to be frightened by what he loved? The one I love has a slave's body, but the beauty of a free man. You see how his hair is like hyacinth, how his eyes gleam beneath his brows like a jewel in a golden setting, his face pink and glowing, and his mouth full of white teeth like ivory? What lover would not pray for sweet kisses from him? In my love for a herdsman, I imitate the gods. Anchises was a cowherd, and he swept Aphrodite off her feet; Branchus used to graze goats, and Apollo fell in love with him; Ganymede was a shepherd, and the king of the universe snatched him away. Let us not scorn a boy who is, we see, obeyed even by his goats as if they love him, but rather let us be grateful to Zeus' eagles for allowing such beauty to remain on earth.'

[18] Astylus laughed pleasantly at Gnathon's fine discourse, and especially at his last comment, and said that Love made men into great orators. He would wait for the right opportunity to speak to his father about Daphnis. But Eudromus had secretly heard everything that passed between the two. He liked Daphnis and thought him a decent, honest young man, and was disturbed at the thought of such a beautiful boy being the target of Gnathon's drunken cravings, so he immediately told him and Lamon all that he had heard. Daphnis was stricken with horror and

decided to risk running away with Chloe or to take his own life and hers also. But Lamon called Myrtale out of the farm and said, 'We're ruined, wife. The time has come to disclose our secret. We'll be all alone and abandoned, you and I, not to mention that the goats will be too, along with everything else. But by Pan and the Nymphs, even if I am left like an ox in the stall, as they say, I shall not remain silent about Daphnis' origins. I'll tell how I found him abandoned, I'll reveal how I found him being nursed, I'll show the things that were left out beside him. Let that disgusting Gnathon learn what sort of person he's elected to love. Just get those tokens ready for me, please.'

[19] They agreed to do as he said, and went back inside. Meanwhile, Astylus made his way to his father when the older man was at leisure and asked him if he could take Daphnis to the city, on the grounds that he was a handsome youth, too good for the country, and could quickly be educated in city manners by Gnathon. His father was happy to grant him his request, and he sent for Lamon and Myrtale and told them that henceforth Daphnis would look after Astylus instead of she-goats and he-goats and that he would give them two goatherds in place of this one. All the slaves now gathered around and were pleased at the idea that they would have a handsome fellow slave, but then Lamon asked for permission to speak and began with these words: 'Listen to the truth from an old man, Master. I swear by Pan and the Nymphs that I am not telling a lie. I am not Daphnis' father nor did Myrtale ever have the good fortune to be his mother. Another father and another mother abandoned this boy, perhaps because they had as many children as they wanted. I found him abandoned and being suckled by one of my she-goats. I buried her at the edge of the garden when she died, loving her because she had done a mother's work. I also found tokens lying beside the child, I admit, Master, and I have kept them with me. They are signs of a higher station in life than ours. I do not scorn that he become a slave of Astylus, in which case he'd be a fine servant for a fine and honest master, but I cannot overlook his becoming a drunkard's butt and let Gnathon take the boy to Mytilene to make him his mistress.'

[20] When Lamon finished, he fell silent and wept profusely, while Gnathon turned belligerent and threatened to strike him. But Dionysophanes was himself struck by Lamon's words, and frowning at Gnathon, he ordered him to be still. He questioned Lamon again and asked him to speak the truth and not to make up a story to keep his son with him. Lamon stood by his account and swore to its truth by all the gods and offered himself up for torture so that they could test him and judge the truth of his words. With Cleariste sitting by his side, Dionysophanes reflected on what they had heard: 'Why is Lamon lying when he can have two goatherds in place of his one? How can a rustic invent such a story? Was it not incredible from the very beginning for so handsome a son to be born to this old man and his plain wife?'

[21] They decided to speculate no further but to inspect the tokens and see if they heralded an illustrious and more distinguished origin. Myrtale went away and brought all the items, which had been kept in an old bag for protection. Dionysophanes was the first to look at them after they were brought in, and when he saw the purple cloak, the golden brooch and the dagger with the ivory hilt, he let out a great shout, 'Lord Zeus!', and called his wife to come over and look. When she saw the objects, she also cried out, 'Dear Fates, aren't these the very things that we abandoned together with our own son? Aren't these the very fields to which we ordered Sophrone to bring them? These are not other things, no, but the very same. My dear husband, the child is our own. Daphnis is your son and he's been grazing his father's goats.'

[22] She was still speaking and Dionysophanes was kissing the tokens and weeping because of his great happiness, when Astylus understood that Daphnis was his brother, and flinging off his coat, he ran down from the garden, wanting to be the first to kiss Daphnis. Daphnis saw him running towards him with many others and crying out 'Daphnis', but he thought that Astylus was running because he wished to seize him, so he threw aside his bag and his pipes and turned towards the sea, with the intention of throwing himself down from the large rock. And

perhaps, as strange as it seems, Daphnis would have been lost on the very day he was found if Astylus had not realized what he was intending to do and cried out again, 'Stop, Daphnis. Don't be afraid. I'm your brother, and your parents are the same people who used to be your masters. Lamon told us just now about the she-goat and he showed us the tokens. Turn around and see, they are coming, look at their smiles and their laughter. But let me be the first to kiss you. I swear to you by the Nymphs that I'm not lying.'

[23] He heard the oath and stopped, at last, then waited for Astylus to run up to him, and after he came up to him, he kissed him. While he was kissing him, the rest of the crowd flowed up, menservants, maidservants, his father himself and his mother with him. All of them threw their arms around and clasped him, kissed him, showing their happiness and their tears together. He embraced his father and mother before all the others, held them close to his breast as if he had known about them for a long time and would not let go of their arms. So quickly does Nature make us learn to trust! Even Chloe was forgotten for a short while as Daphnis went into the farmhouse, put on fine clothing, sat down by his own father and heard him tell the following story:

[24] 'My boys, I married when I was quite young, and after a little time, I became a lucky father, or so I thought. First, I had a son and then a daughter and then, third, Astylus. So I thought that my family was large enough, and when this child was born after the others, I abandoned him, laying out these things not as tokens of recognition but as burial ornaments. But Fortune willed otherwise. My eldest son and daughter were lost to the same illness on one day – and you were saved by divine providence so that we would have more help in our old age. Don't be angry at me, Daphnis, because I once abandoned you; I had no desire to do so. And you, Astylus, don't be annoyed now at receiving a part of my estate rather than all of it; wise men say no possession is more precious than a brother. Love one another. As far as wealth is concerned, you will be able to hold your own

even with princes and kings. I shall leave you vast amounts of land, many able servants, gold, silver, and all the other trappings of the rich. Only, I grant this estate to Daphnis alone, and with it I give him Lamon and Myrtale and the goats that he grazed himself.'

[25] Even before he had finished speaking, Daphnis leaped up. 'Father, you just reminded me, and quite rightly. I'm off to take the goats to drink their water. They're probably thirsty now, waiting for my pipes to give them the signal, and here I am sitting among you.' They all laughed pleasantly because although he had become a master, he was still a goatherd. Another one of the servants was sent to look after the goats, while they offered a sacrifice to Zeus the Saviour and began a party. Gnathon alone did not come to this party; he was afraid and was staying day and night in the temple of Dionysus as a suppliant. Quickly word reached everyone that Dionysophanes had found a son and that Daphnis the goatherd was discovered to be the master of his fields, and so at daybreak people from all parts hurriedly converged there, to share in the young man's pleasure and bring presents to his father. Of these, the first was Dryas, Chloe's foster father.

[26] Dionysophanes made them stay on at his estate to share in his happiness and in the celebrations. He made arrangements to serve large amounts of wine, wheatmeal bread, marsh fowl, suckling pigs and various honey cakes. And many animals were sacrificed to the local deities. Then Daphnis gathered together all his farm possessions and offered them up as dedications to the gods: to Dionysus he dedicated his bag and goatskin, to Pan the pipes and transverse flute, to the Nymphs his staff and the milk pails that he himself had made. And yet, as familiar things give us greater pleasure than an unforeseen or strange prosperity, Daphnis wept as he was parted from each of them. In truth, he did not dedicate the milk pails until he had used them for milking one last time, nor the goatskin before he put it on again, nor the pipes before he played them, and he also kissed all these things and he spoke to the she-goats and called out to the

he-goats by name. He drank too from the spring, because he had done so many times with Chloe. But he did not yet admit his love, and was still waiting for the right moment.

[27] While Daphnis was occupied with his sacrificial offerings, this was what was happening with Chloe. She was sitting and weeping, grazing the sheep and saying things that were entirely predictable in the circumstances: 'Daphnis has forgotten me. He's dreaming of a wealthy marriage. Why did I tell him to swear by the goats instead of the Nymphs? He's abandoned them as he's abandoned Chloe. Not even when he was sacrificing to the Nymphs and to Pan did he feel the desire to see Chloe. Perhaps he's found his mother's maids to be better than I. I say goodbye Daphnis, then. I shall not live.'

[28] While she was saying and thinking these sorts of things, the cowherd Lampis suddenly turned up with a gang of farm workers and snatched her away, supposing that Daphnis would not still want to marry her and that Dryas would welcome him as her husband. And so she was carried off, weeping piteously, but someone who saw what had happened told Nape about it, she told Dryas and Dryas told Daphnis. He went out of his mind, but did not dare speak to his father, nor was he able to suffer the news in silence, and so he went into the yard and lamented to himself: 'This self-discovery is proving to be very bitter! I was better off when I was a herdsman, much happier when I was a slave. Then I could look at Chloe, then I could hear her and her chatter. But as it is, Lampis has snatched her and gone away, and when night falls, he'll sleep with her. And here I am drinking and living in luxury, and my oaths to Pan and the goats have come to mean nothing.'

[29] Gnathon, who was hiding in the garden, heard Daphnis' words, and thought that the opportunity had come for reconciliation with him. He took some of Astylus' young men, went after Dryas and told him to lead them to Lampis' farm. He rushed there with alacrity, overtook Lampis just as he was taking Chloe inside, rescued her and gave the farmers a severe beating.

He was eager also to tie up Lampis and take him away as a prisoner of war, but Lampis was a step ahead of him and ran away first. So Gnathon achieved this great victory and returned as night was falling. He found Dionysophanes asleep, but then he saw that Daphnis was still awake and still weeping in the garden. He brought Chloe to him and as he handed her over, he told him everything; he asked Daphnis not to bear a grudge against him any longer and to consider him a useful slave and not to exile him from his table, in which case he would die of starvation. Seeing Chloe and holding Chloe in his arms, Daphnis realized that Gnathon was now a benefactor and reconciled himself to him. And he also gave Chloe a defence of his own behaviour and of his neglect of her.

[30] They deliberated on a course of action and decided that they would keep their marriage plans secret and that Daphnis would hide Chloe and admit his love only to her mother. But Dryas did not agree and said that they should tell Daphnis' father and promised that he himself would obtain his consent. On the next day, he placed Chloe's tokens in his bag and proceeded to Dionysophanes and Cleariste, who were sitting in the garden, with Astylus and Daphnis himself by their side. Dryas waited for silence and then began to speak: 'I, like Lamon, need to say things that until now have been left in secret. I did not give birth to Chloe, nor did I suckle her; others gave birth to her, and a ewe suckled her as she lay in the cave of the Nymphs. I myself saw this and was amazed to see it and in my amazement I brought her up in my household. Her beauty bears witness to the truth; it is utterly unlike ours. Her tokens also bear witness to the truth; they are finer than anything a shepherd could possess. Look at these things, and seek out the girl's relatives; she might prove to be worthy of your Daphnis.'

[31] Dryas did not throw out this last comment casually. Nor did Dionysophanes listen to it without interest, and when he looked at Daphnis and when he saw him grow pale and weep furtively, he immediately recognized the lover. So, moved more by concern for his own son than for someone else's daughter, he

weighed Dryas' words very carefully. But when he saw the tokens that Dryas had brought with him, the golden sandals, the anklets and the belt, he called for Chloe and reassured her, saying that she already had a husband and would soon find her father and mother. Cleariste took her away and dressed her up to fit the part of her son's future wife. Dionysophanes took Daphnis to one side and when they were alone asked him if Chloe was still a virgin, and when Daphnis swore that nothing more than kisses and vows had passed between them, Dionysophanes was pleased and made them recline at the banquet table.

[32] And then you could learn what beauty can be when properly displayed! After Chloe was dressed, her hair put up and her face washed, she seemed so much lovelier to everyone that even Daphnis hardly recognized her. Even without the tokens anyone would have sworn that Dryas was not the father of such a girl. And yet, Dryas himself was also present, sharing in the feast alongside Nape, with Lamon and Myrtale as drinking companions on their own couch. So again on the following days animals were sacrificed and wine bowls were set out, while Chloe, too, dedicated to the gods her own possessions, her pipes, bag, goatskin and milk pails. She also mixed the wine with water from the spring in the cave because she had been brought up beside it and had washed many times in it, and she placed garlands on the ewe's grave, which Dryas pointed out to her, and then, she too, like Daphnis, played the pipes to her flock, and after she finished with the pipes, she prayed to the goddesses that she would find the parents who abandoned her to be worthy enough for her to marry Daphnis.

[33] When they had had enough of the festivities in the country, they decided to go to the city and look for Chloe's parents and not put off the wedding any longer. So after they had completed their preparations the next morning, they gave Dryas another three thousand drachmas, and they gave Lamon half a share in the harvest and fruit picking of the farm, along with the goats, two new goatherds, four pairs of oxen, winter cloaks, and freedom for himself and his wife. And then they drove their carriages

and horses to Mytilene in great luxury. Since they arrived at night, they escaped the notice of the city's residents, but on the following day, a crowd of men and women gathered around their doors. The men congratulated Dionysophanes for finding his son and congratulated him still more when they saw Daphnis' beauty; the women shared in Cleariste's joy at bringing home both a son and his bride, and were also struck by Chloe's exceptional beauty. In fact, the whole city was set astir by the boy and the girl and was calling their marriage happy already and praying that the girl's family would be found to be worthy of her loveliness. And many a wife, in many of the richest families in the city, prayed to the gods that she might prove to be the mother of this beautiful girl.

[34] Dionysophanes fell into a deep sleep, after being kept awake by his anxieties and thoughts, and had the following dream. The Nymphs seemed to be asking Love to give them his assent to the marriage, finally, and Love had unstrung his bow, set aside his quiver and was asking Dionysophanes to invite all the well-born families of Mytilene to a banquet and then, when he had filled the last wine bowl, to show Chloe's tokens to each guest and lastly to sing the wedding hymn. After he had seen and heard this, Dionysophanes woke up early in the morning and ordered the preparation of a brilliant feast, crammed with foods from land and sea, from marsh and river, and he invited all the well-born Mytileneans to join him as his guests in the celebration. And then when it was dark, and when they had filled the wine bowl from which they used to pour libations to Hermes, a servant brought in the tokens on a silver vessel and, carrying them around from left to right, showed them to all the guests.

[35] None of the others recognized them, but Megacles, who was reclining in the place of honour, last because of his age, recognized them when he saw them, and shouted out very loudly and vigorously, 'What's this I see? What has happened to you, my daughter? Are you still alive, or did some shepherd stumble on these things and carry them away? I beg you, Dionysophanes,

tell me, where did you find my child's tokens? Don't keep me from finding something, now that you've found Daphnis.' Dionysophanes told the man first to relate the story of the child's exposure, and Megacles said, as forcefully as before: 'A long time ago, I used to have very little money to live on, because I would spend whatever I did have on public services such as choruses and triremes. It was in those straitened circumstances that a little daughter was born to me. I declined to bring her up in poverty, but fitted her out with these tokens and abandoned her; I knew that many people were eager to become parents even by this method. And so the child was abandoned in the cave of the Nymphs and entrusted to those goddesses. As for my life since, wealth has come pouring in every day, but I have no heir, and haven't had the good luck to become a father, even of another daughter. The gods must be laughing at me, as it were, because they send me dreams every night that show a sheep making me into a father.'

[36] Dionysophanes shouted out in a voice louder than Megacles' and leaped up and brought in Chloe very beautifully dressed and said, 'This is the child you abandoned. By divine providence, this girl of yours was suckled by a ewe, just as my Daphnis was suckled by a she-goat. Take the tokens and your daughter, but take her and give her back as a bride for Daphnis! We abandoned them both, we found them both and both were cared for by Pan and the Nymphs and Love.' Megacles strongly approved of what Dionysophanes said; he sent for his wife Rhode and held Chloe close to his heart. They stayed and slept there, in the house, because Daphnis had sworn that he would give up Chloe to no one, not even to her own father.

[37] When day came, they decided to drive back to the country. Daphnis and Chloe had begged for this, because they could not take life in the town, and their families too thought it best to celebrate the wedding in the pastoral style. So they went to Lamon's house and introduced Dryas to Megacles, presented Nape to Rhode, and they made preparations for a glittering feast. Her father gave Chloe away in the presence of the Nymphs

and he offered the tokens to them as dedications along with
many other things and he rounded out the earlier gift of drachmas to Dryas, making the sum an even ten thousand.

[38] Since it was a fine day, Dionysophanes spread out beds of
green leaves there, in front of the cave, invited all the villagers
to recline, and served them an extravagant feast. Lamon and
Myrtale were there, Dryas and Nape, Dorcon's family, Philetas
and his sons, Chromis and Lycaenion, and even Lampis, now
forgiven, was there. Predictably, for such a banquet, everything
was celebrated in the rustic ways of the country. They sang the
songs that reapers sing or made jokes heard at the wine press.
Philetas played his pipes, Lampis his flute, Dryas and Lamon
danced, and Chloe and Daphnis kissed each other. Even the goats
grazed nearby, as if they too were sharing in the festivities. This
did not quite thrill the visitors from the city. But Daphnis also
called out to some of the goats by name and gave them green
leaves and took them by the horns and kissed them.

[39] And not only then, but as long as they lived, they spent most
of their time in the pastoral life, worshipping as gods the Nymphs
and Pan and Love, owning flocks of sheep and goats, and thinking of fruit and milk as the sweetest foods there were. And they
placed their baby boy to nurse under a she-goat and made their
baby girl, who arrived later, suck the teats of a ewe, and they
called him Philopoemen and her Agele. They also decorated the
cave, and dedicated statues in it, and raised an altar to Love
the Shepherd, and they gave Pan a temple to live in instead of the
pine, and named him Pan the Soldier.

[40] But it was only later that they did these things and devised
these names. On that occasion, when night fell, everyone escorted
them to the bride-chamber, playing pipes and flutes, or holding
up flaming torches, and when they were near the doors, they
sang in harsh, hard tones, as if they were breaking up the earth
with hoes and forks instead of singing a wedding hymn. Daphnis and Chloe lay down naked together and put their arms
around each other and kissed, and even as they got less sleep

that night than owls, Daphnis did some of the things that Lycaenion taught him, and it was then that Chloe learned, for the first
time, that the things they had done earlier in the woods were
merely games that shepherds play.

ANONYMOUS

LETTERS OF CHION

Letter 1 *Chion to Matris, greeting*

I'd already been in the Byzantium area for three days when Lysis brought me your letter. You make it plain enough that you and the whole family are upset. No doubt someone else would now be employing all the means at his disposal to cheer you up; he would go through the expectations he has of his time away from home one by one, using these to strike a cheerful tone, a 'counterpoise to grief'. I, on the other hand, expect you to provide this sort of thing for yourselves, so that the prize you set up for my aspirations to excellence will become the fact that this makes you *happy* parents. That you expect to get some consolation as a result of my education, some good fortune in the midst of your grief, is not enough. Better to treat me like one who has a history of prizewinning; you'll have to put up bigger prizes to make me a keener competitor for them. So get yourself in this frame of mind, Father, and cheer mother up. She belongs in the ranks of the comforted, so you'd better enlist in the brigade of comforters.

Letter 2 *To the same*

Thrason does business trips to the Black Sea, but he strikes me as far more principled than you'd expect of someone in that profession. And now that I'm in Byzantium, I have reason to be grateful to him. When I wanted to see whatever in the district was worth seeing, he showed me around; in fact he took charge of everything, ensuring that the excursion would not be arduous or too much like a hunting trip but a far more luxurious affair

thanks to the carriages and other things he managed to get hold
of. Now that he's heading your way I thought I should send him
along equipped with this testimony to his services, so he can
receive the same consideration in return. I guess he won't want
to go sightseeing since he has a long record of successful
campaigning in the Black Sea area, but I'm sure you'll be only
too willing to look after him in your customary way.

I'm keen to set sail myself, but can't get a suitable wind.

Letter 3 *To the same*

[1] I'm really grateful to the winds which held me up and forced
me to stay on in Byzantium – though at first I was very annoyed
with them because I was in a hurry. But in fact an excuse worth
an even longer delay appeared in the person of Socrates'
acquaintance Xenophon.

This Xenophon is one of those Greeks who went on the
campaign against Artaxerxes, fighting on Cyrus' side. At first he
was simply there with one of the commanders, not sticking his
nose into anything beyond the proper concerns of an ordinary
soldier even though he was one of those to whom Cyrus showed
great respect. When Cyrus was killed in the first battle and the
Greek commanders, contrary to the agreed terms of surrender,
were beheaded, he was elected commander in consideration of
his courage and general sound judgement; they thought he would
work out the best way to rescue the Greek contingent. And he
didn't let them down in the hope they had placed in him, either;
he led this small force right through the middle of enemy territory, each day pitching camp in close proximity to the king's
commanders, and got them out safely.

[2] This was remarkable enough, but even more remarkable and
momentous was what I now saw with my own eyes. The Greeks,
tired out by their long and arduous campaign, found that they
were getting no reward for facing these dangers other than being
rescued from them. Seeing that the Byzantines were diffident about

taking them in, they decided to ransack the city, which threw the Byzantines into sudden panic. The intruders had armed themselves, the trumpeter had given the signal; I grabbed shield and spear and rushed on to the wall, where I'd seen some of the young men stationed. Of course it was no use guarding the wall when the enemy were in control of the city! Nevertheless, we thought it would be easier to defend ourselves where we had the advantage of space – at least it would take them longer to kill us.

[3] In the midst of all this, with the Greeks on a rampage, we saw a long-haired fellow, very good-looking and of mild appearance, walking among them and restraining them one by one from their assault. This was Xenophon. The soldiers were aggressively demanding that he as one individual should obey the majority and give them at last some respite from their tough and oppressive wandering. But he said, 'Step back a bit and think about it! Don't worry; we're in charge of the situation, and that's not going to change while we think about what to do.' This was a request they felt too embarrassed to refuse. So Xenophon went into the middle of the group and produced a wonderful set of arguments – well, the outcome showed they must have been, although we couldn't hear them very well. For those very people who a little while before had been bent on sacking the city were now to be seen going around the market politely buying what they needed just like any other Byzantine, their warlike lawlessness and rapacity quite vanished.

[4] What I had seen was a demonstration of Xenophon's true character, an ability to think things through and to communicate. There was no way I was going to let him pass me by without speaking to him, particularly given that he had done me as good a turn as he had the Byzantines (since thanks to the winds, I too was one of those in line for pillaging), so I introduced myself to him. He kept recalling your friendship with Socrates and trying to recruit me for philosophy, talking on these and other topics not like a military man, by Zeus, but in the manner of a highly cultured person. He is now taking his troops to Thrace; Seuthes, the Thracian king, is at war with some of his neighbours and so

sent a request for them, promising full pay. They accepted the offer, since they don't want to find themselves penniless on their discharge; this way they can get some reward for their exertions while they are still a united group.

[5] So you can now be assured that I'm all the keener to sail to Athens and take up philosophy. I'm sure you remember how, when you were constantly pushing me towards philosophical study and waxing lyrical about those who had devoted themselves to each and every branch of it, you had me convinced in all respects bar one; and this I was most apprehensive about. You see, it was my impression that while otherwise it clearly made those it touched morally superior – indeed, I thought mankind could not imbibe sound-mindedness and a sense of justice from any source other than philosophy – it tended to deprive one's character of energy and the ability to act, soothing one into a state of quiescence. After all, you used to tell me that quietude and abstaining from politics were things philosophers deemed exceptionally praiseworthy!

[6] I saw it as a serious drawback if being a philosopher meant that, while I would be better in those other ways, I could no longer be a brave soldier and display heroism where necessary – that I would let all that go, bewitched by philosophy as if by some incantation that expelled all thought of nobler action from my mind. I didn't know that practising philosophy made people better with respect to courage as well. This lesson, hard though it was, I learned from Xenophon – and it wasn't through his talking to me about it but from his demonstration of the sort of man he actually is. For in spite of heavy involvement in conversations with Socrates, he is quite capable of rescuing both armies and cities, and philosophy has in no way made him less able to look after both himself and his friends.

[7] Now it may well be that quiescence is more productive of happiness. But the man who will successfully accomplish each of his undertakings is the one who is able to put his quiescence to good use. If one could conquer greed and desire and the other

passions by which even those victorious in war are overcome, one would be greater than a military commander. So what do I expect from practising philosophy? I expect to be better in all those other things and to retain my courage – though I may lose some of my rashness.

Well, that's more than enough by a long, long way. I just have to tell you that I am now on the point of sailing; this aura of auspiciousness has even extended to the winds!

Letter 4 To the same

[1] As we happened to meet Simos and his crew who are heading your way on a business voyage, I thought I would tell you about our adventures in Perinthos, too.

The evening setting of the Kids was upon us. I was cautioning the sailors in our group against immediate departure from Byzantium, particularly given that we were able to stay on there; but they didn't take any notice of me. In fact they made a big joke of my forewarning, saying I had a bad case of star-gazer-itis contracted from the astronomer Archedemos. I held out for a while, but as I was getting beaten in this naval engagement I surrendered to them. To tell you the truth, I wasn't sure myself if my caution had any validity, and the following wind that then blew up with its prospect of a good voyage made my predictions even less credible.

[2] As we put out to sea, and all the way until we passed Selymbria, I was ridiculed for my foreboding; in fact it was my heartfelt prayer that this ridicule would continue until we disembarked. But when we had progressed about thirty stades further, a dreadful storm fell upon us. For ages we couldn't bring the ship to land anywhere and were in dire straits; but eventually we got a vague glimpse of Perinthos in the distance. We had to become good oarsmen to force our way towards it, since the wind was far too strong for sails. To cut a long story short, after a terrible struggle we made land at Perinthos around midnight and fell

asleep. But another storm was heading our way, no easier to deal with than the one at sea: Perinthos was under attack from Thracians. Although we had spent twelve days in Byzantium no one had told us about this, so we knew absolutely nothing; it would appear that this barbarian incursion had been very sudden.

[3] Well, we got up and went off to see the city, or so we thought. There was me and Herakleides and good old Agathon, along with some of our attendants: Baitylos, Podarkes and that bold fellow Philon. We were unarmed, but each of our attendants had a long knife at his side, and Philon was carrying a spear as well. We hadn't gone far from the harbour when we spotted a military encampment quite close to the city, and what was more problematic, three horsemen quite close to us. Philon passed his spear over to me so that he could run faster and fled to the ship. Myself I couldn't hope to outrun a horse, so wrapping my cloak round my arm I held the spear at the ready and stood my ground. The attendants did likewise, while Herakleides and Agathon provided themselves with stones and took cover behind us.

[4] The Thracians rode towards us, but before they came in range they each hurled three javelins which hit the ground just in front of us. Then, as if they had completed their mission, they turned round and rode back to the camp. We picked up the javelins, headed back to the ship, untied the mooring ropes and set sail. And as the winds treated us very kindly throughout our voyage, we are now in Chios.

So you can tell Archedemos that an evening setting of the Kids signifies not only bad storms at sea but even worse ones on land. You can have a bit of fun with him out of what happened to us.

Letter 5 To the same

We have arrived in Athens and are enjoying conversations with Socrates' acquaintance Plato. He is a wise man in every respect, but especially in this: to those who associate with him he makes philosophy not something that is in the final analysis apolitical, but rather something with two facets, suited both to the life of activism and to that of inactive quiescence. You wrote to me on the subject of a friendship with him, saying that I would find your close relationship with Socrates a great advantage in setting this up. So I can tell you that he places great value on all those who have had an association with Socrates, even if it only lasted a day, and that he does not attach himself more closely to anyone than to those he thinks are best able to benefit from him. Accordingly I have made it my business not to be backward in forming a friendship with Plato, but rather to enlist in the ranks of those who, he says, do him good because he can do them good. In fact he says that there is just as much happiness in making people good as in becoming good oneself. And so he provides for those of his friends who are capable of it the opportunity to be benefited, and from those who are capable of being benefited he derives no less a benefit himself.

Letter 6 To the same

Phaidimos brought me a box of dried fish, five jars of honey, twenty flagons of myrtle-flavoured wine – and to cap it all three talents of silver. Him I praise for his honesty; you I acknowledge for your generosity. Now I am indeed happy for you to send me a selection of our home-grown produce as a kind of 'first fruits' offering, if the season justifies it; I can delight my other friends with these and also circumvent Plato's habit of not accepting gifts. But for money I have no desire whatsoever, particularly now I am in Athens and having conversations with Plato. It would be a bit pointless for me to have sailed to Athens in order to become less money-conscious, only to have that same money-consciousness sail over to me from the Black Sea. So I'd prefer you to send me things that remind me of my homeland, not of my wealth.

Letter 7 To the same

[1] Archepolis was born and raised in Lemnos (or so he says);
but he is a worthless individual with nothing to recommend him.
He's at odds with everyone, and most of all with himself. In
addition to this, he is uncontrollably reckless, he blurts out whatever comes into his head and he invariably has the most stupid
ideas. As I understand it he started out as a finance official in
Lemnos, holding a number of such posts, but conducted himself
inappropriately. He then decided to show his contempt for
philosophy as well, and sailed to Athens. Once there he made
himself a great nuisance to Plato and spread numerous slanders
about us; he didn't see any advantage to be gained from us, as
our conversations were all about virtue rather than how to get
rich.

[2] Now he says he's going to the Black Sea to do some trading
– not a bad idea, if he's finally worked out that this is the only
thing that is right for him. But his unstable and flighty character
makes it impossible for him to judge what sort of person he is
and what he might be good at. He's always being carried away
by some crazy scheme or other. This is the person – conveniently
forgetting the outrageous things he said about me – who
approached me and asked me to write you a letter of recommendation for him. Deserving of it though he was, I resisted the
temptation to re-enact the Bellerophon scenario, and instead
gave him a separate letter in which the deception is of a very
different kind. This present one, though, I am putting in the
hands of Lysis, who is setting out ahead of him.

[3] I think you ought to receive the fellow with all courtesy and
then at the end say, 'This is how Chion repays those who have
slandered him. You remember all those precepts you used to
scoff at? Well, this is one lesson he has learned from them: that
one should not go so far in paying back an evil person as to
become evil oneself. And this will be avoided if we repay them
with good deeds.' Now I know he won't comprehend any of

this, since his nature is so stupid as to be impervious; neverthe-less, for our sake let this be your policy.

I have exercised neither constraint nor concealment in telling you about him, but I have at no stage said anything damaging to anyone else, though the facts would support it. I just felt I should tell you what I think simply and clearly, without dressing it up in fine language.

Letter 8 To the same

The bearer of this letter is Archepolis of Lemnos. He is journey-ing to the Black Sea on business and has asked me to recommend him to you. This I do gladly. He does not happen to be a friend of mine; however, I regard it as great profit to acquire the means of making someone a friend who was not so before. You will share this profit with me if you treat him with courtesy. I would add that I believe he is fair in his business dealings; he studied philosophy before he became a businessman.

Letter 9 Chion to Bion, greeting

Such indifference towards me is something I wouldn't have expected from you, and I'm reluctant to accept that this is how you feel. But I'm left wondering how it could happen that no letter from you has reached me in all this time, especially as my other friends are constantly writing. Well, as far as the past goes, I'll write your excuses myself; but from now on, no excuse. If the problem lies with couriers failing to deliver, the solution is to write constantly (that way you're bound to light on *some* who will do their job); but if the problem is your not writing, you'd better resolve that too – the solution is easy enough. I really would have thought there was enough substance in our friend-ship to overcome difficulties. Or have you forgotten the Heraion, the Kallichoros, Kallisthenes' lectures, and all those others with

whom we mixed our very souls? Or is it not that you have
forgotten, but that you assume that I, now that I have tasted
philosophy, have put them out of *my* mind? You really shouldn't
regard our friendship as so trivial a thing, nor imagine that I am
doing so either. It should be on your mind as much as it is on
mine; write on that assumption, and write more often.

Letter 10 *Chion to Matris, greeting*

Plato has four great-nieces. He married the eldest of these to
Speusippos along with a reasonable dowry of thirty minas,
money which Dionysios had sent him. Seeing this as the moment
I had been waiting for, I added a talent to the dowry. For a long
time he refused to accept it, but I breached his defences with an
argument most just and true. I said: 'I make this contribution
viewing it not as a sum of money but as a matter of human
kindness, and gifts of this sort must be accepted. For they will
increase one's reputation, whereas other kinds bring dishonour.
You must admit that, while you may regard wealth as dishon-
ourable, you hold kindness in high repute. You have already
betrothed the other girls to the noblest men in Athens; but they
are rich, while Speusippos, although nobler still, is poor.'

  This was profit indeed, and I thought I must let you know
about it. I can't imagine that in my entire life anything greater
than this can be left for me . . .

Letter 11 *To the same*

Bianor delivered your letter to me. In it you ask me to come back
home, saying that five years is a long enough time for any travel
abroad, and that my status as a foreigner is now beginning its
sixth year. You know perfectly well how I long for you and for
my own country – and yet this very longing seems to be forcing
me to spend more time in Athens. I want to be of more use to

those I feel close to, and only philosophy has the power to effect this. Father, I would regard a five-year period as not enough for someone to study business (at least not if they were serious about it), let alone philosophy! And what they are being sent after is the cheap stuff, whereas we are trading for virtue, something you can purchase with no other commodity than natural ability, a love of hard work and time. In the first two of these I am not totally deficient; but I do need more time. So I'm going to spend another five years here, and then, if God preserves me, I'll come home. Remember the thinking that helped you pull through when you said goodbye to me in the first place; you'll have to rely on that to ease your pain at my prolonged absence. Just bear in mind that it's not the journey to a place of education that makes people good, but spending time energetically devoted to that education.

Letter 12 To the same

My last letter advised you of my earlier decision to return to you only after completing ten years here. Now, though, after hearing about the tyranny, I couldn't endure being in a safer position than that of my fellow citizens, so when spring comes (again if God preserves me), I shall set sail. (It's still midwinter, so I'm unable to leave at the moment.) It would be quite out of the question for me to act like those who take any escape route available when there is trouble in their native land, rather than make sure I'm there when there is the greatest need for men who can be of use. And even if 'being of use' falls absolutely in the realm of impossibility, at least I would feel that choosing to share the suffering puts me close to virtue – poor favour though it may be.

I have expressed myself to you the more boldly, since Lysis is delivering this letter.

Letter 13 To the same

[1] Just as you wrote, Clearchus really does feel less apprehensive about Silenos seizing his citadel than about me engaging in philosophy! As I understand it, he has not yet despatched a siege party to deal with Silenos, but Kotys the Thracian, who I later found had become one of Clearchus' bodyguards, came to deal with me. He attacked me shortly after I'd sent that letter telling you about my illness (I had by then sufficiently recovered). It was around midday and I was walking up and down in the Odeion pondering some philosophical problem, when he came at me out of the blue.

[2] I immediately realized what the situation was. He had a short sword and was reaching for it with obviously evil intent, so I first confused him by screaming at him and then ran up to him and grabbed his right hand which was already grasping the weapon. After that, by a combination of kicking him and bending his arm back, I forced him to drop the sword. I took some damage to my foot as I brought him down, but nothing serious. He was pretty groggy, so I was able to twist his arms behind his back and tie him up with his own belt. I then took him to the authorities, from whom he received due punishment. I have in no way lost heart for my voyage but will set sail as soon as the etesian winds drop, whatever the state of my health. It is out of the question that I should be enjoying life in a democracy when my country is subject to a tyrant.

[3] As far as I am concerned, no matter what happens, I remain fully determined: in life and in death, I shall be good. So that I may make some political move on my country's behalf, you must convince Clearchus that now I am a philosopher I crave quiescence, and that right to the core of my being I am utterly non-political. Someone you could also use to convince him of this is Nymphis; while he is aligned with us he also belongs to Clearchus' family, and so would put us far beyond the bounds of any suspicion on his part.

I haven't made any attempt at concealment here, since I am

putting my letters in the hands of people I can trust – and, as you did well to tell me, Clearchus is showing no interest in these exchanges.

Letter 14 To the same

[1] My voyage to Byzantium was certainly quick if somewhat risky, but at least I arrived safely. I've decided to stay here as long as I think appropriate and to send my attendant Krobylos on to you, so that we can arrange my return in a way that best advantages our country. As far as our security is concerned, Clearchus is not the problem – but now that I've gone this far, I'd better clarify my thoughts on the matter.

In my view there is enormous danger for our country arising out of its current unhappy state. In the short term, as I see it, it has to endure the slaughter and banishment of individuals, the loss of its best citizens and subjection to those who have no sense whatever of justice or piety. But in the longer term the risk it runs is even worse, in that following the success of this person, others will conceive a lust for power while the rest become habituated to their loss of freedom, and the end result will be an autocracy that is too entrenched to remove.

[2] Even small shifts in the balance can lead to long-lasting, not to say interminable, troubles, and have a very similar effect to diseases in the body. In their initial stages diseases are easy for people to throw off, but once they are established they become hard to cure if not completely incurable. It is the same with sickness in the state. For a while memory of freedom remains strong and keeps impacting upon one who has been deprived of it, and there is strong and willing opposition on the part of the people. But once the evil has become too well-established and what occupies the people's mind is not how they should rid themselves of it but how they can most easily live with it, then we can say without reservation that the disease is terminal.

[3] Such are the troubles and dangers that beset our country. So
how do I stand personally? If you take my situation on its own,
I am in no danger of being similarly affected. You see, I confine
the term 'enslavement' to something that subjugates the soul
along with the body, since in my opinion an 'enslavement' that
does not affect the soul in any way but possesses the body only
is really no enslavement at all. And here is proof: If there is some
evil in enslavement, it must reach as far as the soul, since otherwise it would not be called evil. To one enslaved in this sense,
there are two things that are truly terrible: the fear that one will
undergo suffering and the pain of experiencing suffering. So – if
one does not fear what is to come as an evil and is not pained
by what is happening now, then will one be enslaved? Of course
not, since the evils of enslavement are absent.

[4] So you can rest assured that the effect of philosophy on me
has been such that even if Clearchus imprisons me and does the
most awful things to me, he will never enslave me. For he will
never gain mastery over my soul, which is where the distinction
between enslavement and freedom is to be found. It is the body
that is ever at the mercy of external happenings, even when it is
not subjected to a tyrannical regime. And if he kills me, then he
will be granting me absolute freedom. How could that which
the body did not habituate to its own slavery while it was enveloping it lack the capacity to function once it is separated from
the body, do you think? Not only will I be free, whatever I suffer,
but Clearchus, however he deals with me, will be enslaved; for
he will deal with me as he does out of fear, and fear has no part
in the freedom that is the soul's.

[5] So if you do take my situation on its own, you can see that
being acted upon gives me more security than acting does Clearchus. Concern for me is absolutely unnecessary – don't give it a
thought. For such concern even to cross one's mind would show
that one is not completely free. And yet I feel ties to my country,
and these do not allow me to enjoy absolute freedom; rather
they impel me towards political activism and courting danger
– and here I am not worried about anything that might happen

to me, but that I might find myself unable to help my country in its time of suffering. This is why, although I have no fear of death, I must nevertheless take precautions not to die before I can die for my country. So towards the tyrant adopt the policy I suggested to you in my last letter, that is, to convince him that I am in love with quiescence. And if anything else pertinent to the political situation there occurs to you, write and tell me. To achieve my country's freedom requires me to curtail some of my own as I sit here turning all this over and trying to work out what to do.

Letter 15 To the same

[1] So the tyrant has let himself be persuaded by what you have been saying to him about me? What a great thing for our country! And as you suggested, I'll write myself as well, drawing him as far as I possibly can away from the truth. If I were to do the opposite, I would be guilty of gross deception in cheating my fellow citizens and friends of what they hope from me, and they don't deserve to be deceived in that regard.

In my view it's more to our advantage if the tyrant does a thorough job of being cruel and harsh instead of trying to make himself popular by assuming a mask of moderation.

[2] The reason is that the harsh ones are quickly eliminated; or, if they are not deposed, they at least bequeath to the people a hatred of tyranny and by their own efforts succeed in giving one-person rule a very bad name indeed. And as a result it turns out (for the future at least) that everyone plays a greater part in guarding and taking precautions to preserve their democracy. But when someone who has enslaved the people ingratiates himself with those he has enslaved, even if he's quickly overthrown he nevertheless leaves many evil taints of tyranny in each individual; they are incapable of perceiving the common good, some because they crave the future benefit they have been led to expect, while others have been subjected to the distraction of

populism. And when he *is* overthrown, they feel pity for him because he did rule moderately; they do not guard against tyranny as an unbearable evil, because they are ignorant of the fact that even the tyrant who observes moderation in every respect must be deposed. Why? Because the position he holds gives him the *power* to be harsh.

[3] With Clearchus we have one who is cruel, so he'll be easy to deal with himself (because he's hated) and also make it harder for anyone else to establish a tyranny. If on the other hand he'd pretended to be moderate, he would have enjoyed the fruits of a good reputation himself and also left behind easy access to the acropolis for other would-be tyrants. But this must be obvious to you as well.

I'm glad you now find both my style of discourse and my method of delivering these letters safe and secure, and are finally admitting that it was not just some crazy idea of mine. I'm also sending you a copy of my letter to Clearchus. You'll notice its somewhat bombastic tone; I did that on purpose so he would write me off as some kind of mad professor.

Letter 16 Chion to Clearchus

[1] While I was residing in Athens engaged in philosophical studies, my father and certain others of our common acquaintance wrote informing me that you had some grounds of suspicion against me and urging me to refute them; this, they said, would both be the appropriate course of action and work to my advantage. I have no doubts whatever as to the correctness of their advice; but unfortunately I am ignorant as to the basis upon which my reputation has suffered, and this creates a problem for me in composing my defence. I was away when you came to power, and as I was away I could not have opposed you; indeed, no word or action of mine could have had any possible relation with what was occurring over there. I am unaware of any transmarine opposition a man engaged in foreign

travel with few servants might have exerted against someone with absolute power, and this is why I have that problem with my defence: I do not see any charge that can be laid against me.

[2] Let us suppose I am suspected of plotting. That would cause me no difficulty, because I have never entertained the idea; indeed, I have a wealth of arguments at hand to convince you that no such designs could gain access to my soul. Philosophical considerations aside, it seems to me that the fact you have done me no harm should be sufficient proof that I have no hostile feelings towards you. Even those who have no philosophical training – unless that is they are completely insane – do not embark upon enmities because they get some sort of pleasure out of it, nor do they cherish a love of hatred of the kind they have for their boyfriends – far from it, because they are very much aware that nothing brings more pain to humankind than enmity. It is only when something irremediable occurs that divides men's souls from each other that they become enemies, and even then only reluctantly.

[3] As far as you and I are concerned, right up to the present day we have committed no act of enmity against each other, neither great nor small; on your side you have nothing more than assumption and speculation, while on mine I keep my soul pure even from these. What motive could I have for suddenly mounting a challenge against you, particularly since your conduct of state affairs is something I have taken no interest in either before or now? By Zeus, you must think all these triremes and horsemen are giving me big ideas, so that unable to light on anything else you've got it into your head that I have the resources to be your enemy! In fact I left home with eight attendants and two friends, Herakleides and Agathon, and two of those servants I dismissed before setting out on my return journey. I really don't know how people can convince you that this is a sufficient force to use against you.

And here is another thing you are not taking into account. If I were conscious that someone was justified in regarding me with suspicion, would I be voluntarily putting myself in the hands of that very person?

[4] Or is it that I am so in love with enmities that instead of nurturing any friendship that might exist towards me I voluntarily hand my body over to those who will with reason exact vengeance upon it?

The above considerations will constitute a sufficient – nay, more than sufficient – defence, even for those who have not studied philosophy.

Ah, philosophy. When I found I had a natural inclination for the good things philosophy can bring, I did my very best to foster what nature had given me. In particular, when I grew to be a young man I eschewed the path of public office and advancement-seeking; instead I straightaway fell in love with the notion of contemplating the nature of reason. This love brought me to Athens and made me a friend of Plato; even now after all this time I cannot get enough of him.

[5] My natural instinct for quiescence was such that even in my earliest youth I would look down on everything that might potentially lead to some perturbation; and when I went to Athens, I avoided hunting; I did not join up in the Athenian navy to go and fight the Spartans in the Hellespont; I enrolled in no course of instruction which would make me hostile to tyrants and kings, but instead spent my time engaged in dialogue with a man who is himself a lover of quiescence and assimilating the most heavenly doctrine imaginable. The very first thing he told me was to crave quiescence. 'This,' he would say, 'is the light that reveals philosophical reason, whereas political activism and officiousness act like a dark cloud to conceal it and render it undiscoverable to those who are trying to track it down.'

[6] Along with being aware of my natural affinity for it, I was also conscious that to be fully convinced about it would require serious effort. So during this time I have been learning about God who oversees all things and about the way the universe is structured, I have been looking into the basic principles of nature,

and I have been receiving instruction on the proper veneration of righteousness and all the other virtues that philosophy teaches. Nothing is more worthwhile than knowledge of these things – except making the effort to acquire such knowledge. Man may be mortal by nature but he has a portion of God intermingled within; what can be nobler for such a being than to devote the time at his disposal exclusively to the immortal parts of himself and join them to that with which they are cognate? – for I say that those divine parts are cognate with God.

[7] This is what I was both praying and struggling to learn. As for politics – and I hope you won't take umbrage if I speak my mind here – I didn't consider it worth even a thought. But among the many things I did learn are the ones I am now going to put to good use in my relationship with you: that if a person is not doing you wrong, you should treat that person with respect; that when a person is doing you wrong, the best response is to requite him with good deeds, and if that is impossible, with doing nothing; that you should consider a friend to be your most valuable possession; that you should make no one your enemy; that if you do have an enemy you should make him your friend; that you should think nothing so great an evil as that which creates perturbation in your soul and distracts it from its proper function. Knowing that I know this, do you really think I am engaging in some plot against you? No way! Let the activities of war and politics be your domain; all I want is a little slice of your realm, just enough for one who is unperturbed to continue his life of quiescence therein. And if you allow me to talk with my friends, I am confident that I can make them as docile and apolitical as you like; such are the eulogies I will deliver on quiescence, that subject forever so dear to my heart. If I were otherwise minded, it would be the height of ingratitude on my part.

[8] Yes, ingratitude. Suppose my mind were perturbed in the way you suspect it is, and while in such a state the gentle goddess Quiescence were to come and stand next to me. What would she say? 'What an ungrateful wretch you are, Chion! You have

forgotten all that wonderful learning; indeed, you have completely forgotten who you are. When you were devoting yourself to me, you practised righteousness, you acquired soundmindedness, you learned about God, you revived that part of you that is cognate with Him and you came to despise as beneath you such things as ambition, wealth and the like which so impress others. Yet now, at the very time when with your newly elevated principles and strengthened soul, you should be returning thanks to me by associating and conversing with me, you are about to desert me, putting out of your mind the fact that philosophy has taught you not just all those other things, but also and especially the right way to seek out what you do not yet know. And how would you go about this process of seeking and discovering if you deprive yourself of me?'

[9] If she were to speak to me like this, how would I justify myself to her? I can't see any way I could.

You may rest assured that these are the things I am constantly telling myself (and no one can conceal his real thoughts from himself). May I never be found wanting where they are concerned! So you have no valid reason to be apprehensive about me; my quiescence will have no point of contact with your busyness.

Farewell.

Letter 17 *Chion to Plato, greeting*

[1] It is two days before the Festival of Dionysos, and I am despatching to you my most trusted attendants, Pylades and Philokalos. At this festival I intend to make an attack on the tyrant, now that I have for so long worked him into a position of not suspecting me. On that day there is a procession in honour of Dionysos, and I am assuming that while it is going on there will be less vigilance on the part of the bodyguards. Of course I could be wrong; but even if we have to go through fire, we shall not flinch nor shall we bring any shame either on ourselves or on your philosophy. Our conspiracy is strong, a strength

derived from the trust we have in each other more than from numbers.

[2] I know that I shall be killed; my only prayer is that I succeed in killing the tyrant before that happens. If I depart from human-kind after bringing down this tyranny, I would be leaving life accompanied by hymns and prizes of victory. Omens from sacri-fices and the flight of birds, in fact all forms of divination, indicate to me that success in this undertaking will be followed by death. And I myself had a vision, clearer than you'd get in any dream. It was a woman, glamorous, tall, a marvel to look at; she garlanded me with wild olive and headbands, then after a little she showed me a strikingly beautiful tomb and said, 'Chion, when your labour is done, you must come and rest in this tomb.' After such a vision I have strong hopes of dying a noble death, believing that no divination of the soul can be misleading since you too profess this view.

[3] I also believe that if this prophecy proves to be true, I shall reach the pinnacle of blessedness – far more than if I were allowed to live on to old age after killing the tyrant. After so great an achievement it is better to take my leave of human beings rather than continue to share the benefit with them for some unknown period of time. Anything I succeed in doing will be reckoned far more significant than what will be done to me, and my reputation among those I have benefited will be all the greater if I purchase their freedom at the cost of my own death. Beneficiaries feel they have done better out of the transaction if the benefactor has no share of the profit. And so I eagerly await the death that has been prophesied for me.

Now I must bid you farewell, Plato. May you have a happy life and a fulfilling old age. These are my last words to you; of that I am convinced.

Glossary of Personal Names

The meaning of names and mythological figures is explained in the Notes.

CALLIRHOE

Adrastus lawyer
Aphrodite goddess of love and desire; from the first century AD identified with the Roman Venus
Ariston Chaereas' father and rival of Hermocrates
Artaxates chief eunuch of the King of Persia
Artaxerxes Artaxerxes II Memnon, King of Persia; Great King
Bias chief magistrate of Priene
Callirhoe Sicilian girl
Chaereas Sicilian youth
Demetrius Egyptian philosopher; *see also* Theron
Dionysius nobleman in Ionia; based on the historical Dionysius I of Syracuse
Hermocrates ruler of Syracuse and father of Callirhoe
Hyginus servant of Mithridates
Leonas steward of Dionysius
Megabyzos husband of Rhodogune
Mithridates satrap of Caria
Pharnaces ruler of Lydia
Phocas steward of Dionysius' estate
Plangon servant of Dionysius and wife of Phocas
Polycharmus close friend of Chaereas
Rhodogune beautiful Persian woman, sister of Pharnaces
Stateira wife of Artaxerxes, King of Persia
Theron pirate chief (uses the pseudonym Demetrius)
Zopyros Persian aristocrat and father of Rhodogune

DAPHNIS AND CHLOE

Amaryllis girl beloved by Philetas
Astylus son of Dionysophanes and Cleariste
Bryaxis commander of a marauding band from Methymna
Chloe shepherd, 13 when novel begins
Chromis farmer; husband of Lycaenion
Cleariste wife of Dionysophanes
Daphnis goatherd, 15 when novel begins
Dionysophanes owner of the estate on which Daphnis' family works,
   lives in Mytilene
Dorcon cowherd who is in love with Chloe
Dryas shepherd; adoptive father of Chloe
Eros god of love and lust
Eudromus a messenger of Dionysophanes
Gnathon Astylus' companion; a parasite
Hippasus commander of the Mytileneans
Lamon goatherd; adoptive father of Daphnis
Lampis cowherd and suitor of Chloe
Lycaenion glamorous city lady; wife of Chromis
Megacles leading citizen of Mytilene
Myrtale wife of Lamon; adoptive mother of Daphnis
Nape wife of Dryas; adoptive mother of Chloe
Nymphs female divinities associated with nature and companions
   of Pan
Pan god associated with shepherds, hunting and the 'pan pipes'
Philetas old countryman and adviser of Daphnis and Chloe
Rhode wife of Megacles
Sophrone nurse who exposed the baby Daphnis
Tityrus little boy; the youngest of Philetas' children

LETTERS OF CHION

Agathon Chion's friend who accompanies him to Athens
Archedemos Heraclean astronomer
Archepolis failed philosophy student from Lemnos
Baitylos Chion's attendant
Bianor deliverer of letters
Bion Chion's childhood friend
Chion young aristocrat from Heraclea with aspirations to excellence

Clearchus aristocrat from Heraclea, reputedly himself a student of Plato, but with ambitions for political rather than philosophical success

Herakleides Chion's friend who accompanies him to Athens

Kallisthenes Heraclean schoolmaster

Kotys agent of Clearchus and would-be assassin

Krobylos Chion's attendant

Lysis deliverer of letters

Matris Chion's father

Nymphis Clearchus' relative

Phaidimos deliverer of letters

Philokalos Chion's attendant

Philon Chion's attendant

Plato Athenian philosopher, author of many philosophical works and founder of the Academy

Podarkes Chion's attendant

Pylades Chion's attendant

Seuthes Thracian king

Silenos opponent of Clearchus

Simos deliverer of letters

Socrates Athenian philosopher, teacher of Plato

Speusippos Plato's nephew and successor as head of the Academy

Thrason Byzantine businessman

Xenophon Athenian philosopher, military commander and historian

Notes

CALLIRHOE

BOOK 1

[1]

I am Chariton: The first sentence is a pointed allusion to the opening sentence of Thucydides' *History of the Peloponnesian War*. This is a means of self-authorization, but also signals a significant change in prose writing: Chariton's work is as important as that of Thucydides, but will deal with love, not war. See also note to 8.8. For Chariton and the implications of his name, see Introduction.

the city of Aphrodisias: Aphrodisias (near the modern village of Geyre in Turkey) has a privileged place in the history of Greek fiction, being the probable hometown both of Chariton and the author of the *Ninus* romance, an early work of which only fragments survive. It has a claim, therefore, to being the birthplace of the novel. Aphrodisias had a major cult to the goddess that gave the city its name. This fostered a special relationship with Rome, as Aphrodite (Venus) was the mother of Rome's legendary founder, Aeneas.

who had defeated the Athenians: In the 'Sicilian Expedition' during the Peloponnesian War; see Introduction.

a Nereid: A sea nymph.

Aphrodite herself when she was in her prime: Literally, *Aphrodite parthenos* which can mean 'Aphrodite the Virgin'. An unlikely epithet for the goddess of love, this description is, however, reminiscent of the times Aphrodite has appeared to mortals in the guise of a maiden (in the *Homeric Hymn to Aphrodite* and Virgil, *Aeneid*, 1.315).

Achilles, Nireus, Hippolytus and Alcibiades: All renowned for their desirability: Achilles and Nireus were the most handsome of the Greek army at Troy (Homer, *Iliad*, 2.673–4), Hippolytus proved irresistible to his stepmother Phaedra (in, e.g., Euripides, *Hippolytus* and Seneca, *Phaedra*) and Alcibiades was a famously charismatic Athenian politician who planned the Sicilian expedition (see, e.g., Plutarch, *Alcibiades*, 1.3 and Diodorus Siculus 13.68.5).

the first time Callirhoe had attended a public festival: Elite women typically only went out in public to attend religious functions.

Eros was the agitator: Literally, 'Eros was the demagogue'. The political language and context here underlines that marriage was a civic as well as a personal union.

'At this her knees and her dear heart were loosed': Quotation of a Homeric phrase that occurs several times in *Iliad* and *Odyssey* (e.g., *Odyssey*, 4.703) and which is here signalled by Omitowoju's addition 'To quote the bard'. The formula is repeated at *Callirhoe*, 3.6 and 4.5 with somewhat different wording (as is true for other quotations below), and this is the first of many quotations from Homer: what Homer has been to Greek poetry Chariton will be to Greek prose.

darkness poured down over her eyes: A Homeric formula: see *Iliad*, 5.696. Chariton uses it again at 2.7, 3.1 and 4.5.

just as when Artemis appears to huntsmen in a lonely spot: The goddess Artemis was associated with (among other things) hunting and virginity. It could be dangerous for mortals to see her, as Actaeon discovered, but Callirhoe's audience remains safe.

wedding of Thetis: Thetis was a Nereid whom Zeus impregnated with Achilles. Before the baby was born, Zeus arranged for her to marry a mortal man, Peleus. This was a common subject in poetry, e.g., Catullus, poem 64.

goddess Strife: Strife was the only deity not to have been invited to the wedding of Peleus and Thetis. She turned up anyway and threw a golden apple into the crowd, bearing the motto 'To the fairest'. When the goddesses Athena, Hera and Aphrodite fought over it, Zeus instructed the shepherd Paris, son of Priam of Troy, to be the judge, and his verdict (for Aphrodite) led to the abduction of Helen of Sparta and the Trojan War. See also note to 8.1.

[4]

Thus he spake . . . face: Quoted from *Iliad*, 18.22–4, where Achilles learns of the death of his beloved Patroclus. Quoted again at 5.2.

catch the adulterer red-handed and kill him: In classical Athens (as in Augustan Rome), it was probably legal to kill an adulterer caught in flagrante delicto (though our main evidence for this law, Lysias, *Against Eratosthenes*, is controversial).

he kicked her: This act of what would now be called domestic violence characterizes Chaereas as a tyrant. (Nero is said to have kicked his wife in the stomach: Suetonius, *Nero*, 35.3, Tacitus, *Annals*, 16.6.1.) It may also evoke the violence suffered by Hermocrates' historical daughter who was assaulted so viciously by Syracusan enemies of her husband that she committed suicide: see further Hunter 1994, p. 1080.

[5]

Rumour: In this novel Rumour largely serves to spread news of Callirhoe but the personification recalls Virgil's (more sinister) Rumour (Fama) in the *Aeneid*.

interrogated the maidservants with torture: It was established practice for slaves to be tortured in judicial contexts; their testimonies were not believed otherwise.

he wanted to kill himself: One of many episodes in which Chaereas contemplates suicide. To many ancient (and modern) sensibilities, this would seem unheroic behaviour, but the Stoics believed that death offered freedom from unbearable sorrow: see Judith Perkins, *The Suffering Self: Pain and Narrative Representation in the Early Christian Era* (London, 1995), pp. 94–103.

archons: Public officials.

Stone me to death: This kind of self-condemnation is common in Greek fiction (cf. Achilles Tatius 7.7, Heliodorus 8.8.5). Herodotus' story about Adrastus, who unwittingly killed Croesus' son and then killed himself on the young man's tomb, may lie behind (and provide a contrast with) Chaereas here: see Hunter 1994, p. 1082.

[6]

sleeping Ariadne: Ariadne famously slept on the beach at Naxos giving Theseus the opportunity to slip away from his lover. Her pose was a popular subject in art. See also *Daphnis and Chloe*, note to 4.3.

[7]

Let the die be cast!: Said to have been uttered by Julius Caesar as he led his army across the river Rubicon and into civil war; it signifies the point of no return (Suetonius, *Caesar*, 32).

Messanian: Messana, a city in Sicily; modern Messina.

Answering in turn: A Homeric formula (from, e.g., *Odyssey*, 8.500); also used at 5.7 and 8.7.

[10]

Are you telling us now to be philosophers: How philosophers should behave is the subject of the *Letters of Chion*; in Chariton, as elsewhere in the Greek novels, to act 'like a philosopher' is a derogatory phrase.

[11]

Their high court: The Areopagus.

stades: A stade is an imprecise unit of measurement that equalled 125 paces and was equal to roughly .9 of a km.

[12]

he dreamed of locked doors: Dreams and their interpretation are a common feature of Greek fiction. *The Interpretation of Dreams* by Artemidorus, written in the second century AD, details dreams and what they may symbolize and is said to have influenced Sigmund Freud.

the Great King: The standard title for the King of Persia.

Sybaris: A city in southern Italy that no longer existed by the dramatic date of the novel but whose reputation for hedonism (hence 'sybarite') serves Theron well here.

[14]

the registration certificate: To prove that the buyer had purchased a slave, since enslaving a citizen of free birth, except foreigners captured in war, was a crime.

a talent in cash: Silver worth 6,000 drachmas: an exceptionally large amount of money to pay for a slave at the time of Chariton's story.

set sail as quickly as possible before they were discovered: An echo of Thucydides 3.30.1.

BOOK 2

[1]

outstanding . . . for . . . his culture: Education, knowledge and social graces showed a man had *paideia*, 'culture'. A badge of elite status, Callirhoe is also said to have *paideia* at 6.5. Longus' Gnathon is the only character in *Daphnis and Chloe* to be described as having *paideia* (4.17), but in that novel it is a dubious distinction.

not possible for someone who is not freeborn to be physically beautiful: The idea that physical appearance was an index of character and status was common in the ancient world and a motif in Greek fiction.

[2]

radiant in its white brilliance: The description of Callirhoe taking a bath uses language familiar from art criticism and envisages her as a work of art, probably evoking the famous statue of the Aphrodite of Cnidos.

[3]

Like strangers . . . men: Quoted and adapted from *Odyssey*, 17.485–7.

just as it works for a king-bee in a hive: As in the Greek (we now know that the chief bee is female). The same image is used at Xenophon, *Cyropaedia*, 5.1.24.

[4]

a contest between reason and emotion: The ability to debate within oneself was seen as the mark of a cultured man.

satraps: The title of governors of territories known as satrapies.

[5]

Alcinous: King of Phaeacia, in Homer, *Odyssey*, 6–9. He gave the shipwrecked Odysseus generous hospitality before helping him to return home to Ithaca.

[6]

Menelaus . . . Helen: Menelaus was proverbially happy, despite his wife Helen's infidelity with Paris, an infidelity that instigated the Trojan War. However, in desiring a married woman, Dionysius is (unintentionally) more a Paris than a Menelaus.

242

[7]

supplication: A form of ritual pleading.

[9]

Medea . . . the Scythian: Medea was notorious (since Euripides' *Medea*) for being a mother who killed her children to wreak revenge on her unfaithful husband, Jason. Medea was actually from Colchis (on the southern coast of the Black Sea), rather than Scythia (southern Russia), but the reputation of Scythia for cruelty lends rhetorical punch here.

Zethos and Amphion: Twin sons of Zeus by Antiope, they were exposed at birth but rescued and grew up to become rulers of Thebes.

Cyrus: Cyrus the Great (*c.* 600–529 BC) provides a historical example of someone who was exposed at birth but grew up to become a great ruler; he founded the Persian empire.

like unto him . . . his limbs: Quotation from *Iliad*, 23.66ff. describing the ghost of Patroclus.

[11]

sweeter to me than parents, fatherland and child : Echoes *Odyssey*, 9.34.

triremes: The trireme was a swift and agile warship with oarsmen arranged in three rows on each side.

BOOK 3

[1]

Helios: The god of the sun to whom people prayed for prosperity (and, ironically, the grandfather of Medea).

[2]

"for the begetting of children": The standard formula in marriage contracts and frequently used in New Comedy.

the temple of Concord: Concordia was the goddess of marital and social harmony

[3]

It was like Dionysus took Ariadne . . . and Zeus took Semele: Both Semele and Ariadne were mortal women who became deified, which is the ultimate point of Chaereas' comparisons. However (perhaps to mark his distress), it is an unusual version of mythology that is offered here.

I am a Cretan: Theron's lying story reminds us of Odysseus' lying 'Cretan tales' in Homer's *Odyssey*.

[4]

The whole speech had scarce been spoken: A Homeric formula (used, e.g., at *Odyssey*, 16.11 and *Iliad*, 10.540); also at 7.1.

[5]

Child, respect . . . your cares: Chaereas' mother supplicates him with the same gestures and words as Hecuba begs Hector not to go and fight Achilles in *Iliad*, 22.82–3.

Poseidon: God of the sea.

[6]

a gold statue: It was highly unusual for statues of mortals to be made of gold, a material typically used to represent the gods.

His knees . . . faltered: Quotation from *Iliad*, 21.114, the description of the death of Lycaon.

[8]

none . . . has shown Artemis or Athena with her baby: Because both were virgin goddesses.

Nemesis: The personification of divine retribution. Dionysius is praying to her lest his joy in Callirhoe's beauty exceeding that of statues of the goddesses Artemis and Athena be viewed as hubris (arrogance towards the gods) and lead to punishment.

[9]

we are all ready to believe the thing we want to be true: An echo of Demosthenes, *Olynthiacs*, 3.19; also echoed at 6.5.

BOOK 4

[1]

"Bury me . . . Hades": From *Iliad*, 23.71, where Patroclus' shade speaks to Achilles.

So that . . . high seas: From *Odyssey*, 24.83, of the tomb of Achilles.

Leda: The mother of Helen of Sparta by Zeus, who grew close to her in the guise of a swan.

'white-armed' . . . 'lovely ankled': The first is a common epithet in Homer to describe Hera, queen of the Olympian gods; the second is a Homeric epithet used of a number of female characters in the *Odyssey*.

[4]

Would like . . . marry her: From *Odyssey*, 15.21, spoken by Athena to Telemachus.

[5]

Bias: Means 'Man of Force'.

[7]

Like unto Artemis or golden Aphrodite: The description of Penelope at *Odyssey*, 17.37 and 19.54. Chariton uses Homeric allusions to depict Callirhoe alternatively as the chaste Penelope and as the adulterous Helen, with her fidelity and desirability in tension.

When it . . . his arms: Quotation from Menander's comic play *Misoumenos*, 9.

BOOK 5

[1]

Bactra and Susa: In the Persian Empire, Bactra was the most important city of Bactria (in what is now north Afghanistan) and Susa was the capital of Elam (now in south-west Iran).

[2]

With both hands . . . face: See note to 1.4.

[3]

trying to kiss the car itself: Allusion to a famous romantic departure scene: Panthea kissing farewell the carriage of her husband Abradates in Xenophon, *Cyropaedia*, 6.4.9–10.

[4]

Eleusinian Nights: Annual religious festival in honour of the goddess Demeter at Eleusis near Athens; often known as 'the Eleusinian Mysteries'. See also *Daphnis and Chloe*, note to 4.13.

Seated, the gods . . . centre: Quotation from *Iliad*, 4.1, when the gods debate the fate of the city of Troy.

[5]

With Priam, Panthoos and Thymoites: Quotation from *Iliad*, 3.146, describing Helen looking down from the wall of the city with the Trojan elders.

Everyone prayed . . . her side: Quotation from *Odyssey*, 1.366 and 18.213, describing the suitors' designs on Penelope.

[10]

Protesilaus: The first Greek to be killed at Troy; so great was his wife's grief that he was allowed to return to the land of the living for one day only.

Even if they forget the dead in Hades: Adapted from Achilles' words about the dead Patroclus, at *Iliad*, 22.389–90.

BOOK 6

[1]

Sometimes lying . . . face down: Quotation from *Iliad*, 24.10–11, describing Achilles after the death of Patroclus.

The Sun, your ancestor: According to Plutarch, Cyrus' ancestor and namesake took his name from the Persian word for sun (*Artaxerxes*, 1.2).

[2]

the prize was not the olive bough . . . pine cones: The olive was the prize awarded at the Olympic games, apples at the Pythian and pine at the Isthmian.

The savour . . . the smoke: Quoted from *Iliad*, 1.317.

[3]

"*the one who deals the blow, heals it*": A refrain that originates in the tale of Telephus (the subject of a lost tragedy by Euripides), who was injured by the hero Achilles with a wound that would not heal. The Delphic oracle (or, in another version of the myth, Odysseus) suggested this remedy and Telephus was cured with rust taken from Achilles' spear.

[4]

Tyrian: The city of Tyre was famous for its production of purple-red dye. See also note to 7.2.

Chinese workmanship: Contact between the Greco-Roman world and China is attested from the late first century BC.

She will come . . . swift deer: Quotation from *Odyssey*, 6.102–4, a description of the princess Nausicaa. The shift to Homer's words provides Dionysius with a pleasingly (and teasingly) educated climax to his fantasy about Callirhoe.

[6]

O treacherous beauty: Recalls Helen, in *Iliad*, Book 3, who also blames her beauty for her misfortunes.

[7]

the two paths: The choice put before Callirhoe (sleeping with the king in return for material gain and the husband of her choice or excruciating torture) recalls that put before Gyges, in Herodotus 1.11–12. He chose a wife and a kingdom over death; by contrast, Callirhoe's choice shows her courage and nobility.

Marathon . . . Salamis: These battles (in 490 and 480 BC respectively) were the most significant victories of the Athenians over the Persians during the Persian Wars.

[8]

Egypt . . . huge revolt: Egypt frequently rebelled against Persian rule. However, scholarly attempts to determine a particular historical event lying behind the fictional revolt are inconclusive.

Memphis . . . Pelusium: The capital city of Egypt, and a coastal settlement on the far eastern tributary of the river Nile.

Ecbatana: The capital of Media and site of one of the Persian royal residences (modern Hamadan in Iran).

scythed: Scythed chariots (war chariots with blades fixed to the axles) are described in some detail in Xenophon's *Cyropaideia*, 6.1.28–30.

BOOK 7
[1]

Medes and Persians: The Medes were an ancient Iranian people related to the Persians and incorporated into the Persian empire. From a Greek perspective, Medes and Persians were so closely associated that their names could be used interchangeably.

[2]

May I not . . . to come: Hector's last words before he went into combat with Achilles and so to his death (*Iliad*, 22.304-5).

Tyre: Phoenician city (about 80 km south of modern Beirut). It features more prominently in Achilles Tatius' novel, *Leucippe and Clitophon*.

Heracles: The deified hero of the Greeks was identified with the Phoenician god Melkart.

the security of their fortifications: The description of Chaereas' siege of Tyre in this and the following section recalls that by Alexander the Great in 333/2 BC.

[3]

We two . . . of god: Adapted from *Iliad*, 9.48–9, where Diomedes defies Agamemnon's proposal to abandon the war at Troy rather than face defeat.

Dorian: Dorians were a politically important tribe of Greeks (that included Spartans and Corinthians as well as Sicilians) whose clash with Ionian Greeks resulted in the Peloponnesian War.

There are not five million: The number of Persians at the battle of Thermopylae according to Herodotus' implausible account (*Histories*, 7.186).

Othryades . . . Leonidas: Othryades led 300 Spartans and joined with 300 Argives to take possession of Thyreae (Herodotus 1.82). Leonidas famously led his 300 at the battle of Thermopylae. They provide uncertain models for Chaereas' future: Othryades was the sole survivor of his troop and committed suicide at the shame of it, whereas Leonidas died a hero's death in combat.

[4]

Shield pressed . . . on man: A Homeric formula (*Iliad*, 13.131 and 16.215).

He struck . . . from them: Another Homeric line used of Odysseus' slaughter of the suitors (*Odyssey*, 22.308 and 24.184) and of Diomedes' killing of the Thracians (*Iliad*, 10.483). The simile of the lion that follows echoes that in *Iliad*, 10.485ff.

In the midst of this indescribable confusion: Taken from Xenophon, *Cyropaedia*, 7.1.32.

Sidon: The second most important city in Phoenicia, after Tyre.

Arados: An island city, the modern fishing town of Arwad.

[5]

Their minds were focused on nothing trivial: Appears to be a quotation from Thucydides 2.8.1, describing the Athenians and the Spartans at the beginning of the Peloponnesian War, but the text is uncertain here.

[6]

he will make sure you are treated kindly: The praise of Chaereas' good character to Stateira seems to have been modelled on a similar episode in Xenophon where Cyrus is praised to Panthea (*Cyropaedia*, 5.1.6).

BOOK 8

[1]

nor with Dionysus as a bridegroom: According to myth, after her desertion by Theseus Ariadne was married to Dionysus.

Alexander who is known as Paris: Homer and other writers refer to Paris by the name Alexander. Aphrodite's gift to Paris was Helen of Sparta.

it contains the resolution of all the problems: Literally, it will 'cleanse away' (*katharsion*) all the problems in the previous books. This is a clear allusion to Aristotle's famous theory of tragedy, in which he argues that through its evocation of fear and pity, tragedy gives its audience some kind of relief or release (*Poetics*, 1449b28). The catharsis that the novel will bring about is very different; it will provide relief through pleasure and a happy ending.

Rejoicing, they . . . marriage bed: Quotation from *Odyssey*, 23.296, the reunion between Odysseus and Penelope.

[2]

Paphos: Coastal city on the south-west of Cyprus. The mythical birth-place of Aphrodite, so there had been a shrine since early times. The port, however, was built later than the time of Chariton's story.

Brasidas: A Spartan general in the Peloponnesian War.

[4]

You have . . . a daughter: Mentioned in 1.12; in Greece half siblings by different mothers could marry.

[5]

'*With Stateira . . . own losses*: Adapted from *Iliad*, 19.302, when the women grieve ostensibly for Patroclus but in reality for their own losses.

as if it were Callirhoe herself: The extraordinary power of letters to make their writer present is worth bearing in mind when reading *Letters of Chion*.

'*dandled him in his arms*': Quotation from *Iliad*, 6.474, when Hector plays with his infant son Astyanax.

[6]

Aphrodite herself rising up out of the sea: According to myth Aphrodite was born from the foam of the sea off the coast of Cyprus. A more precise image may be evoked here: *Aphrodite Rising from the Sea* by the painter Apelles.

[8]

Polycharmus shouted out my name: An inconsistency with events as they were reported in 4.2.

my sister as a wife: The first mention of Chaereas' sister, but ending the romance with a double marriage looks back to Menander's *Dyscolus* and forward to Jane Austen's *Pride and Prejudice*.

I have to write: The last word in the Greek text (write) is the same word used by Thucydides in the opening sentence of *History of the Peloponnesian War*. The allusion is pointed: see note to 1.1 (*I am Chariton*). The ending is the very first romantic happy ending in Greek prose literature.

DAPHNIS AND CHLOE

BOOK 1

Daphnis and Chloe: The only Greek novel to open with a formal
   prologue.

Lesbos: Renowned for being the birthplace of the archaic Greek poets
   Sappho and Alcaeus, in the imaginative geography of Greek literature
   it was a place charged with eroticism.

Nymphs: Female divinities associated with nature. Connected in myth
   and cult with various gods, they had special relationships with Pan
   and with Dionysus and Apollo (who were sometimes called 'Nymph-
   leaders'). They were worshipped all over Greece, including Lesbos.

the desire took me to repaint the painting: Introduces the narrative as
   being an extended description and interpretation of a painting. Repre-
   senting a picture in words was common in imperial literature, but
   here the narrator is not just attempting to reproduce the visual
   through the verbal, but to outdo the splendour of the painting. See
   also the Introduction.

Love and . . . the Nymphs and . . . Pan: In Greek, Love (Eros) is both
   a god and an emotion. Pan is a god who protects shepherds and
   whose domain is the pastoral world. As his half-man, half-goat
   appearance might suggest, Pan has a less benign aspect: his myths
   (some of which feature in the novel) often involve the victimization
   of Nymphs.

possession from which all men may derive pleasure: A striking echo of
   the famous proposition by the historian Thucydides (1.22.4) that his
   work be 'a possession for all time'. This is an ironic touch: Longus
   is writing a very different type of narrative, concerned with very
   different pleasures.

[1]

Mytilene: The largest and most powerful city on Lesbos was still flour-
   ishing in Roman times, but Longus avoids any mention of the
   contemporary city or its Roman rulers; his Mytilene is an independ-
   ent city-state, set in an indeterminate, classical Greek past.

stades: See *Callirhoe*, note to 1.11.

[3]

Myrtale: An aromatic plant; with erotic as well as pastoral connotations, as the plant was associated with Aphrodite, goddess of desire.

Daphnis: A typical name for a shepherd, meaning 'Laurel' or 'Bay', and it commonly features in the pastoral poetry of Theocritus' *Idylls* and Virgil's *Eclogues*. More pointedly, Daphnis was also the name of the mythical founder of pastoral poetry. In broad outline, the myth tells that Daphnis was the son of Hermes and a nymph and was raised by Nymphs (or shepherds), having been exposed at birth. He fell in love with a nymph and swore to be faithful to her, however, either willingly or seduced while drunk, broke his promise. As punishment he was blinded, and he sought respite in composing pastoral poetry. See R. L. Hunter, *A Study of Daphnis and Chloe* (Cambridge, 1983), pp. 22–31, for the different versions of the story and its impact on Longus.

[4]

Dryas: 'Oak'.

[6]

Nape: Continuing the countryside motif in the characters' names, means 'Glen'. Some groups of Nymphs were called Dryads, others Napaea: the names of Chloe's adoptive parents thus link her even more closely to the deities.

Chloe: 'The budding of spring', with connotations of youth and freshness.

[7]

Daphnis was fifteen . . . Chloe two years younger: Many works of Greek fiction are concerned with couples on the brink of adulthood and the rites of passage they undergo. The legal age for marriage in the early empire was 15.

[8]

the winged boy: Recognizable to the reader (but not to the uneducated adoptive fathers of Daphnis and Chloe) as Eros: the wings and bow were common attributes of the god.

[9]

the beginning of spring: Unlike the other Greek novels, whose plots advance around movement through space as their characters travel abroad, in Longus it is time, and the changing seasons. Book 1 is shaped by early spring and summer and ends with the onset of autumn, 2 sees harvest time, 3 winter, another spring and summer, and in Book 4 events come to fruition in concert with a second harvest.

[10]

He would cut slender reeds: Daphnis is making pan pipes, also known as pan flutes, or *syrinx*. These consist of five or so reeds, bound together and tuned to scale by being cut to unequal lengths (although here Daphnis does not cut them). The sound is produced when the player blows across the top of the open reeds. According to myth Pan first invented the pipes (see 2.34).

[13]

her heart was vexed: Chloe's symptoms conform to the established literary repertoire of symptoms for lovesickness from lyric and Hellenistic poetry (cf. J. R. Morgan (ed.), *Longus: Daphnis and Chloe* (Oxford, 2004), p. 159).

[15]

Dorcon: 'Male roe deer', appropriate to this story, though not found elsewhere in pastoral literature.

bacchant's: Bacchants, also known as maenads, were female devotees of Dionysus and renowned for their sensuous abandon.

[16]

Zeus: Myth has it that Amalthea (represented as a nymph, or as a she-goat) suckled the infant Zeus in Crete. It was said to be one of Amalthea's horns, broken off, that became the 'Cornucopia', the 'Horn of plenty'.

Dionysus: Most of surviving images of the god of wine and revelry (as well as the theatre and ecstasy), largely from vase paintings of the archaic and classical periods, portray Dionysus as bearded (in contrast to the god Apollo, who is shown as a beardless youth). However, later representations commonly depict him without a beard. See also note to 2.2.

Satyrs: Mythological half-men, half-beasts associated with Dionysus and Pan. Sexual predators, they frequently chased Nymphs and bacchants. See also 2.2.

[17]

paler than summer grass: A close allusion to one of Sappho's poems in which she describes the effects of love: 'I am paler than grass' (31.14) or 'I am more moist than grass' (the Greek comparative adjective *chloroteros* clearly denotes a visual property of grass, though whether this is pallor, greenness or moisture is not possible to say for certain).

[18]

Daphnis withers away: Allusion to how love causes the cowherd Daphnis to wither away in Theocritus, *Idylls*, 1.66–141 and 7.71–7.

[22]

from the jaws of the wolf: A proverbial expression, for someone who was unexpectedly lucky, derives from the fable of Aesop (156 in *Aesopica*, ed. B. E. Perry 1980; repr. (Urbana, IL, 2007) in which a heron puts his head into the mouth of a wolf to remove a bone. When the bird claims his reward, the reply is that he should be satisfied with having safely escaped the wolf's jaws. Here Longus plays with the proverbial and the literal.

[27]

Pan and . . . Pine: This is the first of three aetiological myths, all involving Pan and the metamorphosis of a beautiful girl, and all of which invite comparison and contrast with the experiences of Daphnis and Chloe (see 2.34 and 3.23 and notes). Mentioned, but not related here, is the myth that Pan desired the Nymph Pine (the English translation for the Greek name Pitys), but she, in order to escape his advances, turned into a pine tree (cf. Lucian, *The Dialogues of the Gods*, 22.4, Virgil, *Eclogues*, 7.24).

[28]

pirates from Pyrrha: Not known for piracy, and some disagreement in the manuscripts makes Pyrrha an uncertain textual reading. This is not of great importance: pirates are a staple threat in Greek fiction.

[30]

Ox-ford: Captures the etymological pun in the Greek, 'Bosporus', the name of the narrow strait that connects the Black Sea and the Sea of Marmara, which means 'Cow crossing', a reference to Io who, according to myth, swam the strait in the form of a heifer.

[32]

Love's piracies: In the original, 'love's piracy' but the plural reads
better. This closing image equates Love with the threat of violence.

BOOK 2

[1]

new wine: That is the harvest of the first vintage. The second vintage
is described in Book 4.

[2]

festival of Dionysus: A wine festival in honour of the god of the vine
also takes place in Achilles Tatius, *Leucippe and Clitophon*, 2.1. See
also note to 1.16.

dogs off the leash: Aristotle quotes this simile from Androtion's speech:
when Idrieus was released from prison, he behaved like dogs off the
leash, which bite when they are set loose, i.e. viciously hostile (*Art
of Rhetoric*, 3.4).

[3]

Philetas: The historical Philetas (or Philitas) of Cos was a renowned
erotic poet of considerable influence on Theocritus' pastoral poetry
and other writers, including, almost certainly, Longus. Philetas' work
has not survived, so it is impossible to trace the extent of Longus'
engagement with his poetry.

I have come to reveal to you: Philetas is an *erotodidaskalos* or *praecep-
tor amoris*, a teacher of desire. This is a figure with an established
literary (and philosophical) history, notably Diotima in Plato's
Symposium, the poet in Ovid's *Ars Amatoria* and Clinias and Menelaus in Achilles Tatius' *Leucippe and Clitophon*. Philetas is one of
the instructors; the other is Lycaenion: see 3.17–19.

I have a garden: Gardens in ancient fiction are typically erotic and
highly symbolic spaces. See also 4.2–3.

[4]

a boy: A puzzle to Daphnis and Chloe, but of course, Eros.

[5]

older than Cronus: Cronus, youngest son of Gaia (Earth) and Ouranos (Heaven), was said to have ruled the universe for a time before Zeus assumed sovereignty. There is untranslatable punning in this sentence: 'I am older than *Cronus* and all time (*chronos*) itself.'

Amaryllis: A conventional name for a shepherdess, familiar from Theocritus' *Idylls* and Virgil's *Eclogues*.

[7]

what power he had: The most straightforward translation, but the phrase could also mean 'what [the word] eros meant'.

my soul fell sick: The symptoms of lovesickness that Philetas describes recall Sappho fr. 31.5–6.

I praised Echo: This line is reminiscent of Virgil, *Eclogues*, 1.5, probably due to a lost common source, possibly the poet Philetas. For the story of Pan and Echo, see 3.23.

[12]

Methymna: The second most important city on ancient Lesbos; now modern Molivos.

obols: Common currency in ancient Greece; six obols = one drachma.

[15]

puts his goats to pasture by the sea: Literally, 'on the sea' and the sense is unclear, but there may well be a pun on the Greek word *aiges* meaning both 'goats' and 'waves'.

[19]

taking the role of suppliants: Supplication is a form of ritual pleading.

[26]

flowering ivy on their horns: Ivy is usually associated with Dionysus rather than Pan. This episode is reminiscent of the *Homeric Hymn to Dionysus*, in which Dionysus tells of when, abducted by pirates, he made ivy climb up the mast of the ship, and turned the crew into dolphins (see also 4.3).

[28]

Bryaxis: 'To luxuriate', part of Longus' characterization of the Methymnaeans as hedonistic.

[34]

Pan . . . Syrinx: An explanation of the origins of the pan pipes, but also a myth of eroticism and violence that provides a sinister counterpoint to the courtship of Daphnis and Chloe (as is emphasized in their acting out of the myth at 2.37). Achilles Tatius gives a similar account (*Leucippe and Clitophon*, 8.6.7–11); the version in Ovid's *Metamorphoses* (1.689ff.) is less violent.

[35]

showed every skill in pastoral music: There is punning here (and elsewhere) in the Greek that is hard to render in translation: the word *eunomia* means 'lawful behaviour', 'good pasturing' and 'skilful tune', all of which are connected in the novel.

BOOK 3
[6]

an ill-omened moment: A joke: in the ancient world the behaviour of birds was studied by priests and interpreted as auguring well or badly for the future.

[11]

'Iacchus!' . . . 'Evoe!': Ritual cries in the Dionysiac cult.

[12]

the nightingales to sing . . . 'Itys': Allusion to the myth of the origin of the nightingale: Tereus, the King of Thrace, married the Athenian princess Procne, but then raped her sister Philomela and cut out her tongue. Philomela wove the crime into a tapestry and the sisters then enacted revenge on Tereus by killing his son, Itys, and serving his flesh at a banquet. When Tereus realized what he had eaten he pursued the sisters, and all three were turned into birds. Procne became a nightingale, Philomela a swallow, and Tereus a hawk or a hoopoe. The nightingale's cry 'Itu, Itu' is said to be Procne mourning her dead son: 'Itys, Itys'. The story was the subject of Sophocles' lost

play *Tereus*, has its most lurid treatment in Ovid's *Metamorphoses*
(6.422–674) and is told twice in Achilles Tatius' *Leucippe and Clitophon* (5.3.4–8, 5.5.1–9).

[15]

Lycaenion: The second of the novel's instructors in love. Her name,
'Little wolf', hints at her sexual predation, and makes her a female
counterpart to Dorcon (1.20).

[18]

guided him on the road: This captures perfectly the Greek text's shift
into euphemism here.

[23]

Echo: This tale is only found in Longus. Elsewhere, Echo is also associated with Pan but more commonly with Narcissus, whose rejection
of her love made her waste away until all that remained was her
imitative voice.

the Muses: Deities who presided over the arts and sciences.

her limbs, still singing: There is a pun in the Greek: *mele* means both
'limbs' and 'songs'.

[27]

three thousand drachmas: The sum is large enough to impress Dryas,
but small change to the wealthy Methymnaeans: it is one of the
occasions where Longus emphasizes the disparity in privilege between
city dwellers and country folk.

[33]

an apple that hung: The description of the apple is strongly reminiscent
of a similar image in a famous wedding song by Sappho (fr. 105 LP).

[34]

this prize that Aphrodite took for her beauty: A reference to the judgement of Paris: see *Callirhoe*, note to 1.1 (*goddess Strife*).

BOOK 4

[3]

paintings of Dionysus: These depict episodes from Dionysus' life. *Semele giving birth*: A mortal woman impregnated by Zeus who visited her in mortal guise, Semele was tricked into demanding that Zeus reveal himself in his true magnificence, and when he did she was burnt to a crisp. Zeus plucked the foetus from the cinders and sewed it into his thigh until it was ready to be 'born'. *Ariadne sleeping*: Dionysus took Ariadne as his lover after she fell asleep on the island of Naxos and was abandoned by the hero Theseus. *Lycurgus in chains*: The ruler Lycurgus (whose name means 'Wolf-worker') tried to ban the Dionysiac cult from Thrace. Driven mad by Dionysus, he attacked his family and eventually the people of Thrace had him dismembered by wild horses. *Pentheus being torn apart*: King of Thebes, he, too, resisted the cult of Dionysus, with the result that Dionysus drove his mother mad and she tore him apart (the subject of Euripides' *Bacchae*). *Indians in defeat*: Dionysus waged war in India and triumphed: the subject of Nonnus' epic *Dionysiaca* (fifth century AD).

[5]

Eudromus: 'Good Runner'.

[8]

flayed like Marsyas: A satyr who challenged Apollo to a flute contest; the god won and had Marsyas flayed alive.

[9]

foster-brothers nursed on the same milk: Eudromus' birth mother, presumably one of Dionysophanes' slaves, was wet nurse to Astylus.

[10]

Astylus: 'City-slicker'; his name contrasts him with the rustic Daphnis.

'parasite': One who sponges off the wealthy; a stock figure in ancient Greek comedy.

Gnathon: 'Jaws', a common name for the parasite: a stereotypically gluttonous character.

[11]

a pederast by nature: That is, a man who has sexual relations with boys
who are on the brink of manhood. Ancient pederasty maps uneasily
on to modern paedophilia (which is often synonymous with child
abuse) and modern homosexuality (sexuality in antiquity being
conceived more in terms of sexual acts than sexual orientations), so
the meaning is difficult to convey accurately here. Male same-sex
relations were usually acceptable, and indeed celebrated, in classical
Greece. However, at the time when Longus was writing, attitudes
were changing, and Greek fiction shows a romanticizing of hetero-
sexuality and a sidelining, or even, as here, caricaturing, of same-sex
relations.

[12]

it was fine for he-goats to mount she-goats: Arguments 'from nature'
against same-sex relations go back to Plato's *Laws* (8.836c) and
anticipate modern arguments that take similar lines, and are, of
course, anthropomorphizing and highly selective ('bisexual' gorillas
are rarely held up as an example); the joke here is that nature has
repeatedly failed to teach the youths how to act upon their desire.

needing a man's hand: The translation hints at the sexual innuendo
intended here.

[13]

Dionysophanes: Literally, 'Dionysus Manifest', a name that has encouraged some to read the novel as encoding the Dionysiac cult, or
perhaps the Orphic cult (Phanes was a deity central to Orphism, as
was Dionysus). However, Dionysophanes is also an attested aristocratic name, which gives this lord of the manor a suitable *deus ex
machina* quality.

Cleariste: 'Renowned for Excellence', a commonly attested aristocratic
name.

Demeter: Goddess of agriculture and harvest.

[14]

Apollo . . . worked for Laomedon: As punishment for rebelling against
Zeus, Apollo and Poseidon were ordered to serve Laomedon, King
of Troy, for a year. In Homer's *Iliad* (21.444ff.), Apollo is described
as herding cattle as part of his penance.

[17]

Anchises . . . Aphrodite: Anchises, mortal lover of Aphrodite, and father
of the hero Aeneas, was said by Homer to have been an ox-herd
(*Iliad*, 5.312ff.).

Branchus . . . Apollo: Branchus was said to have been a shepherd whom
Apollo loved and endowed with the gift of prophecy; he founded an
oracle at Didyma, near Miletus.

Ganymede . . . Zeus': The young Ganymede was said to have been
shepherding flocks when Zeus, in the form of an eagle, swooped
down and abducted him to be his lover.

[18]

Love made men into great orators: Literally, into sophists, professional
teachers, in the fifth and fourth centuries BC, who travelled from
place to place and had a reputation for twisting arguments.
There was a long tradition of associating *eros* and sophistry; in
Plato's *Symposium* (203d) where Eros is famously described as a
sophist who is always philosophizing, and, in Achilles Tatius, Eros
is himself described as a sophist (*Leucippe and Clitophon*, 1.10.1,
5.27.4).

left like an ox in the stall: A proverbial expression meaning 'to be left
in a useless position'.

[20]

offered himself up for torture: See *Callirhoe*, note to 1.5.

[21]

Dear Fates: The Fates (Moirai) were personifications of destiny. Their
invocation is colloquial here.

Sophrone: A name commonly used of nurses in New Comedy.

[34]

Hermes: A god who (among other capacities) presided over sleep; hence
the last libation is to him.

[35]

Megacles: 'Very famous', an aristocratic name.

public services such as choruses and triremes: Wealthy citizens gained kudos by funding public services, including the theatre (choruses) and military (triremes: see also *Callirhoe*, note to 2.11).

[36]

Rhode: 'Rose', associates Chloe's birth mother with the natural world.

[39]

Philopoemen . . . Agele: 'Lover of shepherds' and 'Flock', respectively.

[40]

games that shepherds play: The word for 'games', *paignia*, is also a literary term, used in the titles of Hellenistic poems to mean something like 'literary amusements'; the final word thus reflects on the novel's own literary status, as well as playfully glossing the climax of the erotic education of Daphnis and Chloe.

LETTERS OF CHION

Letter 1

The first letter makes none of the concessions to the reader that the openings of the prose novels usually do: introducing the characters and setting an agenda. Rather, we are left to piece together why Chion's parents are upset and to contemplate his character, much as we might do if we really were illicitly to read another's correspondence.

'counterpoise to grief': Quotation from Sophocles' *Electra*, 120. The intention is to distinguish Chion from the outset as an educated and well-read young man.

Letter 2

To the same: The manuscript tradition has this heading where the addressee is the same as that of the previous letter, while a real letter would begin with a proper address. The heading breaks the epistolary fiction but also enhances the sense that the letters are to be read as a collection.

testimony to his services: The first of three letters of recommendation to Chion's parents; it foreshadows Letters 7 and 8.

Letter 3

[1]

Xenophon: The philosopher, soldier and historian (*c.* 430–*c.* 350 BC), an example of a philosopher who is also an activist. Much of this letter recalls episodes in Xenophon's *Anabasis*, in which he tells of how he joined the Ten Thousand, a large army of mercenaries hired by Cyrus the Younger, in an expedition to seize the throne of Persia from Cyrus' brother Artaxerxes II. The mission was a failure but Xenophon distinguished himself as one of the leaders who led the army to safety and then on to fight for Seuthes II of Thrace.

[3]

In the midst . . . quite vanished: Cf. *Anabasis*, 7.1.18–31. Chion's implication that it is through Xenophon's use of Socratic arguments that he prevents the Greek army from sacking Byzantium is different from the account in the *Anabasis*, perhaps reflected in the humorous touch of Chion being unable to hear them.

[6]

I could no longer be a brave soldier: The relationship between the philosophic and the active life was much discussed in ancient philosophy. Cf. Plato, *Republic*, 519c–521b and 539e–540c, where Socrates insists that philosophers must be active in the service of the state, both in politics and war. The most concentrated treatment may be found in Aristotle's *Nicomachean Ethics*, 10.6–9.

bewitched by philosophy: The Athenian politician Alcibiades expresses the same fear that Socrates will bewitch him away from public life, in Plato, *Symposium*, 215b–216b.

[7]

my courage . . . my rashness: On the distinction between them, see Plato, *Laches*, 196e–197c. Chion seems to be taking the position of Nicias: that it is knowledge that distinguishes the one from the other.

Letter 4

[1]

the Kids: A constellation of stars. To associate bad weather with the setting of the Kids is a poetic conceit based on Callimachus, *Epigrams*, 18.5: 'Sailor, avoid mixing it with the sea when the Kids are setting.'

[2]

stades: See *Callirhoe*, note to 1.11.

under attack from Thracians: Selymbria and Perinthos feature in Xenophon's narrative of operations around Byzantium in collaboration with Seuthes (*Anabasis*, 7.2.8, 11, 28; 7.4.2; 7.5.15; 7.6.24), but there is no question of any Thracian attack on the town. Perhaps the author's emphasis on the fact that Chion and his companions had heard nothing about it is an acknowledgement of its fictionality.

[4]

as the winds treated us very kindly: Chion seems to ignore the inconsistency with his earlier meteorological predictions.

Letter 5

He is a wise man: In comparison with the vivid and laudatory introduction to Xenophon, this description of Plato is rather underwhelming. While Chion may admire him as a philosopher, he clearly regards Xenophon as his true role model.

Letter 6

Chion alludes to Letters 6 and 13 of Plato's *Letters*.

Letter 7

[2]

his unstable and flighty character: Ancient theorists of letter writing emphasize its suitability for describing and revealing character (*ethopoieia*). This letter illustrates a good, if priggish, man (Chion, who shows generosity to those who have ill-treated him) and a bad

man (Archepolis, whose contempt for philosophy is one of many
flaws). In the characterization of Archepolis as someone who does
not learn from philosophy, the author suggests that Plato's teachings
do not necessarily bring about good for society and strongly anticipates the characterization of Clearchus.

the Bellerophon scenario: Death by letter. Myth has it that Bellerophon
rejected the advances of the wife of Proteus, King of Tiryns. Piqued,
she falsely accused him of rape; Proteus responded by sending Bellerophon to her father bearing a sealed letter containing instructions to
kill its bearer (see *Iliad*, 6.152–202).

Letter 8

A short, formal letter whose meaning is explicable when one reads the
previous letter (Cf. Letters 15 and 16).

Letter 9

the Heraion: The sanctuary of Hera.

the Kallichoros: A river near Heraclea where there was a cave sacred
to Dionysus (Apollonius of Rhodes, *Argonautika*, 2.904–10).

Letter 10

In the Platonic *Letter* 13 (361b–e) 'Plato' tells Dionysios that he intends
to use his 30 minas for this purpose, but goes on to say that the other
girls are not yet of marriageable age.

Letter 11

a five-year period: This and Letter 12 suggest that Chion's stay in Athens
was of five years' duration. However, the meeting with Xenophon
in Byzantium can only have occurred in late 400 BC (late in the year
being suggested by the astronomical reference in Letter 4). On time,
see the Introduction.

natural ability, a love of hard work: For their importance to the trainee
philosopher, see Plato, *Republic*, 535c.

Letter 12

after hearing about the tyranny: Clearchus has staged a *coup d' état*, which is Chion's reason for cutting short his philosophical training and returning home. See also note to Letter 11.

since Lysis is delivering this letter: Chion obviously trusts this courier (see Letter 7.2). One of the several acknowledgements that letters may be intercepted and fall into the wrong hands: an effective technique for cranking up the tension.

Letter 13

[1]

after I'd sent that letter: One that got lost in transit?

the Odeion: Also known as the Odeum, a small theatre or covered hall used for music competitions and meetings.

[3]

he also belongs to Clearchus' family: An ironic detail, as Memnon (*FGrH* 434.3) suggests that Chion was also a relative of Clearchus, which is omitted from *Letters* (see the Introduction).

Letter 14

[1]

an autocracy that is too entrenched to remove: According to historical record this is indeed what happened. After the assassination of Clearchus, his brother Satyros seized power, and Heraclea was thereafter subject to a succession of tyrants until it was taken over by Lysimachus at the beginning of the third century BC.

[2]

It is the same with sickness in the state: The analogy between body and state is common in ancient writing: see, e.g., Plato, *Republic*, 556e.

[3]

no enslavement at all: The idea that the wise are free but the immoral enslaved is discussed by Plato and was also promoted by the Stoics

(see, e.g., Diogenes Laertius, *Lives of the Ancient Philosophers*, 7.121;
Epictetus, *Discourses*, 1.19, 4.1).

[4]

Clearchus . . . will be enslaved: Recalls Plato's suggestion that tyrants
are enslaved (Plato, *Republic*, 579d–e).

Letter 15

Like Letters 7 and 8, Letters 15 and 16 are to be read together.

[2]

they do not guard against tyranny: Anticipates Brutus' 'serpent's egg'
argument (Shakespeare, *Julius Caesar*, 2.1.28–34).

Letter 16

This letter is full of Platonic resonances but has no coherent Platonic
agenda.

[3]

all these triremes and horsemen: Chion pretends that Clearchus must
be assuming he is spending his time in Byzantium hiring ships and
cavalry to stage a counter-coup, the precedent being Seuthes hiring
survivors of the Ten Thousand (see Letter 3.4).

[5]

fight the Spartans in the Hellespont: A reference, perhaps, to the operations of Thrasybulus around the Hellespont in 389 BC (Xenophon,
Hellenika, 4.8.25ff.), which among other things succeeded in bringing Byzantium back under Athenian influence and restoring
democratic government (4.8.27).

[8]

were to come and stand next to me: In Plato's *Crito* (50a–54c), Socrates similarly imagines the Laws of Athens coming to give their
opinion on the proposal that he should escape from prison. There
are a number of echoes of their speech here.

[9]

Farewell: The standard epistolary courtesies; it is possible that he also
began the letter with 'Greetings' (as two manuscripts have it).

Letter 17

[1]

Our conspiracy is strong: Unlike in other accounts, co-conspirators are
not named nor does anyone else play any significant role (see the
Introduction).

[2]

hymns and prizes of victory: A pointed echo of the prizes for acquiring
virtue in Letter 1.

I myself had a vision: An allusion to the dream recounted by Socrates
to Crito in Plato, *Crito*, 44a–b. Chion's vision contrasts sharply with
the dream that Clearchus was said to have experienced shortly after
meeting Plato: 'Clearchus saw a dream: a woman saying to him,
"Disobey the Academy and flee philosophy; for it is not right for you
to enjoy her; she views you as hostile." Having heard this, he returned
to Heraclea' (Aelian = *Suidae Lexicon*, ed. A. Adler, 5 vols. (Stuttgart,
1928–38), s.v. Clearchus). The differences between these two visions
underline the different reactions of the men to Plato's philosophy.

After such a vision: Malosse and Michael Trapp (ed.), *Greek and
Roman Letters: An Anthology* (Cambridge, 2003), see an evocation
of Plato, *Timaeus*, 71a–72b, together with *Phaedrus* 244a–e and
Apology, 33c (to which one might add *Republic*, 571c–572a), but it
may well be that the author is looking no further than the *Crito*
passage mentioned in the previous note as evidence for Chion's asser-
tion. The irony here is that given what we know of the aftermath of
the conspiracy it is unlikely that Chion would have received a tomb
of any kind.

a noble death: Chion was certainly represented as a noble assassin by
Trogus (Justinus, *Epitome of Pompeius Trogus*, 16.12), but in the
Letters of Chion the moral issue is not so clear-cut (on which see
John Penwill, 'Evolution of an Assassin: The Letters of Chion of
Heraclea', *Ramus*, 38 (2009), pp. 24–52.

THE STORY OF PENGUIN CLASSICS

Before 1946 ... 'Classics' are mainly the domain of academics and students; readable editions for everyone else are almost unheard of. This all changes when a little-known classicist, E. V. Rieu, presents Penguin founder Allen Lane with the translation of Homer's *Odyssey* that he has been working on in his spare time.

1946 Penguin Classics debuts with *The Odyssey*, which promptly sells three million copies. Suddenly, classics are no longer for the privileged few.

1950s Rieu, now series editor, turns to professional writers for the best modern, readable translations, including Dorothy L. Sayers's *Inferno* and Robert Graves's unexpurgated *Twelve Caesars*.

1960s The Classics are given the distinctive black covers that have remained a constant throughout the life of the series. Rieu retires in 1964, hailing the Penguin Classics list as 'the greatest educative force of the twentieth century.'

1970s A new generation of translators swells the Penguin Classics ranks, introducing readers of English to classics of world literature from more than twenty languages. The list grows to encompass more history, philosophy, science, religion and politics.

1980s The Penguin American Library launches with titles such as *Uncle Tom's Cabin*, and joins forces with Penguin Classics to provide the most comprehensive library of world literature available from any paperback publisher.

1990s The launch of Penguin Audiobooks brings the classics to a listening audience for the first time, and in 1999 the worldwide launch of the Penguin Classics website extends their reach to the global online community.

The 21st Century Penguin Classics are completely redesigned for the first time in nearly twenty years. This world-famous series now consists of more than 1300 titles, making the widest range of the best books ever written available to millions – and constantly redefining what makes a 'classic'.

The Odyssey continues ...

The best books ever written

PENGUIN CLASSICS

SINCE 1946